TOUCHSTONE BOOKS
Published by Simon & Schuster
New York   London   Toronto   Sydney   New Delhi

THE
SKELETON
BOX

Bryan Gruley

Touchstone
A Division of Simon & Schuster, Inc.
1230 Avenue of the Americas
New York, NY 10020

First Touchstone hardcover edition June 2012

TOUCHSTONE and colophon are registered trademarks of Simon & Schuster, Inc.

For information about special discounts for bulk purchases, please contact Simon & Schuster Special Sales at 1-866-506-1949 or business@simonandschuster.com.

The Simon & Schuster Speakers Bureau can bring authors to your live event. For more information or to book an event contact the Simon & Schuster Speakers Bureau at 1-866-248-3049 or visit our website at www.simonspeakers.com.

Designed by Renata Di Biase

Manufactured in the United States of America

10 9 8 7 6 5 4 3 2 1

ISBN 978-1-4165-6366-2
ISBN 978-1-4165-6402-7 (ebook)

for kimi, karen, kathleen, mike, and dave
and in memory of our father

THE
SKELETON
BOX

Father, forgive me, for I have sinned. I have succumbed to the temptations of the flesh, to the venal allure of physical pleasure, to the enrapture of lust and all that goes before it, and with it, and alongside it. I have let sin reign in my mortal body and I have obeyed its desires. I have committed atrocity and tolerated it and sought the false and sinful asylum of denial. I have made company with men who would do the same while demanding my silence and wicked acquiescence. I seek your divine mercy and everlasting forgiveness as I write these things down on the twenty-first day of August in the year 1950. . . .

MARCH 2000

4TH BINGO BREAK-IN STRIKES FEAR INTO TOWN OF STARVATION LAKE

By Lucas B. Whistler
Pilot Staff Correspondent

The Bingo Night Burglar may have struck again.

In what appears to be the fourth such break-in since the New Year, the Pine County Sheriff's Department said an intruder entered the home of John and Mary Hodges on Sunday evening while the retired couple was at bingo at St. Valentine's Catholic Church.

The burglary wasn't technically one because, as in previous break-ins, nothing was taken. As before, the intruder appears to have rummaged through file cabinets and desk drawers containing personal and financial documents.

"I don't know why, but that's even scarier than if they walked off with our TV," said Mary Hodges, 178 Little Twin Trail.

Pine County sheriff Dingus Aho released a statement saying, "The department is treating these various incidents as burglaries." He declined to comment further. All four break-ins have occurred while the occupants of the homes broken into were at bingo. Police have no suspects.

Bingo attendance has declined, while sales of padlocks have soared at Kepsel's Ace Hardware. "Starvation Lake is scared," said County Commissioner Elvis Bontrager. "Sheriff Aho ought to start doing his job, or we'll find someone who will."

Before a Jan. 9 break-in at the home of Ted and Gardenia Mapes, Starvation Lake hadn't had one since 1998. B and E's followed at the homes of Bill and Martha Nussler on Jan. 16 and Neil and Sally Pearson on Feb. 6.

"I hope the police catch somebody soon," Sally Pearson said. "One of these times, somebody could get hurt."

TWO

We ignored the first knock. The punk who drove the Zamboni had been barging in and yelling at us about leaving empties in the dressing room. So we started locking the door.

"Soupy?" I said. "Cold one?"

I reached into a plastic bucket filled with ice and fished out a Blue Ribbon. My squad, the Chowder Heads of the Midnight Hour Men's League, had just beaten the Ice Picks of Repicky Realty, 7–0.

"Pope shit in the woods?" Soupy said. I tossed him the beer. He slumped on a bench between Wilf and Zilchy, his hair a sweaty blond tangle, his hockey socks bunched around his ankles. The room smelled of mildew and tobacco dip. I grabbed myself a beer, the ice stinging my knuckles, and dropped my goalie mask into my hockey bag.

Soupy hoisted his can toward me. "You stoned them tonight, Gus. When's the last time you had a shutout?"

I shrugged. "I think I was still living downstate."

I had left our little northern Michigan town, Starvation Lake, in the 1980s and worked at a big Detroit newspaper. I came home after getting in some trouble on the job. I could have gone a lot of places—Battle Creek, Toledo, Daytona Beach. But I returned to Starvation.

I'd been back only two and a half years, and at times it felt as if I'd never left. Which was frightening, if I let myself think about it. At other times I felt as if I'd wanted to come back all along, as if I had some unfinished business, some question I had to answer about myself. Meantime, I played goaltender at night and spent my days as executive editor of the *Pine County Pilot*, circulation 3,876 and falling.

"Speaking of goalies, where was Tatch?" Wilf said.

Tatch was the Ice Picks goalie. He'd been a no-show that night.

"Goalies," Soupy said. He took a pull on his beer, the liquid clicking inside the can, then thrust it up over his head. "The hell with them. How about them Rats?"

Most of us had played for the River Rats, the local youth team, as teenagers. We'd lost the 1981 state final on a goal I should have stopped.

"State finals, baby," Wilf said, "right here in beautiful Starvation Lake."

There was another, harder knock at the door. Then a voice.

"Police. Open up."

"Hell, it's just Skipper," Soupy said. "Game tomorrow's at seven. Pre-game at my bar. The Enright's Pub shuttle will leave for the rink at six-thirty sharp. Adult beverages will be provided." He looked at me. "You coming?"

"Yeah, right." As a Rats assistant coach, I didn't drink much before games.

"Pussy."

The door swung open and Pine County sheriff's deputy Skip Catledge stepped into the room. I saw the Zamboni punk slink away with a ring of keys. The deputy pointed at me. "Get dressed."

"He wasn't drinking, Skip, honest."

"Shut up, Soup. Let's go, Gus. We have a situation."

I thought of my mother. She was watching TV in her pajamas when I left for the game. Our next-door neighbor, Phyllis Bontrager, had come to sit with her.

"A situation where?"

"I'll be outside," the deputy said. "In two minutes, I'll come in and haul your butt out."

Cop flashers blinked in the distance as Catledge steered his sheriff's cruiser off Main Street and onto the beach road along the lake's southern shore. The lake itself was invisible in the blackness beyond the naked trees. Twin bands of packed snow ran down the asphalt lanes between the steep banks on both shoulders.

The deputy, his hat perched on the dashboard, had spoken barely a word since we'd left the rink. He had had me sit in the front next to him. Not a good sign.

"Are those flashers where I think they are?" I said.

"We'll be there in a minute."

Half a mile ahead, the flashing lights obscured my mother's little yellow house. I imagined what might have happened. A greasy pan Mom had left burning on the stove. A fireplace flue she had neglected to open. A door she had forgotten to lock. Dammit, Mother, I thought, then immediately felt bad about it. We'd never had to lock our doors in Starvation Lake. Then the break-ins had begun.

"Why no siren?" I said.

"No need to wake up the whole town."

"Skip, if it's—"

"Gus, I don't know, OK? Sheriff told me not to call him and he hasn't called me. He's probably keeping it quiet so every old lady with a scanner doesn't show up to watch."

"Watch what?"

He stepped harder on the gas. The trees and houses flew past, cozy log cabins and plank board cottages built in the 1940s and 1950s, and makeover mansions of red brick and cut rock and cantilevered decks built in the 1990s. We were heading to Mom's house, all right. There were no flames that I could see. I told myself Mom was all right.

Catledge grabbed his hat and set it on his head. We slowed. A hundred yards ahead, another deputy emerged from the shadows along the road shoulder, a flashlight beam bouncing in front of him. Catledge blinked his headlights. The beam waved us through.

Some of Mom's neighbors stood along the road, pajamas and bathrobes sticking out from under winter coats. As we passed, one spied me and shook her head and brought her hands up into a clasp at her face.

"Christ," I said. "What the hell's going on?"

Static crackled on Catledge's shoulder mike. I heard the Finnish lilt of the sheriff's voice. "Deputy," it said. "Did you collect Mr. Carpenter?"

Mom's house sat on a snow-covered bluff overlooking the lake. Now it was surrounded by five police cars, two ambulances, and a fire truck. The swirling blue and red lights striped the aluminum siding and roof shingles. Why two ambulances? I thought.

We stopped at the end of Mom's driveway. One ambulance was parked there. The other waited in the snow in Mom's front yard, one of its twin rear doors swung open. I saw sheriff's deputies moving around in the light blazing inside the house.

As I climbed out of the cruiser, I heard a woman's sob, sharp and halting, as if she were trying not to cry. I knew that sound. I looked in the direction of the ambulance in Mom's yard.

"Darlene," I said, then louder. "Darlene."

A door slammed. The ambulance eased out of the yard onto the road. I turned to Catledge. "Where's Darlene?"

Darlene Esper was another Pine County sheriff's deputy. She was also my ex-girlfriend and the daughter of Phyllis Bontrager—Mrs. B to me—the next-door neighbor who had been with my mother that night.

"I don't know," Catledge said. He took my elbow and nudged me toward the house. "The sheriff's waiting."

"I heard her in that ambulance," I said. "They must have—shit. Is Mrs. B in that ambulance?"

Pine County sheriff Dingus Aho stepped into the muddy snow outside the sliding glass doors to Mom's dining room, a walkie-talkie squeezed in one pork-chop hand. He was a big man who looked bigger silhouetted against the backlit wall.

"I can't go in?" I said.

Dingus shook his head. "I'm afraid it's a crime scene."

"It's my family."

"I'm sorry."

I had glanced into the kitchen as I passed, noticed a glass casserole soaking on the counter next to the sink. Yellow police tape was strung everywhere. The dining room, except for a cop flashlight resting on the table, looked to be in order. Beyond there, officers wearing latex gloves shuffled in and out of the bathroom next to Mom's bedroom.

"Where's my mother? Is she in one of those amb—"

"No. She's fine. Phyllis Bontrager is on her way to Munson."

Munson was the medical center in Traverse City, forty miles west. You didn't go there for cuts and bruises.

"What happened?"

"There was a break-in."

"I want to see my mom."

He hooked his walkie-talkie on his belt. "Calm down."

"What's the big fucking secret, Dingus? It's another Bingo Night Burglary, isn't it?"

Dingus stepped toward me. The sweet aroma of Tiparillo floated off of his handlebar mustache. "Watch your language," he said.

"You mean 'bingo night'?"

My newspaper had made the connection between the break-ins and bingo night. That had not pleased the sheriff, who was up for re-election and didn't appreciate headlines reminding voters that he had no clues, no suspects, no idea why someone was breaking into homes, rifling through personal papers, and then leaving empty-handed. "Bingo Night Burglaries" was catchy and I'd heard people saying it at the rink and Audrey's Diner and Fortune Drug and imagined that it might help circulation.

"We're not sure what happened here," the sheriff said. "As I've said, bingo night is a coincidence. There's bingo every night somewhere around here."

Mother had been waiting when Darlene, the sheriff's deputy, had arrived, heeding Mom's 911 call, he told me. Darlene found her mother lying unconscious on the bathroom floor. Questioning my mother so far had proved fruitless.

"She's a little confused," Dingus said.

"You know Mom's got memory issues."

She was going on sixty-seven. Her memory had always been selective, but now she wasn't always certain what she should be selecting. Sometimes she was all there, sometimes hardly at all. The illness played tricks on her, and Mom tried to play tricks back, often in vain.

"I understand."

"Is Mrs. B going to be all right?"

The sheriff looked away, into the house. "Doc Joe's on his way to Munson."

Doc Joe Schriver was the county coroner.

Mrs. B had been stopping by at night to make sure Mom had turned off the stove, doused the fire, and done whatever else she needed to do before bed. Sometimes Mrs. B stayed for a while and sat in the rocking recliner to read while the fire died. I pictured her sitting there in her favorite winter sweater, the red one knitted with the shapes of reindeer heads.

I felt a pinprick of sleet on my cheek. "The guy attacked her?"

"We don't know it's a guy. We don't—"

"Gus!"

The voice came from the road. Dingus and I both turned to see Luke Whistler, the *Pilot* reporter I'd hired four months before. He was standing with the bathrobes outside the police tape. Whistler had written most of the Bingo Night stories. The cops weren't fans. I waved and called out, "Go to Munson."

Whistler pointed his notebook at the deputies keeping him and the crowd back. "They won't let me in," he said.

"Just go," I said.

I looked down the road and was relieved not to see the Channel Eight TV van. I turned back to Dingus. "Murder?" I said.

He couldn't bring himself to look at me. "Maybe we can get you in to see your mom for a minute."

In the other break-ins, the intruder or intruders had come when no one was home. Maybe they'd come tonight thinking Mom would be at bingo. She went most Sundays but hadn't tonight. The only light likely to have been burning was the one on the end table by the chair where Mrs. B did her reading. I imagined Mom dozing in bed, maybe watching something on the tiny black-and-white tube that sat atop her dresser, Mrs. B in the living room, absorbed in Maeve Binchy.

"That would be good," I said.

"Just do me a favor. Try not to jump to any conclusions."

THREE

C an you leave us alone for a few minutes, please?"

The paramedic, a woman I did not know, glanced at the doorway to Mom's bedroom, where Skip Catledge stood guard.

"If you're done," the deputy said.

"Surely."

She gave me a sympathetic nod on her way out.

Catledge stepped out and slid the bedroom door closed. Mom sat up against the headboard, her eyes closed. "Gussy," she whispered.

I sat on the edge of the bed, took one of her hands in mine. "Mom, are you all right?"

She wore the button-down pajamas she wore every night from October through April, off-white flannels printed with floral designs so faded that you couldn't tell the shapes were flowers anymore. I had bought the pajamas for her sixtieth birthday.

Mom shook her head. Her eyes were puffy and red. Wads of used tissue cluttered the nightstand. Her shoulders rose and fell with her breathing.

"She was my best friend," she said.

"I know."

"Is she going to be all right? She wasn't . . . she wasn't moving when they took her."

"It's not looking good, Mom."

"What am I going to do?" I had no answer but to squeeze her hand. "From the day your father died, Phyllis has been my rock."

A single tear dripped off her face onto her arm. I snatched a tissue from the box. Mom balled it up in her right hand and held it in her lap.

I thought of the two of them, Phyllis and Bea, sitting next to each other at the end of our dock, the sun golden on their backs, their hair tied back in twin ponytails, their feet dangling in the water. They wore one-piece bathing suits and drank lemonade from tall pink plastic cups.

They'd sit for hours, talking about what was in the paper that day, who gossiped what about whom at euchre night, how Mr. B had to go to the doctor about the lumbar pain that turned out to be cancer, which salads and Jell-O molds they would make for the town's annual Labor Day picnic. About Darlene and me, and when we would both finally decide that we were made for each other and do something about it. When the late August sky blew chilly on their shoulders, they wrapped themselves together in a towel and kept talking.

Mom looked up. "Darlene," she said. "Where is she?"

"On her way to the hospital with Mrs. B."

"Oh, God."

"You know Darlene. She'll just funnel it all into finding out what happened."

"That poor girl. She'll be all alone."

Mom dabbed at her eyes. I was all she had left now. The Damico family who had adopted her sixty-four years before were all dead but for a stepbrother in Oregon she hadn't seen in years. She had plenty of friends, but none so close as Mrs. B.

"So what happened, Mom?"

She glanced at the bedroom door, leaned in close to me. "I don't think Sheriff Aho is very happy with me. He kept asking questions: 'Who was it? Did you see a face? Did you hear a voice? Was it someone you knew?'"

"Were you asleep?"

"Yes. Then I woke up, because I had to pee. I'd had an extra cup of tea."

"And you found her."

She swallowed a sob, her eyes welling again. "There was—there was so much blood."

"Mom."

"I was useless. Useless to my best friend."

"Mom, it's not your fault."

She picked up her hands then and held them in front of her face. She stared at the palms, then turned her hands over and stared again.

"What's the matter?" I said.

She let her hands fall. "If only she hadn't been here."

"Why didn't you go to bingo?"

"She shouldn't have been here. I am not her responsibility."

No, I thought, Mom was *my* responsibility. That's what I heard her saying, whether she meant it or not.

"I'm sorry," I said. "Do you want me to move back in? Maybe just till summer breaks?"

"I'll be fine, son. They won't come back."

I wasn't so sure. I heard the door slide open behind me.

"Gus," Catledge said.

I gave Mom's hand another squeeze. "I love you," I said. "I'll find out what happened."

"You always do."

Catledge took me through the dining room and outside.

I had sat at Mom's dining room table that Sunday morning, with Mom and Mrs. B.

I'd come with a copy of Saturday's *Pilot*. A few days before, a snowplow had flattened the blue plastic *Pilot* tube in front of Mom's house, then dragged it halfway around the lake. Saturday's delivery guy was probably too hungover to bother to stop his station wagon and carry Mom's paper to her door. The *Pilot* came only twice a week, on Tuesdays and Saturdays. Mom hated to miss one.

When I walked in, Mom was talking in a low voice, almost a whisper.

"Shush," Mrs. B said. "You're imagining things, Beatrice."

"Why aren't they taking things?" Mom said. "Can you—" She cut herself off when she noticed me coming in.

"Maybe they are," Mrs. B said, "and the police are just keeping it quiet."

I set the fresh *Pilot* on the table where they sat on either side of a corner behind cups of tea.

"Good morning, Gussy," Mom said. "Do you want some tea?"

"No thanks. Keeping what quiet?"

"You," Mrs. B said, "until I get my hug."

I smiled and went over and hugged her from above, smelling her hair spray mixed with perfume. She looked dressy in a silver necklace bedecked with peridots over a lavender turtleneck. She had been to nine o'clock Mass.

Mom had not. My mother had stopped going to church when I was a boy. She never said why and I hadn't asked, because I didn't like going anyway. I figured her adoptive family had worn the Catholic out of her, with years of grade school, weekday Masses, then years working at the church rectory. She didn't talk much about any of it. Every few years, Mrs. B would drag her to Mass, and Mom would swear off it again.

Still, she liked the Epistles and Gospels and Psalms. Mrs. B stopped by every Sunday to fill Mom in on the readings over tea and coffee cake. "I'm happy to hear what God has to say," I'd heard Mom declare a hundred times. "But I can do without the priests grubbing for money. I give them plenty at bingo anyway."

On that Sunday morning, I helped myself to a slice of poppy-seed Danish and gazed out at the evergreens along Mom's bluff. They threw blue-hued shadows on the untrampled backyard snow. I imagined how different they would look in summer, how they'd dapple the grass shimmering green in the sun. Mom and Mrs. B chattered away about a recipe for vegetable lasagna, which sounded terrible to me.

Mom had read somewhere, probably something ping-ponging around the Internet, that vegetables were good for people with memory issues. She'd been eating a lot of broccoli, carrots, and cauliflower, so I'd been eating a lot of broccoli, carrots, and cauliflower, because I made sure to visit Mom for dinner at least twice a week, less for the cooking, which wasn't as good as it once was, than to check in.

"Are you making it tonight?" I said. "Maybe I'll bring some Italian sausage to go with it."

"Tonight is bingo at St. Val's," Mrs. B said, pushing her goggle-sized glasses up on her nose. "There's a potluck before."

Mom was frowning. "I don't feel like cooking."

"I have a nice pot of goulash already made, dear."

"I'm not sure I'm feeling up to it."

"Oh, boo, Beatrice. You have to get those old bones up from that chair and out of this stuffy house." As Mom of late had found less energy for going out, Phyllis had happily become her scold, because she thought Mom needed to get out, needed to see people, needed to keep her mind working. She reached over and patted my mother's hand. "I'll pick you up at six sharp."

Mom stared at the hand Mrs. B had placed on hers. I heard snowmobiles whining their way past the house on the lake below.

"I don't like church," Mom said.

"We're not going to church. We're going to bingo."

"We shouldn't leave the house on bingo night."

"How else are we going to go to bingo?" Mrs. B said. "Maybe Gus will babysit."

"What about my house?" I said, grinning.

"Right," Mom said. "That's what the burglar must be looking for—smelly old hockey equipment."

"I'll have my lovely daughter swing by," Mrs. B said. "I think she's on duty tonight."

"I have a game," I said. Mom was staring at Mrs. B's hand now. "Mom?"

"I don't like the mothballs," she said.

Mrs. B gave me a reassuring glance, then addressed Mom. "There are no mothballs, Bea. That was a long time ago."

"We kept the robes in mothballs."

She was talking about the job she'd had at the church rectory, many years before I was born. She did this from time to time, slipped back into the long ago like falling backward off of our dive raft into the lake. On recent Sunday mornings, I had noticed, she was more likely to go back a long way. Then she'd suddenly arrive back in the moment, as if she'd emerged from a time machine, as alert as if she had never left.

"Yes, I know," Mrs. B said. "The mothballs are gone now."

Mom pursed her lips, thinking. I hesitated as I might with someone having a nightmare. I had heard you weren't supposed to wake them up. I didn't know what to do. The doctors weren't sure, either.

"Mom?" I finally said. "Are you all right?"

"Bingo?" she said. "Phyllis?"

"That's right, tonight," Mrs. B said. "I'll be here at six."

Mom folded her arms. "Call me at five. We'll see."

I recalled that morning and how sweet Mrs. B had smelled, as I steered my pickup truck west on M-72 through sleet as thick as oatmeal.

I had hesitated to go, but Dingus, who probably didn't want reporters around anyway, had assured me a nurse and a deputy would stay with Mom through the night.

I pushed my truck as fast as I safely could on the slippery road to Munson Medical Center in Traverse City. I had tried to call Darlene on the way but she didn't answer.

My cell phone burbled as I swung south onto U.S. 31.

"Darlene?"

"Dude." It was Soupy. In the background I heard laughter and music and clinking glass. He was at Enright's, the bar he owned on Main Street. "Man, I've been trying to call."

"Had my cell off."

"One of your mom's neighbors just came in." He stopped, sounding choked up, but mostly drunk. "I'm so fucking sorry. Mrs. B was the best."

"Yeah."

"Who the hell would want to do that?"

"Nobody."

"How's your mom?"

"As you might expect."

"Mrs. B was her best pal."

"Yeah."

"And you're— Hold on." Soupy muffled his phone but I heard him anyway, taking an order for a round of shots. He came back on. "Sorry, man. I mean, what was I saying?"

"Nothing. I've got to go."

"Jesus, Trap, let's get"—he was choking up again, one of his late-night jags coming on—"let's get together tomorrow."

"Right."

I tossed the phone on the passenger seat. Two hours from closing time and Soupy was shitfaced in his own bar.

I steered along the shore of the east bay, trying to focus on the driving, trying to think of anything but how it could have been Mom instead of Mrs. B on the coroner's table.

I imagined Mrs. B cutting through Mom's yard in the dark that evening with her casserole in one hand, her other arm outstretched for balance as she minced through the snow in her brown galoshes with the undone buckles clacking. She would have let herself in and slipped off her galoshes before sliding the casserole into the oven. *Hello, honey,* she would have said. Always honey or dear or sweetheart or sweetie-pie.

Sweetie-pie.

They were the first words I had heard when I awoke in a hospital bed after getting my tonsils out. I was seven years old, somewhere in Detroit, a faraway city with big buildings and the Red Wings and doctors who promised my throat would stop hurting.

Do you want ice cream? Chocolate or vanilla or strawberry? Mrs. B asked as she held both my hands in one of hers, smiling down at me. *Your mother will meet us downstairs soon. Chocolate? Would you like chocolate, honey?*

My father had died barely a year before in that hospital, and Mom could not bear to go inside, so Mrs. B would go with me, and Mom would be waiting when I came out.

Can I have two? I asked. *May I? May I have two? Of course, sweetie-pie.* Mrs. B fed me vanilla and strawberry in slow, alternating spoonfuls, telling me to let it melt in my mouth before I swallowed so it wouldn't hurt as much. I watched her face as she fed me. I swirled the ice cream around on my tongue. I forgot about my throat.

Who could have killed that kind, precious woman?

I pounded the heel of my hand against the steering wheel. My throat constricted. A sob forced its way up. Then came another, and another, and finally I couldn't stop them.

I pulled my truck onto the shoulder along the bay. But I veered a little too quickly, forgetting the sleet, and my rear end fishtailed left and right and then left again and I felt the truck slipping and grinding toward the blackness of the water. "Goddammit!" I shouted, stomping the brakes and wrenching the steering wheel to get one of my tires back onto the asphalt.

The truck crunched to a halt just short of the knife-edged rocks along the water, my headlight beams disappearing in the gloom beyond. "Fuck me," I said, and dropped my head to the steering wheel, crying to the plinking of my hazard lights.

FOUR

S orry. Hospital's closed. Nobody's going in."

Sheriff's Deputy Frank D'Alessio stood with his arms crossed in front of the double glass doors at Munson's emergency entrance.

"Hospitals don't close, Frankie," I said.

"They do today. Especially to vultures."

As he swayed to and fro on his heels, his forehead moved in and out of the light thrown by an overhead lamp.

I held up my empty hands. "No pen, no notebook. I just want to see Darlene."

She was standing with her back to me down the corridor behind D'Alessio, talking to a nurse. Doctors and cops milled in the hall beyond her.

"Your mom doing OK?" D'Alessio asked.

"As well as can be expected."

"Good. Go home and take care of her."

"I need to see Darlene."

He glanced over his shoulder. "She's with her mother. Why don't you leave her alone?"

"Have they pronounced her dead?"

"I'm not at liberty to say."

"A little ticked you're not working the scene, Frankie?"

"What scene? A bunch of people stumbling over each other. I'm fine right here."

What an asshole, I thought. But that was Frankie. I'd played hockey against him for years, and he was no different on the ice. My pals in the Midnight Hour Men's League referred to him as a short little prick with a short little prick.

"So when are you going to announce?" I said. "Noon tomorrow would be perfect, don't you think? By then, every voter in the county will have heard what happened tonight."

D'Alessio was the subject—and probably the source—of rumors about a possible election challenge to Dingus. The two had never gotten along. For many years, running against Dingus, who stayed on budget and made sure locals didn't get too many speeding tickets, would have been futile. The burglaries had changed that. Murder would change it more.

"No comment," D'Alessio said.

"Right. So I won't quote you in the *Pilot* on your fellow deputies stumbling around and you let me duck in and see Darlene. OK?"

"How about, Sorry about what happened but go home."

"Whoa," came a voice behind me.

"Mr. Whistler," D'Alessio said.

"Deputy," Luke Whistler said.

Of course they knew each other. Whistler had gotten a few scoops on the Bingo Night stories and I figured his source was D'Alessio, who was leaking stuff to make Dingus look bad. Whistler hadn't had anything juicy for a while, so I assumed Dingus was now keeping D'Alessio in the dark.

"What's going on here?" Whistler said.

He wore a drab down vest patched in four or five places over a faded navy-and-orange sweatshirt announcing the Detroit Tigers as American League Champions, 1984. Sleet had mussed his white hair and streaked it dark along the sides of his boxy head. His retiree's gut pushed the sweatshirt's belly pocket out so that I could see the outline of a tape recorder inside.

"Sorry, no reporters allowed," D'Alessio said.

"Of course not," Whistler said. "Big story. No reporters. Who needs reporters?" He waggled a ballpoint pen in one hand and clutched a notebook in the other. He looked at me. "Sorry, boss. This can't be easy for you."

"I'm OK."

"Your mom's all right?"

"Yeah. Where were you?"

"Stopped at the cop shop." He held up his notebook, open to a blank page. "Here's what I got—squat. Nobody talking. How about you, Deputy?"

"Talk to the sheriff," D'Alessio said. "Anyway, your boss isn't here for the big story. He came to see his ex-girlfriend."

Darlene Esper, née Bontrager, had been my first love. We'd broken up the first time, years before, when I'd left Starvation to be a big-shot reporter in Detroit. After I'd come home, chastened, I found Darlene in an unhappy marriage, and we found our way back to each other. But by the time her divorce was final, we were apart again. I'd come to the hospital more out of a sense of duty to her mother than to her. At least that's what I told myself.

"Sure he did," Whistler said. "Her mother's dead. I'd just like to talk to the next of kin, whoever it is. That's what reporters do."

"Parasites."

"Been called worse by my exes, believe me. But you'll be the first to pick up the paper and look for your name, won't you, Deputy?" Whistler turned to me. "Shall we go?"

I took a last look into the hospital. There was Darlene, halfway down the corridor, facing my way. She raised a hand in a halfhearted wave, bit her lip. Then a doctor approached her and she disappeared around a corner.

"How'd the game go tonight?" D'Alessio said. "I was working."

D'Alessio skated for the Ice Picks.

"You had no goalie, so we won easy," I said.

"Where was Tatch?"

"Hell if I know. Probably with his fellow born-agains."

"Frigging goalies."

As I pulled out of the lot behind Whistler's gigantic sedan—an Olds Toronado, black with red pinstripes, 1970 or 1971—the Channel Eight TV van was trying to pull in.

Tawny Jane Reese was hanging out of the front passenger window, yelling and gesturing angrily at two Traverse City cops waving the van away from the lot. She stopped for a few seconds to give Whistler a look as he slid past. It usually felt good to see my competitors hitting a stone wall. Tonight, nothing felt good.

* * *

I parked on Main in front of the *Pilot*. The sleet had stopped. A snow-plow's brake lights made red needle points in the dark two blocks down. I stood on the sidewalk watching the plow veer along the lakeshore, toward Mom's house.

The street lamps had gone black at ten p.m., one of the austerity measures adopted by the town council. The late night darkness lured high school kids out for impromptu beer bashes on the beach, which required police visits, which probably cost more than the council had saved on shutting the lamps off. It made for decent copy in the *Pilot*.

I let my eyes adjust to the darkness until I could make out the snow-mottled beach, the frozen gray scar of the lake's edge beyond. The two-lane street stretched back from the beach, flanked on both sides by two-story clapboard-and-brick buildings. The marina, a bait shop, Repicky Realty, a vacated lawyer's office. An abandoned movie theater, Fortune Drug, Kepsel's Hardware, a vacated dentist office, Sally's Dry Cleaning and Floral, and Kate's Cakes, closed for the winter. Between them all, empty storefronts like missing teeth in a hockey player's mouth. Behind the shops on my right, the Hungry River flowed unseen beneath a crust of ice.

I smelled dampness in the air.

Fuzzy amber light glowed in the front window of Enright's Pub. I wondered if Soupy had forgotten to turn it off or had just passed out in his office. Two doors down, Audrey's Diner was dark, but in an hour or two, the lights would flick on and the proprietor would bustle about preparing for the breakfast rush of old men and their old wives.

On this particular morning at Audrey's, there would be less of the usual jabber about the River Rats' chances in the state playoffs, or how the weather was helping or hurting the tourist business of snowmobilers up from downstate. The men and women would lean on the counter together and listen as the little radio Audrey kept over the griddle told them that one of their own, a woman who had sat with them eating French toast with powdered sugar, never syrup, had been found dead in the home of Bea Carpenter.

It was my job to tell them what had happened and why. Whether they wanted to hear it or not. Whether I wanted to or not. Through the *Pilot* window I saw light bleeding from the newsroom into the reception area. My watch said 2:27 a.m.

"Shit," I said, and fitted my key into the door.

Luke Whistler kept tapping on his keyboard as I threw my jacket over my chair and sat. I looked at my blank computer screen, considered having to write the obituary of Phyllis Marie Snyder Bontrager. Behind me, the tapping stopped. I heard the deadening hum of the fluorescent lamps overhead.

"Hey, guy," Whistler said.

I heard him from behind the notes and files and newspapers and fast-food wrappers heaped on his gray metal desk. All I could see of him over the pile was the sheet-white top of his head.

"Yeah?"

He leaned back so that I could see his face. "Really sorry for what happened," he said. "I couldn't really say much back there with the copper."

"Thanks."

"You want to figure this out, boss?" He pushed his swivel chair out from behind his desk, the metal chair wheels crinkling the sugar packets scattered on the tile floor. "Huh? Me and you?"

I let out a breath. I didn't want to break down in front of Whistler.

"Yeah. Hell yeah."

"Good. Listen to these."

Whistler stood, still in his down vest, and hit some buttons on the phone on his desk. A dial tone blared on the speaker. He was calling our voice mail system. Usually it was filled with people complaining about soaked papers and missed deliveries.

Now the automated voice said we had thirty-two new messages.

"That a record?" I said.

"Hang on."

He played message twenty-one. "When are you guys in the media going to pick up the damn ball and run with it on this bingo guy? Our alleged police department can't police a damn thing, and I don't know what the hell we're paying them for. We need you to find this bingo guy."

"Yes, sir," Whistler said.

He played message twenty-two. This voice was muffled, like one you'd hear coming from the other side of a motel wall. "Anyone checking on those whackaroonies at the Christian camp? They're all agitated with the county. Maybe they're just messing with us, and now they made a big damn mistake."

Message twenty-three. A woman this time. "I can't leave my house and go to bingo? Have you asked the church . . . Saint, Saint, oh, I can't remember the name, I'm not Catholic . . . but have you asked the church—" A burst of static obliterated the rest of what she said. Whistler turned it off and sat. "Crazy, huh?"

"The natives are restless."

"The natives are shitting their pants. But we're going to figure it out."

"Let's do it."

Luke Whistler had come to me, at the age of fifty-six, from the *Detroit Free Press*. Thirty years before, he had been the youngest *Free Press* staffer ever to be a finalist for a Pulitzer Prize, for a series of stories he wrote about a Washtenaw County detective's obsession with finding someone who was raping and killing young women in Ann Arbor. Whistler had never quite matched that performance, at least in the eyes of the Pulitzer judges, but his byline inspired awe and trepidation in the newsroom of my paper, the *Detroit Times*, because invariably it sat atop investigative stories that we wished we'd had the vision and courage and persistence to have pursued ourselves.

Whistler was nothing if not relentless. He had a reputation for immersing himself in stories so deeply that editors worried he'd have trouble resuming a normal life once he'd finished them, not unlike undercover cops who find themselves thinking more like the crooks than the good guys. Whistler hung around an emergency room for six months and came out knowing how to suture switchblade gashes and clean gunshot wounds. He became desperately ill from an ammonia leak while working undercover in a chicken processing plant for a story. Long after his stories about the Washtenaw detective had run, Whistler still met him once a week for double Crown and Cokes at the Tap Room in Ypsilanti. The serial killer was never caught.

I'd also heard he had a penchant for smashing computer screens. All reporters fantasized now and then about driving a fist into a balky monitor on deadline. I'd never known one who actually did it. Then came Whistler. He hadn't been at the *Pilot* a month before I came into the newsroom one day and found a handwritten note on my keyboard. "Sorry about the computer," he had written. "Thing kept freezing and I got carried away. Will pay for it." I walked over to his desk and saw the shattered monitor, jagged cracks spidering out from a black circle at the center of the screen. Now that's passion, I thought. I told our parent company, Media North, that the thing shorted out and blew up, and accounting reluctantly paid for a replacement.

I could have been just as good as Luke Whistler, or at least I liked to think so. But I had gone places I shouldn't have, broken the law, and wound up back in Starvation Lake.

Finding Whistler's résumé in the mail the previous fall had surprised me. I was usually forced to choose between journalism school grads who couldn't latch on at a decent paper and old ladies who wanted to use the columns of the *Pilot* to opine on the way teenagers dressed. I didn't really vet him, didn't bother calling his boss at the *Freep*, a know-nothing named McFetridge who couldn't cover a house fire but had been promoted high enough that he could no longer do much damage. I knew Whistler's clips and his reputation and, I had to admit, there was something perversely delicious about hiring him away from the *Free Press*, the competition I had so loathed and occasionally feared during my Detroit days. Besides, with the budget year nearing an end, I had to hire somebody or risk having the bean counters take the slot back. When I offered Whistler the job in a phone call one day, he told me, "They say all journalism careers end badly, it's just a question of when."

"Never heard that," I said. "Funny."

"Well, I'm going to prove them wrong."

He insisted he'd come to Starvation not to retire, no, not a chance of that, but rather just so he wouldn't have to worry every day about the *Detroit Times* or one of the network affiliates beating him to a story he'd been working on for weeks or months. His doctor had warned him about his blood pressure; strokes ran in his family, he said. Better to walk away now, settle into something less stressful, still be able to do what he loved, maybe have time for a little fishing, maybe read a book now and then.

Yet no one who had seen him around town, literally trotting from new source to new source, would think this hoary-headed guy in the ratty down vest and low-top sneakers had lost his passion. Whistler could get just as excited about a story on the new four-way stop at Horvath and Hodara roads as he could about the school millage vote that had split the town so savagely that Dingus assigned an extra deputy to the polling station. Hell, Whistler had happily written our annual story about the turkeys that survived Thanksgiving at the Drummond farm north of Mancelona.

Despite what he'd said about fishing and books, he was usually in the newsroom late at night, banging out the stories he had collected during the day. I would come in at 8:30 in the morning to e-mails and voice mails he had sent me just a few hours earlier. He avoided the place during daylight hours. "No news in the newsroom," he liked to say.

I looked around the newsroom now, smelling old coffee and potato chip grease. There were three desks, some squeaky swivel chairs, a copier-and-fax machine that actually worked once or twice a week, and an old mini-fridge that made beers into slushies if you kept them in there too long.

"Can you hear those fluorescent lamps?" I said. "I hate that damn buzzing."

Whistler shrugged. "Newsroom," he said. "You know, I obviously didn't know her well, but Phyllis was a good lady." Mrs. B had worked the front counter at the *Pilot*. "I enjoyed getting to know her a little better at your mom's the other night."

Mom had had us both to dinner, and invited Mrs. B.

"Yeah."

"Tell me. What's the nicest thing she ever did for you?"

Someone who didn't know Whistler might have told him it was none of his business. But I knew him, at least a little, and I knew he could not keep his curiosity bottled up.

"The nicest thing." I thought about it. The story about getting my tonsils out was too personal. "When I was a kid," I said, "she fixed one of my goalie gloves. My lucky glove."

"Which?"

I flapped my right hand. "The stick hand."

"Still got the glove?"

"Nope."

"You know," he said, "you remind me a little of Tags."

"Who?"

"My old partner. Byline, Beverly C. Taggart. We'd be on some story, and she'd be acting all indifferent, but really she was the kind of reporter who wanted to knock on the door of somebody who'd just lost a daughter or a husband, maybe they didn't even know it yet. Get there before the cops. She was good at that. Creepy good."

"Before the cops? That's out there."

"Yeah. That's probably why I married her."

"She was one of your exes?"

"Both, actually. Married her twice. Divorced her twice."

"You mean she divorced you."

"Takes two," Whistler said. "But I wouldn't want to be married and divorced twice to any other woman in the world."

"And I remind you of her why?"

"Well, you don't have her caboose," Whistler said.

I waited.

He said, "You're not letting on how much you care. I mean, sorry for saying it, but what happened tonight could've happened—perish the thought—to your mother."

I had let that notion curl into a ball in a dark corner of my mind. Better to imagine that the whole thing was some case of mistaken address or identity. I glanced at the ceiling, a suspended grid of warped beige panels that looked like they'd been dipped in piss.

"I don't know why anyone would want to kill Mrs. B," I said. "Or my mother."

"Your mother have a safe?"

"A safe? Right. Only the bank has a safe."

"Valuables?"

"Define valuables. Her cross-stitch collection? She cashed in her jewelry a few years ago for like four hundred bucks and gave it to the Salvation Army. She's got a coin collection she hasn't looked at since my dad died. And a bunch of pictures of me in hockey gear."

"Guns?"

"No. I mean, a twenty-two, for shooting muskrats and chipmunks, but they give you a twenty-two here when you get out of fourth grade."

Whistler clapped his hands on his knees and rose from his chair. "OK then. We'll talk tomorrow." He zipped up his vest. "I suppose the next step is to figure out what this has to do with the other burglaries."

"It happened on bingo night."

"Yeah, but people know we already made that connection, so it's a convenient cover."

I hadn't thought of it that way.

"Anything to that Scratch guy not showing up?" he said.

"Who?"

"The hockey guy D'Alessio was talking about."

"Oh, Tatch. A born-again Christian who plays goalie? Harmless."

"If you say so."

My cell phone rang. Mom, I thought. "Excuse me," I said. Into the phone, I said, "It's Gus." It wasn't Mom. I listened. I hung up.

"Who was that at this hour?" Whistler said.

"No one."

"You're the boss," he said. "Just tell me what you want me to do. We'll get out there and dig some dry holes. You know what I say."

"Can't find a gusher without digging a few dry holes."

"Yes sir."

He went out the back door. The clock on the wall over the copier-and-fax said three minutes after three. I wanted to go to bed, but Darlene was waiting.

FIVE

The tree house," she had said on my cell phone. "Ten minutes."

Beneath four months of snow, the one-car garage seemed barely more than a bump on a hill. If you didn't know it was there, with a 1969 Pontiac Bonneville parked inside, you probably wouldn't have thought it was anything more than a gigantic snowdrift.

I felt a tinge of regret seeing the shrouds of snow drooping from the eaves. My dad would have wanted me to climb on top of the garage and push the snow off so the weight didn't cave the roof in. He had built the garage when I was two or three years old. On the back he had attached a platform of planks ringed by a wooden railing. He called it his "tree house."

From up there you could peer across the tops of shoreline trees and see the southwestern corner of the lake, watch the falling sun play its last orange and purple sheen across the water's mirror before going away. Dad spent many a summer evening up there, smoking cigars, drinking Stroh's, listening to Ernie Harwell narrate the Tigers. Mom almost never went up, which I think was how Dad wanted it, though I never heard him say so. "Girls don't really get it," he would tell me with a wink on the nights he let me come up. He'd pop me an Orange Crush and we'd clink bottles in the dusk.

I had brought a shovel from my pickup. I used it to dig my way through knee-deep drifts to reach the side door. The door was unlocked. I shoved it open. The smell of gasoline washed over me. I stepped inside.

"Hey, old girl," I said.

The Bonneville was gold with a cream vinyl roof. I pulled the driver's door open and sat down. The keys were in the ignition. I had been starting the Bonnie every few months since moving back to Starvation. I had taken it out only once, two years before, for a long drive that almost killed her. After that, I let a mechanic have at her, and she'd come back almost as good as new. But now I hadn't been out to the tree house in so long that I worried her battery had succumbed to the winter damp.

I turned the key. There were a few clicks. Then nothing.

"Shit," I said. "My fault. Sorry."

"What are you sorry for now?"

Darlene was silhouetted in the gray light framed by the side doorway, in uniform, a badge glinting on the furry front of her earflap cap. Her face was obscured in the shadow, but I could feel her gaze, pensive and wary and sad.

I got out of the Bonnie, pushed the door closed behind me.

"Hey, Darl," I said. "I'm—"

"Don't."

"Why?"

"Please."

Darlene took off her cap and her dark hair fell around her shoulders. Her hands trembled as she held the cap, every muscle in her face straining to keep it from cracking. She started toward me and, as she did, she dropped the cap, as if it was too heavy to hold. I bent to pick it up but she fell to one knee and snatched it up in both hands, lifting it to her face, where she buried her eyes in its fur, her shoulders heaving.

"Darlene," I said. I started to lay a hand on her left shoulder but hesitated, unsure whether I should.

"I can't," she said.

"You can't what?"

She stood. She wrapped her arms around me, pressed her face into my chest.

I remembered the night after her father's funeral. We were in my dad's garage. It was two or three in the morning. Darlene hadn't spoken a word since we'd left the community hall where my mother and Soupy's mom had stayed close to Mrs. B while the other ladies clucked around Darlene, telling her what a wonderful man her father had been. We left our clothes down in the garage and climbed the short stairway to Dad's tree house. We fell asleep in the humid dark, waking just before dawn. Then she curled her body into me, shivering against the dew.

Now she lifted her head and stepped back, fitted her cap back on. "I don't know," she said.

"I'm sorry I don't have a hankie or something," I said.

She wiped a coat sleeve across her face. "I don't want it to freeze there," she said.

"Why did you want to come here?"

"I didn't want them to see me."

"Who? See you what?"

"The first thing Dingus did, after telling me he was so sorry about Mom, was tell me to stay away from you."

Because Dingus didn't like the *Pilot* reporting things until he was ready to have them reported. Especially now.

"That's Dingus," I said. "Look, Darl, I really am— I don't know how to say it. About your mom. You know I loved her."

Darlene turned away, fighting more tears, and took off her cap again, set it on the roof of the Bonneville. She laid her hands on the roof and stood there staring into the car through the driver's window.

I looked in, too. The eight-track tape player was still bolted to the underside of the dashboard. During our college summers, before I left Starvation to work at the *Detroit Times*, Darlene had liked me to blast Elton John doing "Bennie and the Jets." I hated the song, and she knew it, and when the tape got tangled up so badly that it wouldn't play anymore, she accused me of messing it up on purpose. I told her I hadn't but wished I had. The fight ended in Dad's tree house sometime after midnight.

"Why didn't they go to bingo, Gus?" Darlene said.

"I don't know. Mom was in one of her crabby moods."

"Don't you usually go over for supper?"

"Usually. But I had a game."

"It doesn't matter. It's done. You weren't there."

"Wait. Weren't you the one always telling me I had to cut the apron strings? Telling me, Come on, you want to live with your mommy all your life? You can't pin this on me."

"No." She looked around the garage, finally let her eyes settle on mine. "I miss you."

"You miss me. You've been missing me? Or you miss me now?"

"There aren't many people left in the world who know me. Who really know me."

I was not about to go into how she had ignored my calls for weeks, how she had stolen out the back of Enright's the one Saturday night I had spied her there, how I had finally accepted that we were to be nothing more than failed lovers who through the happenstance of necessity would inhabit the same crowded space while barely acknowledging each other.

Now here she was, seemingly opening the door again.

"How did you hear?"

She looked at the floor. "I found her."

"You mean you were there first?"

"Yes."

"My God, Darl."

"I was out on patrol when the call went out from dispatch. Your Mother had called nine-one-one. When I got there, there was just the one light on in the living room."

"Where was my mother?"

"In the bathroom. With my mother." Darlene's lips were trembling now. "There was a lot of blood." She put a forefinger to her left eyebrow. "She had a gash here." She drew the finger away, held it half an inch from her thumb. "About like this. Like she was hit with something."

"Like what?"

"I don't want to think about it."

She covered her face with her hands. I moved closer, wanting to embrace her, unsure whether I should. Darlene shook her head, dropped her hands. "I tried to show her a hundred times what to do if she was ever . . . ever in trouble."

"How to defend herself."

"She told me, 'I know where a man's privates are.'"

"So she—"

"He must have hit her in the head. Or he hit her and she fell and hit her head. Or both. Detectives are working on it."

"No knives or guns?"

"Not that we can tell. We took . . . we took the rug."

"The rug?"

"It was soaked."

"Ah. Me Sweet Ho," I said, and Darlene smiled wanly, beautiful even then.

My mother knitted the rug many years before. A little yellow house sat on a pond ringed by pines over the legend "Home Sweet Home." Over years of wear, the house blurred into the pond and trees, and some of the letters in the words faded into the fabric. When we were a lot younger, Darlene had liked to needle me about it.

She reached into a back pocket and produced a cell phone. She punched a few buttons and held it up in front of me.

"Listen."

I moved closer and bowed my head to the phone. There was a beep. A few seconds of silence gave way to a woman's voice.

"Darlene," it whispered.

"Jesus," I said. The voice belonged to Mrs. B.

"Listen," Darlene said.

"There's someone here," Mrs. B whispered. She had to have been hiding. But why hadn't she called 911? Maybe because her daughter was, after all, a cop.

The call went silent but for the sound of Mrs. B's breathing. Hearing those shallow breaths must have been torture for Darlene, for they told her that her mother was frightened in the final moments of her life. I heard the creaking hinge of a door. I knew that sound. One of the two doors to Mom's bathroom. There was a footstep. I pictured Mrs. B ducking her head out, stepping into the hallway, peeking around the corner into the living room.

If she saw someone, she didn't say.

The door creaked shut.

There was silence again, then the sound of the other door opening. Mrs. B started to cry out but something muffled her voice. There was a brief scuffling, then a thud, then silence.

"My God," I said.

"Wait."

A few seconds passed. Then came a single word, in a barely audible whisper, a word I had never heard before. It sounded like "nye-less." Like the name Silas, but with an "n." Then, sounding barely able to speak, Mrs. B uttered it again: "Nye-less."

Darlene ended the call.

I wanted to reach out and hug her, for what had happened to her mother, and for what she must have felt for not having picked up her mother's call. Would she have made it to the house in time? Would she have been able to get an ambulance there faster?

"I'm sorry you had to hear that," I said.

"I heard it ring, figured it was Mom, but . . . I was chasing a raccoon out of Mrs. Morcone's house. She left the door open again. I thought I'd call Mom when I was done."

"What was it she said? Nye-less? What is that?"

"I have no idea. I've listened to it a thousand times."

"Can your tech guys make it clearer?"

"They can barely do a reboot."

"Maybe it's a name."

"I thought of that."

"What about the state cops? They have a lab."

She didn't say anything.

"Darlene," I said. "You haven't told anyone yet, have you."

She had come close to losing her job the year before for failing to pursue a lead in the case of a close friend's apparent suicide. She had let it become personal. Dingus gave her a break, knowing himself how hard it was for a cop to keep the proper distance in a place that could feel as crowded as New York City, minus the convenience of anonymity.

The case had also been the proximate cause of our second breakup, because my own investigation had exposed Darlene's apparently willful negligence. So we'd gone our separate ways, or at least she had gone hers.

"No, I haven't," she said.

"It's evidence. They're going to run a check on the phone. They'll see she called you."

She yanked her cap back on her head. "I'll tell them. It's just—it was my mother."

"So you're on the case?"

"Damn right I am."

"How's Dingus? I'm thinking he's afraid of losing, eh?"

"Heck, I'm afraid he'll lose. I couldn't work for that jerk D'Alessio. I wouldn't."

"So . . ."

"I'd need a job somewhere. With Mom gone . . ."

I felt a little shiver of panic. "There's plenty of time for all that," I said.

"We have to solve this, Gus."

"Why don't you let the police—"

"Dammit," she said, "I am a police officer. I'm not about to go home and fucking cry into my pillow. My mother didn't bring me up like that."

No, she didn't, I thought. "Do you think it's the same guy who did the other houses?"

"That assumes just one person did all the other houses."

"It wasn't?"

"Whoever it was, in all these break-ins, has been very careful. No prints, no nothing, nothing stolen."

"DNA?"

"Working on it."

"Did the neighbors see anything?"

"The Grays are in Florida, the Cerrutis were in Detroit at a hockey tournament."

"You've taped off the yard."

"Routine. But it'll discourage somebody if they decide to come back."

"They're not coming back."

"I don't think so."

"Can I put any of this in the paper?"

"I told you we were off the record."

Actually she hadn't, but I wasn't about to push it. I was glad she'd come to me. "OK."

"Please be careful what you report. This is my mother."

"I know. I will."

"Come here."

She put a hand on my chest, feeling for my heart. It was pounding.

"You matter to me," she said.

"Do you want me to stay with you?" I said.

"I'm going back to work. Nobody wants you there, believe me."

"Are you going to be all right?"

"No."

I leaned out the doorway and watched her hike down the path to her car, thinking about her mother and about my mom and about that word: nye-less.

SIX

The little bells on the door at Audrey's Diner jangled as I stepped inside.

"Ask him," somebody yelled in my direction, and a bunch of other people sitting at the tables and along the counter yelled, too.

"Ask me what?" I said.

I had come from Mom's house, where I'd sat by her bed watching her sleep for an hour, then made sure the sheriff's deputy watching her knew how she took her tea. I thought I'd stayed long enough to miss the morning rush at Audrey's. But I'd never seen the diner like this, not even on Saturdays when Audrey made her egg-pie special. Every stool at the counter and every seat at every table was taken. The tables were arranged in a haphazard semicircle so everyone could face the man standing a few feet away from me in a brown-and-mustard Pine County Sheriff's Department uniform.

"Take a seat, Gus," Sheriff Aho said.

"Ask *him* if that's a good idea, Sheriff." It was Elvis Bontrager, Mrs. B's brother-in-law, Darlene's uncle, and a Pine County commissioner.

"What idea?" I said.

Audrey DeYonghe emerged from behind the counter wiping her hands on the white apron she wore over a sky-blue smock. "Oh, dear," she said, taking my face in her damp hands, then pulling me into her arms for a hug. "This is so sad. It's so, so terrible."

"Yes."

"I almost decided not to open today, but I thought, well, this would be a good place for people to blow off steam. How is Darlene?"

I glanced at Dingus. He was listening. "OK, I hope."

"And your mother?"

"Not so good. She was sleeping when I saw her this morning."

"I don't suppose there are any funeral arrangements yet."

"That's going to take a while. The cops have to do their work first."

Audrey squeezed me again before letting me go. She reached behind the counter and pulled out a wooden stool. "Here, honey, set this over there. I'll get you some coffee."

"Thank you."

I set the stool by the window near the end of the counter and sat. Dingus was still looking at me, waiting. I reached into my back pocket and pulled out a notebook.

"No," Dingus said. "We're off the record here."

"What's going on?" I said.

"The sheriff's trying like hell to save his job is what's going on," Bart Fleder shouted from the back of the room. Then everyone started to yell again. I couldn't make out everything they said, but I heard "bingo" and "murder" and "Phyllis" and "incompetent." I could barely believe I was in Audrey's. The faces around me were pinched with fury and fear. Two women looked as if they had been crying.

"Please," Dingus said, holding his palms up for quiet.

"Tell us what you got, and we'll stop," Fleder said.

Elvis turned to me, his belly straining against the suspenders clipped to his jeans. "The sheriff wants to cancel all bingo. Just shut it off. Like that's going to catch this guy. Brilliant, huh?"

"Elvis," Dingus said. His cheeks had flushed red behind his handlebar mustache. He wasn't used to this sort of treatment. When he spoke to audiences of more than three or four people, he was usually the welcome guest handing out a safety award or posing for photographs with schoolchildren.

Floyd Kepsel piped up. "I think what Elvis is trying to say, Sheriff, is that we couldn't give a hoot about bingo being canceled. But is that it? Is that all you have for us?"

"I'll tell you what I'm trying to say, Dingus," Elvis said. "Do you see my wife here today? Huh? Do you? She comes here every day"—Elvis rapped a forefinger on the table with each word—"because she loves this place and this town because it's quiet and peaceful and you don't have to lock your doors and we have places like this where nice people come to have a nice breakfast and talk about their grandkids. But she's not here today, Sheriff, because she can't get out of bed, she can't move, she can't do anything but cry."

"I'm sorry, Elvis. You know—"

"Sorry? I'll tell you what's sorry. What's sorry is you coming here like this is some damn campaign stop and telling us *we're* the problem, *we're* the ones who have to be confined to our homes." The yelling started up again. "What if the guy starts breaking in on bowling night, huh? You going to shut the bowling alley, too? And what about hockey? We got a big game tonight and everybody's going. You going to order us to forfeit so we all stay home because you and your overpaid deputies can't catch a thief who doesn't even take anything?"

"He's not a thief," Dingus said. "If he was, we'd have—"

"No, he's a murderer."

It was Sally Pearson. Her home had been broken into on a bingo night in February. She rose from her table. The room quieted. Behind her, I saw Jo Evangelista dabbing at her eyes. I felt a catch in my throat and started taking notes to distract myself.

"A murderer, Dingus," Sally said. "And he killed one of the best of us."

"I realize that, Sally. We're doing everything we can."

"We don't have murderers in Starvation Lake. It can't be one of us."

"Probably not," Dingus said. "But we have to look at all of the possibilities."

"Do it, Dingus. And do it quickly. Because we can't have this hanging over us in our town. We've had our problems with the economy and the real estate but we get through it because we know what we have here, a little piece of heaven on earth."

"And there are no murderers in heaven, sir," Elvis said.

Sally sat. Dingus fingered the brass mitten-shaped clasp on his tie. "I'm deeply regretful that we haven't solved this—these cases," he said. "And I understand your concerns. But I'm afraid I must go ahead with my decision to cancel bingo until we have a better handle on this."

"What's to stop this guy—"

"Enough, Elvis." Audrey barked it from behind the counter.

Elvis turned in his seat. "Now, come on, Aud—"

"I said, enough. Phyllis was my friend, too. Dingus is doing his best. If that isn't good enough, you'll have a chance to let him know at the polls. But now let's let the poor man do his job. If you still insist on second-guessing him, that's up to you, but you'll do it somewhere else from now on. And Sheriff?" She turned to Dingus. "I'll thank you to refrain from calling meetings in my establishment. The same goes for Frank D'Alessio."

"Yes ma'am," Dingus said, giving a little bow. "With that, I'll take my leave." He picked up his hat and jacket off a chair and had opened the jangling door halfway when he looked at me. "You," he said. "Out here."

I followed the sheriff down Main. He veered into the narrow alley between Repicky Realty and a defunct antique shop, waving me along.

"Where are you taking me?" I said, but Dingus ignored me until he turned onto the walkway along the Hungry River and stopped. He peered over the railing at the river gurgling to the lake. He shook his head and leaned his elbows on the railing. Green paint was peeling off in spots because the town had only enough money to repaint once every two years.

"My loyal deputy was in there earlier," he said, "stirring up the rabble."

"D'Alessio?"

"The one and only."

"The guy's dumber than a sack of hockey pucks."

"Which never hurt a politician before, so far as I can tell. I wasn't going to do any dog-and-pony shows, but Skip was in there getting a coffee and saw D'Alessio and gave me a jingle and said, 'Boss, you better get down here before they hang you in effigy.'"

"Jesus."

"Yes. Frank's treating all these crazy ideas—Phyllis got shot with a hunting bow, she got sliced up with a cheese grater—like they're all real possibilities. He doesn't know a thing."

"What did—"

"The guy may have slammed her head into the bathroom door, and then, we think, into the floor. He may not have meant to kill her, but he did."

We stood watching the water for a moment. I'd never seen Dingus so worked up. "When was the last murder in Starvation?" I said.

"In 1973," he said. "A couple of brothers arguing over natural gas rights. Drinking, of course. One grabs a shotgun out of his gun cabinet and shoots the other across the kitchen table. I think he's out of prison by now."

"That the only one?"

"Before that, we had a man accused of murdering a nun at St. Val's back in the forties or fifties. He got into it with somebody at the jail and got his throat cut. It was kind of a big deal at the time, though more because of the nun than the guy who killed her."

"And now you have this."

"Yes." He came up from the railing. "And you are going to help me."

Dingus and I had a special relationship. Sometimes he helped me, mostly he didn't. But when he did, he expected something in return, usually more than what he gave up. It never would have worked for a marriage, but as cop-reporter romances go, it was about as good as it gets.

"Am I working for you or something?" I said.

He stepped in closer. "Can it. You want to solve this as much as I do, whether it's in your paper or not."

"Go ahead."

"Your mother. She knows things. I know she knows them. She knows she knows them."

"Not always. She—"

"Pipe down. I know about memory problems. My mama had them, too, may she rest in peace. But Bea, forgive me for saying, she knows more than she's letting on."

"Sometimes she can't dredge it up."

"Yeah, well." He leaned his face in close. I smelled the Tiparillos again. "Maybe you can help her."

"And then what?"

"Then you pass it along to your friendly neighborhood sheriff."

"So, Dingus, do you have any clues at all? Do you know why they're not taking anything?"

A frown bunched his mustache at his lips. He wasn't going to respond. I considered asking about nye-less but didn't want to expose Darlene. And I didn't want to give away the only lead I had. "So, can I take off?" I said.

"How about your friend Tatch?"

My phone buzzed in my pocket. I let it go.

"What about him?"

"We got a tip he didn't show up at the rink last night. That so?"

A tip? Shit, I thought, that had to be D'Alessio, who'd heard from me that Tatch was a no-show. Then I recalled the message left at the *Pilot* the night before: *Anyone checking on those whackaroonies at the Christian camp?* Meaning Tatch. His camp.

"Tatch wasn't at the game," I said. "But he's not the most reliable guy on the planet."

"Uh-huh. He's a goalie, isn't he? Like you? I'm no hockey expert, but it's pretty unusual for the guy who guards the net to miss a game, isn't it? Kind of puts his team at a disadvantage?"

"Kind of. What do you want from me?"

"Just ask him a question or two."

"Why don't *you* ask him a question or two?"

"He's your buddy. Couple of goalies, you think alike, right? If 'think' is the right word for goalies."

"That's funny."

"Just do it, huh?"

A breeze off the river washed cold along the back of my neck. "I'm going out to his camp later anyway. I'll see what I can find out."

"Good," Dingus said. "You been out there before? I have nothing against born-again Christians, but I'll tell you, that place is just a tad creepy."

SEVEN

After Dingus cleared out, I headed down the river to Estelle Street, where I turned toward Main and the Pine County Courthouse.

My chat with the sheriff had reminded me to pick up some documents. The week before, I'd requested several years' worth of tax reports on properties owned or formerly owned by Stewart and Bernice Edwards, Tatch's parents, or owned by Roy Edwards, Tatch himself. He and his little camp of born-again Christians were fighting the county over an increase in taxes on the property where their trailers huddled on a wooded hill above the lake. They were arguing that they were a religious organization that shouldn't have to pay taxes at all, and certainly not more than before. Now that Dingus seemed the least bit suspicious of Tatch—even if I didn't think Tatch clever enough to break into a house without getting caught or mean enough to hurt a flea—I figured I ought to have those documents handy, just in case.

The redbrick courthouse stood over a square guarded by oaks and crosshatched with sidewalks blotched with dirty snow. I remembered the call I'd ignored and pulled out my phone to check messages. Luke Whistler had left one.

"Hey, boss," he said. I heard the sound of a truck rumbling past him, wherever he was. "Popped a story online about what happened last night. Hope that's OK, Mr. Sleep-All-Day. I'm headed out to the territories. Talk later."

I pocketed the phone, thinking, how the hell could a fifty-six-year-old reporter be so chipper day after day? His beloved "territories" were anyplace outside the newsroom—the courthouse, the pizza joint, the cop shop, Audrey's, the high school, Enright's, wherever there might be someone willing to whisper in Whistler's waiting ear.

Although the *Pilot* published on Tuesdays and Saturdays, our bosses at Media North let us post stories on the Internet each morning.

Whistler loved having a place to counter Channel Eight's ability to go with a story the minute they got it. So what if Channel Eight was also owned by Media North. I thought Whistler also liked having the freedom once in a while to post stories without showing them to me. "Always first," he liked to say, "and frequently right." I'd tell him I hoped he was joking, and he'd grin and assure me he was.

Vicky Clark wrapped both of her fleshy hands around mine and tugged me toward her across the glass-topped counter in the Pine County Clerk's Office. My forearms tensed a little as my fingertips neared the cleavage jiggling in her low-cut sweater.

"Gus, I am so sorry," she said. "So sorry."

"Thanks."

"Such a caring lady. I hope I can be so caring one day."

I tried to slip my hands free but Vicky tightened her grip and pulled me closer, her perfume so sweet I thought my eyes might water.

"You'll let me know about arrangements?"

"Sure."

The deputy clerk had three fat youngsters and an on-and-off boyfriend named Sully who spent weekdays working road construction downstate and weekends fishing, drinking, and shooting pool with his old high school pals in Starvation. On balance, I figured Sully had a better life than Vicky, which was probably why she imagined it couldn't hurt to try to draw me into hers, via her boobs. I couldn't blame her for assuming that I, too, was stuck in Starvation forever, since I had already made my own downstate foray and it had ended badly.

I liked Vicky. We had a sort of understanding in our mutual stuckness. But I had no serious interest in her beyond friendly chitchat and extracting whatever I needed from her office. Especially if it meant I could avoid dealing with the clerk herself, a brittle stick of a woman who happened to be Vicky's mother, Verna Clark.

Vicky gave me a smile, her tomato cheeks squeezing her eyes nearly shut. She loosed my hands. "One of these nights," she said, "I have to have you over for dinner. In all modesty, my chicken and dumplings is to die for."

"I love chicken and dumplings," I said, while thinking, But not that much. "Hey—do you think I could get those documents I asked for last week?"

"Did you fill out a form and give it to me?"

"It was me," Verna Clark said. The county clerk emerged from the rows of file cabinets behind her daughter, wearing the same drab gray woolen dress she seemed to wear every day. Here we go, I thought.

"Good morning, Mrs. Clark," I said.

She peered up at the clock on the oak paneling over my head. "Nearly noon, Mr. Carpenter, and our lunch break. I'm afraid you'll have to come back later."

It was vintage Verna. She couldn't legally withhold the records, but she could make it difficult for you to actually put your eyes and hands on them. Complicating matters with formal paperwork gave both her and her daughter more things to do and the county commission reason to keep them on, when in fact one member of the Clark family could probably have handled the clerk's office on her own, especially now that so little property was being bought and sold in Starvation anyway.

"I'm sorry, I can't come back later," I said. "I have to get back to my mom's."

"I'm very sorry to hear about the incident at your mother's house," Verna said. She stood pole straight at the counter, her reading glasses dangling from a frayed silver strand. "But we cannot allow the vagaries of daily life to disrupt our procedures."

"Excuse me?"

Two lawyers stepped into the office and set briefcases on the floor.

"You'll have to come back at one p.m.," Verna Clark said.

"Why? I filled out the request forms a week ago. What's the holdup?"

That was the wrong thing to say. Verna pursed her lips, then turned to Vicky. "You may take lunch now, but"—she looked at the clock again—"be sure to be back six minutes early."

I glanced at the lawyers waiting by the double doors. They were smiling. I felt the seconds ticking off the clock.

"Bye, Gus," Vicky said.

Verna waited for her to leave, then leveled her gaze on me. She'd been county clerk for as long as I could remember. She won re-election each time partly because she kept her office on budget, partly because her demeanor made her job seem so grim that nobody could work up the energy to mount a challenge. Verna herself seemed to operate on a limited budget of smiles and helpfulness that she rationed for county commissioners.

"For your information, Mr. Carpenter, there is no holdup," she said. "You made a rather extensive request for records. We've processed them once and I need to check them over one last time to make sure that we've given you precisely what you asked for."

"Forgive me, Mrs. Clerk, I mean Clark," I said. "I'll take whatever you have now."

"As you know, the county is strict about closing times, given our current budget situation. I know you're familiar with our budget, Mr. Carpenter, because you've written extensively about it, and opined extensively about it, too."

The *Pilot* had published an editorial the previous November recommending that voters reject a tax increase that would have shored up the county budget. Someone at Media North headquarters in Traverse City had written the editorial, not me, but that distinction wouldn't have mattered to Verna Clark.

"Yes ma'am. But if I could just—"

"The truth is, Mr. Carpenter, another individual was in to look at a number of the same records earlier today—after filing the proper request forms prior to you—and the files have yet to proceed through reprocessing."

"I thought you said they were processed."

"Yes, but not reprocessed."

Oh, for fuck's sake, I thought.

"Besides," Verna continued, arching a thin eyebrow, "why is it

necessary for the newspaper to monopolize the viewing of certain records?"

"Monopolize? What are you talking about?"

She took a set of keys from a pocket in her dress. "For someone who
renders such harsh verdicts about our county's operations, you appear to
run a remarkably inefficient operation yourself. Perhaps you, too, should
try being prudent."

The word "prudent" had been in the headline of that damned editorial. "Are you telling me someone else from the *Pilot* was here?"

"This is apparently a very popular batch of records. I seem to recall
someone from downstate requesting the very same papers not two years
ago."

"Really?"

"Really. We are now closed for the lunch hour, sir. You'll need to
leave."

"Wait, Vern—Mrs. Clark. Are you saying my colleague was here?
Luke Whistler?"

Her face betrayed the faintest hint of a smile. She was enjoying this.
Verna Clark may have been a bitch, but she was a smart bitch.

"Unfortunately, I'm not at liberty to discuss individual requests for
records. But you seem like you're at least intelligent enough to put two
and two together." She pointed a finger past me. "I'll thank you for closing the door on your way out."

I walked out thinking, Whistler wanted those records? For what?

"Poppy," I said into my phone as I swung my pickup onto Main.

"Hey," said Dick Popovich, head coach of the Hungry River Rats. I
helped him with the goaltenders. "I'm so sorry about what happened."

"Yeah."

"Phyllis was all class. Good to the town. Good to the hockey program."

Mrs. B wasn't a big hockey fan, but she had worked the ticket table in
the rink lobby since I played for the Rats, and brought big boxes of her

molasses cookies and chocolate-covered macaroons to the Rats' annual preseason fund-raiser. Whenever people in Starvation Lake wanted to raise money, they went to Mrs. B for cookies. She never said no. A hundred people must have told her she should open her own cookie shop, to which she would always say, "I bake cookies. If I could bake money, I would bake money."

"She was," I said. "I wanted to let you know I might be late to the pregame skate. Got a few things to do."

"Understood. Glad you called, though. We gotta have a talk with Tex."

Matthew Dobrick, sixteen years old, was the River Rats' big, fast, crafty left wing. His teammates had nicknamed him "Tex" for the garish green-and-gold Dallas Stars jacket he wore. He insisted he had won the jacket new in a raffle downstate. But the seams coming apart along the shoulders and the torn left pocket made me think it had been plucked from a bin at a consignment store.

Tex had never known his father. His mother, from what I had heard, had played the role of dutiful hockey mom, shuttling her son from practice to game to practice while carrying on an affair with a team dad who worked as a shoe salesman by day and dealt marijuana and cocaine on nights and weekends. When the police appeared at his apartment one evening with a search warrant, Tex's mother was there and, maybe because she was using, took a swing at one of the cops. It was not the first time she'd run afoul of the law. Even after she had ratted out her boyfriend, the judge sentenced her to eighteen months at the prison in Decatur.

So Tex had come to Starvation Lake to live with his uncle Roy, known to us as Tatch, and just like that, for the first time in almost twenty years, the River Rats were contenders for the state championship. In his first and only season with the Rats, Tex had scored more goals than the rest of the team combined. Unfortunately, he had also tallied the most minutes in penalties, which was why Poppy and I needed to have a talk with him.

"Yeah, but let's go easy," I said. "The kid plays angry. It helps him."

"It doesn't help when he's sitting in the penalty box. Mic-Mac knows his deal. They'll be goading him. He's got to keep his cool."

Mic-Mac, a scrappy bunch of bumblebees from Detroit's northwest side, was to be our opponent in the state quarterfinal that evening.

"I'm taking his skates out to him in a bit," I said. "You want me to say something?"

"Going up to that religious camp?"

"Yeah, part of the drill. The kid plays superstitious, too."

As I approached Mom's little yellow house, I looked through the bare trees to the frozen white crescent of the lake curling north and then west. A crow settled in the branches of a beech, a black blot on the smoky quilt of sky.

You have a nice, simple life, I thought as I watched it.

I wanted to check on Mom before I took Tex his skates. Then I had to drop by the pregame skate, then get back to the *Pilot* and move a few stories for the next day's paper. I wanted to get to puzzling out what or who nye-less was. Maybe just the gibberish of a woman who'd suffered a serious blow to the head. Or maybe not.

I pulled onto the shoulder just short of the driveway and the do-not-cross tape ringing the yard of grass and trees between Mom's house and Mrs. B's. As kids, Darlene and Soupy and I had called it the "big yard," and we'd spent a lot of time there, building snow forts in winter, racing our bicycles between the trees in summer.

One late evening, I had tried to kiss Darlene as we balanced next to each other on our bikes watching the sun dip behind the bluffs across the lake. "Ewww!" she yelled, punching me in the chest before I could get my lips on hers. I toppled over into a pricker bush and scrambled out bleeding while Darlene pedaled away laughing.

Would she really leave Starvation Lake?

I shut off my truck and sat there a minute, thinking. The tape strung closer to the house was at the end with the dining room and bathroom and Mom's bedroom. The cops must have figured the intruder had entered through the glass door into the dining room; otherwise, the kitchen would be taped off, too, wouldn't it? Mom normally locked the door, but the lock had been sticking, so she might have left it undone. I had been promising to fix it but hadn't gotten around to it.

I heard rapping at the passenger-side window and turned to look. Luke Whistler was standing there, notebook in hand. I rolled the window down.

"What are you doing here?" I said.

"Isn't this where the story is?"

I rolled up the window and got out, walked around to Whistler. Under his down vest today he wore a black Detroit Police Athletic League sweatshirt striped with bleach stains.

"Did you talk to my mother?" I said.

"Nah," he said. "This is as close as I got. Channel Eight came by, too. T.J. tried to sweet-talk her way in, but the cops wouldn't budge."

"T.J.? You know her?"

Whistler grinned. "A little."

"What's that mean, 'a little'?"

"She likes white wine," he said.

He was sleeping with Tawny Jane Reese? Every loser in Starvation Lake had jerked off at least once to Channel Eight's slinky, fortyish reporter.

"No way," I said.

"She has a police scanner on her nightstand. So do I."

"When my mother's house was—wait. I don't want to hear this."

I put my hands in my coat pockets and walked toward Mom's, stopping where the driveway met the road. A sheriff's cruiser and an unmarked police car sat there, flashers on. I saw Mom sitting at the dining room table in her fuzzy blue bathrobe.

"How's she doing?" Whistler said.

"Who? Tawny Jane?"

"Come on, man."

"You got anything more for tomorrow's paper?"

"Matter of fact, might have a little scoop." He pulled a watch out of his sweatshirt belly pocket. "See you back at the shop?"

"What's the story?"

He grinned again. For someone like Whistler, getting a scoop was just as good as getting laid. I'd known a lot of guys like that in Detroit. A few women, too.

"Has to do with the sheriff."

"If you're getting it from D'Alessio, he better not hear you're bopping Tawny Jane. He's been trying to get up her skirt for years."

"So I gather."

"Let me handle Mom myself, OK?"

"Sure. Sorry."

"That's all right. Hey—hold on." I moved closer to Whistler, looked over his shoulder to see whether any cops were around. "I got a little tip."

"What's that?"

"It's not much. Just a word. Apparently, Mrs. B—Phyllis—said something about it before she died."

"Really? She saw the guy?"

"Maybe, maybe not. All we got is this, and I don't know if it's a name or what: nye-less."

Whistler's eyebrows crinkled. "Say again?"

I said it again.

"Huh," he said. "Spelling?"

"No idea."

"Weird. But I'm headed back. You want me to check into it? Not sure what to do exactly. Maybe run a few different spellings through a search engine or something."

"Try it out. Maybe we get to it before the cops do."

"Always first," he said. "I'm on it."

"Why was that man here?"

Mom sat across from me, a cup of tea at her elbow, speaking in her normal rapid-fire staccato, which meant she was probably thinking clearly, though that was prone to change in an unpredictable instant.

"Whistler?"

"Can't you keep your own reporters away?"

"He won't be back. I can't help with the TV crews."

"I thought they worked for your company, too."

"They don't work for me."

The inside of the house was a snarl of yellow tape. The police had strung a narrow pathway from the kitchen to the dining room to Mom's bedroom. Deputy Skip Catledge sat in the kitchen, waiting for something in the microwave. Outside the picture window facing the lake, a detective paced the deck while talking into a cell phone.

"My God," Mom said. "Mavis Schmieder just called to extend her condolences. She said she was at the IGA this morning and Frank D'Alessio was standing out front, handing out copies of some story from the Internet."

D'Alessio must have stopped there after Audrey's Diner. He'd probably been handing out printouts of our story on the break-in, turning up the heat on Dingus.

"Good old Frankie," I said.

The microwave dinged. I turned and saw Catledge remove a ham-and-cheese sandwich on an onion roll.

"Is that it, Skip?" Mom said to him. "He's using Phyllis's death to get elected?"

Catledge looked surprised that someone had bothered to ask him. "I don't have the slightest idea what goes on in that man's head, Mrs. Carpenter."

"He hasn't even announced he's running yet," I said. "Maybe it'll backfire."

Mom sipped her tea, set the cup down. "That man is familiar," she said.

"D'Alessio?"

"No." She nodded toward the window. "Your reporter."

"He was here for dinner last week. He loved the meatballs, remember? I think he went home wearing one on his vest."

"Yes, Gussy. And you might also recall that I asked him if he had family ties here."

"He said he didn't think so."

"I heard him. But we had a Whistler family here a long time ago. I remember a woman at the church. She had a funny name."

"Hmm," I said. I took one of my mother's hands in mine and smiled. "Do you think she could have been Whistler's mother?"

Mom slipped her hand away from mine and sipped her tea. I wanted to ask her about nye-less, but Catledge was standing six feet away. Instead I said, "How are you feeling?"

Her eyes focused on the cup as it plinked in the saucer.

"Phyllis was my rock," she said.

"I know."

"No, you don't know."

She picked up her empty cup and saucer and stood. "I would love to take a shower, but my bathroom is police territory," she said, glaring at Catledge. "At least they let me use the toilet." Skipper stayed focused on his sandwich. "So I'll just freshen up in the kitchen sink, and then I'm going to Murray and Murray." The funeral home. "I told Darlene I'd look into arrangements."

I doubted she would be able to arrange anything until the coroner was done with Mrs. B, but it wasn't worth saying. I was glad she'd be occupied. "Darlene will be checking in on you," I said. "I'll be back tonight after the game."

"Nobody needs to be checking on me. I've already told the police I want them out of here by sundown."

"I'll sleep in my old room."

"You will not. You will get out there and get to the bottom of this. How are you going to do that sitting here with an old woman?"

I looked at Catledge after Mom had gone into her bedroom. "How's Darlene doing?" I said.

He thought about it for a moment, then said, "She's tougher than I'd be. One hell of a police officer, if you ask me."

EIGHT

The rusted metal step creaked as I lifted my boot onto it. I stopped and looked around, hoping I'd chosen the right trailer. Four were arranged in a ragged circle in the clearing that was home to Tatch's camp.

The trailers sat amid oaks and beeches and birches on a flat interruption of an incline that rose from the lake's northeastern shore. Soupy's parents' house, vacant since their deaths, sat just beyond the crest of the ridge, a few hundred yards up.

I heard something from the other side of the trailer where I was standing. There was a chugging sound, like machinery, and the clank and scrape of metal. Someone was clapping and shouting something I couldn't quite make out.

"Hey, Gus," Tatch called out. "Over here."

I spun around to see Tatch waving from the trailer at my back. Through the stripped trees behind him I could see all the way down to the white lake.

"Hey, Tatch," I said.

Like some born-agains, Tatch had become one after hitting bottom—specifically, the bottom of Dead Sledder Mile. Dead Sledder was a two-lane corkscrew of asphalt that spiraled between narrow gravel shoulders dropping off forty and fifty feet into thickets of merciless pines. The road got its nickname after a toboggan full of downstate tourists rode it into the grille of an oncoming semitrailer after a long night at Enright's in the 1970s.

Tatch himself awoke one morning in August of 1999 lying between two roadside crosses garlanded in flowers, having been flung from his pickup as it careened off Dead Sledder's last vicious curve. His truck was a steel pancake; Tatch was unhurt except for the hangover throbbing in his head. He swore as he lay there, regarding the markers of two less fortunate souls, that he would never take another drink and that he would seek the Lord as his savior. He would keep one promise more faithfully than the other.

None of it really surprised people in town. Tatch came from a family of devout Christians who read the Bible aloud before and after every meal and led the choir at the Church of the Messiah in Mio. His mother would bellow scripture at Tatch as he played goalie for the River Rats when we were kids, even when he was sitting on the bench and I was in the net. The team favorite was "Save with thy right hand, and hear me." It was only natural, then, that adolescent Tatch would rebel in every way, seeking salvation in Southern Comfort, Stroh's, red bud, and speeders. And it seemed just as natural, at least to the people of Starvation Lake, that Tatch years later would fall back on the only thing he'd ever thought he understood except partying and hockey.

Now Tatch had gathered people he had met at church services and at Alcoholics Anonymous meetings, along with his jailed sister's son, Tex, into a makeshift commune on twenty acres his dead parents had left him. I made my way to him across muddy snow pocked with hundreds of boot prints. Strewn along the ground were a playpen turned on its side, a hockey stick cut short for a little kid, a smattering of dolls in various stages of undress. Two pickup trucks and a Jeep were parked along the two-track road beneath the circle of trailers. Tatch offered his hand.

"Welcome to our little heaven on a hill," he said.

I took his hand and he said, "Come on, buddy," and pulled me in for a hug.

"I'm real sorry about Phyllis," he said.

"Me, too."

He stepped back. "She was all right. I liked them cookies she used to make us. May the good Lord be with her."

"Thanks."

"How's Darl?"

"You know."

Tatch and I had long been friends, but more than that, we'd been goalies who played alongside each other. Even though I had started

many more games than he had, there was an unspoken agreement between us that we were equals. That's how it was with goaltenders. It
didn't matter who supposedly was number one, because we were the
only ones on the team who understood how alone we were between the
goalposts.

I was the better skater, Tatch better at handling the puck. I had
a quicker catching glove; he was more agile sliding post to post. You
wanted me in the crease when the puck was lost in a scramble of players,
but nobody was better than Tatch at stopping a one-on-one breakaway.
Only one of us could play the games, though. That Coach chose me undoubtedly frustrated Tatch as much, at times, as it frightened me.

Yet if I had blocked the overtime goal that lost the Rats the 1981
state title, Tatch would have been the first one off the bench to tackle me
in celebration. Instead, he was the first to find me on the ice and wrap an
arm around me and tell me that I had played the best game I had ever
played and I should never forget that.

When we were kids, Soupy had dubbed him Tatch, short for attachment, as in vacuum cleaner attachment sucking pucks into the net.
It was hardly flattering as goalie nicknames go, but Tatch painted it in
blood red on his goalie mask and had a shoemaker stitch it into his leg
pads. Once he was Tatch and not just Roy Edwards or Roy-Roy or Roy
Toy, he let his hair grow out and his sideburns go bushy, and the next
thing you knew, he was getting hand jobs.

I held up the pair of hockey skates I'd brought. Freshly sharpened
Bauers, size 9.

"Tex around?" I said.

Tatch held his hands up. "I ain't touching those. Bad luck."

"Where were you last night? The Picks aren't much good with you,
but they really suck without a goalie."

A semicircle scar creased the skin above his left eyebrow, the mark of
a goalie-mask screw pounded in by a slap shot. Tatch treasured the scar
as much as his nickname.

"Aw, jeez," he said, scratching the salt-and-pepper scraggle on his
chin. "Had some family stuff."

"You sure?"

"Sure about what?"

"Family stuff."

Tatch screwed his face into a question mark. "Why?"

"Dingus was asking."

"The sheriff?"

"You know any other Dinguses around here?"

"He ain't got better things to do?"

I really didn't think Tatch was capable of breaking into someone's house, especially my mother's. But he also wasn't telling me everything.

"Just letting you know," I said. I looked up the ridge. "What's going on up there? You building a church?"

Tatch looked relieved that I'd changed the subject. "Got a project going."

I counted three men and five women scattered across the wooded ridge. They were digging, throwing aside the two feet of snow and jabbing the blades of their long-handled spades and pickaxes into the stubborn winter soil, their faces ruddy with exertion. All around them the ground was torn into shallow gullies that wound between potholes blackening the snowy surface. A backhoe scooped dirt onto snow-flecked mounds. In the middle of the action stood a thin man clapping and shouting orders over the chuffing machine. I didn't recognize him.

"Busy bees," I said. "Digging for gold?"

Tatch chuckled again. "Not quite. The good Lord blessed us with an early snowfall, insulated the ground so it ain't impossible to get in there."

"But what are you doing?"

"Can't really talk about it."

"It's a secret?"

"You ought to hit the drain commission meeting tomorrow."

"Why?" I watched the man giving the orders. He was facing away from me now, still clapping his hands in rhythm with the clank of the shovels. "This got something to do with your tax issue?"

After Tatch had planted the trailers on his land, removing the wheels and setting them on cinder blocks as if they were permanent,

Echo Township had doubled his assessment, thereby doubling his property taxes. Tatch went before the county tax appeals board in a paisley tie dangling down a yellowed dress shirt he'd probably worn to high school graduation. "Ain't fair to crank up my taxes just 'cause of crummy old trailers," he told the board. "I ain't got that kind of money." Getting wound up, he went on to insist that he shouldn't have to pay taxes at all, as his Christian camp was a religious organization protected by the Fourth Amendment. I think he meant the First. The appeals board members, seeing a scarecrow of a man whom they thought of as better than average at blowing smoke rings, assured Tatch they would consider his request. A few weeks later, Tatch's tax bill showed up, doubled.

From what I saw, I couldn't imagine how someone could justify the hike, especially given how tough things were in Starvation. But it was easier to shake down Tatch than some company that could afford a court fight.

"Can't say," Tatch told me. "Show up tomorrow."

Drain commission meetings weren't one of my favorite things to cover. "Gotcha," I said. I held up the skates. "You want to take these?"

"No way, buddy. Tex's got to take them hisself."

"His first superstition," I said. "A sure sign of maturity."

Helpful assistant coach that I was, early in the season I had done Tex a favor by taking his skates to be sharpened. The next day, he scored four goals and assisted on two others in an 8–2 River Rats' win over a team from Alpena.

Although Tex had the speed and size and smarts to score four goals and two assists in almost any game, he convinced himself that his big night had nothing to do with the talent that was luring college scouts to River Rats games, but with the fact that I had taken his skates to be sharpened. From then on, I always took his skates. Usually I gave them back to him at the rink, but today we had a pregame skate I wasn't sure I'd make, so I'd brought them out to Tatch's camp.

"Did I hear my name?"

Tex bounced out of the trailer behind Tatch in sweats and high-top sneakers, unlaced. He slapped Tatch hard on the shoulder. Tatch lurched forward and I caught him with one hand.

"What's up, Coach?" Tex said.

Tatch twisted around to look at the boy. "You trying to kill your uncle?"

Tex grinned. "Sorry, old man."

"Got your skates," I said.

On the trailer, a shred of cardboard duct-taped over a cracked window waggled in the breeze. I smelled something wafting out, at once acrid and sweet, maybe canned beans burned onto the inside of a pan. A preacher's voice tinned through a transistor radio: "There is no ice in hell . . ."

Tex squirmed past his uncle, towering over both Tatch and me, pale biceps bulging against the threadbare sleeves of his gray Spitfires T-shirt. "Thanks," he said, taking the skates. One by one he turned them over, shut one eye, and peered with the other down the length of each blade. Each time, he nodded and said, "That's it." Then he looked at me. His hair, black as a puck, was matted on one side. He'd been napping.

"Who's Mic-Mac's guy again?" he said.

"Holcomb," I said. "Pinky Holcomb. Number nine."

"Pinky? The guy a fag?"

"Be tolerant, son," Tatch said.

"You don't want to mess with Pinky," I said.

Mic-Mac's captain and top scorer had gotten his nickname after dropping his gloves in a hockey fight and having his left pinky severed by a skate blade in the melee. He wasn't the most skilled player, but he played with unrelenting fire, a little cannonball who would skate through a brick wall for a stray puck.

"Well, only wimps wear nine," Tex said.

I hesitated because Gordie Howe, the Red Wings great, had worn number 9.

"Right," I said.

Tex's eyes focused behind me, his smile fading.

"I'm out of here," he said. "Thanks for the skates."

"Hey there, Mr. Breck," Tatch said. "Was just about to come up."

I turned around. Standing before me was the clapping man from up on the ridge. He wore a long denim coat and a wool cap tight on the back of his head. His too-small wire-rim glasses pinched his face in a way that made him look like a sallow John Denver. I felt unsure that I would like him. He smiled and offered his hand. I took it.

"Mr. Gus Carpenter," he said. "Of the *Pilot*."

"That's me."

"I am Mr. Breck."

"You've seen my byline?"

"Some, yes. Forgive me, but I find that newspapers offer little of value. There is no salvation to be found on the sports page."

"Hard to argue with that."

"What brings you here?"

The way Breck had commandeered the conversation, with Tatch just standing meekly by, made me wonder if Breck, not Tatch, was actually in charge.

"Brought Tex his skates," I said. "He's a little superstitious."

"Matthew," Breck said.

"Matthew."

"He's got a warm-up skate before the game on account of it's a play-off tonight," Tatch offered, sounding apologetic.

Breck folded his arms and looked at the trailer behind Tatch. "We need his strong shoulders on the hill. Everyone's working hard. We cannot count on the county to do the right thing. We will have to force their hand."

"I'll get him going," Tatch said.

"Thank you, Mr. Edwards."

"What about the county?" I said.

Breck turned back to me. "Your town," he said. "You come looking for a boy to bring you a trophy so you can hoist it high over your head."

"Excuse me?"

"You ask a boy to carry your town on his shoulders."

"Actually, I just did him a little favor."

"On the contrary, Mr. Carpenter, you did yourself a favor." He smiled again. "You have a mistaken idea of what a messiah is. You and everyone down there."

I gave Tatch a who-the-hell-is-this-guy glance. "Well," I said, "I'm not sure what to say. It's just a game."

"Indeed," Breck said. "You, of all people, should understand that."

Tatch touched my elbow. "Mr. Breck's been a good friend since he come to us a few months back. Met him at a Christian convocation down to Monroe. He's helping us out with our tax issue, the legal stuff."

"Have you told him?" Breck asked Tatch.

"No," Tatch said, looking guilty nevertheless. "Told him he might want to attend that drain commission meeting tomorrow."

"I see."

"You from around here?" I said.

"I am now," Breck said. "We are building a Christian community. I'm sure it doesn't look like much to you. But we are working hard. Our faith sustains us."

"And a backhoe?"

Breck twisted his glasses off and turned and pointed them at the ridge. I saw shovels flinging dirt and the backhoe shuttling backward and up. Many a developer had begged Tatch's father to sell the land, but he refused to do anything but put his trailer and a pole barn on it.

"The Lord helps those who help themselves," Breck said. "Do you see that line of trees there, the one that tops out with the oak on the ridge?"

I looked up. I felt my breath catch. I hadn't noticed before. The trees were filled with crosses. Christian crosses. Dozens of them. Small ones made from two-by-twos, larger ones from two-by-fours. Painted black, white, red, gold. Nailed into the tree trunks at twenty, thirty feet above the ground, out of reach without a ladder. Some facing down on the clearing, some facing up toward the sky.

"Mr. Carpenter?"

"Yes," I said. "I see."

"Do not judge, so that you may not be judged," Breck said. "Where

I'm pointing approximates the property line on the western edge of the Edwards's parcels. On the other side of that line is land owned by your friends in Pine County."

I was less interested in the property line than in those crosses on the trees.

"The county purchased it in the nineteen-seventies when the economy was poor and the land could be had cheaply," he said. "Of course the people who run the county could never decide what to do with it, so it sits."

"Why are you telling me this?"

"Long ago, a handful of homes once stood there, and beneath them a septic field. We believe it to be leaking."

"Thus the backhoe and the shovels."

"It's bad enough, wouldn't you agree, that the county wants us to eat their property tax crap." He glanced at Tatch. "Please forgive the language."

"They just want us out of here," Tatch said.

"Mr. Edwards."

"Praise Jesus," Tatch said.

"If the land is so polluted," I said, "who would want to buy it?"

"Hard to believe in this country, but there are motives aside from strict financial enrichment," Breck said. "Perhaps we're mistaken about the septic matter, but if we're not, well, we may have to take the matter up with the drain commission, or the county itself, or whatever collection of cronies currently mismanages things. Perhaps we'll need to avail ourselves of the courts."

"So you're a lawyer?"

He fitted his glasses back on, adjusted his cap. "I apologize for my earlier stridency. We actually would just like to be left alone."

"Until there's a fire in one of the trailers, or rain washes out that two-track. Then you'll be calling for help."

"We have work to do." He looked at Tatch. "Please get Matthew."

Tatch shifted uneasily in the mud. "I think he's resting up."

"For what? His warm-up? Why must he play twice in the same day?"

I wanted to tell Breck that lots of teams had pregame skates, but I thought I might get Tatch in more trouble than he was already in.

"I'll get him," Tatch said. "Take her easy, Gus. God bless."

He went into the trailer.

Breck said, "Why are you running errands, Mr. Carpenter, bringing skates to boys?" He nodded in the direction of the town. "Don't you have more pressing matters to attend to?"

"I do."

Breck turned and started to walk, then jog, toward the ridge. He resumed the clapping as he disappeared behind a trailer. The women and men seemed to shovel harder. He was an interesting stranger, this Breck who'd come to Starvation not long before the break-ins began. Maybe his arrival was mere coincidence. My gaze drifted up to the crosses. I felt myself shudder as I turned away.

NINE

"Soup? You back there?"

I called down the whiskey-colored bar that ran the length of the tunnel of week-old smoke that was Enright's Pub. A crash came from the office and storeroom behind the bar, like a stack of boxes had toppled.

"Son of a bitch," I heard Soupy say. "Fucking closet."

Foghat was grinding out of the jukebox. An old woman sitting at the other end of the bar nodded at me. Stalks of white hair stuck out from beneath her orange LaCoste Builders cap.

"Angie," I said.

She knew my name but probably didn't want to take the trouble to recall it. Instead she lifted her tulip glass of beer in a halfhearted toast, took a sip, and set it back down next to her cigarettes and Bic lighter. She returned to staring at the soap opera flickering soundlessly on the television over the bar. Beneath the TV hung a sign that said "If you're drinking to forget, please pay in advance."

I didn't have to worry about a lunch rush at Enright's. There hadn't been one since the griddle stopped working in December. I'd been there that evening, awaiting a patty melt. Soupy was standing in front of the griddle, spatula in hand, watching a burger fry when the sizzling ebbed and then stopped altogether. He stared at the half-cooked meat for a minute, then tossed the spatula aside with a clatter and started fiddling with the griddle controls. "What the fuck?" he said. He stood there another minute staring at the grill, then picked up the spatula and scooped the meat into a garbage can. "Fuck it," he said. "Go to McDonald's." He went back to his office and came out with a piece of cardboard he had torn from a gin box. "Grill Not Working—SORRY" was scratched across it in felt-tip pen. He stuck it to the wall over the back bar with a piece of white hockey tape.

The sorry sign was hanging there still when I walked in that afternoon looking for a Coke and a bag of Better Mades to take to the *Pilot*. Soupy hadn't yet fixed the griddle, saying he didn't have the money. That was undoubtedly true, but even if he did have the money, I doubted he would've squandered it on necessary repairs when he could be investing it in booze and the Bay City stripper who came up every other Monday to screw him, ignorant of the fact that Mr. Big Shot Resort-Town Tavern Owner was in Chapter 11 bankruptcy and might never emerge. "I know what happens in Chapter Eleven," Soupy liked to say. "Who knows about Chapter Twelve?"

Today he came out of his office sucking on a finger. He wore an apron stained with ketchup, or maybe blood, over an old Hershey Bears T-shirt. The Bears were the last minor league team Soupy had skated with before he walked away from his once promising hockey career for the more reliable pursuit of hungover weekday mornings.

"You hurt yourself?" I said.

"Shit, Trap." He flicked on the cold water in the bar sink and let it run over his finger. "Need a damn chain saw to cut into those booze boxes. If they used the same glue on the space shuttle, we'd never had a problem."

He turned the water off and reached into a fridge beneath the back bar. "Soup," I said. "Just a Coke. I'm working."

Soupy popped the caps off of two Blue Ribbons on an opener bolted to the sink. He slammed mine down so that foam slopped over the lip.

"Don't be a pussy, Trap," he said. He held his bottle out to me. "To Mrs. B."

"Not fair."

"She was a sweetheart."

I clinked my bottle into his and took a swallow. I usually loved that first burning cold gulp of a beer, but this one was as lukewarm as a Detroit Lions fan.

"Did you pay the electric bill?" I said.

"Are you my mother?" Soupy said. "The lights are still on, aren't they? Why don't you go back to the fish-wrapper and fix this fucked-up town?

Jesus, can't the cops get anything right? People think they have to stay in their goddamn houses every night instead of going out for a drink with their friends. It's tearing up the social fabric. Now Mrs. B is dead? It's killing me."

I had heard Soupy's rant before. He must have heard "social fabric" on some talk show on the bar tube. While it was true that some people were staying closer to home, I doubted the old folks whose houses had been broken into had set foot in Enright's since Reagan was president. But Soupy needed someone to blame besides himself.

"Who the hell would want to kill Mrs. B anyway?" he said.

"Nobody."

"How's Darlene doing? She talking to you now?"

"Yeah."

"I figured she'd be back."

"She's not back the way you mean, but at least we're talking." I wanted to change the subject. "How about you? Get your mom's house sold yet?"

Soupy's mother had been dead for nearly two years, his father almost three, and Soupy was finally selling the house they had lived in for more than forty years. It sat on a few acres on the back side of the ridge above Tatch's camp. Soupy hadn't lived there in a long time and said he didn't want to live anywhere his old man had lived. And he needed the money.

"Working on it," he said. "Was over there yesterday, digging through Mom's shit. What a pack rat. Stacks of magazines from the sixties, Liz goddamn Taylor on the cover, and she's not as big as a house. And, oh, hey—I found the old Bobby Hull."

"The table hockey game?"

"Yeah, man, with the little metal players. I thought it was long gone, but there it was, all covered with dust under the basement stairs. Way to go, Ma."

As kids we'd played hundreds of games on that table. Soupy had nicknamed his goalie "Tommy Trapezoid." When I started to play goalie myself, he started calling me Trapezoid, too, and soon shortened it to Trap, which he called me still.

"We'll resume the series," I said. "I'm up like two twenty to two hundred five."

"Bullshit, man, I was way ahead. You couldn't handle my right-wing-to-center move."

"Whatever. When's the garage sale?"

He'd been talking about having a garage sale for months. I couldn't imagine Soupy actually going to the trouble of making price tags and haggling with old ladies over an ancient ottoman or toaster oven. More likely, he would load everything into his pickup and take it to the county landfill. Even more likely, load everything up and tote it around for a few months.

"Rethinking that," he said.

"How come?"

"Not sure."

He turned to the back bar and started rearranging schnapps bottles.

"Not sure about what?" I said.

He turned back around, glanced down the bar at Angie, lowered his voice.

"Really don't want all these local assholes talking about my business," Soupy said.

"You got a buyer?"

"Kind of out of nowhere. Yeah. Five above asking."

That was a good price in Starvation, where houses for sale sat for months, even years, without an offer. The Campbells' place, a two-bedroom with water-stained clapboard walls and a roof enveloped in vines, wasn't even on the lake.

"They must love that knotty pine paneling, eh?" I said. "And the cigarette smell. Who's the buyer? Do I know them?"

"I'm dealing with some law firm downstate."

"You get me the name, I might be able to check it out for you."

Soupy studied the rim of his bottle.

"Thanks. Don't want to jinx it just yet," he said.

You don't know a guy for thirty years and not know when he's bullshitting you. Especially Soupy, who, except when he had a hockey stick in his hands, wasn't nearly as clever as he imagined. I let it go for the moment.

"Rats going to do it tonight?" he said.

"I think so."

"Best thing that could happen around here, Rats win the state title. Good for the soul, good for the economy. Mrs. B would've wanted it that way."

Mrs. B wouldn't have given a rip, I thought. "I was just out giving Tex his skates," I said.

Soupy flipped his empty at the overflowing barrel of garbage next to his office door. The bottle clanged off of another and nestled against a pizza box.

"Out where?" he said.

"Tatch's."

"Camp J.C.?"

"Yeah. A little spooky. Have you seen it?"

"Nope." He reached into the fridge for another Blue Ribbon. "But I was out at Mom's the other day and heard them making all sorts of noise."

"They're turning the hill into an ant farm. Got a backhoe going."

"Bunch of crazy Jesus freaks, don't want to pay their fair share." It was Angie, shouting from her bar stool.

"Need a refill, Ange?" Soupy said.

She looked at her glass as if she hadn't noticed it before. "Might as well."

Soupy poured another tulip glass from the Busch Light tap and took it down the bar. When he came back, he said, "Where the hell was Tatch last night anyway?"

"He said family stuff."

"Since when did Tatch give a shit about—" Soupy stopped and turned toward the front door as chilly air washed into the bar. Luke Whistler stepped in and closed the door.

"Gus," he said. "Mr. Campbell."

Soupy grabbed a bottle of Jack Daniel's and slapped a shot glass down on the bar. "Chief," he said, filling the glass and nudging it in Whistler's direction.

Whistler looked at it for a second, smiling uncomfortably, then picked it up and drank it back in one smooth swallow. As he set the glass back down, Soupy held the bottle up for a refill. Whistler pulled the glass away. "No thanks."

"I guess you guys know each other," I said.

"I wouldn't be much of a reporter if I didn't know the town barkeep," Whistler said. Then he said to Soupy, "You're going to get me in trouble with the boss."

"Who, him?" Soupy said. "He's a goalie. He doesn't worry about anybody but himself and his little net. Ain't that right, Trap?" He grabbed the beer I had pushed away and shoved it in front of me. "Drink up. People are dying of thirst in Cambodia."

I grimaced through another tepid sip.

"Saw your truck outside," Whistler said. "Got a little info on that thing you asked about."

Nye-less? I thought. "That was fast."

"I wish I could take credit. This Google thing is pretty nifty."

"What the hell are you talking about?" Soupy said.

"Nothing," I said, standing up and feeling justified in keeping something from Soupy. "Can I have a Coke to go? And a bag of Better Mades?"

"Out of Coke," he said. He snatched the potato chips off a rack on the back bar and threw the bag at me. I caught it in my left hand. "Nice save," he said.

"You going over to the shop?" Whistler said.

"Yeah."

"I'll meet you there in five."

Soupy grabbed my bottle, downed the dregs, and flipped it at the trash barrel. It bounced off the pizza box and shattered on the floor.

"Fuck it," I heard him say as I went out the door.

The *Pilot* front counter was buried. There were newspapers—the *Free Press*, the *Times*, the *Traverse City Record-Eagle*, shoppers from Kalkaska and Bellaire—the weekend mail, and our weekly bundle of memos from corporate headquarters in Traverse City.

Plus the remembrances for Mrs. B: Bouquets of flowers. Baskets of dried cherries and fudge. A frozen casserole that must have come from some well-meaning lady who didn't understand that Mrs. B was Darlene's mom, not mine, or who just didn't know what else to do when someone died but bake something stuffed with cheese and potatoes and offer it to the bereaved.

I needed to hire a replacement but didn't want to think about it yet.

Whistler was hunched over his keyboard, batting away with his two forefingers. The plastic clacks of the keystrokes were punctuated by the metallic clicking of a fat gold pinkie ring slapping the shift key. A foam cup of coffee steamed next to him; he wouldn't touch it until the steam was gone and the coffee was about the temperature of that beer I'd choked down at Enright's. He said he'd gotten used to lukewarm coffee on winter stakeouts in Detroit.

I went to my desk and dumped the mail across my blotter. There were three March of Dimes solicitations; the spring sports schedule from Pine County High School; and press releases from an advertising agency in Traverse, the Meijer supercenter in Charlevoix, the winter park in Petoskey. At the bottom of the pile lay a manila envelope tied with string. It contained the ad layouts for the next day's paper. I already knew what it would tell me: We had barely any ads, which meant fewer pages and less space for stories.

"Hey," Whistler said. "Just sent you a story."

The shrinking news hole hadn't been a problem until Whistler showed up and started writing more stories than we had space for. It forced me to trim his stories, or hold them for the next paper, or just keep them out altogether, hoping someone would find them on our website. Whistler had complained only once so far, when I held a story he'd written about a road commissioner's secret financial interest in an asphalt company in favor of an advance story on the River Rats' chances in a Christmas tournament.

"Public service ought to trump kids' play," he'd said.

Hockey, I had replied, is more than kids' play in Starvation Lake.

Now I hit a key and Whistler's story appeared on my computer screen.

> Pine County sheriff's deputy Frank T. D'Alessio will challenge the incumbent sheriff—his boss—in November's election, according to papers expected to be filed with the county clerk and disclosed exclusively to the *Pine County Pilot*.

Whistler was big on self-promotion, constantly mentioning the *Pilot* in his stories, what the *Pilot* knew "exclusively," what it had reported before. I figured he did it because he had come from Detroit, where chest-thumping was part of the newspaper game. I usually sliced it out. Besides the AP guy in Grand Rapids, who seemed to come north only after the temperature hit eighty, we had no real competition except for Channel Eight. Readers and advertisers weren't going away because we weren't getting stories first. They were just going away.

I spun in my swivel chair to face Whistler. "Nice," I said. "But do we have to do the commercial so high in the story?"

He propped a sneaker on the edge of his desk. "Why not tell the readers we're kicking ass on their behalf?"

"I think they can see the paper they're holding in their hands is the *Pilot*. Besides, doesn't everyone know Frankie's going to run?"

Whistler smiled the smile of a reporter who knew his boss was clueless. "According to the clips I read, everyone knew he was going to run last election, too. And he didn't run."

"He backed out because he knew he didn't have a chance."

"Correct. But everything's different now, isn't it?"

He had me there. The second and third paragraphs of his story were all about the break-ins, the murder, and Sheriff Dingus Aho's inability so far to figure out what was going on. D'Alessio will love that, I thought.

"The story doesn't quote D'Alessio and the department spokesman declined to comment," I said. "So I'm guessing your main source is Frankie."

Whistler shrugged. He took the pinkie ring off, rubbed the finger, put the ring back on. "I shouldn't talk about my sources. But you should know that our friend from Channel Eight is snooping around, too."

"Your friend," I said. I tore open the bag of chips and popped a handful into my mouth. "You better hope D'Alessio doesn't find out about you and your close relationship with her police scanner."

"Ha," Whistler said. "We better get that thing online, eh?"

"You think D'Alessio would do any better than Dingus?"

"I have no idea. Just a good story."

I looked at the clock on the wall over the copier. Eight minutes after three. "Tawny Jane doesn't have a program till five, but she could do a bulletin. Let me give this a quick read."

I read the story through, fixed a few typos, and hit Send. A goateed twenty-two-year-old at the main printing plant would have it on the Media North website in minutes.

"Done," I said. "Another Whistler scoop."

"That's nice," he said, "but really, BFD, you know, all we did was beat another reporter."

"Isn't that the idea?"

"Well, yeah. 'Always first.' But it's one thing to beat a competitor. They're just journalists, after all. It's another thing to beat the cops."

"Right. Like your ex-wife."

"Tags."

"Yeah."

"Which brings me to this," Whistler said. He kicked away from his desk, rolled over to me, and leaned forward in his chair. He had a printout folded in one hand. "Did a little Internet search."

"You are cutting-edge for an old man."

"Funny. Write this down."

I picked up a pen.

"N-I-L-U-S," he spelled.

I looked at it written on my blotter.

"Nilus," I said. "As in nye-less?"

"Nilus Moreau," Whistler said. "Father Nilus Moreau."

"A priest?"

"He was the pastor of St. Valentine's."

"Here? In Starvation Lake?"

"A long time ago. I only did a quick search. Been spending most of my time calling around to cop shops that might be hearing echoes from Dingus and his guys." He handed me the printout. "Found an obit in the *Marquette Mining Journal*, 1971."

I scanned it quickly, three short paragraphs on an inside page of the *Mining Journal* from Michigan's Upper Peninsula. Father Nilus Moreau had come to Starvation Lake in the early 1930s before it was even called Starvation Lake. He led the effort to build a new church at St. Valentine's in 1951. He died in a nursing home in Calumet at the age of sixty-nine.

"So what?" I said.

"Where did you get this Nilus tip?" Whistler said.

I thought of Darlene. "I shouldn't talk about my sources either. But it wasn't D'Alessio."

"OK. But you ought to run it down from here, don't you think?"

"Fair enough."

A priest? I thought, and an image of the crosses in the trees at Tatch's camp popped into my head.

"Speaking of churches," I said, "I was out at that born-again camp today."

Whistler's white eyebrows went up. "Whatever for?"

"One of the kids on our hockey team lives there. Took him his skates."

"I'll bet that was interesting."

"A little weird, actually. Reminds me: Were you trying to get the records on that land?"

I could tell Whistler hadn't expected that question. "I might have seen them if the wench clerk had let me."

"You didn't say anything to me."

"Sorry, boss. I always go looking for the documents. The docs can't kiss your ass and buy you lunch and make you write like a wimp, like

those auto reporters back in—" He caught himself, perhaps remembering I had once covered that industry. "Oh, sorry."

"I wish writing like a wimp had been my problem."

"Anyway, I got nowhere with Verna the Vault. But it's a story, right?
The born-agains want to get out of paying taxes, or at least pay less.
Kind of a sore subject in this economy."

"Yep. They apparently have a lawyer now, an out-of-towner named
Breck."

Whistler sat back in his chair. "Breck?"

"Like the shampoo. Didn't get the first name. Know him?"

"Nope."

"Seems like he's running things out there. They've got a backhoe tearing up that hill."

"Really? Building themselves a church?"

"Nah. Something about a septic field leaking into their land. They're
going to try to use it to squeeze the county for some cash."

"You can't get blood from a stone."

"Right." I ate another chip. "But they might be making some hay
about it at the drain commission tomorrow. You want to go? This Breck
guy's supposed to be there."

"The drain commission? Hmm." Whistler pedaled his chair back to
his desk. "I'm going to be a good guy and let you do it, how's that?"

"Thanks a million."

"But tell you what. I've got a source in the archdiocese from covering
the pope's visit to Detroit way back when. If he's not dead, I'll call him,
see what I can find out about this Nilus character."

"Did you check the old papers downstairs?"

"In the morgue?"

"Nobody calls it a morgue anymore."

"What you got downstairs ought to be one, as cold and damp as
it is. I got allergies. The last time I went down there, I sneezed for a
week."

"I'll look. There's probably something."

Whistler stood up. "I've got to see a man about a horse," he said. "But one thing. If you're poking around back in whenever Nilus was here, you might stumble over my mother."

"Your mother?"

"Yeah. She lived nearby for a little while in the forties. Matter of fact, I lived here, but we moved away when I was a little shaver."

So Mom's recollection of a Whistler in Starvation Lake was not mistaken. I said, "But didn't you tell my mother—"

"I know, I fibbed to your mom. I'm sorry. See, unlike your mom, mine was nothing to be proud of. Spent most of her life in a bottle. I just, I don't know, I didn't know how well your mom knew her, and I didn't want to get into it."

"Gotcha."

"How is your mom anyway?"

"Getting through it. I've got to check on her."

Whistler yanked keys from his vest pocket. "Will let you know what I find out. Let's get there before the cops, eh, boss?"

I finished up the next day's paper. Wrote a few headlines, some photo captions, a brief on the high school girls' basketball team going to Big Rapids for a game. Then I went to the back of the newsroom and descended a set of creaky stairs to the basement.

At the bottom I reached up and pulled on a string that lit a single overhead bulb. The air tasted of chalk. Black binders filled with old newspapers lay in racks along two walls. The binders went back only about forty years, so I doubted they'd help me much. In the darkest corner of the room stood a pair of wooden file cabinets, painted green. Index cards taped on the drawers were marked with letters in alphabetical order. I pulled open the drawer marked Na–No and flipped through the file folders inside.

I found the file I wanted about two-thirds deep in the drawer: "Moreau, Rev. Nilus." I pulled it out and opened it, praying it would hold a yellowed, cut-out clip or two. The file was empty except for an index card. I pulled the card out and walked across the floor to read beneath the lightbulb. The typewriting on the card said:

```
St. Valentine's Welcomes New Pastor,
    November 2, 1933.

Nilus Expands Orphanage with Children from
    Midland, January 20, 1934.

Town Searches for Missing Nun; "No Stone
    Unturned," Priest Vows, p. A-1,
    August 17, 1944.

Hope Ebbing in Search for Nun, p. A-1,
    August 28, 1944.
```

"Holy shit," I said. I flipped the card over. The list continued on the back:

```
Gardener Arrested in Disappearance of Nun,
    p. A-1, August 5, 1950.

cf. Accused Killer Murdered in Pine County Jail,
    p. A-3, August 7, 1950.
```

This had to be the nun Dingus had told me about, and the guy who'd gotten his throat cut in the jail. I did the math in my head. Mrs. B and Mom were the same age, sixty-six. They had known each other since they went to the school at St. Val's together. The school had closed sometime in the 1970s. Mom and Mrs. B would've been eleven years old when the nun vanished. I wondered if the nun had taught at St. Val's, if Nilus had. Did he know Mrs. B as a little girl?

I flipped the index card back to the front. A faded blue stamp in the upper right hand corner said MICROFILM.

"Shit," I said.

I slipped the card into my shirt pocket. I ran up the stairs and sat down at my desk and picked up my phone. I felt a little burst of that energy I'd felt at the *Detroit Times* whenever I thought I was on to a good story. I wanted to tell someone. For a second, I thought about calling Whistler and telling him too bad about your allergies.

Instead, I dialed the clerk's office.

"Pine County Clerk," Verna Clark said.

I hung up and looked at the clock. Three forty-five. The pregame skate had already begun. I had to get going. I dialed again.

"Clerk," Verna Clark said.

I couldn't afford to wait again. "Vicky, please."

"Vicky?" her mother said. "Is this a personal call?"

I screwed up by hesitating. "No. Not really."

"Not really? Well then, perhaps I can help you if whatever you need is doable within the next hour and fourteen minutes. After that, I'm afraid you'll have to call tomorrow."

"It's Gus Carpenter, Verna."

"I am aware of that."

"Can I speak to the deputy clerk?"

"May I?"

"May I speak to the deputy clerk?"

"She's busy at the moment. How can I help you?"

If I told Verna Clark what I really wanted, which was to look at the microfilm of those newspaper clips in the county archive, she would have informed me that I would need to come to the office the next morning and fill out a request form and then wait a week or ten days or whatever she decided would be long enough to frustrate the hell out of me. Silently I cursed the Media North bean counter who had decided the *Pilot*'s oldest stories could be most efficiently stored where Verna could lord it over them. The *Pilot* actually *paid* the county for this privilege.

I had to throw her off somehow. So I said, "I need to ask Vicky about a recipe."

"A recipe? This is not Audrey's Diner."

"Yes, but—"

"I'm sorry. Is there any official county business I could help you with, sir?"

"Could you tell your daughter I called?"

"Excuse me?"

Verna Clark hated to be reminded that her deputy also happened to be her daughter. Her opponent in her last election had run an attack campaign based largely on nepotism, and Verna had been forced to nearly drain her election fund defending herself. She even had to stoop to buying ads in the *Pilot*, which must have infuriated her.

"Could you please—"

"I heard you the first time, Mr. Carpenter. The Pine County Clerk's Office will welcome your request in person. We close in one hour and thirteen minutes and reopen tomorrow at nine o'clock sharp."

She hung up. But I had gotten her to speak my name aloud. My phone rang again a few minutes later. Vicky Clark whispered it: "Are you ready for chicken and dumplings?"

Pucks boomed off of the rink boards as I pushed through the double-door entrance to the Starvation Lake Arena. It felt reassuring. There would be no talk of burglaries or murder there.

Through the lobby windows I saw Tex on the ice, bearing down on the goalie, Dougie Baker. Tex faked to his right, then dragged the puck the other way with the toe of his stick. Dougie slid with him. The puck hit a rut in the ice and rolled up on an edge. Tex tried to snap it between Dougie's legs but got only half of the tumbling puck. It flip-flopped up and Dougie snatched it with his catching glove.

"Fucking bullshit," Tex yelled. He turned hard, spun behind the net, wound up with his stick, and, as he came around the other side of the net, swung the shaft across the goalpost with an echoing crack. The broken-off blade went flying. Tex skated to the bench.

We really did have to talk with him.

Refrigerant stung my nostrils as I hustled across the black rubber-mat floors past the benches beneath the big gold-and-blue Home and Visitors signs. I had relished that whiff of chill since I was a boy and the town rink, about the same age as me, hadn't yet been closed in on the ends.

My dad took me to my first River Rats game when I was five. By the second period, I had taken my hot chocolate and climbed down from the bleachers to stand along the glass behind the Rats' goalie, a short kid with quick hands named Ronayne. I was fascinated by all the straps and buckles and laces that attached his leather and plastic armor to his arms and chest and legs and how it made him seem so much bigger than when I had seen him walking along Main Street.

I liked how he tossed his head around between face-offs, twisting his neck this way and that, his face inscrutable behind his molded white mask, the sweaty ends of his stringy hair flopping on the back of his jersey. It wasn't long before I was strapping on the goalie pads and squatting, alone, between the goalposts.

Now I laced my goalie skates on in dressing room 3. I heard Coach Poppy blow two blasts on his whistle. The skate was nearly over. I shoved on hockey gloves, grabbed a stick, and clomped out to the ice.

The seventeen young River Rats were kneeling around Poppy at center ice in their blue-and-gold helmets, gloves, and sweats. High above their heads hung a faded banner declaring the Rats the runners-up in the 1981 Michigan state championship. My team. A team I wished had been forgotten, but was not.

"On your feet, buckets off," Poppy said. I skated up and stood facing him from the other side of the players' circle. The Rats doffed their helmets, hair stuck by sweat to their necks and foreheads. "Let's have a moment of silence for Coach Carpenter. He lost a good friend who was a good friend to the River Rats."

Tex and the other boys lowered their eyes. I saw stickers on the sides of their helmets bearing the initials PMB. I wondered if any had known Mrs. B. I wondered what they would have thought if they knew that, the morning after our loss in that state final so long ago, she'd come to our house with a plate of peanut butter cookies she must have gotten out of bed at dawn to make. I petulantly refused to eat. Later I felt sad that she had been so kind and I had turned her away. I walked next door and, while Darlene watched, I apologized to Mrs. B. She laughed and told me she was glad I hadn't eaten those cookies because it wasn't her best batch and she'd given one to the dog and thrown the rest away.

The team assembled around me now was poised to wipe out the memories of the team that had come so close but fallen short. These Rats were as quick and hungry as their namesakes and, to the delight of the fans, as nasty, too, certainly tougher and scrappier than any of the teams that had preceded them. For years, the mighty squads from Detroit—Little Caesars and Slasor Heating, Byrd Electric and Paddock Pools—had intimidated the Rats with their jutting elbows and chopping sticks. But these Rats weren't afraid to meet a slash with a slash, a cross-check with a cross-check.

Best of all, it was Tex, their leading scorer, their most skilled player, who inspired their toughness, though not only with his heavy slap shot or his fast feet or his knack for finding the back of the opponents' net with the puck. Unlike many a star player, Tex refused to let his teammates fight his battles.

Early that season, he'd scored two goals and an assist and the Rats were finishing a 5–2 win over Detroit's Byrd Electric when a double-wide defenseman named Cranch, nicknamed "Crunch," gave Tex a whack to the back of a knee. Tex collapsed and slid into the side of his own net. The crowd howled for a penalty, but no ref had seen. Cranch skated away with a smirk between his chapped-red cheeks. Tex struggled to a knee, then to both feet, and started wobbling down the ice after Cranch. "No, Tex," Poppy screamed from the bench, and I joined him, yelling, "Come to the bench—now!"

Cranch was curling out of a corner with the puck, his head down, when Tex hit him. Tex's hard plastic right shoulder pad drove into Cranch's chin and snapped his head back so hard that his helmet flew off and cracked against the boards. Then Tex grabbed him by the collar of his jersey and flung him to the ice and pummeled his face with punch after punch, opening cuts that would require twenty-four stitches. Cranch was unconscious by the time the two refs and Poppy tore Tex off. Poppy appealed the three-game suspension ordered by the league, to no avail.

After that, the Rats were never the same, never again the talented but tame youngsters from up north who went into games against the downstate teams hoping merely to stay close and get a bounce or a ref's call that would help them win late. The Rats began to play in the spirit of the logo they wore on their jerseys: a snarling, snaggle-toothed rodent wielding a hockey stick like a pitchfork.

The fans loved it, our players reveled in it, Poppy and I worried about it. Both of us knew there's a thin line in hockey between playing tough and playing stupid. If the Rats got a reputation, deserved or not, as dirty players, opposing coaches would whisper to the refs, who would then look for the first chance to whistle us for a hook or an elbow. We didn't have the depth on our bench or the kind of stand-on-his-head goalie to survive too many penalties.

Because Tex was our best player, we were in even deeper trouble when he went to the penalty box. Yet three times that season, he had taken major penalties of five minutes each because he'd let his temper get the best of him. With Tex sitting uselessly in the box and the Rats forced to play short-handed for long stretches, we had lost all three games.

Mic-Mac, the team we'd face in the state quarterfinal that night, was well aware of Tex's weakness. They would keep a shadow on him, try to deny him the puck, shove a butt end in his ribs, or give him a face wash with a glove whenever the refs were looking elsewhere, hoping to get him riled, get him to take a penalty, at least get him thinking about something other than taking the puck to the Mic-Mac net.

"OK, gentlemen," Poppy said. He wore a Rats sweat suit. His head, a tousle of thinning gray, was bare. "What's the most important thing?"

"The puck," the Rats answered in unison.

"That's right—the puck. Because the best defense . . ."

"Is to have the puck on your stick."

"If we have the puck, we cannot lose, am I right?"

"Yes sir, Coach."

"And we move the puck to the open man because . . ."

"The puck has no lungs."

"That's right, the puck never gets tired." He grabbed his whistle, blew another short blast. "Tex, hang around," he said. "Everybody else, be back here no later than six-fifteen."

The Rats scattered. Tex slipped a glove off and held his right hand in front of his face, frowning.

"What's the matter?" I said.

He showed me the skin between his thumb and forefinger. "Blister," he said. "On my shooting hand."

"From breaking your stick in half?"

"Freaking digging."

"At the camp?"

"Yeah. Bunch of bullshit. That Breck dude is a dick."

"Whoa there, partner," Poppy said. "Tape it up and forget it. You're going to have a big game tonight."

"Yeah."

"The Mic-Macs are going to be all over you, trying to get you to do something stupid."

"I won't."

"Yeah, well, listen up."

Poppy had told me about his plan earlier. It stemmed from his own youth skating for the old Detroit Junior Red Wings. Poppy had been a brawler then, assigned to beat up opposing players who hassled the Junior Wings' stars, like Gordie Howe's son Mark. Poppy had some wicked scars on his knuckles to prove it.

If you pushed him, Poppy would talk about those days, but it was clear that he had regrets, that he wished he hadn't established himself as merely a fighter, a reputation that followed him into the low minor leagues but never propelled him even close to the NHL. Back then, their fighters came from every corner of Canada but never from the United States.

"I want you to keep your cool," Poppy said. "When you get honked off at some guy for putting his stick up your butt, count to three, call him an asshole, walk away."

"I can do that."

"But just in case." Poppy moved in close to Tex. "Just in case you feel like you can't hold it in, here's what I want you to do."

Tex waited.

"Do not drop your gloves. Do you hear me? Under no circumstances will you drop your gloves. Got it?"

"Got it."

"Instead, if some guy gets you to the point that you're just dying to blast him, I want you to do this. I want you to hit the guy once, as hard as you can." Poppy threw a slow fake punch just short of Tex's face. Tex did not flinch. "Just once. As hard as you can. Then head directly to the penalty box. Do not pass go."

Tex smiled. "You sure about this, Coach?"

"It ain't funny, son. I don't want you to lose it at all out there. I don't want you in the penalty box. But I'd rather you took a two-minute penalty than something that sits you down longer or gets you tossed."

"Do you understand, Tex?" I said.

"Yeah. One punch, go to the box."

"Especially with that Holcomb guy."

"Pinky?" Tex said. "What a wuss. I'll take him and—"

"No," Poppy said. "The point is not to go head-hunting. The point is to stay calm, focus on the puck, but if you feel the dam bursting, you know what to do."

"OK, Coach."

"Control yourself. Be a man."

For some reason I thought of my reporter's propensity for smashing computers. Whistler, who was forty years older than Tex.

"I've got to fix this hand," Tex said.

As he skated away, Poppy said, "You think he'll get into it with Pinky?"

"Of course," I said. "Just a question of how much."

"God help us. I worry about him up there with all those crazy people. He's a good kid. Not sure he's cut out for that."

"Me either. Listen, Pop, I might be a little late tonight. Got some stuff to take care of."

He looked taken aback for a second, then said, "Got it. Hey—we're going to have a moment of silence for Phyllis again, right after the anthem."

"Great. Ring me between periods, will you?"

"Will do."

"Don't forget."

My phone rang as I was pulling out of the rink parking lot.

"Whistler here," the caller said. "Got lucky again."

"With T.J.?"

"Good one. No. With this Nilus guy. My source at the archdiocese is retired, but he remembered him from way back. Said to check a couple of counties for lawsuits. I left a note on your desk. Maybe you want to run them down. Or I can."

"Lawsuits against Nilus?"

"Concerning Nilus, supposedly, though I doubt he's the only defendant, because as a priest he wouldn't have two nickels. The church or the diocese would be the deep pockets."

"What did he supposedly do?"

"Not sure. The guy was a little squirrelly. Might be nothing—you know, a property dispute or something. Maybe somebody got pissed that he made him say too many Hail Marys." Whistler laughed at his little joke and, as he laughed, I heard a snatch of music, the opening riff of a Procol Harum song. I imagined him standing outside Enright's.

"I'll check it out," I said. "I found out some interesting stuff myself."

"Cool. What do you got?"

A snowplow rumbled past, a pair of fluttering River Rats flags attached to the cab windows.

"Not much yet," I said, "but the clips—well, the headlines—filed downstairs, you know, the morgue, said Nilus was around when some nun disappeared years ago. Then they got the guy who killed her and he got killed in jail."

"Whoa. Awesome shit, man. You get it in tomorrow's paper?"

"No." I looked at my watch. "Two minutes to deadline, and I don't really have it nailed."

"Always first," Whistler said.

"And frequently right."

"Let's hope Channel Eight doesn't have it."

"I've got to go. Thanks for the good work."

"You got it," he said. "Tough story, but a good story."

"Yeah."

"And, Gus, next time you go down to that basement, let someone know so we can send down a search team if you don't come out."

* * *

Besides two moldering tomatoes and half a head of slimy lettuce, all I could find in my fridge were two cans of Blue Ribbon, a month-old package of Swiss cheese, a jar of dill pickles, and some Miracle Whip. It would be enough. I was starving.

I had planned to shop for groceries that weekend but got busy. Before going to Mom's Sunday morning, I'd had to dump a quart of 2 percent milk that had soured before I'd even opened it. My one loaf of bread was nearly stale, but I figured it would be fine toasted, at least until it started growing mold, so I'd stuck it in the freezer.

Now I took it out and put two hard, frosted slices in the toaster on the counter next to the fridge. The kitchen, with its drab green walls and fake petunias hanging in a plastic basket over the sink, wasn't all that big, but bigger than the one I'd had when I'd last lived alone, in an apartment over the *Pilot*, before spending a year back at Mom's.

I had moved out of Mom's six months before and rented one of the old Victorians on Main a few blocks from the *Pilot*. The rent was cheap because the landlord lived downstate and he liked having someone there to make sure the pipes didn't freeze and the roof was shoveled. I could walk to work, which helped clear my mind for rewriting press releases and arm wrestling with corporate and cops and town council members.

Some mornings I would be sitting in that kitchen eating a bowl of Cheerios, hearing the ticking of the grandfather clock in the living room, imagining it was growing louder by the tick, and I would feel oddly certain that somebody else should have been there, that I shouldn't be sitting alone in a house that big, in a town that small, and I would get up and turn on a radio or, if it was warm enough outside, open a window so I could hear cars and trucks passing on Main.

Now, while the bread toasted, I spun the lid off the Miracle Whip and shoved my nose inside. It didn't smell life threatening yet. I cut two dill pickles into thin slices and set them on a paper plate festooned with little Santa heads.

I gazed out the window over the sink. Across the way I could see the Andersons sitting down to dinner. Two towheaded boys and a teenage girl waited at the table while their mother set a casserole in the middle.

Beef stew? I wondered. Scalloped potatoes? Darlene made terrific scalloped potatoes with ham.

The boys and the girl were wearing matching River Rats sweatshirts. The father, Oke, came in talking into a cell phone. His wife gave him a look and he smiled and dropped the phone into a pocket and sat down. I'd gone to high school with the guy. He used to come to Rats games back then. He and his buddies would sit in the very top row at one end of the stands, avoiding teachers because they'd had a little pregame party in the woods near Jitters Creek.

Oke ladled the casserole onto the kids' plates. I imagined him and his wife and the boys sitting in the bleachers across from the Rats bench while the girl—I thought her name was Jo, and like a lot of the girls she was sweet on Tex Dobrick—squeezed along the glass with all the other high school girls in the corner near the concession stand.

My toast popped up.

I laid the pieces of bread down side by side and used a spoon to slather Miracle Whip on both. I laid a slice of cheese on each piece, the pickles on one, and mashed the whole thing together.

Miracle Whip splatted out one end of the sandwich into my palm as I took the first bite standing at the sink. I finished it in six bites and leaned my head under the faucet for a long drink of water. Dinner was done.

My phone rang. After I'd spoken with Whistler, I had tried and failed to get both Mom and Darlene. I hoped this was one of them.

"What do you got for me?" Dingus said.

I wished I hadn't answered. "Not much," I said. "Tatch said he had family matters the other night."

"What family matters?"

"I didn't ask."

"You call yourself a reporter?"

"It's Tatch, Dingus. You were right about his camp."

I wondered if Darlene had told Dingus about Nilus by now, if they'd figured out he might be a priest who once lived in Starvation.

"How about Bea?" he said.

"She might have told me more if you didn't have Catledge hovering."

"It's for her own safety."

My phone beeped. Another call was coming in, but I couldn't hang up on Dingus.

"I appreciate it," I said. "Mom did say she heard Frankie was out campaigning."

"Yeah, waving your stories around," Dingus said. "Thanks for the help."

"We have a story tomorrow saying he's going to make it official."

"Stop the presses. That guy's been up my butt for months."

"Solve the case. He'll go away."

"I do hope your mom talks, Gus. Because I'd hate to have to bring you in."

"Bring me in for what?"

"For questioning."

"You might want to reread the First Amendment, Dingus."

"Uh-huh. The shield of shields. Who the heck's going to wield that for you, son? Your lawyers? The last time you were in my office, you had to borrow a pen."

Which was true.

He ended the call with a satisfied grunt.

I dialed voice mail. There was a message from Darlene.

"Gus," she said. "I hope you're making more progress than we are, and . . . I hope you're doing OK and Mom C's all right." Seconds of silence followed. "I might try to stop by the rink, but . . . we'll see. We've got extra patrols out in the neighborhoods, in case this guy tries another house while everyone's at the game. Talk later."

I hit Replay, listened again. It hurt to hear Darlene in pain, but hearing her voice also felt good. She hadn't spoken to me that softly since she'd ended things the year before. I hoped it wasn't only because of her mother.

I went upstairs to my bedroom, brushed my teeth, ran a hand through what remained of my hair. Mom always said I looked better with my hair short anyway. "My own little Paul Newman," she would say.

I heard cars honking outside on Main Street.

I grabbed my River Rats jacket, a blue-and-gold satin number with "Coach Carpenter" stitched in cursive over the left breast. Beneath that, another line of script said, "State Runner-Up 1981." Poppy had had it put on. I told him I wished it wasn't there, and he told me, Grow up, Gus, that was the greatest Rats team ever.

I went downstairs and stood at the bay window watching the cars and pickups and SUVs inching down Main toward the rink, an actual traffic jam in Starvation Lake. Horns blared. Kids hung out of windows waving Rats pennants. People stood curbside, thigh deep in snowbanks, clapping their mittens together and chanting, "Gooooo River Rats! Beeeat Mic-Mac!"

A sheriff's cruiser whooshed by the line in the left lane, lights flashing.

The people of Starvation Lake had set their new home alarm systems and fastened the new padlocks on their doors and set out for a night of forgetting. Of forgetting about the vacant storefronts down the street, the For Sale signs on the lake, the high school having too little money to continue shop classes, the plastics plant closing and taking its fifty-eight jobs to Alabama. Maybe they couldn't forget the break-in that had left one of their own dead, but they could channel their fear and confusion into cheering for the long-haired, pimply-faced boys taking their first step toward the town's first state title.

I really wanted to join them, but I had something else to do.

ELEVEN

The kicked-up wind churned whorls of snow along the walk from Main Street to the Pine County Courthouse. I'd parked at one of the meters the county had installed in the 1980s when the town was flourishing, with rich downstate people coming up to buy property and houses on the lake. Now the meters stood there like antiques. Some county worker went around each week and collected the quarters. One week in January, he gathered a total of seventy-five cents.

Vicky Clark had propped a back door open with a phone book. I'd persuaded her to meet me in the clerk's office to see if she could help me. Then we would go to her place for that dinner she had offered. That's what I'd told her.

I smelled her perfume from the dark hallway outside the office. I hesitated, thinking maybe I shouldn't do this after all. We weren't all that different, Vicky and me. I'd left town for good, or so I thought, and made mistakes and come groveling home. She'd been a pianist with a scholarship to a music academy when her triplets made their unexpected appearance. Now here we were, chasing what we wanted amid the long evening shadows in the clerk's office.

Vicky jiggled into the corridor and winked at me. "Pine County Clerk's Office," she said. "How can I help you?"

"Hi."

"Aren't you missing the big game?"

"Duty calls," I said. She giggled.

Two microfilm machines squatted on the back wall of the office behind eight long rows of file cabinets. Vicky leaned over my shoulder as I sat winding a plastic handle that scrolled through the microfilm of old

Pilots projected on a screen. I'd gotten used to her perfume, but I shivered when I felt her hair tickle the back of my neck.

"Can I ask why you're so interested in all this ancient stuff?" she said.

"Just some background for some stories I'm working on."

"Oh. It doesn't have anything to do with Phyllis, does it?"

"I don't know."

"This is exciting," she said. "You have an exciting job."

"Trust me, Vick, that's rarely the case."

"My mother would absolutely kill us."

"I'll bet. What time do you need to get home to your kids?"

"Don't worry about that, sweetie. My girlfriend picked them up. They're having a pajama party tonight." Vicky leaned over further until I turned to look at her. She must have put lipstick on while I was scrolling. A blob of it had coagulated between her front teeth. Sympathy mixed with nausea in the pit of my belly. "You know," she said, "I heard you had a little pajama party yourself a long time ago. Right here."

She grinned and nodded toward a door with a frosted-glass window on the back wall. It led to a corridor where there was a janitor's closet. As a college student working one summer at the *Pilot*, I had hid in that closet so I could get my hands on some files a clerk named Verna had refused to let me see. The night turned eventful when a young part-time security guard caught me. That was Darlene.

"Ah," I said. "I never kiss and tell."

"Good," she said, nudging me with a hip and almost knocking me off of my chair. "I don't either."

Focus, I told myself. I looked at my watch. I decided I wouldn't take any notes, I would simply make copies of the stories and escape before I got into real trouble.

One by one, I found the stories listed on the index card I'd taken from the *Pilot* basement. I hit the button to copy each and waited while the machine hummed, the images disappearing and then reappearing on the screen. Vicky collected the black-on-gray pages churning out of the machine and handed them to me.

I flipped through the first few pages, finding the August 17, 1944, story, "Town Searches for Missing Nun." It was bannered across the top of the front page, with the headline and a deck and a three-column photo of a priest addressing a throng of mostly men. He wore a black cassock and a black three-cornered hat. His long, pointed nose divided knife-sharp cheekbones on a narrow face. He stood outdoors atop a short flight of wooden stairs leading to a pair of tall doors. A crucifix hung over the apex of the clapboard arch above him. One of the priest's arms was outstretched, his sleeve billowing below his elbow, and the other was hidden inside his cassock above his belt.

The caption identified the building as St. Valentine's—the old church, I thought—and the priest as Father Nilus Moreau.

I didn't have time, but I read the story anyway. Sister Mary Cordelia Gallesero had come to Starvation Lake from the Detroit suburb of St. Clair Shores, just before FDR's Civilian Conservation Corps diverted the Hungry River to form Starvation Lake. She was nineteen years old and barely five feet tall. A photograph showed a pale smiling face and hopeful eyes floating inside the black-and-white frame of her habit. "Her rosary probably weighs more than her," said another nun who was quoted. I wished I had spent a few more minutes in the *Pilot* basement looking for stories about the nun.

"Vicky," I said, "could you do me a favor?"

In a few minutes, we were both scrolling away. Vicky leaned over and said, "Look, your mom." She shoved a copy of a story from November 1941 in front of my face. "Sr. Cordelia Takes Spellers to Roscommon Bee," the headline read. A photo showed a bunch of girls in plaid jumpers over white blouses standing with a nun and a boy who seemed a bit older than the girls, maybe because he looked so studious in his white shirt and tie and horn-rimmed glasses. Vicky folded the sheet so as to block out the caption.

"Let's see if we can guess the other ladies in the picture," she said.

I wanted to get done and out of there, but I said, without looking, "I bet one's Louise Campbell. And Phyllis Bontrager—or Snyder, back then."

"So sad," Vicky said. "Who's this one, with the pigtails?"

"I don't know, who?"

"You know what? I think it's Sally Pearson. She even has a flower in one of her pigtails—and now she's a florist. How about that?"

"Pretty amazing," I said, still not looking.

Vicky took the page away and sat back in her chair. I looked up and saw that her plump face had puckered into a pout. Christ, I thought.

"I'm sorry," I said.

"You asked me to find these stories," she said.

"Yes, I'm a jerk. Let's see, who else is in there?"

Vicky unfolded the sheet and read the caption aloud. "'Bee-Ing Good Spellers,'" she said. "'Sister Mary Cordelia of St. Valentine's Catholic School with her best spellers. From left, Phyllis Snyder, Beatrice Damico, Gardenia Lawton, Louise Ellison, Mary Kentwood, Martha Yeager, Sally Wentzel, and teacher's helper Horace Gallagher.'"

"Judge Gallagher?" I said.

"Oh my God, Horace," Vicky said, pointing to the boy who still wore horn-rimmed glasses as the county's longtime circuit judge. "Can you believe he got to be a judge?"

"More amazing that he *stayed* a judge with all the goofy high jinks he pulls in court."

"Ha. You got that right."

"Martha Yeager is who now?" I said.

"Nussler. After losing that Brenner guy from Mesick."

"He cheated on her with old Tillie Spaulding. And it's Gardenia Mapes now, right?"

"Was. She died last year. Alzheimer's."

I remembered writing about her death. Someone in her family, knowing of my mother's issues, had called to ask that I handle the obituary. With the family's permission, I had spoken with Gardenia's doctor, who also happened to be my mother's doctor, who told me that Gardenia was further along than my mother in her disease, but that I could expect much of the same.

"That's weird," I said.

"What?" Vicky rolled her chair closer to mine. Her perfume washed over me again. I wasn't getting used to it.

"My mom's a terrible speller," I said. "Whenever she writes me a note or a letter, there's always at least one thing wrong."

My favorite was Mom spelling drawers as "droors," maybe because it rhymed with "doors."

"I can't spell for beans either," Vicky said.

I picked up the story headlined "Hope Ebbing in Search for Nun."

"Let's see here," I said.

On August 15, 1944, Sister Cordelia had disappeared. According to the *Pilot*, no one actually saw her leave. The last person to see her was a gardener named Joseph Wayland. Police said Wayland had told them he waved hello to Sister Cordelia as he was hoeing a tomato patch and she was passing on her way to the church sacristy. He offered her a tomato but she begged off, saying she was late to see Father Nilus. She never arrived at the sacristy and she was never seen, at least not in Starvation Lake, again.

Father Nilus organized a party of hundreds of men and women who came from Kalkaska, Kresnak Lake, Mancelona, Sandy Cove, and Grayling, and as far away as Frederic and East Jordan, to help search for the nun. She was known to take solitary walks along the lakeshore and into the swampland beyond the lake's northwestern corner. There were worries that she had fallen into a bog and drowned, or she had surprised a coyote or a badger and been bitten and bled to death.

"We will not relent," Nilus was quoted as saying. The story went on, "The priest has worked like a madman, sleeping and eating but a portion of the time. After saying his Masses Sunday, he tramped through the woods with the rest of the searchers."

Boats were dispatched. More than one hundred men donned waders and formed a sweeping line that moved step by step through the swamp. They found nothing but the rotting carcass of a fawn that had been gnawed by a predator.

After six days of searching and no sign of the nun, Starvation Lake's uglier side began to emerge. It was inevitable. The locals needed rumors to explain their failure to find Sister Cordelia: She had grown disillusioned with the church and stolen away in her guilt and grief. She had fallen in love with a wealthy summer visitor from Muskegon and left to marry him. The possibility that she had been murdered was generally dismissed. Murders didn't happen in young, hopeful Starvation Lake, certainly not to a nun.

Her students, who called her "Nonny," a nickname that was not explained, were devastated, according to the story. The story said she was known best for teaching reading and writing. There was mention of a Saturday morning class called Letters to the Lord that students actually attended, even in summer. Sister Cordelia rewarded pupils with perfect attendance at those sessions with rosaries engraved with their initials. Eleven-year-old Beatrice Damico was quoted as saying, "I miss Nonny. She was so nice."

I sat back in my chair. "Man," I said.

"Aw." Vicky placed a hand on my shoulder. I felt the edges of the rings she wore digging into my skin. I twisted my body around so that her hand came away.

"Let's keep going," I said. I switched out the roll of microfilm. I looked at my watch. Where the hell was that call from Poppy?

"Now what?" Vicky said.

"They caught the guy who killed the nun."

"Oooh. Who knew microfilm could be so much fun?"

I spun the handle. The pages blurred past. I stopped every few to see where I was: March, May, July. Now the year was 1950. I stopped on August 5. Two stories dominated the top of the front page. "Gardener Arrested in Disappearance of Nun," ran across five of the eight columns. The other, which I had not seen in the *Pilot* catalog, ate up the other three columns: "Arrest Boosts Sheriff's Bid for Re-Election."

"Look at that," I said.

"What?"

"History really does repeat itself."

I spun the handle again. The next story would have to have everything the arrest story had and more. I stopped at August 7, 1950.

ACCUSED KILLER MURDERED
IN PINE COUNTY JAIL

By Carl L. Wick
Pilot Staff

STARVATION LAKE—The man accused of the long-ago murder of a young nun was killed in an apparent fight at the county jail here.

Joseph E. Wayland, 51 years old, died of internal injuries allegedly inflicted by another inmate at the Pine County Jail. Pine County sheriff R. Lawrence Spardell said the two had a disagreement over a game of craps.

Wayland was stabbed in the throat with a crude weapon the other man had fashioned from a spoon smuggled out of the jail mess, Spardell said.

The sheriff declined to identify the other man, pending an arraignment scheduled for Wednesday before Pine County circuit judge Franklin Carey.

Wayland was arrested last week on charges of first-degree murder in the disappearance of Sister Mary Cordelia Gallesero.

Sister Cordelia, as the Felician nun was known at St. Valentine's Catholic Church here, was reported missing in August of 1944. She was 30 years old at the time. The nun's body was never found despite a massive search.

Wayland worked as a gardener at St. Valentine's at the time of the nun's disappearance.

Charges were filed based largely on the testimony of an unnamed Catholic parish priest who said Wayland confessed to the crime during the sacrament of penance.

The unnamed priest told police that Wayland revealed in the church confessional that he had bludgeoned the nun to death with a shovel after she rejected his romantic advances, and disposed of her body in Torch Lake.

Fr. Nilus Moreau, pastor of St. Valentine's, referred questions to the Archdiocese of Detroit. Fr. Timothy Reilly, a spokesman for the archdiocese, denied that a priest had violated the sanctity of the confessional, but said, "We pray for the Lord's love and tender mercy for Sister Cordelia, the men in the jail, and their families."

Pine County prosecutor Michael Carey said plans were being made to dredge Torch Lake, but he wasn't optimistic about finding the nun's body so long after her murder.

Of the jail killing, he said, "This unfortunate turn of events appears to close the case of Sister Cordelia's demise, and I sincerely hope we won't have to speak of it again."

Wayland has previously been convicted twice of public intoxication and was acquitted in 1939 of a charge of aggravated assault after allegedly striking a man with a bar stool.

His wife of 28 years, Esmerelda, died in childbirth in 1930. He is survived by a daughter, Mrs. Susan Breck of Plymouth, Michigan, and a grandson.

"Whoa," I said, forgetting Vicky.

"What?"

I was focused on the last sentence of the clip. Breck, I thought. Again I did some math in my head. The Breck at Tatch's camp could have been Wayland's grandson.

"Nothing," I said. "Just . . . I can't believe I never knew about this."

"It probably wasn't something people were proud of," Vicky said. "Anyway, it happened a million years ago. Did you see those clothes in the pictures? Crazy."

I reread the story, focused again on the last sentence, and tried to get into my reporter's garb, distance myself, be objective. Could it be mere coincidence? Could this Susan Breck be unrelated to the Breck who had insinuated himself into Tatch's camp and convinced its dwellers that they could dig their way to liberation? Was Breck somehow connected to Nilus and, therefore, to Mrs. B? What was he really digging for?

"Are you getting hungry?" Vicky said.

"Huh?"

My phone rang. Thank God, I thought.

"For chicken and dumplings?"

"Hang on."

I may have grabbed the phone a little too eagerly. Vicky folded her arms in that pose women adopt when they have an inkling that they're about to be handed bullshit.

"Yeah?" I said into the phone.

"We're down one-zip after two," came the voice. It was Poppy. He was yelling. I flattened the phone hard against my ear.

"Excuse me?" I said. "This is Gus Carpenter."

I could hear the din of the crowd across the ice from Poppy, who was probably standing by our bench, scanning statistics. "I said we're down by one," Poppy said, louder. "Dougie had a rough start, and they've got Tex all bottled up. But we're still in it."

"I appreciate that," I said.

"You what?" Poppy said. "Gus?"

I waited as if listening to someone filling me in about something. I knew I was being a shithead, but I felt I had no choice.

"You there?" Poppy said.

"I understand," I said into the phone. "Of course."

"Let me guess—this involves a woman," Poppy said. He hung up. I stayed on, knitting my brows. Vicky moved closer.

"All right, understood," I said. "I'll be there as soon as I can." I clicked the phone off.

"You have to go?" Vicky said. She looked skeptical.

"Something's going on with Mom."

"Is she all right?"

"Well . . . I'm not sure."

"Who was that?"

"Somebody at the sheriff's office."

"Oh. Your ex, I suppose?"

I decided that by saying nothing I would let her think that.

"I can't believe she could just throw away a good man like you."

I stood. "Sorry, Vick. I'll have to take a rain check."

"How about tomorrow? Sully's gone till Saturday."

I busied myself with folding up the copies and finding pockets for them. I couldn't look Vicky in the eye anymore. "We'll see."

"No. We won't, will we?"

"Come on, Vicky. It's my mom."

"Oh, of course. Did you get what you wanted?"

"Yes. Thank you so much."

"I'm so glad. What are you waiting for?"

"I'm sorry."

"You're sorry all right. Just leave."

I should have felt worse than I did, but I was too busy thinking. As I walked to my truck through fluttering snowflakes, it struck me that if Breck was connected to Nilus and to Mrs. B, he might also be linked, in some way I couldn't fathom at the moment, to my mother.

TWELVE

When I slipped into the rink through a door near the Zamboni shed, the game clock said eight minutes, seventeen seconds to go with the River Rats trailing Mic-Mac, 1–0. I peered down the boards to the Rats' bench. They had a chance. It was only one goal. The Mic-Mac goaltender might've been playing the game of his life, but he still had a weak glove and he kicked rebounds right back out in front of the net. One little bounce, a deflection, a mishandled rebound, and the Rats could be back in the game.

But the disconsolate way they were sitting told me they were bracing for a loss. I'd seen it before, the heads down, the barely discernible slump to the shoulders, the eyes straying to the clock. Poppy had called a time-out and was barking orders at the skaters gathered around him. He wouldn't have called a time-out with so much time left if the Rats weren't struggling. Tex had his right glove off and was examining the blister he'd gotten digging at Tatch's camp. I looked into the stands. Tatch usually sat one row beneath the press box at center ice, where he could easily see his nephew at either end of the rink. But Tatch was not there.

I watched from a corner of the arena where there were no fans and I was breathing Zamboni oil and gas. The rink was as packed as I had seen it since I'd played net for the Rats on our failed title run. The bleachers were dressed in Rats blue and the throng swayed along with gold banners blaring "Welcome to Starvation—we're hungrier than you!" I saw Soupy and Wilf and Zilchy and Stevie Reneau, wearing their old, frayed, too-tight Rats jerseys and passing around a water bottle. In the past it would've been filled with Beam and Coke, but Soupy couldn't afford the good stuff anymore, so it was probably cut with Ten High or worse.

Instead of joining Poppy at the bench, I decided to stay where I was.

Poppy didn't need me now, and I preferred not to be seen by someone who might tell Vicky I was there. And if Darlene called, I wanted to be able to exit without being noticed.

It quickly became obvious to me what the Rats' problem was. They couldn't get the puck to Tex. And if Tex didn't get the puck, the Rats had trouble scoring. It was a team of grinders and muckers who were good at keeping the other squad off the scoreboard and, usually, finding ways to put the puck on the stick of our best player.

Mic-Mac had that figured out. Every time Tex touched the ice, Pinky Holcomb, number 9, was on him, always within a stick's length, chirping in his ear between whistles. Before a face-off in my corner, Pinky sidled up next to Tex on the edge of the circle as the ref prepared to drop the puck. They were just a few feet away from me on the other side of the glass. Pinky turned his head sideways and talked into Tex's ear. Tex fixed his gaze on the players taking the face-off.

"Hey, shit-teeth," Pinky said. "Maybe I can fuck your mommy when she gets out of jail, huh? She'll probably need it after licking all that prison pussy, eh?"

Tex turned his head to Pinky. I pushed my face into the gap between two sheets of glass. "Tex, don't do it," I said.

Tex glanced back at me, then turned back to the face-off. The ref dropped the puck. "Pussy," Pinky told Tex.

Little Davey Straub, standing just to Tex's left, had heard everything. As Pinky chased the puck into the corner, Davey chugged up from behind and pasted him across the boards. "Fuck you," Davey said as Holcomb went down. Number 22 for Mic-Mac smacked the puck behind the net and around to the opposite corner. Holcomb got to one knee and watched Davey skate away as the refs cleared the zone. Then he jumped up and zeroed in. Coming up from behind Davey, Holcomb swung a vicious hack across the back of his left leg. Davey crumpled. Holcomb flew past, cackling. The slash was risky with a one-goal lead, but the refs didn't see.

Tex did, though.

The next thing I knew, Tex was standing face-to-face with Holcomb at the near blue line. It was too far away for me to say anything, but I heard Poppy screaming, "No, not now, Tex, no." Tex wasn't saying a word. Holcomb was smirking and yammering and did not expect the punch. Tex's gloved fist hit him square on the chin. He dropped. Tex turned and obediently headed for the penalty box. I looked over at Poppy. He had his eyes closed, shaking his head. Tex had done exactly what he'd been told, but his timing was not good. It looked like the Rats would have to play short-handed for the rest of the game.

But Pinky Holcomb, thank God, had an even nastier temper than Tex.

Pinky bounced up, juked around a ref, and tackled Tex from behind. Tex tried to right himself, but Pinky grabbed the back of his jersey collar and slammed Tex's helmeted head into the ice, once, twice, again. Tex took it. It took two refs to peel Pinky off. "Straight to the box, Tex," Poppy was yelling. When Tex got there, I saw him wipe his mouth. He held his hand up for a ref to see the blood.

The officials took a few minutes to sort out the penalties. Tex got two minutes for roughing. Holcomb was assessed a five-minute major because he had drawn blood, a ten-minute misconduct, and a game misconduct. He skated off, still screaming curses at Tex and Poppy and the refs as he disappeared into dressing room 1. Later we would learn that he had turned to one ref and said, "Did the other coach suck your cock before the game?"

Thank you, Pinky. The Rats now would have a power play, five skaters against four, for the last three minutes of the game.

Everything changed then. Now the Rats were carrying the play and Mic-Mac was chasing. With one minute, forty-two seconds to go and the Rats swarming the Mic-Mac net, Davey Straub tipped a Tex Dobrick slap shot up and over the falling goaltender's left shoulder to tie the game. The arena shook, our old runner-up banner trembling in the rafters. I glanced at the Mic-Mac bench. Now they had the slumped shoulders.

With just over thirty seconds to go, Tex scooped up a rolling puck at our blue line. Butterfly bandages had closed two cuts under his left eye.

He leaned his long body into a churning circle, cradling the puck on his stick with one hand, then exploded out of the turn at center ice, blowing past a Mic-Mac winger as if his skates were set in concrete. Tex zigged left, cut right, head-faked a center, flipped the puck high off the glass, zoomed around a defenseman, and caught up to the puck with the other defenseman in futile pursuit.

The Rats on the bench jumped to their feet. I actually felt a fleeting pang of sympathy for the Mic-Mac goalie. He must have been praying that Tex's shot would hit him in the head, the neck, the chest, somewhere, anywhere, because there was no chance that he was going to see it.

Tex dipped a shoulder. His wrists snapped. The goalie flailed. The black blur of puck grazed the inside of the near post and tore into the mesh at the back of the net.

The game ended twenty-seven seconds later, Rats 2, Mic-Mac 1.

Gloves and helmets and sticks littered the ice around the blue-and-gold mound of players swarming Tex. Some of the younger fans vaulted the glass and shuffled across the ice in their shoes and threw themselves onto the pile, while the rest of the fans stamped their feet, chanting, "Let's go, Rats! Beat Pipefitters! Let's go, Rats! Beat Pipefitters!" In Thursday night's state semifinal, the Rats would face the Pipefitters, their old nemesis from downstate, the team the Rats had never beaten, the team that stole the title from us in 1981.

I slipped out through the Zamboni shed.

I called Mom as I walked to my truck.

"I'm going to bed," she said. "The police keep driving by."

"They're just doing their job," I said.

"They're irritating."

I wondered how she would even know they were driving by. She would have had to stand in the kitchen to see the road. She was usually in bed by nine.

"I'm coming over."

"No. I'm fine. I have things to do."

"I thought you were going to bed."

The phone fell silent. Then Mom said, "Just be sure to lock the door. And make your bed in the morning."

A single light burned over the kitchen sink at Mom's. The house was quiet. I locked the kitchen door, slipped off my boots, turned my phone off, and tossed it on the snack bar. I opened the fridge. It was packed with platters and casseroles wrapped in cellophane and foil that neighbors had dropped off. I chose a chicken dish with broccoli and noodles and slid it into the microwave over the stove.

Walking through the bathroom with its doors at each end, I saw a balled-up clump of police tape in the wastepaper basket next to the toilet. The tile floor was bare, the Me Sweet Ho rug having been confiscated as evidence. The door to Mom's bedroom was closed, but I inched it open and peeked in. She was asleep, faced away from me toward the lake side of the house. A paperback by Jacquelyn Mitchard rested on her nightstand.

It gave me a little start. Mom had given me my first book, *From the Rocket to the Jet: Hockey's Greatest Heroes*, when I was six. I almost didn't read it because the title didn't include the greatest player of them all, Gordie Howe of the Red Wings. Mom told me not to judge a book by its cover. I read it. Gordie was in it after all.

Mom bought me another book, *The House on the Cliff*, and then another and another until I was reading them so fast that my parents couldn't afford to keep buying them and I got my first library card. I thought of the sixty-year-old photograph I had seen at the clerk's office showing a young woman, a nun, who had done the same for my mother. If Mom had ever said a word about her, I had missed it, or forgotten.

I shut Mom's door.

Back in the kitchen, I scooped a heap of the chicken casserole onto a plate and poured myself a glass of milk. A set of headlights eased past the house. I went to the window and squinted into the dark to see if it was a Pine County sheriff's cruiser but it was gone before I could be sure. I took my plate and glass into the living room and sat in the recliner and grabbed the TV remote. I clicked the volume low and pushed Channel Eight for the news. The set blinked on to a hockey game, the Wings playing the Blues in St. Louis, late in the third period, Wings up, 4–2, and Stevie Yzerman squatting for a face-off.

I tried to clear my mind for a few minutes of everything I had seen and heard and read in the long day behind me. The casserole was delicious. The Wings were about to win. I set the plate on the end table next to me and picked up the remote. Maybe I wouldn't bother with the news after all. Maybe I could find a Seinfeld rerun instead. The Blues pulled their goalie for an extra skater. I shoved myself back in the recliner, thought I wouldn't mind if I fell asleep right there.

Less than twenty seconds remained in the game when a ribbon of words began to scroll across the bottom of the TV screen. "CHANNEL EIGHT BULLETIN YOUR NEWS NORTH SOURCE CHANNEL EIGHT BULLETIN," they began. Not another snowstorm, I thought. The string went blank, then these words rolled across: "BINGO NIGHT KILLING LINKED TO LATE PRIEST." I bolted up in the recliner. "What the fuck?" I whispered. I waited. "CHANNEL EIGHT BULLETIN YOUR NEWS NORTH SOURCE CHANNEL EIGHT BULLETIN," it repeated while my stomach twisted into a knot. The next line rolled past: "POLICE INVESTIGATING CONNECTION TO FR. NILUS MOREAU. DETAILS AFTER THE GAME."

I jumped to my feet, thinking, How the hell could they know that? It had to be Tawny Jane Reese reporting. There was no way that Darlene would have told her, or that D'Alessio would have known now that he was openly campaigning against Dingus. Vicky Clark? Could Vicky have figured out what I was really doing at the clerk's office? And even if she had and then had thought to call Tawny Jane, Tawny Jane couldn't have reported it based solely on a secondhand tip from a deputy county clerk.

The only other person who knew was Luke Whistler.

I went into the kitchen, turned on my phone, dialed Whistler.

"Where the hell were you?" he answered.

"Did you just moan it out when she was going down on you?" I said.

"Settle down, junior," Whistler said. "I didn't tell her a thing. She told me. I got it out of her. I tried to call you from her bathroom."

"Bullshit."

"I left you a message about twenty minutes ago."

I pulled the phone away from my ear. The message light was blinking. Shit, I thought. "I don't give a damn," I said. "You told her."

I looked through the kitchen and dining room to the TV. There was Tawny Jane on the screen, microphone in hand, doing a stand-up in front of St. Valentine's. Goddamm it, I thought.

"The next time you accuse me," Whistler said, "I'm gone, and you can fill your little rag by yourself. If you'd had your phone on—"

"Shit!" I said, spluttering it.

"If you'd had your phone on, you could've beaten her to the punch on the Web and I'd be getting my ass chewed by her instead."

"Then how the hell did she know, Luke?"

"Are you watching her now?"

I walked into the living room. Tawny Jane was signing off, her brows furrowed into their deepest crease of seriousness. "Yes. Fuck."

"She didn't have anything more than what we already knew. I'm betting you've already made some progress in your reporting, am I right?"

"Some. But how did she know? Really."

"She wouldn't tell me. But I'm betting it was D'Alessio."

"Come on. Dingus has got to be totally shutting him out."

"Maybe he has his own department mole."

I considered this, doubted it, but didn't know what else to think. I shut the TV off.

"Should we pop something online?" I said.

"That would just be an admission of defeat. And it'll be seen by about six people. Might as well stay on the trail and do a better story when we got it. Look, partner, T.J.'s good."

"I'll bet."

"Enough," he said.

He was right. Tawny Jane Reese could be a good reporter, as I had learned from hard experience. "All right," I said. "Let's talk in the morning."

"Get back on the horse."

The kitchen filled with the glow of headlights. I heard tires crunching snow. I started walking to the kitchen door.

"And look, I'm sorry," I said. "But you've got to understand—"

"Yeah, I know, I know. I can see how you'd jump to the conclusion. But, look, I'm on your side."

Darlene was standing outside Mom's kitchen door. She didn't look happy. I unlocked the door, swung it open, stepped outside, pulled the door closed. Her cruiser was idling, the exhaust a coiled wraith in the dark. "Good night," I said into the phone, hanging up. Midnight cold enveloped me. I wrapped my arms around my chest.

"Checking in with T.J.?" Darlene said.

"That was Whistler," I said. "We got scooped big-time."

"Really? How would the TV bitch know about Nilus if you didn't tell her?"

Oh, holy shit, no, I thought. "I didn't tell her anything."

"Do you get extra points at work for helping Channel Eight? Do the bosses send you an attaboy? Or maybe T.J. has one for you, huh?"

I couldn't believe this was happening. "I'm not sleeping with Tawny Jane, Darl." I decided against telling her about Whistler and T.J. "She knew on her own. Whistler's as pissed as I am."

"Uh-huh."

She didn't look convinced, but what else could I say?

"Did you hear what she said?" Darlene asked.

"I saw the bulletin and got on the phone. Why?"

"She said the Catholic Church may be implicated in my mother's murder."

"She what?"

"The Catholic Church, Gus. My mother loved the church. She believed. She had faith. She'd be horrified at this crap coming out of the TV."

"That's just TV hype," I said. "As you may know by now, there was a Nilus here who was pastor at St. Valentine's when our mothers were girls. But I don't see how that connects him to what happened."

"That's all you know?"

"So far."

"I believe, too," Darlene said. She'd gone to Mass with her mother almost every Sunday. The church was a subject on which we'd long ago agreed to disagree.

"I know," I said.

"This may force our hand."

"What does that mean?"

"This is not easy for me. Please don't make it any harder."

"I'm not."

"Just do your job, and I'll try to do mine."

I watched her taillights recede on the shore road toward town. When I turned to go back inside, I saw Mom standing in the kitchen in her bathrobe.

Mom sat on the footstool in front of the recliner, facing me. The remnants of my chicken and noodles sat on the end table.

"I'll clean that up," I said.

"Why are you here?"

"I told you I was coming over."

"It's late."

"I'm here because of Father Nilus Moreau," I said. "Does that name mean anything to you?"

Mom considered it. "He was at St. Val's when I was a girl. I worked for him for a few years at the rectory. Why?"

"He was your boss?"

"I guess. Grandma Damico liked him, but she liked all the priests."

She meant her adoptive mother, my grandmother.

"What's Grandma D got to do with it?" I said.

Mom shook her head. "She never liked Rudy, you know." My father.

"What? Why are you—"

"She would never let us be alone in the house. It was fine for my brothers. They could have their girlfriends in at all hours when Mama and Papa weren't there. But Rudy had to stay away."

"Why are you telling me this?"

"You asked."

"No. I asked about Father Nilus."

"Grandma Damico liked him."

Grandpa Damico died of a heart attack before I was born. Grandma D lasted until I was almost seven. I remembered how she looked too fat for her tiny kitchen and how her apron smelled of garlic and how disappointed I was that she gave me socks and underwear for my sixth birthday and then again for Christmas a month later.

"Why does that matter?" I said.

"She got me the job with Nilus. She said she wanted me busy, but really she just wanted me away from all the boys. 'Boys bad,' she used to say. 'Boys bad.' She was right, of course, as her own sons proved."

"So you knew him pretty well?"

"Who?"

I told myself to be patient. It was late, Mom was tired, I was testing her.

"Nilus," I said.

She placed her hands palms down on her knees and assessed them. "He was my friend, for a while," she said.

"You never mentioned him before."

"I suppose not. He went away when I was, oh, I don't know, sixteen or seventeen? I wrote him a few letters, but he never wrote back. So I guess he wasn't my mentor. Maybe I had the wrong address."

"Where were you writing?"

"Why are you asking me these things?"

I studied her face. She wasn't going to say more until I answered.

"During the break-in," I said, "Mrs. B tried to call Darlene. Darlene didn't answer so her mom left a message. She mentioned this Nilus. At least we think she did."

Mom looked away. "Why?"

"Why what?"

She looked back at me. "Why would Phyllis say something like that?"

"I don't know. That's why I'm asking you. Did she know this guy, too?"

"Of course. We went to the same school. We went to Mass every day."

"Did something happen that would have—"

"A lot happened," Mom said. "But then it was over, and we went on with our lives."

"Are you talking about the nun? Sister Cordelia?"

Now Mom studied my face.

"How do you know about her?"

"I read about her at the—in old newspaper clippings."

"It was quite a story."

"You knew her?"

"We all knew her. She taught us."

"Reading and writing and spelling, right? Did you like her?"

Mom nodded. "She was nice. She brought us cake on our birthdays."

"Did Grandma Damico like her?"

"No. She thought Non—Sister Cordelia was too pretty to be a nun."

"She did look pretty in the picture I saw. She took you on a trip for a spelling bee."

"Really?" Mom thought about this. "I'm sure it will come as no surprise to you that we lost."

"Why didn't you ever tell me about any of this?"

Mom lowered her eyes, and the fine features of her face—the high cheekbones, the thin-lipped mouth—narrowed into a concerted frown, as if she was trying to remember something. She began to rock gently on the footstool. She raised her right hand in front of her face and looked at the backs of her fingers. She rotated her hand slowly one way, then the other. Then she turned it over and curled her fingers into her palm.

"Mom," I said.

"My fingernails," she said. "I have to wash my hands. Look at my nails. They're filthy."

I leaned over and looked. Her fingers and her palm were clean. Her unpolished nails, too. "They look fine," I said.

"I need the hard brush. The bristles get under the nails."

I had learned not to argue about things she believed she saw or heard that no one else could see or hear. They would go away on their own. I wanted to put my arm around her, but that wouldn't have done any good either. I waited. She stared at her fingers a little longer, then let her hand fall back into her lap. The rocking stopped.

"I wish Phyllis were here," she said.

"So do I," I said. "Can you tell me anything more about Nilus?"

"Why are you so concerned with a priest who's been dead for years?"

"How did you know he was dead?"

"I don't know. He was old."

"I thought he never wrote you back."

"He didn't."

"Where was he?"

"I don't know."

"Where'd you send your letters?"

"Detroit." A muscle in her jaw pulsed. "The archdiocese."

"What's the matter?"

"Nothing. I'm tired."

"That's not why you stopped going to church, is it?"

"Because he didn't write back to me? No." She sighed. "No, he was a help after"—she paused—"after Sister Cordelia left. For a while."

She'd never told me exactly why she had walked away from the church. She and Mrs. B had their occasional debates, of course, and almost every time Mom would say of St. Val's, "There's nothing in there but a frustrated man and his expensive geegaws." I never knew if she meant the pastor or God himself.

"Nilus died in the U.P.," I said. "In 1971."

"Hmm," she said. She looked past me and I turned to see headlights moving past the house again. "When will the police stop?"

"Why do you care so much?"

"I want my life to go back to normal."

It would never be normal again without her best friend, but I didn't need to say that. "You'd better get some sleep," I said.

"Yes," she said. "How is Alden?"

My mother was one of the only people in the world who called Soupy by his given name. "He's fine. I mean, you know, he's in bankruptcy and his life's a total mess, but nothing out of the ordinary."

"I worry about him."

"Why?"

"Because I do. He's selling his parents' property, isn't he?"

"He has an offer. Why?"

"He needs to be careful."

"Don't hold your breath."

Mom stood, gathering her robe around her. "I'll stay at your place tomorrow night, if that's all right."

"Of course. Any particular reason?"

"I'm tired of the police watching my every move."

"They're not watching you, Mom. They're watching over you."

"Millie's coming to get me in the morning," she said. "We're going to have breakfast at Audrey's, then go to the funeral home."

"I thought you were going there today."

"Where?"

"The funeral home."

Mom thought about this for a moment. "Well," she said, "I didn't."

"How come?"

She looked past me into the kitchen again, as if she hadn't heard my question. "Tomorrow night," she said, "I'll need you to help me with something."

"All right."

"After it's dark." She leaned over and kissed me on the cheek. "I love you," she said.

"I love you, too."

I scraped my plate and put it in the dishwasher, then dialed voice mail on my cell phone. Sure enough, there was Whistler's voice, telling me at ten fifty-two that Tawny Jane Reese was about to clobber us with the Nilus scoop.

"Damn," I said, and shut the phone off.

THIRTEEN

M y phone was ringing when I came through the back door to the *Pilot* newsroom. Only one person, my boss, called me on the line that was blinking. I grabbed it.

"Hey," I said.

"I've been trying to call you," Philo Beech said.

"I've been busy."

Millie Bontrager had picked Mom up just as I was dragging myself out of bed. I'd hugged them both and told Mom I'd call her in the afternoon. Now I had a few things to do at the *Pilot* before I went to the drain commission meeting where Breck was supposed to make an appearance. I had a few questions to ask him about a murdered murderer who might have been his maternal grandfather.

"No, I'm sorry," Philo said. "How's your mother doing? It seems like every time I look at my computer, something else bad has happened over there."

"Mom's OK."

Philo would have been standing at the fourth-floor window of his corner office in Traverse City, tall and gawky in a sleeveless argyle sweater, peering down on Front Street as he talked. Seven years my junior, he was enthralled with the idea that he was at corporate, with his own office and a shared secretary, after his promotion from the *Pilot* to Media North assistant vice president for news and innovation. As a reporter, he'd barely been able to cover a high school volleyball match. Now he was in charge of telling editors and reporters like me which stories to cover and how. It was actually the order of things at newspapers big and small. The guys who couldn't skate or shoot or stickhandle often wound up running the hockey team.

I needed a fresh notebook for the drain commission meeting. We'd run out of the latest ration corporate had shipped, but Whistler hoarded them, so I walked over to his desk. I didn't see any unused notebooks. But there on his calendar blotter sat the fat gold pinkie ring he was constantly taking on and off. His Toronado was parked out back, so I figured he was in the john.

"I hope they find whoever caused all this trouble," Philo said. "And I hope everything works out for your mother, and for you."

I cradled the phone on my shoulder and picked up Whistler's ring. Its heft surprised me. Either Whistler had a thick pinkie or the ring had a lot of real gold in it. I rotated it in front of my eyes. Up close, it was far from perfect, closer to oval than round, with hairline streaks of scarlet and silver flecking the gold. Carved on the inside were four letters in uppercase italic: *EJPW.*

"Thank you," I said.

"Interesting story on Channel Eight last night, eh? The Catholic Church?"

This was Philo's way of asking me why the *Pilot* hadn't had the story first.

"Tawny Jane may be out on a limb on that," I said. "But we're on it."

Philo cleared his throat. It was time for the business part of the call. I heard the toilet flush in the john and set Whistler's ring down on his blotter.

"This probably isn't the best time, but there is something I—we—need to discuss."

"Shoot."

"The Media North board of directors, as you know, meets this afternoon."

I didn't know or care, but I said, "Yeah." *EJPW.* Initials, I assumed. But for what? Whistler's high school? An old girlfriend? An ex-wife? His ex, I recalled, was Barbara or Beverly something, so it wasn't that ex.

"One item on the agenda," Philo continued, "is a discussion of how to rationalize our print and Internet platforms."

That got my attention. "Rationalize platforms? You mean shut the paper down?"

"Calm down, Gus. You're jumping to conclusions again."

"Our readers aren't ready for point and click. They're old, like three times your age. I know you find that hard to imagine, but technology's not their thing. They still get freaked out by antilock brakes."

"Nobody wants to close the paper."

"It's March, ads are in the shitter, so the bean counters get panicky, and the fastest way to fix things is to kill the dinosaur, whack the printing and delivery, all that bothersome expensive stuff, and just put the whole thing on the Internet. Then we'll all get rich."

"No, we won't."

Whistler came out of the john. "Morning," he said.

I nodded at him. He went to his desk, put his ring on, fished his car keys out of his vest. He waved and started to leave, but I held up a finger for him to wait. He shrugged and sat on his desk.

"Damn right," I told Philo. "Because Audrey's Diner and Kepsel's Ace Hardware and Sally's Floral aren't going to pay squat for Internet ads, are they?"

Philo sighed.

"So what's the discussion about?"

I heard a chair squeak—Philo sitting—and then clacking on a computer. I sat at my desk. Whistler had left a page torn from a notebook on my keyboard. A bunch of names and numbers were scratched across the page in black pen. I set it aside and flicked on my computer. At the top of my e-mail queue were two from a former *Pilot* reporter now working at my old paper in Detroit, the *Times*. The tapping on Philo's end stopped.

"Look," he said. "We're just trying to envision the best way to go forward. Ignoring the Web would be—"

"We're not ignoring the Web. For Christ's sake, it's what got you your promotion. We posted twice yesterday and we'll be posting more today."

Whistler smiled and winked and gave me a thumbs-up. I gave it back.

"Please listen," Philo said. "There'll be a broad discussion of where we go with our online platform, how gradually or not we migrate content—"

"Can you speak in English?"

"Can you shut up?" He waited. So did I. He continued. "The board is going to talk about what we're doing and how, what we ought to do about costs, whether we should start charging for the paper on the Internet."

"Who the hell's going to start paying for something they already get for free?"

I toggled to e-mail and opened the first of the two topping the queue. It had come in the night before:

hey, stranger. got two tix for wings this sun v avs. leave the rat(s) race behind and come down. Will buy you a beer. Or three. We'll have fun.

—j

Philo ignored my rhetorical question. "Well, Gus, I have to tell you that part of what got this whole discussion going was our CFO noticed some rather large and, frankly, rather disturbing cost spikes at your operation."

Nothing good ever followed the word "frankly."

"Here?" I said. "You've got to be kidding."

I scoured my brain for what I'd recently put on my Media North credit card. All I could come up with was two beers and a basket of fried dill pickles at Enright's for me and some real estate guy trying to unload the empty strip mall outside of town.

"There was that monitor your reporter destroyed," Philo said.

"That was last year's budget. Wait—I did buy a month's worth of toilet paper the other day. But at least it was Costco."

"This is no joke. Your costs are out of control. Long-distance calls. Copying and printing. And a consultant? In Grosse Pointe, for Pete's sake? Who authorized that?"

"I don't know what you're talking about."

"We have three credit-card charges totaling four hundred fifty dollars."

"For what?"

"Hard to tell. All it said was 'Information services.' Some consulting firm."

I looked at Whistler. He, too, had a Media North credit card. It wasn't supposed to be used for anything but gas on long-distance trips and the occasional coffee or lunch with a source. Certainly nothing over fifty bucks.

"That's got to be a mistake," I said, lowering my voice so Whistler wouldn't hear. "Hell, Luke used his own cell phone until the end of the year when he could've been using ours. It's not like he's trying to screw us. Someone probably got our credit card mixed up with somebody else's."

"Do you personally approve *Pilot* expense reports?" Philo said.

"Of course."

That was technically true. My two employees—Whistler and, previously, Mrs. B—filed their infrequent reports online and zapped them to me. The supremely efficient paperless process required so many clicks and strokes to scrutinize each entry that I gave up and just approved the reports without looking. Which was even more efficient, as I saw it.

Philo waited. He knew I was full of shit. He knew all I cared about was writing stories.

"I'm worried about you," he finally said.

"Why?"

"I know you've had a rough—a very rough—couple of days."

"I hear a 'but' coming."

"I fibbed before," he said. "There is very serious consideration being given to putting the *Pilot* on the Internet only."

"No shit."

"No shit. They want to try it with one of our papers to see how it goes. Fuqua's running the numbers now."

Fuqua was Media North's CFO. Fuckward, I called him. He had been hired away from a chain of fudge shops. He had never worked at a newspaper. Based on the memos he e-mailed about how to be more "smart" and "productive" about covering news, I had come to doubt that he had even read a newspaper.

"So the *Pilot* would be a pilot project, huh?"

"I hope not," Philo said. "I actually don't think it makes business sense, at least not yet. But you're not helping me with four hundred fifty dollar bills."

There was no use arguing.

"Understood," I told Philo. "I will check into it."

"I'm going to try to head this thing off for now," he said. "But this train's going to arrive sooner or later."

"What was that all about?" Whistler said after I'd hung up.

"Bullshit," I said. "Listen, I hate to ask, but did you put a bunch of charges on your credit card for some consultant or something?"

Whistler gave me a look. Great reporters never liked being questioned on such unimportant details as how much money they spent chasing stories. Nor did I. But things were different now. If the *Pilot* went online only, the bean counter Fuqua would shut the newsroom, sell the desks and chairs and copier, and make us work from home. Or, worse, Traverse City.

"I did," Whistler said. "A guy downstate who helps me with Freedom of Information requests. I was going to put it on my Visa, but it was on some sort of frigging hold."

Reporters, I thought. They could write story after story eviscerating a county board for running a budget deficit but couldn't get their own bills paid on time.

"Goddamn, Luke," I said. "You've got to be more careful. The budget hawks are circling."

"Gotcha."

"The scanner, too." Media North had been on me about our utility bills. Whistler was always leaving the police scanner on overnight. "Just turn it off. Humor me."

I felt like a mope saying it. How much electricity could a scanner use anyway?

"Sorry, boss," he said.

I picked up the page of notes he'd left me. "Midland County? Around the thumb?"

"Somewhere over there. My archdiocese guy said to check that and the other."

"Marquette County, in the U.P. According to his obit, Nilus was living up there when he died. What are these other numbers? Case files?"

"Yeah," Whistler said. "Listen, I'm supposed to be at some little college in Roscommon talking about journalism careers. I'll knock that out and be back on the case in a couple of hours, and we'll lap those bastards at Channel Eight."

He was sleeping with one of those "bastards," I thought, but let it go. "What are you going to tell the kids?" I said.

He grinned. "Try blacksmithing."

I heard his Toronado growl to life as I swiveled back to my computer and opened the second e-mail from the reporter at my old paper:

hey, sorry for being so chipper in my earlier e. just heard about what's going on up there. holy crap—bingo nights? is your mom ok? was that your neighbor? i'm trying to get my editor to send me up there. call me!

—joanie
Mobile 313 555 6758

I sat back in my chair. Did I really want Joanie McCarthy coming back to Starvation Lake? I couldn't stop her. In my experience, nobody could stop Joanie from doing what she wanted to do. But I didn't have to encourage her either.

I scribbled her number on my blotter, picked up the phone, and dialed the clerk's office in Midland County. I had no idea what I was looking for, but hoped I might learn something about Father Nilus Moreau.

* * *

Frank D'Alessio was standing in front of the Echo Township Hall where the drain commission met when I parked on the snowy shoulder across the road. He wore a white shirt and red tie beneath a dark top-coat. He was shaking hands and handing out big sheets of paper that flapped in the morning breeze.

Campaigning again, Frankie? I thought. I rolled my window down to watch, thinking of the "anonymous" tip he must have given the cops about Tatch missing hockey the night of the break-in at Mom's house.

"It's right there, people, right there in black and white," I heard him shout. He'd printed out copies of the online version of Channel Eight's scoop on Nilus. Just what I needed. "Morning, Carol, Edgar . . . hey, Channel Eight's on the case, but what's our sheriff doing? Probably sitting in his office stuffing crullers in his face."

I rolled up my window, opened the door, and walked up to the hall, a converted firehouse that sat in a clearing of pines. The glassed-in bulletin board on the front of the hall read "Pine County Drain Commission," and just beneath it "Phyllis Bontrager, We Loved You," and beneath that, "Go River Rats! Beat Pipefitters!"

"Frankie," I said. "Don't you have a shift coming up?"

"Took a leave of absence as of today . . . Morning, Mrs. Jargon, here you go . . . Unpaid leave, incidentally, in case you see fit to mention. By the way, good game last night. Damn glad you weren't in the net."

"Smart move, Frank. Insult the local paper."

"Like you matter . . . Hey there, Mr. Bradley, how's by you? Take two, they're free."

"Come on, Frank, you work there. Why don't you bring the burglar in?"

"Man, they've shut me out completely. I can't get Dingus to tell me what he wants in his coffee . . . Morning, Mrs. Baranowski."

"They appear to have a lead."

"Yeah, sure, maybe this priest came back from the dead and did it. That's what they're doing, chasing ghosts. Look, Carpie, you're just sucking up to Dingus because you're afraid if he gets booted, the love of your life will be out of here, too."

"Mr. D'Alessio?"

Breck had come up from behind without a sound. He carried a brown satchel under his right arm.

D'Alessio stuck out his hand and Breck took it. "Yes sir, Frank D'Alessio, running for Pine County sheriff, nice to meet you."

"Mr. Breck. May I?"

D'Alessio gave him a printout. Breck held it in front of his face. I watched his tiny eyes dart back and forth behind his wire-rims. He turned and offered me the sheet.

"Good morning, Mr. Carpenter. Have you seen this? Do you believe it to be true?"

I looked at Breck for some sign of what he thought about the Nilus story, whether it was familiar to him, but saw nothing. "I'm still reporting," I said.

"I didn't see it in your paper."

"Nope." I reached into the back pocket of my jeans for the notebook I had dug out from under my truck passenger seat. "Can I ask you a couple of questions?"

"Excuse me," he said. "I have to prepare for the meeting."

He walked to the hall, stopped, opened one of the double doors, stepped to one side, and, with a wave of his satchel, ushered two women inside.

"Who's he?" D'Alessio said.

"The new guy at Tatch's camp."

"One of those Jesus people, huh? Why do you want to interview him?"

"You going inside?" I started walking. "Or you got another rally at the IGA?"

"Keep sucking up, pal."

Pine County Drain Commission chairman Les Cronholm looked around the Echo Township Hall and reluctantly rapped his gavel.

"Do we have any public comment?" he said.

Breck set his satchel on the floor. "Thank you, Mr. Chairman."

He had waited for nearly an hour, sitting on a wooden folding chair in the front row, satchel on the floor between his knees, while the commission passed a unanimous resolution commemorating Phyllis Bontrager as a model citizen who had given generously of her time to many a community cause. Chairman Cronholm, who owned a plumbing company now doing most of its business in Traverse City, told of the time he was sick for a week with the flu, and Mrs. B came to his house with a pot of his favorite meatball soup. As other commissioners offered their own fond tales, I thought they could as well have been talking about my mother.

The five commissioners sat at a long table behind pieces of white cardboard bearing their names. On the wall behind them hung a banner reading "Pine County Drain Commission: Fresh Ideas, Fresh Water." Each of them wore a black armband over some form of River Rats apparel—a golf shirt, a sweatshirt, a button-down—and they passed a resolution commending the Rats for their "courageous" victory the night before. I thought "lucky" might have been a better word. They also debated, without deciding, whether to lower the water level in Walleye Lake, how to assess property owners for a new drainage district near the Hungry River, and, for the hundredth time, who should clean up the runoff mess left when Norbert Plastics vacated its plant in Starvation. Breck sat through it all without a trace of expression on his face.

Now he rose from his chair.

"Yes sir," Cronholm said. "Can you identify yourself, please?"

"Mr. Breck, sir. I represent the taxpaying citizens who live on the Edwards parcels on the northeastern corner of the lake."

Each of the thirty-odd citizens sitting in the neatly arranged rows of chairs turned to see Breck. They usually came less for commission business than for free coffee and a slice of pie baked by Chairman Cronholm's wife, Cara. Today, they had a man they'd never seen before to go with their huckleberry pie. There was nothing like a stranger to get the attention of the people in Starvation.

"Maybe I heard wrong," Cronholm said. "But I thought you just wanted to be citizens, without the taxpaying part."

"We respectfully object to the recent increase in the assessment of the Edwards parcels, which we consider to be extortionate," Breck said. "And we also believe, separately, that as a nonprofit faith organization we are quite possibly exempt from taxes altogether."

"What did you say your name was, sir?"

"Mr. Breck."

Cronholm fingered his gavel, irritated. "Your full name, please."

"Breck, sir. Wayland Ezra Breck."

Yes, I thought. He had to be Joseph Wayland's grandson, named with his grandfather's surname and a derivation of his grandmother's given name.

"Thank you, Mr. Wayland Ezra Breck," the chairman said. "'Extortionate' is a two-dollar word if I've ever heard one. You're a lawyer then?"

"Yes sir."

"Registered or whatever with the state bar?"

"Yes sir."

"How can we help you?"

Breck wasted no time explaining. Soil samples taken from the ground beneath Tatch's family's land had shown evidence of contamination by sewage runoff. He reached into his satchel and produced an old plat map. He unfolded it and held it up with one hand while indicating certain parts of it with the other hand.

Here, he said, etching an imaginary circle, is land the county purchased years ago. And here, he said, waggling his finger in a portion of the circle, is where an old septic field lies underground. A septic field, unused for years, but now leaking into an area where twenty-some people, including five children, were living.

The commissioners mulled. Then Don Champagne took his River Rats cap off of his liver-spotted head and waved it dismissively in Breck's direction.

"I'm sorry, Mr. Wayland, but I can't get my head around this," Champagne said.

"Mr. Breck, Commissioner. Get your head around what, please?"

"This so-called septic field. First of all, how the heck are you digging out there with the ground frozen up like rock?"

"The insulation of early snow. Elbow grease. Persistence. Teamwork. We've also been able to secure the use of a backhoe."

"Impressive," Champagne said. "So you can afford a backhoe to dig around looking for ways to sue somebody, but you can't afford to pay your taxes?"

"This is about our fair share of taxes."

"Maybe you can tell me why anyone in his right mind would allow a septic field to be installed on a ridge that slopes down toward the lake?" Champagne chuckled as he fitted his hat back on his head. "Just doesn't make sense."

"I don't know, Commissioner. Who in their right mind would let a man fond of young boys coach a boys' hockey team?"

Silence fell over the room. Breck had spoken of something from the town's past, something no one spoke of anymore. He knew more about us than we did about him.

Champagne glared. Cronholm rapped his gavel once. "All right, Mr. Breck, the commission would appreciate it if you would come directly to the point."

"The point, Mr. Chairman, is this," Breck said. "Your septic field is leaching poison into our property, contaminating our wells, and potentially compromising the health of our children. Yet you are trying to make us pay more to live on polluted soil that is obviously worth less now, not more. I would submit that *that* just doesn't make sense."

Commissioner June Jones leaned forward on her arms. "We are the drain commission," she said. "We don't do taxes. You should be talking to the tax assessment appeal board. I believe they meet on the third Thursday of each month."

"Thank you, Commissioner. We have pursued that and been, to put it lightly, ignored."

"I'm sorry about that," Jones told Breck. "But I don't know what you expect us to do."

"We expect to be treated as God-fearing Christians who have done our fair share for this community, despite our increasing skepticism that your countless boards and commissions and councils and committees and subcommittees serve any purpose other than to give you all something to do besides shovel snow."

"That'll be quite enough," Cronholm said.

"Lord, deliver us," Champagne said. He turned to Cronholm. "Lester? We have bigger fish to fry."

"Furthermore," Breck continued, "while this board may be technically powerless to act on our tax predicament, each of you is related by blood or marriage or both to one or more members of the appeal board and/or the Pine County Commission, so I'll appreciate your sparing me the pretense that you are helpless."

Cronholm looked down one end of the table, then the other, staring the board into silence. Then he said, "Thank you, Mr. Breck. We will take your suggestions under advisement. Do we have any other public comment?"

I saw Verna Clark rise from her seat in the front row opposite Breck. She walked to one end of the commissioners' table and handed a scrap of paper to Commissioner Jones. Jones nodded thanks and looked at the paper. She smiled before she passed it toward Cronholm.

Breck remained standing. "Excuse me, Mr. Chairman, but what do you plan to do and when can we expect to hear back from you?"

"You've had your say, Mr. Breck. Please sit down."

"I gather from your attire that you all are fans of the local hockey team. Let me ask: do you think your team can win tomorrow night without the services of its best player?"

Tex? I thought. Was Breck saying Tex would not play?

"Lester," Champagne said, "can you shut this guy's mouth?"

"Excuse me," Cronholm said. He took reading glasses from a breast pocket and peered through them at the note Verna had passed along. He looked over the top of his glasses at Verna and furrowed his brows. She nodded. Cronholm turned to Breck.

"I'm sorry, Mr. Breck, but your beef—and understand I'm not saying whether it's legitimate or not—is not with the county."

"You represent the county, sir, and—"

"Quiet, please." Cronholm held the piece of paper up. "According to our very conscientious county clerk, as of last week, the county does not own that land anymore. It's been purchased, along with several other parcels in the area. You'll need to speak with the new owner about your septic problem."

For a moment, Breck seemed unable to speak. Finally, he said, "Mr. Chairman, would you mind telling me who the buyer is?"

"Not at all. Looks like a legal firm: Eagan, MacDonald and Browne. Detroit."

I had tangled with that firm during my time in Detroit. Eagan, MacDonald & Browne couldn't have been buying the land for its own purposes; it had to be representing someone or something wishing to remain anonymous. I recalled, too, that Soupy had said a downstate law firm was interested in buying his parents' house.

"Want me to spell it?" Cronholm said.

Breck pulled his wool cap onto the back of his head and picked up his satchel.

"That won't be necessary," he said, turning to leave. Cronholm asked if there was any more public comment. Breck stopped in the center aisle and turned again to face the commissioners.

"You brood of vipers," he said.

"Pardon me?" Champagne said. Mrs. Jones snarled, "How dare you?" Cronholm banged his gavel as a murmur moved through the room. Someone behind me muttered, "Goddamn Holy Rollers."

"We'll thank you to leave quietly," Cronholm said.

"Good luck Thursday night," Breck said.

I followed him out. "Breck," I called after him. He kept walking toward the street. I came up behind him. "Breck. Your grandfather?"

He stopped without turning to face me. I came around and stood in front of him. "Joseph Wayland," I said. "He was killed in the Pine County Jail after they arrested him for killing a nun. A long time ago."

Breck gave me a long look. "I am truly sorry for your loss," he said. "But what business could that possibly be of yours?"

"It might have something to do with what happened to Mrs.— Phyllis Bontrager."

"Why would you think that?"

"I have my reasons."

"Ah, your inscrutable reasons. But you expect me to tell you all about mine, is that it? Does the public have some inalienable right to know?"

He wasn't going to answer my question. Not yet. Sometimes you had to ask a question more than once, in different contexts, to get an honest answer. Sometimes you never got an honest answer. But I was sure now that Breck was Joseph Wayland's grandson, and that he had some purpose to being in Starvation Lake other than locating a septic field. "You aren't really going to hold Tex hostage, are you?"

"His name is Matthew."

"He's just a kid."

"We are all children in God's eyes. You and the rest would do well to remember that."

"Come on. Does Tatch—?"

"Matthew is no more to you than I am, or Mr. Edwards, or anyone up on that hill. Young Matthew is but a means to an end, isn't he?"

"You're angry, Breck. Are you angry about your grandfather?"

"Are you even remotely aware, Mr. Carpenter, of how you are being led astray?"

"Huh?"

"Of course not. None of you are. Good day."

He started to walk away. My phone rang in my pocket.

"How about Nilus, Breck?" I called out. "Father Nilus Moreau? You know that name?"

He slowed his gait for a step but did not stop until he climbed into a mud-stained Jeep on the road shoulder. I pulled my ringing phone out, watched Breck make a U-turn. A yellow frame around his rear license plate bore the name Strait Dodge. I knew it. Bob Strait Dodge sponsored the Strait Arrows, a men's hockey team in Livonia, near Detroit.

"Yeah?" I said into my phone.

Luke Whistler said, "The shit has hit the fan."

FOURTEEN

Whistler leaned against his Toronado in the road outside the sheriff's department, his breath billowing white around his white head. I rolled up in my truck and eased the window down. The winged wheel of the Detroit Red Wings logo peeked out from inside Whistler's vest.

"What are you doing out here?" I said.

"The cops aren't letting us in. There's a press conference in a few minutes."

Catledge and another deputy were standing guard at the entrance to the department parking lot. Half a dozen cars and the Channel Eight van were parked on the shoulder, reporters standing around with their notebooks and microphones at their sides. They'd come from as far away as Traverse City and Petoskey. No reporters from Detroit yet, but I supposed they'd show up eventually if bad things kept happening.

"What do you know?" I said.

"They grabbed him coming out of the hardware. Apparently bought them out of work gloves," Whistler said.

"In cuffs?"

"Far as I know."

Roy "Tatch" Edwards was in police custody.

"They charge him?"

"Not sure. The sheriff's got to be shaking him down. I guess he shouldn't have missed that hockey game."

I recalled what Darlene had told me at Mom's. "Maybe the Channel Eight story forced Dingus's hand," I said.

"Sure. Leaky department. Connections to priests. Nobody in jail. Got to do something."

"Speaking of priests, your guy at the archdiocese knew where the bodies are buried, all right. Two lawsuits saying our friend Nilus fathered children of local parishioners. In Midland County, 1928. Marquette County, 1956."

"No shit. I didn't know they even had paternity stuff in the twenties. Priests can't use a rubber, eh? Against their religion?"

"Funny. This guy must have been a big problem for the church. I'm thinking he might've had other lucky parishioners in between the twenties and fifties."

"What happened with the lawsuits?"

"Settled, of course. Terms not disclosed, but no doubt the church paid the ladies handsomely to go away."

"Hell of a story, man." Whistler held up a hand for a high-five. I slapped it, feeling the hard edge of his ring. "I wish I'd just done it myself. You put it online?"

"I want to get the lawsuits in hand first. They're overnighting them."

Whistler grinned. "On the corporate card?"

"Screw it," I said. My phone started ringing again, reminding me I wanted to check on Mom. "Besides, don't we have to figure out what the hell it means first? What does Nilus banging parishioners have to do with what happened to Phyllis?"

The door on the front of the sheriff's department opened. Darlene stepped out. She placed something on a lectern set up outside with a microphone.

"Who knows?" Whistler said. "There's got to be something there." He turned toward the department. "Looks like the press conference is getting started."

"I'm going to get this call," I said, picking up my phone.

Whistler waved his notebook at me as he walked away.

"Mom?" I said into the phone.

"No, Gus."

I almost dropped the phone. I thought of yelling for Whistler, but he was too far away. "Tatch?" I said. "Holy shit, where are you?"

"Jail, man. This is my call."

"Why are you calling me?"

"I tried Mr. Breck, but he ain't answering."

"What about the rest of the people out there?"

"None of them got phones. Mr. Breck made us turn them in. Said we had to isolate ourselves from the sinners in civilization."

Shrewd, I thought. "What can I do?"

"Well, first, one thing: I never did nothing at your mom's. You know I wouldn't do anything to hurt Bea or Darlene's mom."

"OK."

"I can't believe this is happening. I mean, I've been in this shithole before, but then I deserved it."

Rolling holy hadn't done much for Tatch's language.

"Did they charge you with something?" I said.

"Nah, this ain't about me. This is about old Mr. Breck. Dingus already told me we're going to be having a talk about him."

As Tatch said it, I saw Dingus come out of the sheriff's department and walk to the lectern, where he picked up the sheaf of papers Darlene had left. Darlene and Catledge stood just behind him. He began to speak into the mike.

"I'm across the road from the jail. Dingus just came out to address the press."

"Aw, hell," Tatch said. "Putting the pressure on. I should've just sold the damn land when I had the chance."

"Somebody was going to buy your property? Who?"

"Yeah, Mr. Breck talked me out of it. Some law firm from Detroit."

"Let me guess: Eagan, MacDonald and Browne."

"Hm. Maybe so—oh, hang on, buddy." Tatch directed himself to someone else. "Gimme just another damn minute."

I watched Dingus reading from a sheet of paper, Whistler bowed to his notebook, TV lights glaring in the gray noon, Tawny Jane waiting with her own mike.

Tatch came back on. "Gusser, 'fraid I have to go."

"I saw Breck at the drain commission," I said. "He told them he's not going to let Tex play tomorrow."

"No way."

"Oh, yeah."

"What the hell," Tatch said. "The guy's got some kind of hard-on for the whole town. It ain't just the tax thing. Something's got him honked off at everyone here."

Whatever it was, I thought, had something to do with his grandfather.

"Speaking of hockey, where were you Sunday night anyway?" I said.

"Got stuck. Slipped off the road. Like a damn tourist."

"And you didn't have a cell phone to call."

"Yeah."

"But you told me you had family stuff."

"I know. Sorry, man. I had me a couple of nips to steady my nerves before the game. Couldn't be saying that around Mr. Breck. He don't like us drinking."

"Tell me, buddy," I said. "What the hell were you thinking?"

"When?"

"When you let this Breck guy cut your balls off and take over?"

I didn't mean to embarrass Tatch, but his pause told me I probably had.

"Shit, you know. We were living on fumes out there. Mr. Breck came with cash. I couldn't look at another can of SpaghettiOs."

"So, was it him at my mom's?"

"He was at the camp Sunday night. Everybody said so."

"So what do you want me to do?"

"Shit, I don't know. I wish to heck Mr. Breck would've just picked up."

"You want me to call Terence?"

Terence Flapp was a local lawyer who knew Tatch only too well.

"You sure about what you said about Tex? He ain't going to let him play?"

"That's what he said."

"That's bullshit, man. Yeah, call Terence."

"How's the digging going?"

"Oh, don't get me start— Hey, wait—"

The call ended. I dialed Flapp and left a message.

* * *

As I walked up to the press conference, I heard Whistler asking whether the sheriff would confirm Channel Eight's report about Father Nilus Moreau. His question surely annoyed the hell out of Tawny Jane, who was standing in the semicircle of reporters, photographers, and cameramen gathered around the lectern, kept at a distance by Catledge and Darlene.

Dingus peered over the half-moon glasses perched on his tulip bulb of a nose. "I have no comment on that report, sir," he said in his Finnish lilt. "I can tell you, however, that the department has conducted administrative discipline on certain personnel."

"Deputy Frank D'Alessio?" Whistler said.

"Next question."

"So," Whistler persisted, "you *cannot* confirm the Channel Eight report, and we should regard it as inaccurate? Is that what you're saying?"

I glanced at Tawny Jane. She kept her eyes on Dingus, pointedly ignoring Whistler's insult so as to assure the rest of us that her scoop was good.

Dingus ignored Whistler and pointed at Chester Pavich, a young reporter from Petoskey. With shirttails flying out from beneath his corduroy jacket, Pavich always looked like he was in a hurry, which could've meant that he had ambition and was going places, or that he was struggling to keep up and doomed forever to chase chicken-dinner news at dinky papers up north. Both were familiar to me.

He asked, "Is the man you've arrested considered a suspect in the murder of Paula Bontrager?"

Phyllis, I thought, and then, Doomed.

"As I said," Dingus said, "we have in custody a person of interest."

"Hold on." It was Tawny Jane, her microphone thrust forward like a sword. "Sheriff Aho, would you tell Channel Eight's viewers whether charges will be filed?"

"Ma'am," Dingus said without looking at her, "as a deliberative police force, we need to investigate first, charge second, if we charge at all.

Operating on rumors and speculation would be a poor use of taxpayers' hard-earned dollars."

Tawny Jane hated to be called ma'am, and Dingus knew it. "Well then," she said, "what other than rumors and speculation are the basis of this arrest?"

"We had an anonymous tip and, upon further investigation, it turned out to be more than a rumor. That's all I can say for now."

I heard a car passing and looked behind me. A Jeep slowed almost to a stop before moving along. Breck. I pictured him gathering the adults and children at the camp, fixing them with his cross-eyed stare, telling them the townspeople were determined to stop them from living their lives, from practicing their faith, and now had captured one of their own to demonstrate their power and instill fear.

Tawny Jane furrowed her penciled-in brows and cocked her head just so. "Sheriff Aho, isn't this just a reaction to your opponent's charges that you haven't responded aggressively to the recent break-ins? To the point that now a murder has occurred?"

"Excuse me, Sheriff," Whistler interrupted. Tawny Jane looked at him as if she might shove her mike up his ass. "Your opponent has told the *Pilot* you may not have the right person in custody. Would you like to comment on that?"

Dingus's face turned redder than a goal light. "I would not."

"So do you or don't you believe you've arrested the Bingo Night Burglar?"

Tawny Jane jumped in. "Will you tell our viewers that your investigation has nothing to do with a certain Father Nilus Moreau?"

I looked at Darlene. She must have had enough of the back-and-forth—I certainly had—but her face remained expressionless. I thought of her waking that morning and remembering, in an instant, that her mother was gone. Or maybe she hadn't slept, maybe not since the night of the break-in, as the creases beneath her eyes suggested. She was tougher than me, tougher than anyone I knew, to stand there next to Dingus without losing it, without coming close, in front of all the professional voyeurs. Her mother would have been proud. I sure was.

"I cannot and will not comment on speculation," Dingus said.

"Will you be giving us regular updates?" Pavich asked.

Dingus pursed his lips, pressed his hands together, and forced a smile. "The Pine County Sheriff's Department is nothing if not transparent," he said. "But we hope that all of the God-fearing people of Pine County will remain calm and rational as we sift through the evidence."

"Is that a yes or a no?"

"Thank you."

Darlene and Catledge followed Dingus back inside.

"Where'd you find him?" Tawny Jane asked me as Whistler shuffled off to his Toronado. He'd whispered that he was going to put a story online and I should delay Channel Eight.

"He's quite a character," I said.

"You were awfully quiet today."

Generally, I didn't say much at press conferences. It gave lousy reporters an edge if decent ones were asking questions. But I said, "It was more fun to watch you and Luke go at it."

"Is that supposed to be funny?"

"No," I said, then realized she was referring to "go at it," and said, "Sorry."

She pulled her hair back with the hand holding her microphone, revealing silver wisps along her neck. Seeing Tawny Jane Reese up close always made me think, man, she must have knocked them dead when she was twenty-five, how did she get stuck up here? I had heard that she still stayed late at the station to make tapes she sent to stations in every major market in the country, hoping someone would notice.

Whistler's car pulled away.

"Forget it," she said. "How's your mom?"

"OK."

"It's one heck of a story."

"Yeah. Nice scoop last night, by the way."

I was thinking I'd try to scoop her back with what I'd learned about Nilus's serial womanizing, as soon as I figured out what it meant.

She shifted her Channel Eight equipment bag from one shoulder to the other. "I don't know what it's got to do with anything, but I'll take it. It's been getting a lot of Web traffic."

"Really? I never keep track of that stuff."

"Maybe because your job is safe."

"No safer than yours."

"Really? Do they want to make you the weather bitch?"

"Huh?"

"They want me to do the weather, Gus."

"You mean like—"

"Yes. They want me to give up news and become the weather bitch. You know, smiling and waving my arms around like a goddamn cheerleader."

"Jesus. Why?"

"I don't know. My numbers are down, they have new bimbos to try out, they want to yank my salary back to poverty level. Depends what time of day you ask. Either I beat everybody on this story or I'm going to have to get new boobs."

She wasn't kidding. No wonder she was sleeping with the competition.

"Sorry about that, T.J."

"You know," she said, "when you came back here a few years ago, I figured you were going to make a quick stop, get your shit together, and get out of Dodge."

"I probably thought that, too. But here I am."

"Yeah, well, I am not going to be the weather bitch." She stuffed the microphone in her bag. "See you in the trenches."

FIFTEEN

My mother picked up as I was parking on Main in front of the *Pilot*.

"Is that you, Gussy?" she said.

"Are you at my place?" I said.

"I am. Why are all these boxes here? There's nowhere to sit."

On the floor and the sofa in my living room were four or five boxes I hadn't gotten around to unpacking. "Sorry," I said. "I'll be there in a little while."

"You're not going to throw away your old report cards, are you?"

The old hockey tape box on the sofa was filled with junk from my boyhood that Mom had salvaged. "I'll look through it soon," I said. "I've been kind of busy."

Mom told me about her day as I went inside. She and Millie had had a nice late breakfast in an empty Audrey's Diner and done some shopping and then gone back to Millie's and played cribbage and talked.

"When's the funeral?" I said.

"Pardon me?"

"You said you were going to Murray and Murray to see about arrangements."

"Oh, yes. Millie called over there. They said Darlene was handling it."

I couldn't imagine how. "I thought you were helping."

"Dingus arrested the Edwards boy?" She was changing the subject. "Whatever for?"

"I'm looking into it," I said.

Neat stacks of mail crowded the *Pilot*'s L-shaped front counter. The baskets and bouquets were standing on the floor in the corner. Whistler must have tidied up.

"Can you imagine what Bernice would think?"

If she were around, Tatch's mom would have been at the press conference shouting biblical quotes. "I'll get to the bottom of it," I said.

"Good," Mom said. "Tonight we have to go somewhere."

The door swung open and the postman dropped a bundle of mail bound with rubber bands at my feet. "Do you need something at the store?" I said.

"No. As soon as it's dark, we have to go. Before someone else gets there."

"Someone else gets where?" I said, but Mom had hung up. "Everything's a mystery," I said to myself, shaking my head. I turned off my phone and picked up the bundle of mail. "Luke?" I called out. There was no answer.

A turquoise sweater, fuzzy with lint, one button missing, was draped over the back of the stool facing Mrs. B's computer. I set the bundle on the chair and idly punched the space bar on her keyboard. The screen stayed black.

Mrs. B had stood there greeting customers, trading gossip, taking classifieds, paying the weekly bills until Media North automated the ads and bills and Philo asked me if the *Pilot* really needed Mrs. B anymore, if we shouldn't just stand a placard on the counter with a list of phone numbers that visitors could call for their needs. "And who exactly will explain to Mrs. Evangelista why we moved the crossword from A2 to A8 and have her go back out the door smiling?" I had said.

Philo never brought it up again.

Next to Mrs. B's computer stood three photographs in fake wooden frames she probably had bought off the dollar shelf at the drugstore. One was of Darlene, looking solemn on the day of her graduation from police academy, her hair in a bun, her deputy's hat cradled in the crook of an elbow. Another showed her as a girl crouched inside an inner tube on a boat dock and throwing her pigtailed head back to laugh as her father tickled her from behind.

The last photo was of Mrs. B with my mother and Soupy's mom. The frame was etched all around with the words "friends" and "forever." The women were standing with their arms around one another, my mother at the center, in front of a minivan. I tilted the picture to see their faces better in the shadows. They were all smiling.

I had taken that picture.

It was a Friday in July and I had taken a long weekend off from the *Times* to come north and see Mom and relax by the lake. I was sitting down the bluff on her dock with the *Pilot* and a cup of coffee when I heard a woman's shriek and then another. I dropped the paper and ran up to see Mrs. Campbell, all two-hundred-some pounds of her, lying on her back next to a minivan in Mom's driveway. She was laughing. Mom and Mrs. B were doubled over laughing. "Curly, Curly, Curly," Mrs. B kept saying between gasps of laughter, using Mrs. Campbell's nickname.

"What's going on?" I said, and all of them laughed even harder. Mrs. Campbell got to one knee. She had a wicker purse the size of an Easter basket looped around one arm. Tears glistened on her plump cheeks. Mom and Mrs. B helped her to her feet. They'd been trying, without success, to lift her into the minivan. "Dear lord, Louise," Mom said. "If we don't get you in that van, you're never going to win that million dollars you promised Angus." That brought more peals of laughter. I shook my head and was starting back down to the lake when they asked me to snap a photo.

They had been friends for as long as I could remember. Mrs. Campbell would refer to them as the Three Musketeers and Mom would say, on cue, "Oh no, dear, we are definitely the Three Stooges." Mrs. Campbell was Curly, Mrs. B was Larry, and my mother, of course, was Moe.

Sometime after Soupy's dad died, July 4, 1997, something happened between them that Mom chose not to speak of, at least not with me. Suddenly they no longer were an inseparable trio. Mom still did things with Mrs. B, and Mrs. B with Mrs. Campbell, but Moe and Curly no longer spoke. Thanksgiving at our house that year was quiet, with too much room around the table in Mom's dining room. I missed Mrs. Campbell's creamed onions and cinnamon chocolate cake.

When I asked Mom why Soupy and his mother hadn't come, she told me she'd simply decided to have a smaller dinner and, as was her practiced habit, avoided further discussion. Darlene and I weren't really talking at the time, so I didn't bother asking her, but I did query Soupy, who shrugged and said, "Hell, I don't know. Chick weirdness. Even when they get old, that shit never stops. They'll get over it."

They never did, as far as I could tell. When Mrs. Campbell died the next year, Mom made a brief appearance at the wake but didn't attend the funeral Mass. "You know I don't go to church," she told me.

"What's the matter with you?" I said. "What about Soupy?"

"It's none of Alden's business," she said.

"What is none of his business?"

"It's none of yours either. I saw Alden at the funeral home. He doesn't expect to see me at church, but that shouldn't stop you."

Now I picked up the photograph from Mrs. B's counter. I looked at the smiles the women wore, lacking any trace of vanity or goofy self-consciousness, unlike the smiles men plastered on for photographs. How sad, I thought, that only my mother now remained, that she might never smile so purely again.

I put the photograph back.

I picked up the mail bundle and the rubber band snapped in my hand, the mail spilling across the floor. "Shit," I said, bending to pick it up.

There were two manila envelopes from adult education at Kepshire Community College; a narrow cardboard box, probably containing a pen in the shape of a baseball bat, from the Detroit Tigers Fan Club of Antrim County; and fifteen or sixteen white envelopes of varying sizes. I riffled through those. One said "Attorney Discipline Board, State of Michigan." Was some local lawyer in trouble? I slipped it out of the stack.

It was addressed to Lucas B. Whistler.

If I had thought about it for more than five seconds, I probably would have set it on the counter or on Whistler's desk. I told myself it was also addressed to the *Pine County Pilot*, of which I was an official representative. Nowhere was it marked "Personal and Confidential." I remembered the conversation I'd had with Philo about expenses.

I tore the envelope open. I flicked on a desk lamp next to Mrs. B's computer and scanned the page in my hand. It was dated the prior Friday.

Beneath Whistler's address it said: "RE: Case No. B-MI-8675309-01. Wayland E. Breck."

I looked over my shoulder through the newsroom door at Whistler's desk. At Enright's, I'd asked Whistler if he knew Breck. *Nope*, he had said.

The letter didn't say much: "This is to acknowledge receipt of your February 23, 2000, request for additional information regarding Case No. B-MI-8675309-01. We will evaluate your request and reply as promptly as required by law. Please be advised that, due to staffing shortages necessitated by budget reductions, our backlogs are currently running longer than usual."

That was all.

I put the letter back in the torn envelope and stood there thinking. Twilight was falling on Main Street. The dim glow from Enright's glimmered on the *Pilot*'s front window.

Whistler had known Breck, or had known about him, before I had. For some reason he'd kept that from me. I took out my cell phone to dial Whistler, then changed my mind.

I went back to my desk and slid the letter beneath some file folders in a drawer. I wanted to know more about Breck; more about his grandfather; more about Nilus and his women; more about who was behind Eagan, MacDonald & Browne's stealthy efforts to buy up the land above the northeastern corner of the lake; and if and how it was all connected. I thought I might make a quick run downstate. And I would not tell Whistler.

I made a mental note to call Millie Bontrager after dinner and ask if she could stay with Mom the next day. Then I sat down at my computer and called up the last e-mail from Joanie McCarthy. I hit Reply and typed:

Joanie,

Good to hear from you. Mom's as OK as can be expected. Thanks for asking. I hear you're kicking some butt down there. That's great—but no surprise. Matter of fact, I might be able to use your help. Call me asap.

* * *

My pickup truck fishtailed on the slippery washboard of Trimble Trail, an ignored gravel road that meandered through the low hills south of the lake.

Mom sat next to me, watching the trees pass.

We had had a quiet dinner of cheese-and-mushroom pizza I had picked up at Roselli's. Mom had barely eaten. She had seemed preoccupied. *Why do you keep looking out the windows?* I had asked, and she had told me to finish my pizza. *How was your day?* I had said, and she said her day would not be over until she ran the errand she wanted me to run with her. I had asked her where we were going and why and she had said, with great and specific determination, *Just do what I say for once, please.*

So I did. If Mom was imagining something, it wouldn't hurt to indulge her. If she was not, then I wanted to know what it was. Maybe it would shed some light on the priest and the dead nun and whoever had killed her and what, if anything, it all had to do with the death of Mrs. B. Or, more likely, it would tell me nothing.

I pulled the truck over just after Trimble veered north in the direction of the lake and just before it began to run parallel to South Beach opposite a thick pine stand. I parked far enough away from the snowdrifts on Mom's side of the car so that she had plenty of room to get out. It didn't matter that the car sat near the middle of the road. Snowplows were the only vehicles that plied Trimble and, if Pine County's finance manager had his way, they wouldn't be seen on that road again either.

Mom stood at the edge of the road shoulder, peering into the woods. I closed her door, which she didn't seem to notice was open. I glanced up the slope creeping from her feet to a ridge in the gloom. I knew there was a footpath that wound up through the trees, but it was barely visible in the snow.

"Why didn't we just take Horvath?" I said.

"For the same reason I wanted to stay at your place," Mom said. "The nosy police." She squinted in the direction of the snow-covered path. "Did you bring the flashlight?"

"Yes." I flicked it on, pointed it into the forest. Snow glistened on the trees.

"Your father used to come up this way when he got off work early and didn't want me to know. As if I couldn't smell the beer and cigars on him when he came in."

"Boys will be boys."

"For ever and ever." She took the flashlight. "Let's go."

I tried to take her by one arm but she shook me off. I actually wasn't worried about her being able to make the climb. Her body, although frailer than a year before, was still in decent shape for a woman going on sixty-seven. It was her mind that worried me, whether it worried her or not.

We trudged our way up in snow to our knees. Mom's left foot kept slipping on the incline, and I noticed she had tucked her corduroys into black rubber galoshes that I had worn as a boy. For Christmas I'd bought her a pair of insulated, waterproof boots for something like ninety bucks at a mall in Traverse City. Why hadn't she worn those? She kept turning the flashlight on and off. She'd stop and turn it on, then turn it back off and we'd stumble ahead for five or six steps, then she'd turn it on again.

"Mother," I said, "just keep it on."

"Someone will see," she hissed.

"Who? The police?"

"They're watching."

"Who are 'they,' Mom?"

"Quiet."

We reached the top of the ridge. Beyond the treetops I could see the lake's frozen expanse, as blank as fresh newsprint. An image flashed in my mind of Soupy and me squatting there on a summer night, drinking the Goebels or Black Labels we'd stolen out of some left-open garage, and plotting the rest of the evening without a thought to the rest of our lives. Mom pointed the flashlight down the slope. The beam fell on the trapezoidal white shroud of Dad's extra garage, his beloved tree house. Only a flagpole jutting up from the outer deck had gone untouched by snow.

My cell phone blurted from my jacket pocket.

"Gus," Mom said. "What are you thinking?"

"Sorry." I pulled the phone out. She grabbed at it. I yanked it away.

"Off now," she said, handing me the flashlight. "You go first on the downhill."

She grabbed a fistful of the back of my jacket and followed me down to Dad's garage. In the faraway distance I heard the sound of a police siren. Probably chasing a drunken driver, I thought. Whistler would probably hear about it on the scanner.

Mom gave me a sudden shove from behind. "Get going," she said.

Inside the garage I flipped the switch to turn on the overhead light, but Mom reached around me—"No"—and snapped it off. She felt her way to the Bonneville's trunk. She dug in her coat pocket and produced a set of three keys attached to a fob holding a photograph of our long-dead dogs, Blinky and Fats. The chain, which also held a key for the basement door and one for the boathouse, usually hung on a key-shaped wooden rack next to the back door at Mom's house. She held the keys in front of her face and selected a red one and inserted it into the lock on the Bonnie's trunk lid.

"Oh," she said, surprised. "It's already unlocked."

I stepped around to where she was standing. The trunk lid came open with a rusty groan. The smells of oil and hockey mildew wafted out. Normally a tiny light on the underside of the lid would have blinked on. But it remained dark.

"Ah," I said. "That's why the battery was dead. I didn't close the lid tight."

"Flashlight," Mom said.

I pulled it out and pointed the beam into the trunk, as big as a bath-tub. I pictured it stuffed with five hockey bags and half a dozen sticks and, hidden beneath the hockey gear, three or four stay-cold packs of Stroh's for trips downstate in our last season with the Rats. On a wool blanket rolled up in the back of the trunk lay one of Soupy's old hockey sticks, a Montreal Surprise.

Mom pulled the stick away, undid the blanket, tossed it aside. "Help me here," she said, propping a knee on the Bonnie's bumper so she could reach farther into the trunk.

"I can do it," I said.

"Just help me get up here."

I grasped Mom beneath her left arm and hoisted her onto the bumper. She ducked her head and leaned in. I heard the siren again, actually two sirens, closer than before. Stupid souse must be shitfaced enough to think he can get away, I thought.

Mom scraped something across the floor of the trunk. She rose up, careful to keep her head from banging the underside of the trunk lid. "There," she said. In her right hand she held a gray metal lockbox with a slot for a key and a handle folded flat on the top. She turned her head toward the garage door, hearing the sirens.

"Get me down, please."

I helped her out. She reached up and brought the trunk lid down. It bounced lightly on the latch and stayed open half an inch, as it must have been when Mom first tried to unlock it.

"Hold on," I said, moving between Mom and the trunk.

"Hurry, son."

I lifted the lid a foot, flattened my hands on it, and slammed it down. "You've got to really hammer it. Thing never worked right."

Mom handed me the lockbox. "Take this and go," she said.

It didn't feel as if it had much in it. "What is this?"

Mom reached into the neck of her coat, down into her sweater, and came out with another key. This one, blue, looked newly copied.

"And this," she said. "Now you have to— Wait."

"What's going on?"

"Listen," she said. Her eyes darted toward the oval windows on the upper half of the garage door. "Take this somewhere safe. Do not let anyone know you have it."

I looked at the box. "Why can't I—"

She pressed the blue key into my palm. "The police are coming. Listen now."

"They're coming here? No, why?"

"I lost my boot. They found my boot."

"Who? What boot?"

"The police."

She went to the garage door and got up on her toes to look out through the ovals. I saw blue light flicker across her forehead.

"Holy shit, Mom," I said. "What's going on?"

"I thought it was over," she said, coming back to me. "It's not over. That person came for me and got Phyllis instead."

"Who's 'they'? Why would—"

She slapped a palm down hard on the lockbox. "If you want to know about Nilus and about Nonny, you have to take this and get out of here now. Go."

"Are they going to arrest you? Who's Nonny?"

"I'll be fine. You must go, Gus. Go now."

She lunged forward and wrapped her arms around my chest and hugged me as hard as she'd hugged me in years. When she pulled her face away, I saw dampness on her cheeks. "You have work to do," she said.

I could have stood there and opened the door for the police, asked them what the hell was going on. I had no idea why they were descending but, as crazy as it seemed, the fact that they were there made me think my mother was not, at this particular moment, out of her mind. Her eyes were clear. She was speaking in her regular staccato. This wasn't the mother who left the teakettle whistling for hours, who forgot the directions to the IGA, who drifted into unknowable recesses of her memory. This was the mother who had brought me up, who had proudly recited my grade-point and goals-against averages to anyone who asked, who had always remembered to put a roll of white hockey tape in the left pocket of my Rats jacket, a black roll in the right, because I was superstitious that way.

I started to go out the side door we'd entered but through the window saw the beams of headlights bouncing on the tree trunks as the police cruisers struggled up the two-track to the garage. I shut that door and, with the lockbox cradled in my arm, pulled open the door to the short stairway up to Dad's tree house.

I looked back at Mom, who was standing on her tiptoes again, her face aglow in the police lights. "God, Mother," I said. I shut the door behind me and scrambled up the steps to another door that opened onto the outside landing. I twisted its knob and shoved but it did not budge against the snow piled against it on the other side. "Damn," I said.

My heart was racing. Sweat trickling down from under my wool Red Wings cap stung my left eye. I blinked at the sweat and twisted the knob again and drove my left shoulder into the door, trying not to make too much noise. The door moved a little, maybe a quarter of an inch, so I shoved it again, then again, until finally it fetched up against something hard. Sometimes during a thaw, water would overflow from the eaves and form puddles that refroze into ridges of ice on the landing. The door was stuck on one now.

I looked back down the stairs. A thin line of white light shone across the bottom of the door. I listened. I heard the big steel garage door clanking its way up. "Christ," I whispered. I had to squeeze through the six-inch gap I had opened.

The snow on the landing was at least a foot deep. I reached the box around the door and heard it land with a moist crunch. I did the same with my coat. Then I turned myself sideways and stuck my left leg and arm out between the door and the jamb. I grasped at the railing outside but it remained a few inches out of my reach.

I forced my torso into the crack. A splinter on the door's edge stabbed into my back so I squeezed harder against the jamb. I heard voices in the garage. Dingus and Darlene. Holy God, I thought, how could Darlene arrest my mother?

I reached for the railing again and got it with my ring and middle fingers. I relaxed for a second, then held my breath, sucked in what gut I had, and pulled as hard as I could. As I sprang free onto the landing, my flannel shirt caught on the strike plate. The shirt ripped and I heard something bounce into the dark stairwell.

Outside now, I held my breath again, listening.

I shut the door, threw my coat on, picked up the box. Now what? Dad had refused to build an outer stairway. He had said he didn't want neighbor kids or drunken teenagers or other strangers using his tree house when he wasn't around. Really he didn't want anyone using it, except him and the buddies he chose and, once in a while, me. I had to jump the eight or nine feet to the ground.

I slogged through the snow to the railing. The police lights now rippled color across the snow alongside the garage, but the landing remained in darkness. I took out the flashlight and, shielding it with one hand, snapped it on and aimed it at the ground, hoping to see a giant snowdrift I could jump into. There wasn't one.

I turned the flashlight off and tossed the box down. As long as I roll, I thought, it can't hurt much worse than a slap shot to the balls. I jumped. I landed next to the box, rolling, chunks of snow scratching into my neck and down my shirt. I grabbed the box and scuttled up the hill, trying to stay low, dodging trees, praying the cop lights wouldn't find me.

I should have kept running when I crested the ridge. Instead I stopped and squatted with one arm around a birch and peered back down on Mom's latest crime scene. Darlene and Dingus were standing with their arms folded in the shadows at the edge of one cruiser's headlights and Skip Catledge was helping Mom into the back of another car, the lights churning all their faces blue and red. It didn't appear that they had cuffed her, for which I was grateful. She stopped before ducking into the car and nodded at Catledge as if to say thank you. Skipper, polite as ever, nodded back.

The door slamming on Mom made me think of the Bonneville's trunk lid. You had to bang it down hard. Mom wouldn't have known that, because she didn't drive the Bonnie. Dad had driven it, and I had, though not for a couple of years. At some point, she had gone to the garage and put the lockbox I now carried under my arm in the Bonnie's trunk. Hidden it there, actually, where she thought nobody would find it.

But when? And why? And what did she mean, she had lost a boot? And "Nonny"? Where had I heard that before?

I followed a different path out of the woods than the one we had come up earlier, avoiding my pickup, which I figured the police would find and tow. Still in the trees, about fifty feet up from Horvath Road, I pulled out my cell phone and called Soupy.

SIXTEEN

W hat the fuck, Trap?"

Soupy had pulled his pickup over to the roadside near the public access boat ramp on the southwestern end of the lake. I came out of the trees where I'd been waiting in a snowdrift up to my thighs.

"Sorry," I said, shaking the snow off my legs. Soupy hadn't been happy about my call for help, but I rarely asked anything more of him than a Blue Ribbon, so he came. I hoped he hadn't said anything to his customers at Enright's about why he was leaving.

"I had to stick Angie behind the bar," he said, and I caught a whiff of mint laced with liquor. "By the time I get back, I could be wiped out. So where's your truck? What do you got there, a box of cash or something? Treasure in the woods?"

The lockbox was a little too big to hide in my coat, so I had set it on my lap, as if I carried a box like that around with me all the time. "The truck got towed," I said. "The box is Mom's. I don't know what's in it."

Soupy chuckled. "Old Mom Carpenter could probably could keep all her skeletons in a box that small, eh?"

We happened to be passing Mom's house. I glanced across the road into the trees sheltering Dad's garage. I didn't see any cop lights. "Mom's going to jail," I said.

"Get out."

"Yes."

"And you're not going with her?"

"No. I assume they'd arrest me, too."

"Holy fuck. First Tatch, now Mom C? Who's next, Mother Teresa? What did they arrest her for? They don't think—"

"No idea. They just took her in, up at Dad's garage."

"What was she doing up there? That where you got that?"

"Yeah."

"Then what are you doing here?"

"Soup," I said, "you can't go back to the bar and start running your mouth."

"Trap, come on, I love your mother. She's the last person I'd want to hurt."

Soupy really did love my mother, really did care about what she thought about him, even if his actions suggested he never heard a word of what she said about his drinking and slut chasing. It reminded me of Mom telling me she was worried about Soupy selling his parents' place. He had to be "careful," she had said.

"Eagan, MacDonald and Browne," I said.

"Huh?"

"Is that the law firm you're dealing with on your parents' house?"

"Hold on," Soupy said. "You're hiding in the trees like a prison escapee and I'm the one getting questioned? What's in the box?"

"It's them, isn't it, Soup?"

He slowed the truck where the shore road curved into Main at the western end of town. A streetlight illuminated a gnarl of scar on Soupy's cheekbone where a puck had struck him when we were kids. I remembered the blood spurting between his fingers as he clutched at his cheek and how he made himself laugh while our old coach tried to butterfly the gash closed with hockey tape before he took Soupy to the clinic.

"Eagan whatever sounds right," he said. "What do you care? Or that Whistler guy?"

"What about Whistler?"

"He's been asking me about the house, too."

Damn, he's good, I thought.

"Who's the law firm representing?" I said. "They're sure as hell not buying it for themselves."

"They didn't tell old Soupy. Probably some rich guy who's going to tear the place down and throw up a mansion. Who cares? I need the cash. You going to open that?"

Knowing nothing of the lockbox's contents, I had no desire to open it in front of Soupy.

"I don't have a key," I lied.

"I got a crowbar in the flatbed."

"Mom told me to take it and go. You have to give me your truck."

Soupy jammed the accelerator down to blast through the yellow light at Estelle. "Give you my—oh, shit, a cop."

The sheriff's cruiser was parked on Main two blocks down. It waited across from my rental house, where, to my surprise, my truck sat in the side drive.

"Soup," I said. "Turn. Now."

"Where?"

"Here."

"I thought—"

"Now."

Soupy swung his truck right onto Garfield, drove a block, and turned right again onto South, rolling toward the parking lot behind the *Pilot*. I didn't see a sheriff's cruiser there, but I couldn't risk going to the newsroom either.

"Here?" Soupy said.

"Keep going."

He continued past the *Pilot* and turned left on Elm, then went another block to Ambling and turned right toward the lake. Then he pulled over again and parked.

"Trap," he said, "you look like you're going to have a baby. The cops want that box, don't they?"

I had to speak to him in a language he would understand. "Soup, you know how they say every hockey game has like three hundred mistakes?"

"Never heard that," Soupy said.

"I read it in *Hockey News,* and I thought, I bet you two hundred of them happen when you're tired. You know, the other team's in your end, and you're running around and you can't get off the ice, and you're sucking wind, that's when you screw up, make a bad pass, take a bad penalty."

"And you're telling me this because?"

I grabbed the door handle. "Are you going to help me?"

He turned sideways in his seat. "Just square with me. Is Mom C in real trouble?"

"She's in jail," I said. "But there's something else. I mean, she has her memory issues, but she's either gone crazier than a shithouse rat or there's something else going on."

Soupy pointed at the box. "And you think it might be in there?"

"Maybe."

"Jesus Christ," he said. He sighed. Soupy didn't sigh much. "What the hell. Take it." He opened his door and stepped into the street. "You're going to have to fill it."

"What are you going to do?"

"What I always do: wing it. If I need a truck for something, I can borrow one from one of the five hundred people who owe me money."

"Soup—"

"No, man, I mean it, just go." He nodded in the direction of where the cop was parked. "The hell with those idiots. They arrest my buddy, my best buddy's mom. Fuck them."

I slid behind the steering wheel. Soupy extended his hand. I shook it.

"Take the back roads," he said. "I don't want to have to hock the thing back from the cops. Let me know what happens with Mom C."

"Will do."

He slammed the door shut. I gave him a salute. He grinned and gave me the finger.

I didn't pick up my cell phone until Grayling.

Mom's lockbox sat on the floor in front of the passenger seat. It wouldn't fit beneath. It made me nervous sitting there, where a cop could see it if one pulled me over.

Half a mile before merging onto Interstate 75 south, I pulled into a gas station. I leaned into Soupy's narrow rear seat and scooped up the garbage piled on the floor: crumpled Doritos and Burger King bags, empty dip cans, plastic pop bottles streaked with spat dip, a pizza box holding two old slices of pizza and a torn-open condom package, emptied bottles of Beam and El Toro, wads of hockey tape from nights when Soupy was in such a hurry to get to Enright's that he undressed in the truck.

I dumped it all on top of the lockbox. Then I got out and stood by the truck watching for cops while the gas tank gurgled full. Dingus couldn't arrest me in Crawford County, but he'd had me followed in the past. Inside the station, I bought three bottles of Vernors, a big bag of chips, and some onion dip.

Back in the truck, I started to punch a *Detroit Times* number into my cell phone, then decided to check my messages first. There were two. Coach Poppy had left the first when Mom and I were about to descend the hill to Dad's tree house.

"Hey, Gus, got a weird call," Poppy said. "Some woman left a message, said Tex is done playing hockey. Putting away foolish things, she said. Didn't leave a name, but I gather she's from Tatch's camp. I'd heard some talk about this but was hoping it was bull. Without Tex, I'm not liking our chances against the Pipefitters. Give me a shout."

I knew I had more important things to worry about, but the old River Rat in me couldn't help thinking: Damn, the Rats are so close, if they just had Tex, they could actually bring a state title, a little glory, a bit of relief to Starvation.

The second message was from Darlene. My heart skipped a beat when I heard her voice say, "Gussy." She hadn't called me that in a long time.

"I waited outside your house for an hour," she said. Oh, shit, I thought; that was her in the cop car across the street, not someone who'd come to arrest me. She must have made sure my truck made it home, too. "Bea is safe . . . I hope you're safe . . . Be careful, OK?"

It felt good to hear that. I saved the message and turned the phone off, wishing I had the charger, which was plugged into a wall socket at the *Pilot*.

Traffic was light, the weather clear. I stayed in the right lane and kept my speed around seventy-four, a bit over the limit but not so fast as to rouse a state trooper. I almost pulled into the rest stop at Nine Mile Hill, but a state trooper darted into the exit lane ahead of me and I stayed on I-75. Twenty-five miles later, I veered into the rest area at West Branch. Two sedans and a minivan were parked near the restrooms. A pudgy man in a Catholic Central High School fleece was dragging a little girl toward the restrooms. She was throwing a flop-around tantrum and the man was barking something at her that, thankfully, I could not hear. I rolled past them and pulled into a spot about five places down from their minivan.

I left the dome light off. I took a quick look around, checked all the mirrors. The man and the squalling girl disappeared into the glowing restroom hut. The lot sat still and quiet beneath the high street lamps. No cops. Nobody behind me.

I bent to the passenger seat floor, pushed the trash aside, and picked up the lockbox. I set it on my lap and pulled the blue key out of my pocket. I glanced around again before sliding the key into the lock. At first it jammed when I tried to turn it. I jiggled it gently, not wanting to break it off. Who knew when my mother had last opened the thing?

Finally it gave. The lid opened soundlessly. Taped to the bottom of the box was a manila envelope. Scratched on the front in black ballpoint pen, in my mother's cursive hand, was one word: "Nilus."

I felt goose bumps break out along my forearms.

I peeled away the tape securing the envelope inside the box and lifted the envelope out. I ran a palm across the top surface. It was smooth and flat except for a cluster of bumps beneath the paper in one corner. I shook it. The bumps seemed to rattle. I turned the envelope up and the bumps slid down to the other end.

Fresh tape sealed one end of the envelope, as if Mom had recently opened and then resealed it. As I stripped away the new stuff, I saw the speckled gray outlines of past sealings, felt the cracked, yellowed remnants of tape that looked to be years old. I peeked into the open end. It was too dark to see inside. I dipped a hand in. My fingertips brushed over the rough edge of a piece of paper, then across a thinner, softer paper, like old newsprint. I reached into the corner where the bumps had slid. I cupped them in my palm—a necklace?—and pulled my hand out.

Curled in my palm was a rosary.

I took it in two fingers and let it unwind before my face. A crucifix of bronze or something cheaper dangled at the end of a thin metal chain strung with smooth brown wooden beads. As the rosary twirled in the shadows of Soupy's truck, I noticed a gold tag attached to the chain at the end opposite the crucifix. I pinched the tag and brought it close to my face. Something was engraved on it that I couldn't make out in the dark. I reached overhead and switched on the dome light.

I squinted to read the engraving on the face of the little tag, bracing myself for the possibility that it might read "Nilus." It did not. The engraving bore only three letters: *BCD*. For Beatrice Clare Damico, I assumed. My mother's maiden name.

"Man," I said to myself. I turned off the dome light.

I tried to recall Mom saying the rosary. I could imagine a woman kneeling before a statue of the Blessed Mother at St. Valentine's, her head bowed and her eyes shut, her lips forming shapes of the words in the Hail Mary, a rosary laced in her fingers. But I couldn't tell if it was actually Mom before she walked away from the church, or an image I had conjured from a book or a movie or my own scant memories of services. I held my hand up, let the rosary slide down between my fingers, closed my hand into a gentle fist. Why had my mother saved it? Why had she felt the need to lock it away?

I dropped the rosary back into the envelope. I reached in and pulled out one of the pieces of paper. Out of the corner of my eye I saw the glass door on the restroom building flash in the light. The father and his daughter were coming out. He was carrying her now, and she was eating a candy bar. The door of the minivan opened and a woman stepped into the light, smiling. The father set the girl down and she ran to her mother, who gathered the child into her arms.

The piece of paper was a rectangle. One of the two long edges looked as if it had been folded and then carefully torn along the fold. I decided

I was holding one third of an eight-and-a-half-by-eleven-inch page. I turned it sideways so a short edge was on top. At the top of the rectangle were a faded stylized capital "S" and part of a small "a" along the torn edge. Below those were color pictures, cut in half by the ripped edge, of what looked like ice-cream confections, maybe a sundae and a soda.

Sanders, I thought. The classic Detroit ice-cream and candy palace. I had tried to take Mom there on one of her rare visits when I worked at the *Times*. But she had demurred, calling the place a tourist trap. It was funny to hear that from someone who lived in a town desperate to be a tourist trap. We got ice-cream cones at a Baskin-Robbins instead.

But now in my hands was what looked like a placemat from a Sanders restaurant, maybe the very one I had tried to take Mom to. The mat had to be old, maybe as old as me, because I could see parts of the prices of the items, and each carried a cents rather than a dollar sign.

I flipped the paper over.

On the back was some sort of drawing—or, again, part of a drawing, because I had in my hands only about a third of a page. I switched the dome light back on and leaned into it. As I looked more closely, the drawing appeared to be a map of some sort, drawn in ballpoint ink. It looked as though someone might have carefully traced over the lines and letters on the drawing, perhaps because the earlier version was fading.

In the upper left corner of the page was an arrow pointing up and marked alongside with a capital "N." For north, I assumed. A smaller arrow beneath it pointed down and off the left side of the page, and beneath the arrow was the word "LAKE," written in my mother's hand.

A car pulled in two spaces to my right. I lowered the paper to my lap and waited while a stooped old man emerged from the Chrysler and made his way slowly toward the restrooms. He wore an orange hunting cap with a picture of a deer over the bill. He peered at me as he passed. For a second I thought he might stop, and I started to slip the paper back into the envelope, but he just smiled and nodded, and I gave him a polite smile and pointed at the restrooms as if I were waiting for my wife. He kept walking.

I looked back at the map. Beneath the arrows, a curving line traced the upper portion of an irregular oval from the bottom left of the page up and around to the bottom right. Within the oval my mother had scratched three X's and some squiggly vertical lines. Perhaps, I thought, the squiggles signified a hill or a rise. The X's were clustered around those lines, each marked with the name of a tree: "BIG OAK STUMP," "BURNED OAK," and "TWO-TRUNK BIRCH."

The burned oak stood at the apex of a triangle with the other oak and the birch marking the ends of its legs. A scalene triangle, I thought, remembering my mother saying it to me over my ninth-grade geometry textbook at the dining room table. She was better at math than she was at spelling. The scalene was outlined by dotted lines. A fourth dotted line bisected it from the burned oak down and off the page's ragged bottom edge. To where, or to what, I had no idea.

A treasure map? I thought. It made me recall what I had said to Tatch when I'd visited his camp and seen all the people toiling on the hill: *Digging for gold?* Now I asked myself: Could this crude map my mother had drawn years or even decades ago show Breck and his blindly faithful diggers how to find whatever it was they were tearing up the earth for? If so, it would have to have something to do with Nilus, wouldn't it, or why else would Mom have put it in an envelope labeled as it was?

I slipped the page back into the envelope and pulled out the other paper. It was, as I'd thought, newsprint, a yellowed, one-column clip that had been scissored out of a newspaper, then folded over once. I'd seen it on the microfilm machine at the clerk's office: "Accused Killer Murdered in Pine County Jail." I quickly reread it, noting again the connection between the accused, Joseph Wayland, and his grandson, Breck.

I felt someone looking at me and lifted my eyes to see the orange hunting cap floating in the dark before my truck. The old man grinned and looked back at the restrooms with a shrug, as if to say, "What do women do in there anyway?" I smiled again, nervously I thought, and kept a sidelong gaze on him until his Chrysler pulled away.

Mom obviously didn't want the police to know about what I held in my hands, or else she wouldn't have rushed me out the back of Dad's garage. I imagined her now, sitting in a jail cell, reading a book or a magazine. I pictured Darlene stopping by to see her. I felt relieved. I wondered if the police would release Mom before I returned to Starvation, and hoped they would not.

I put everything back in the envelope, dropped it into the lockbox, locked it, and stuffed it under the rubbish on the floor. The fluorescent glow of the restroom lobby grew dim in my rearview mirrors as I pulled back onto I-75.

SEVENTEEN

I turned my cell phone on after crossing the bridge at Zilwaukee, a bit more than a hundred miles north of Detroit. There were two new messages.

Attorney Peter Shipman said he'd been retained by my mother. Darlene, he said, had called him, God bless her. "Bea's fine," he said. "The cops aren't saying much, and I told her to stay mum for now. No charges yet, but they're holding her for questioning. Between us, I think they think it's for her own safety. She has her own cell and they're treating her with kid gloves. She sends her love."

The young woman on the other message said simply, "Call me when you hit twenty-three."

I dialed Joanie McCarthy when I exited onto U.S. 23 south toward Detroit.

"Thirsty?" she answered.

"Where are you?"

"The newsroom. The desk called me in to chase some stupid *Freep* story we wrote a week ago. Then they decided there was no space for it."

My old newsroom: the wooden desks like steamer trunks, the wires snaking up the ancient pillars, the rattle of keyboards ringing off the tile floors, the smells of bad coffee and old leather and newsprint.

"Sorry," I said. "Just pop it on the Internet."

"Might as well put it in a bottle and throw it off the banks of the Detroit River. You still shoot pool?"

"Not for a while, but it's kind of late, isn't it?"

"Not upstairs at Aggie's. You know it?"

I looked at my watch. After midnight. I had thought I would get a motel and meet Joanie in the morning. But she had stayed up, so I guess I had to stay up.

"Greektown, right? Monroe?"

"Off Beaubien. An hour?"

"Sure. You got some stuff on Breck?"

I heard what I thought was her taking her feet off of a desk, plopping them on the floor. "Altar boy," she said.

"How so?"

"See you at Aggie's. Bring your A game."

I had to hop between three puddles of vomit glistening in the streetlights on the sidewalk outside Aggeliki's Greek.

A man wearing a grease-spattered apron and folded white paper hat came out of Aggie's with a bucket and mop, shaking his head. He looked at me and I said, "Not me, man." He said something in Greek that I didn't understand. His look said fuck off.

I opened the glass door to the vestibule at Aggie's. The restaurant lay beyond another glass door to my right, aglow in white fluorescence, clattering with plates and forks and the babble of the boozed and drowsy. The aroma of garlic filled my nose, and my belly told me pastitsio, please, and dolmades, with a cup of creamy lemon soup. But I turned to my left and pushed through a wooden door that hid a gloomy stairway reeking of cigarettes. At the top of the stairs, I heard the faint din of the Clash on a speaker that must have had a torn woofer, then the dull crack of a rack of pool balls being broken, then the voice of a man saying, "Get in there, sweetness."

I squinted through the haze, thicker even than at Enright's. Behind the balls rolling to a stop on the table, Joanie McCarthy leaned against a paneled wall, a pool stick propped in one hand. Her face was obscured in the smoky radiance of the two bare lightbulbs hanging over the table, but I could tell it was her by the way her wide hips swung to one side over her crossed legs.

I caught her eye. She smiled. I was transported back to the *Pilot* newsroom, two years before, when she had sat where Whistler now sat, daring me to run the stories she wrote that she knew would upset the old fogies who would rather sit around Audrey's bitching about how the politicians were pissing away their tax dollars than have to stomach reading about it in the *Pilot*. On the rare occasion back then when Joanie smiled without sarcasm, I don't know exactly why, but I would feel better about myself, and about her.

Her smile across the pool table now did the same, for a heartbeat. Joanie turned to the guy who had broken the rack. "That's all you got?"

"Loose rack," said the guy.

"Loose? You love loose," Joanie said, allowing herself a quick look at me, almost as if for approval. Now she came off the wall and leaned over the table, scanning the scattered balls. "One off the four," she said. "Four might go, too."

"The queen of slop," the guy said.

His voice was oddly familiar.

Joanie grinned and bent and stroked the cue ball into the one ball. The one glanced off of the four and dropped cleanly into a corner pocket. The four edged toward a side pocket and hung on the lip. Joanie bounced sideways to her left, pointed her stick at the table again. "Two down there, and I'll back up the cue and knock the four in this time," she said.

"Sure you will," the guy said.

The three of us seemed to be the only ones in the place. The floor was covered in shag carpet the color of zucchini and flecked with cigarette burns and stains I didn't want to know the origin of. The walls were bare but for coats hung on nails and a single black-and-white photograph of a woman in an apron, Aggie herself, hugging the Stanley Cup.

The guy playing against Joanie plucked a cell phone off of his belt and punched the keys with a thumb while glaring at me. I looked away, wondering who the hell made phone calls at this time of night?

Joanie kept sinking balls. After each shot, she gave me a fleeting glance, gauging my expression. She knew she was not the Joanie McCarthy I had known, the baby-fat grad-school kid with the bush of flaming auburn hair and gigantic backpack who had spent an eventful year as my junior reporter at the *Pilot*. This Joanie shooting nine ball in an after-hours joint wasn't quite slinky, but she had lost enough pounds to wear her Dearborn Music T-shirt knotted over her bare belly.

Her hair was cropped short and straightened, which made her green eyes seem bigger and brighter. She had never lacked for confidence, at least not around me, but watching her move around the pool table, weighing her options, calling her shots, leveling her stick, I thought she seemed more like a woman, even at just twenty-five, than the impatient girl who had left Starvation for bigger and better, first in Chicago, now in Detroit.

She missed a seven-nine combo that would have ended the game.

"Oh, crap," she said.

I stepped into the light. The piss-yellow felt on the table was threadbare along the rails. "You mean, 'Oh, fuck'?"

She turned to me, brushing reddish bangs from her eyes. "I don't think so."

"It's not a pool stick," I said, mimicking the complaint I had heard from her about obscene words. "It's a fucking pool stick."

She laughed as she came over and surprised me first with a two-armed hug, the tip of her pool stick poking me between the shoulder blades, then a light kiss on the neck that made me shiver a little.

"It's so good to see you," she said.

"You, too." Up close I saw a scar I had never noticed before, an upside-down smile etched between her chin and lower lip. I pointed at it. "Bar fight?"

"Not quite. How was your trip?"

"OK," I said, thinking of the lockbox. "No traffic."

"Excuse me."

It was the guy with Joanie. He was moving around the table. I wasn't in his way, but he wanted me to think I was. I took a step back. He gave me a look, gave a different one to Joanie, who didn't seem to notice. The guy was big. Not athletic big, just lumbering cumbersome big, like a washing machine. He was wearing his olive drab winter coat open. A striped wool scarf dangled from his neck. He snapped the tip of his stick on the table's edge, grabbed the chalk.

"Game over," he said.

Again the voice sounded familiar, but I couldn't place it.

"Good luck," Joanie said. "Hey—meet my friend Gus from up north. Gus, this is Albert Gaudreault."

I started to offer a hand across the table but the guy was already lining up his shot. He jabbed at the cue ball. It struck the seven, which bumped the nine into a corner. He spread his arms and looked at Joanie. "Like I said." He pointed the stick at me then and waggled it.

"Frenchy," he said.

"Pardon?" I said.

"Call me Frenchy."

In my head I repeated the name I had heard: GAW-droh. It, too, sounded familiar, though again not familiar enough that I knew what it meant to me. Frenchy didn't speak with even a hint of a French accent, as did some of the French-Canadians I'd encountered in hockey rinks. If anything, he sounded like he might have come from downriver. Maybe River Rouge, or Woodhaven.

"Gus," I said.

"Yeah." As if he knew me.

Somehow the Clash became Three Dog Night.

"Buy you a beer?" I said.

He looked at Joanie. He had the sad face of a basset hound, but the attitude was more Doberman. He mouthed the words, "This is the guy?"

Joanie stepped over, flattened a hand on the slight curve of his belly, leaned up and kissed him, quickly, on the lips. The hair on the back of her neck parted, revealing the whiteness of the nape.

Frenchy looked past Joanie to me. "No, thanks," he said. "I'm going." Then to Joanie, "Careful now, sweetness."

She laughed as she pushed him toward the stairway. He glanced at me over his shoulder before he disappeared. Then Joanie grabbed me by my belt and pulled me toward the bar.

"Nightcap," she said.

"That your boyfriend?"

Joanie and I half sat, half stood on the rickety stools at the bar, a rectangular box of plywood and two-by-fours hung with a torn Kid Rock poster. The guy I'd seen cleaning up the puke appeared from a back room. His mood had not improved. Blue Ribbon wasn't on the menu, so I ordered a longneck Bud, Joanie a Jack Daniel's, neat.

She shook her head no to my question.

"You know him?" she said. "You know everybody."

I peered at the doorway to the stairs, as if that might tell me. Frenchy was at least ten years older than Joanie, probably older than me. "He looks . . . I don't know."

Joanie shook her head. She obviously liked the guy, but I couldn't tell if there was more than that. In my experience, the only thing that got Joanie going was scoops.

"Poor Frenchy," she said.

"He's not your boyfriend?"

"I don't have boyfriends."

"Really? Does he work for the *Times*?"

"Sort of. Not really."

"Meaning?"

"He used to work there. The *Free Press*, too. Now he does a little of this and a little of that. Kind of a freelancer."

"Ah. One of those guys."

I knew a few. They hopped back and forth between the *Times* and the *Free Press*, playing the papers and their editors off of one another, getting raises and more raises until one day an editor who'd hired them at one paper had a drink with one who'd hired them at the other and halted that little gravy train. Guys like Frenchy wound up hanging out at the Anchor and the Post and the Money Tree, picking up dollar-a-word assignments and pretending they were loving the freelance life while leaving $10 bills on $120 tabs.

"He says the past is the past," Joanie said, and I thought, Were it only so. She inched her stool closer. I caught a whiff of her body wash. Almond. "He's good at computer stuff. You'll see. How are you?"

I told her without telling her anything she didn't need to know. She listened, her chin in one hand, her eyes intent on my face. She asked about Dingus, about the *Pilot*, about my mother. She had gotten to know Mom, and Mom her, while she was in Starvation. When she asked about Darlene, I changed the subject and asked her how she had wound up on the cop beat in Detroit, at the *Times*, after leaving the *Pilot* for the *Chicago Tribune*.

Joanie stirred her whiskey with a forefinger, licked the finger. I remembered how she once had surprised me by chugging a can of Blue Ribbon in the *Pilot* newsroom. "I don't know," she said. "It was more money."

"The way I heard it, the *Times* came after you big-time after you broke some highway construction scam."

"L trains, actually," she said. "But, yeah, I guess. Whatever. The new editor at the *Times* used to be at the *Trib*."

She had been in a hurry since the day I had hired her at the *Pilot*. In a hurry for bigger stories, bigger audiences, bigger prizes. Lots of young reporters were in a hurry, but most were prone to tripping over their own feet. I had once been in a hurry and wound up stumbling all the way back to the small time.

"Don't apologize for success, Joanie."

"Don't be a wimp, Gus."

"What does that mean?"

"You could be back here now. All the people who sold you out are long gone. All you have to do is pick up the phone and you'd be kicking the auto companies' butts again."

"It's not that simple."

"Look what you did in Starvation. You got the bad guy."

"We both did. But I should've gotten him twenty years ago."

"Whatever. It doesn't matter where you are, it's what you do that matters."

I took a drink of my Bud. Warm again. "No complaints here. My mom needs me. I like my life OK. Got a new reporter."

"You mean old reporter, don't you?"

"You know him?"

"Lucas B. Whistler? Are you kidding? The youngest Detroit reporter ever to be a Pulitzer finalist? Prizewinning basher of computer screens?"

"He already smashed one at the *Pilot*," I said. "Sounds like you got Pulitzer envy."

"I have another year to beat him," she said, holding her glass up in a toast, then sipping from it. "And after I actually win, I plan to keep my job longer, too."

"You have a ways to go."

"How did you get stuck with him?"

"Stuck with him? I'm glad to have him. The guy's a pro."

"OK."

"What does that mean?"

She pulled her hair back on her head. "Rumors. I don't know."

"Come on. Anything in particular? Or just beer blather at the Anchor?"

"Evidently he's quite the wheeler-dealer."

That was no surprise. I decided not to tell Joanie about Whistler and Tawny Jane Reese. During her *Pilot* days, Joanie had called T.J. "Twitchy-Butt."

"Well, his clips looked great."

"Yeah?" Joanie said. "How many had solo bylines?"

"There were some JVs in there. The guy was getting ready to retire."

"He's not *that* old."

"Hell, I'm all for retiring at fifty-six. Anyway, he said he was mentoring the youngsters, letting them have bylines."

"Huh. He might've had it backward. I think he smashed more computers in the last few years than he wrote stories."

"This isn't just a *Times* thing, is it?" I said. "You know—he's a *Freep* reporter, therefore he sucks?"

She grinned. "Of course. You want me to ask around about him?"

"Knock yourself out. Did you get me that appointment?"

"I got *us* the appointment."

"Ah." I'd expected that. She wasn't letting me have anything to myself.

"Nine a.m. At a golf course in Redford."

"Redford. Why a golf course?"

"That's what the flack wanted."

"What flack? What do they need a PR guy for?"

"Got me. That's who called me back."

She stood and walked across the room to the nail where her jacket hung. She came back wrapping herself in black leather to her knees. She kept coming until she was standing so close that I could smell the almond wash again. She pointed a fingernail shellacked in scarlet at the half-moon scar on her chin.

"You know how I got this?" she said.

"Nope."

The music, Creedence now, ended abruptly in the middle of "Lodi," the 3:15 silence as sudden as a shriek.

"A puck."

"At a Wings game?"

"My center throws me a cross-ice pass." She took a step back and positioned her hands as if they were holding a hockey stick. *My center throws me a cross-ice pass?* When Joanie was in Starvation, she'd had no use whatsoever for the game I loved.

"I'm about to catch it on my backhand when this idiot from the other team shoves his stick in the way and the puck flies up and catches me."

"Get out of here. You're playing hockey?"

"Novice. Lots of leaners out there."

"Benders," I corrected her.

"Right."

"And tripods."

She pushed her face in close to mine, and for half a second I thought she might kiss me. Joanie McCarthy, who had called me a coward to my face when she had worked for me. Now she was sending me weekly e-mails about my coming to Detroit for a visit. And she was one of only a handful of *Pilot* subscribers who had the paper mailed to her in Detroit. "I'm not a tripod," she said.

"I'll take your word for it."

"See. You really did teach me things." She looked at my beer. "You going to take that with you?"

"I'd rather drink Freon."

"Freon's a gas. You can't drink it. If you want to know more about this Breck dude, you're coming with me."

"I've got to get some sleep. At least an hour or so. I don't suppose the cops would appreciate me snoozing in my truck."

"You're coming to my place. We need a computer. Leave your truck. We're not going to get much sleep."

I had heard that line from a woman or two before, and it hadn't had anything to do with computers. I must have sounded stupid when I blurted, "Why?"

She was already halfway down the stairs. "Now," she said.

EIGHTEEN

Joanie lived in a rented loft apartment near the Eastern Market. The old floors creaked as we made our way down the shadowed corridors. Passing one door, I heard the muted cadence of a weatherman telling Detroit it would be cloudy and cold. No news there. I smelled bread toasting, pictured someone climbing out of a shower.

Secretly, I felt a little nervous as we made our way to the end of one hallway and Joanie's place. I'd once had a girlfriend who had lived two floors up in that very building and, so far as I knew, still did. She worked at the *Free Press* and was often out schmoozing sources this late. I'd shot five a.m. pool with her at Aggeliki's, in fact; she was damn good at sinking the nine on the break.

I was relieved to have Joanie's door shut behind us.

Her apartment was spare and neat, except for the two cheap wooden desks shoved against the wall beneath her loft. A knot of wires and surge protectors surrounded two computer terminals and keyboards crowded atop one of the desks. The other desk was stacked a foot deep with dog-eared files, stuffed into accordion folders. More files were piled on the hardwood floor next to the desk. Leaned against that stack was the backpack from her *Pilot* days.

"Still got that thing, eh?" I said. "It's big enough, you could use it for your hockey gear."

Joanie was lighting a candle. It smelled of tart berries. "The guy next door smokes like a chimney," she said. "Back in a minute." She disappeared behind a door in the wall behind the wooden ladder ascending to the loft.

I listened. From behind the door came a few clicks, then a mechanized voice. "You have one new message," it said. "Call received today at twelve fifty-eight a.m." There came another click, then a whooshing sound, probably traffic, maybe in a freeway tunnel. "Hey, babe," echoed a man's voice. "I think I got what you—"

Joanie cut it off before Frenchy could say anything more. But an alarm of recognition already had gone off in my head. Frenchy was the guy my old girlfriend, the one who'd lived upstairs, had thrown over for me years before. I had never met him. But I had heard that voice, the one I'd heard over the pool table at Aggeliki's, on an answering machine just like Joanie's in an apartment just like Joanie's. My old girlfriend's apartment. He left a lot of messages on that machine. Too many.

He had been a computer tech at the *Free Press*. My girlfriend, whose name was Michele, had called him Albert, or Bert, or Bertie. I didn't remember her calling him "Frenchy." She would have thought it a silly nickname, which it was. Maybe he'd given it to himself later. I did remember the things he had threatened to do to her after she had stopped taking his calls. And how, instead of squealing to her bosses at the paper, Michele instead mentioned the guy's threats to a couple of cops she knew, who had a men-to-man talk with him. After that, she never heard from him again. He eventually left the *Freep* amid rumors that he kept showing up at the college dormitory of a summer intern he'd had a fling with.

I sat down on one of the vinyl-backed chairs at Joanie's kitchen table, wishing I was back in Starvation. Joanie emerged barefoot in gray sweats and a white River Rats jersey striped in gold and blue. I recognized it immediately as one I had worn as a kid. The number, 35, was faded, and the "R" and second "E" in "CARPENTER" across the back had peeled away.

"Where did you get that?" I said.

"Your mom. She sent it with a nice note about the time I spent with her up north. Would you like to read it?" She looked ruefully at her desk. "Not sure I could find it."

"I think I've had enough surprises for one day."

"I think your mom's sweet." Joanie motioned toward the fridge. "Do you want anything to drink?"

"No, but I'm starving."

She reached into a cabinet over the sink and came out with an opened box of brown sugar Pop-Tarts. She tossed it to me. "Sorry, toaster's on the fritz. Let's get to work."

She sat at her computer. I pulled up a chair. She reached under the desk. The machine whirred as she slipped a CD into it. A long minute passed. "Come on, piece of crap," Joanie said. The screen went all white, then all blue. Then some words materialized in white at the top:

Subject: Breck, Wayland Ezra
Social Security Number: 292-41-6654
Date of Birth: 04/26/48
Birthplace: Detroit, Michigan

"So he's . . . fifty-one. Almost fifty-two. He looks younger." Must be the cross-eyed thing, I thought. "Jesus, you have his Social Security number?"

"I'm not going to give it to anybody."

"You just gave it to me."

"Frenchy's pretty good at what he does."

I wasn't a big fan of Frenchy but figured it wouldn't be smart to let Joanie know. "The freelancer, huh? Just how freelance is he?"

"Excuse me?"

"Do you pay him for this?"

She pulled one of her legs up under the other on her chair. The chartreuse polish on one foot's toenails didn't match the frosted pink on the other's. "When you need something fast—you know, background stuff—Frenchy can get it faster than anyone."

"Always first, frequently right," I said.

"How did you know that?"

"Know what?"

"Frenchy says that."

"So does Whistler. Must be a *Free Press* thing."

"Brand X," Joanie said. "Anyway, Frenchy said this is pretty cursory, he didn't have much time, but . . . well, see what you think."

I watched her click through more than forty pages of documents Frenchy had unearthed from the Internet and scanned onto the CD. Some of them—Breck's birth certificate, his home address, a couple of newspaper photos, even the clipping I had seen in Mom's lockbox—came from public sources. Others, like the Social Security number, derived from sources I preferred to know nothing about.

Joanie returned to the first screen. She opened a drawer, pulled out two fresh notebooks, and handed one to me.

"Wow," I said. "You're rich."

"Huh?"

"Nothing."

"Got a pen?" she said. "You can't take the disk."

"I'm not sure I want it. Why are you taking notes?"

"The *Times* covers Michigan, you know."

Same old Joanie. She hit Enter.

Wayland Breck was born to Gregory Breck, a draftsman, and his homemaker wife, the former Susan Veronica Wayland. On the boy's second Christmas Eve, his father was killed in a car crash with a drunken driver, who was issued a ticket and released. When Wayland was five, he moved with his mother to Livonia, a suburb near Detroit's western border anchored by Michigan's only Thoroughbred racetrack, since closed, and one of the first shopping malls in the United States, since demolished.

Breck graduated in 1966 from Livonia's Franklin High, 1971 from Michigan State, 1975 from University of Detroit Law. A grainy copy of a photograph showed Breck in his cap and gown, unsmiling, in front of a stone clock tower.

"Typical lawyer, eh?" I said. "Not making money yet, not happy."

"Maybe he's just itchy in that robe."

By the late 1970s, Breck's name was showing up on state documents registering him as a principal—apparently the sole principal—in a firm called W. E. Breck Legal Associates, with an address in Livonia. Based on what Frenchy had unearthed, Breck did mostly routine domestic work—divorce, probate, minor tax issues, some workers' compensation. His mother died in 1988. He divorced a wife of twelve years in 1990.

Joanie rapped the Page-down key seven or eight times. A series of blank pages flashed on the screen. "Here's where it gets interesting."

There followed a sequence of documents that had been copied and copied over again. As Joanie scrolled down, I saw what appeared to be many pages of legal filings, followed by two or three photocopies of newspaper clippings, followed by more legal filings, then clips, and so forth, until the pages went blank again.

All of the documents were dated in the 1990s.

Joanie backtracked to the beginning of the sequence. She sat back and folded her arms across her Rats jersey. "The guy was doing oppo research," Joanie said.

"Opposition? Digging dirt on someone?"

"Not just anybody." She leaned into the keyboard. "This really sucks, Gus."

"You want—"

"Yeah." She stood. "Take over."

We traded seats. I began to tap through the documents on the screen. They were a collection of affidavits connected to various lawsuits filed in the circuit courts of Wayne and Oakland counties. The plaintiffs' names were blacked out, but the case numbers varied, so I was able to count eight separate lawsuits. In each case, one of the defendants was the Archdiocese of Detroit.

My stomach tightened as the nature of the lawsuits became clear. Eight men, ranging in age from twenty-three to fifty-four, had accused priests at parishes in the archdiocese of sexually abusing them when they were young. Because the original complaints were not included, it was impossible to know the specifics of the charges.

For that, I was grateful.

"My God," I said.

"Just like old times."

In terse, clinical language, the affidavits delineated evidence that the accusers were mistaken, hypocritical, compromised, delusional, lying: "Mr. [NAME REDACTED] was terminated from his job as an assistant foreman at Detroit Diesel on February 4, 1993, because he had repeatedly shown up for work inebriated." In these papers, the victims of abuse were now adulterers, debtors, wife beaters, gambling addicts, tax cheats: "Despite his protestations to the contrary, there is ample evidence that Mr. [NAME REDACTED] disregarded the plain truth in the pleadings related to his ongoing divorce proceedings with [NAME REDACTED]."

Each affidavit was executed and signed by Wayland E. Breck, "Special Counsel," on behalf of the law firm of Eagan, MacDonald & Browne.

"He wasn't part of Eagan, MacDonald, was he?" I said.

"I don't think so," Joanie said. "Looks like he was just a contractor."

"These are bad people, boy."

The affidavits cited little if any supporting evidence for their assertions. Which made me think that the assertions were probably laced with falsehoods and half-truths while containing just enough verifiable fact—a tax document that could be interpreted in various ways, a statement from a jealous coworker, the testimony of an aggrieved wife—to put a scare into these men who already had been scared so badly as boys, to fling them back upon the dark certainty they had carried for most of their lives that whatever misfortune befell them was their fault and theirs alone.

As the archdiocese's hired hatchet man, Breck had assembled affidavits that might give a man pause, especially a man laboring under a burden of guilt laid upon him in a rectory, a sacristy, a confessional. Maybe that man, that accuser, would withdraw lest he be forced to face his supposed flaws in public. Or maybe, at the very least, he would acquiesce in a mutual silence in return for money.

The photocopied newspaper clips that Frenchy had interspersed told this very story. Taken from the *Times*, the *Free Press*, the *Birmingham Eccentric*, the *Northville Record*, the articles, none more than six paragraphs long, told of how each of the men—all of them named in the stories—had agreed to settle with the archdiocese. The accusers declined to comment, in accordance with the terms of the settlements.

Other terms were not disclosed.

Joanie laid a hand on my shoulder and squeezed. "What are you thinking?" she said.

"So the guy was your basic household lawyer for years, then in the 1990s he starts taking on these errands for Eagan, MacDonald."

"For the archdiocese," Joanie said.

I was trying to think about all of it, all at once: Mrs. B dead. Nilus. The murdered nun. Tatch's camp. Breck. The digging. Tatch and my mother in jail. The piece of what appeared to be a map. The rosary. The archdiocese. Breck again.

Joanie clapped a hand on my thigh and leaned in close enough that I glimpsed pale freckles through the laces at the neck of her jersey.

"Wake up, Gus," she said. "Why are you here? Why do you care about this guy? What does all this have to do with what happened to Phyllis Bontrager?"

"My mother knows something."

"About these pedophile priests?"

"No." I shifted my legs so that her hand came off my thigh. "About a nun who was killed in Starvation a long time ago."

I told Joanie about Sister Cordelia and the man who had been accused of killing her, Breck's grandfather. I told her about Nilus and his womanizing. I left the lockbox out of it.

"Is that why you asked about meeting with the archdiocese?"

"I wanted to know more about Nilus."

"Good gut, then."

"Maybe. Interesting that Eagan, MacDonald is their law firm."

"Why?"

"The firm's been quietly buying up land on a corner of the lake. It's not prime land, it's not even on the water, but all of a sudden everybody's interested in it."

"And you're thinking . . ."

"I wonder if they're buying it for the archdiocese."

"Because . . ."

I hesitated, not sure I wanted to say it yet. "I don't know. We can ask tomorrow."

"You mean today." She leaned back to look at the clock on her stove. "Holy cripes, it's almost four-thirty."

Through the blinds on her sole window I heard traffic stirring on the Chrysler Freeway. Her new look aside, Joanie was now the Joanie I remembered, shoving me toward conclusions, as she had when she was at the *Pilot* and we were looking into the past of a hockey coach. She unfolded herself and stood, the Rats jersey falling to her knees. "You know," she said, "I don't miss Starvation much. But I do miss you."

"Sure, as long as you don't have to work for me."

"Time for bed, eh?"

I looked around the room. There was nothing but hard-backed chairs. No sofa, no armchair, not even a beanbag chair.

"Hell," I said, "maybe we ought to just go get some breakfast."

"You don't like Pop-Tarts?" She slid onto the bottom step of the ladder to her loft. "I'm going up. What about you?"

The silence that followed probably was shorter than it seemed to me. "I'll be OK," I said. Joanie regarded me for a second, then started up the ladder. She was cute and tough and passionate, which made her beautiful, in her way. I made myself think of Darlene in Dad's tree house the night her mother died.

I watched Joanie climb away from me.

She stopped at the top. Something, maybe a pipe, made a lurching sound inside a wall. "Nothing has to happen, Gus."

"I know."

She waited. I stayed. "All right," she said. "See you in three hours."

NINETEEN

My cell phone woke me.

"Damn," I croaked. I'd thought I had turned the thing off. I jumped up from where I had dozed off on a wool rug with my coat balled up beneath my head for a pillow. The phone was in my coat. I pulled it out and answered.

"Where the hell are you?" Luke Whistler said. I checked the stove clock. Not quite seven. On the floor at the foot of the loft ladder lay the Rats jersey Joanie had been wearing earlier, covering the boots I'd taken off to sleep.

"I had to run an errand."

"At seven in the morning? You know your mom's in jail?"

"I do."

I heard a chair squeak through the phone. Whistler was at the *Pilot*. "Got the coroner's report."

"They released it?"

"Not publicly."

I glanced up at the loft, turned my body away, lowered my voice.

"How come you bullshitted me about Breck?" I said.

"What are you talking about?"

"I asked you if you knew Breck. You said no. But you've been checking up on the guy."

"You going through my mail?"

"It's *Pilot* mail, pal."

"OK, boss," Whistler said. He sounded annoyed, but I didn't care. "You got me. Although I didn't really lie. I didn't, and don't, know this character. But I was trying to get to know him, for a story."

"What story?"

"He's supposedly in hot water with the state. They might disbar him. Which wouldn't be good for the born-agains' tax appeal."

"First I heard of it."

"Yeah, well, I'm not sure it's true."

"Do me a favor and keep me posted."

"I will. Sorry. Really. If you can't trust a fellow scribe, who can you trust? It's me and you and the rest of the world, right?"

"What about the coroner's report?"

"Confirmed homicide," he said. "Blunt trauma to the head, from a blow and from falling to the floor. She had a pretty bad gash above one eye, but that wasn't the cause."

"It wasn't just a heart attack or something?"

"Everybody dies of heart attacks," Whistler said. "A guy gets shot in the head, he dies of heart failure. Could be the break-in artist freaked out, so it wasn't premeditated. But it's a dead body. Your pal in the pokey may have a problem."

"Have they charged him yet?"

"Nothing yet. And the cops ain't talking a lick. I got in the sheriff's face a little and your girlfriend threatened to usher me off the premises."

"My ex-girlfriend."

"Really? I don't get that impression."

I wasn't about to engage Whistler on Darlene and whatever Tawny Jane had told him across the pillow.

"You don't think they really believe Tatch did it, do you?" I said.

"Nah. I think they want him to give up the other guy. Meantime, some of the local yokels have been making noise about that Tex kid not playing in the big game. D'Alessio's got them all riled up, saying this is all Dingus's fault, he arrested the wrong guy. They're getting up a posse to go demonstrate at the Jesus camp."

"When?"

"This afternoon. People got signs in their windows: 'Free Tex.' Why's he called Tex anyway?"

"Long story. Does Tatch have a lawyer?"

"Had that Flapp guy for a few hours. Then Breck took over. He supposedly told the cops Mr. Edwards isn't going to say a word."

I heard Joanie stir, glanced up, saw her naked shoulders, white as winter.

"Can you do me a favor?" I said. "Check on my mom."

"Sure thing. By the way, your boss called."

"Philo?"

"He sounds barely old enough to drive."

Philo must have been calling about that board of directors meeting. I couldn't believe that that collection of wide-assed retirees collecting per diems for telling the CEO he's a genius would have the guts to switch the *Pilot* to online publication only. They would sit around their mahogany table the size of a rowboat and make their speeches about the future of newspapers until one of them motioned to table the subject until the next month's meeting so they could all retire to the Knife and Fork Club for filets and cigars.

"Hey," Joanie said. She was leaning over the edge of her loft, blanket bunched beneath her chin. "Who you talking to?"

I ignored her. "OK, thanks, I'll check in later." I ended the call.

"You want to shower?"

I looked at the phone, saw it was almost out of power, clicked it off. "No thanks," I said. "Could we get some eggs before our appointment?"

I was swallowing the last of my second fried-egg-and-cheese sandwich as Joanie swung her Malibu off Beech Daly onto Six Mile Road. I followed in Soupy's pickup.

I tossed the greasy sandwich wrapper on the garbage hiding the lockbox and grabbed the foam cup of black coffee from the console. I had checked to make sure the box was still there and kicked myself for having left it in the truck the night before in a neighborhood filled with curious late-night pedestrians. At least I'd thought to lock the truck, something I never did in Starvation.

We had sped down the Jeffries Freeway west through Detroit, an eight-lane gully winding between road shoulders pocked with snow and empty wine bottles, past pawnshops and liquor stores and boarded-up supermarkets and tar-papered houses, some of them charred black and literally falling down, where autoworkers had once laid claim to a good life that eventually slipped from their grasp. As a rookie *Times* reporter covering the cops, I had exited the freeway a few times to interview the bereaved families of shooting victims. But usually the Jeffries had ferried me to hockey rinks in the western suburbs.

Tunneling beneath the underpass at Telegraph Road, we'd crossed from the city into Redford Township, where those same autoworkers— the white ones, that is—had escaped in the 1950s seeking brick ranches and wider backyards. We'd left the Jeffries and turned north on Beech Daly. We passed a Lebanese bakery, a Little Caesars pizza joint, a vinyl-siding shop, a tool-and-die business hung with a For Lease sign, and what seemed like a dozen insurance agencies. I wondered why people in flat, quiet Redford would live in fear of fires and floods.

Six Mile is five gray lanes scarred with oily potholes and rock salt. I steered around a mattress discarded in the middle of the street. We passed a Catholic church and a used car lot and a Presbyterian church and another liquor store and a bar that advertised karaoke every Friday. The only human I saw was a teenage boy swaggering down the sidewalk in a hooded sweatshirt and headphones beneath a Yankees cap perched backward on his head. Only a Yankees fan, I thought, would be dumb enough to wear just a sweatshirt in that cold.

Joanie put on her right turn blinker and veered into a parking lot ringed by a low wooden fence. A curbside sign identified it as Lost Valley Golf Course. The only other car in the lot was a black Cadillac coupe parked in a handicap spot facing the first tee. I slid Soupy's pickup in next to Joanie's Malibu and peeked at the Caddy. I didn't see any handicap tag hanging from the rearview mirror.

Joanie came up to my door, notebook in hand. I stepped out.

"Ever do an interview at a golf course?" she said.

"Chased quotes once when the U.S. Open was at Oakland Hills."

Out on the course, old oaks as big as the ones up north stood guard along a flat brown fairway mottled with snow. A sign planted in front of the first tee announced in big black letters COURSE CLOSED. But there were gouges in the matted grass on the tee, and at the end of the fairway, a red flag fluttered in the breeze. I didn't like golf. If you played a lousy round, you could feel lousy for hours. If you had a bad day on the rink, it went away the second you cracked your first beer.

"Weird," Joanie said. "But the flack insisted. Said the priest would be more comfortable."

I started walking toward the pro shop. "Who's the priest again?"

"Reilly. He's apparently the visiting priest at that church back up Six Mile."

"And the flack?"

"A guy named Regis something."

I stopped. "No way."

Regis Repelmaus greeted me at the door to the Lost Valley pro shop with his usual too-firm, held-too-long, so-sincere-it's-bullshit hand-shake. He wore a dark suit, a starched white shirt, a red tie with pin-point silver polka dots, a Caribbean vacation tan, and a head of brown shoe-polish hair that could have been transplanted from a Ken doll.

"It's been too long, old friend," he said. He smelled of breath mints. "How are the north woods?"

"Like you, Regis," I said. "Cold and dark."

He chuckled. "Ah, well, maybe it hasn't been too long."

Repelmaus wasn't just any flack. He was Detroit's premier public-relations fixer, a lawyer who did not practice law but had glad-handed himself into a position where, whenever a big company or wealthy ex-ecutive got in trouble, he was called upon to prescribe a plan of action or inaction designed to "correct the record," as he was fond of saying, as if he were an historian rather than a $500-an-hour dissembler.

His clients were never companies or individuals themselves, but rather the law firms that represented them. By renting his services out in this way, Repelmaus could pretend he was not defending a company whose poorly built pickup trucks burned people to death or a natural gas executive who used the corporate jet to fly call girls to his Harbor Springs redoubt. No, Repelmaus was representing the law firms, who were, of course, merely defending the law.

I first encountered him one evening in Detroit. I'd just begun covering the auto industry for the *Times*, and I'd gotten a tip that police had picked up the CFO of Superior Motors for smacking his wife around. I started calling cop shops to confirm it. I hadn't made half a dozen calls before Repelmaus called me. He identified himself as a representative for a law firm representing Superior Motors.

"Call me Rep," he said, as cheerful as if I were writing about the company boosting its dividend.

"Rep?" I said.

"Yes, thank you. May I be of help?"

I had to ask the company anyway, so I told him what I'd heard.

"Off the record," he said, "this would certainly be a serious matter, if true, and I will get to the bottom of it and get back to you as soon as possible. When is your deadline?"

I told him I had until midnight and asked if he had heard from any *Free Press* reporters. "I have not," he said. "It looks like you have an exclusive."

My scoop evaporated two hours later. By then I had confirmed with anonymous police sources that the CFO had been arrested and that it wasn't the first time he'd had a boxing match with his wife. There was no Internet then, so my story wouldn't be out there until the papers hit the newsstands in the morning. But around ten thirty, Superior Motors issued a press release saying the CFO had resigned "to pursue other opportunities." It was all over the eleven o'clock news. My editor asked me what the hell happened. When I told her, she said she wished she had known I was dealing with Regis Repelmaus.

The next day, Repelmaus called me and congratulated me on getting the story first. Of course I hadn't gotten the story first. "You screwed me, Rep," I said.

"I totally understand how you could see it that way," he said. He explained that he had dutifully asked his "client" about the matter and the "client" had decided that "getting ahead of the matter" was in Superior Motors' best interest. And you agreed? I asked. Repelmaus told me that, because he also happened to be an attorney, he couldn't comment on that question, as it would violate attorney-client privilege.

From then on, I called him Regis.

I had to wonder why he would show up for a meeting with a priest at a public golf course in a scruffy suburb like Redford. "What are you doing here, Regis?" I said. "Something bad must be going on, eh?"

"The economy's tough," he said, smiling. "I'm taking whatever I can get." He turned to Joanie, extending a daintier hand than he'd given me. "Miss McCarthy."

"Joanie," she said. "Or Ms. McCarthy."

"Whoa, that's quite a handshake. Feel free to call me Rep."

Joanie ducked around him past the glass cases holding golf balls and hats and thirty-five-dollar shirts bearing the Lost Valley crest. "We doing this in there?" She pointed into the grillroom. "Oh," she said to someone I couldn't see. "Good morning, Father."

"Excuse me," Repelmaus said. He took Joanie by the arm to tug her back into the pro shop. "Could we talk about some ground rules first?"

Joanie yanked her arm away. "You didn't say anything yesterday about ground rules."

His smile did not falter.

"I totally understand how you could see it that way."

"We see it that way," Joanie said, "because that's the way it is."

That's why I loved Joanie McCarthy.

"Please, hear me out," Repelmaus said. "We think that once you hear what Father Tim has to say, you'll be considerate of his privacy, and that of the people he represents, so that we may correct the record without undue harm coming to anyone."

I brushed past him and went into the grill.

"Wait, Gus, please . . ."

I smelled frying onions. The room was dark with green carpeting, dark paneling on the walls, a low ceiling framed by dark wooden beams, and stilled ceiling fans, the only light leaking in through the windows and off some Christmas decorations strung along the wainscoting. Four stools upholstered in fake brown leather stood at a short bar stacked with red plastic burger baskets.

The priest hunched in a heavy wooden chair at one of the little round tables, gazing through a picture window at the first tee. White curls lapped the rim of his plaid flat cap. A coffee cup and a bottle of Jameson whiskey stood beside each other on a green vinyl tablecloth. His pale hands, riven with blue veins, gripped the blade of a pitching wedge propped between his knees. Bits of grass and mud were strewn on the carpet around his two-toned shoes.

"How'd you hit them?" I said.

He turned. I saw the Roman collar beneath his Lost Valley fleece. He smiled, his cheeks pink. He looked tired.

"Not as bad as yesterday," he said. "See, they let an old man come play the first hole a couple of times a day, and I say an extra prayer for them at morning Mass."

"Nice arrangement."

"Had a birdie on the first try and then, of course"—he looked heavenward—"a double bogey, to set the world back on an even keel."

I extended my hand. He took it. "Gus Carpenter, Father."

"Apologies, Father, he just barged right in." It was Regis, but the priest's eyes stayed on mine. "Yes, Mr. Carpenter," he said. "I'm Father Timothy. Please." He gestured for me to sit. I did, to his left. He looked up at Regis and Joanie, standing at my shoulder.

"You must be Ms. McCarthy," the priest said, offering his hand. "My mother was a McCarthy, and she was just as redheaded and lovely as you, if you don't mind my saying."

"Not at all," Joanie said. She sat down across from me and set her notebook and pen down in front of her.

Father Tim looked up at Repelmaus. "Well, Mr. Repelmaus," he said. "Are you going to join us?"

"Of course," he said, sitting. "I was hoping we could establish a few ground rules first."

"Give it up, Regis," Joanie said.

Regis started to say something, but Father Tim interrupted, speaking to me, "Are you a Catholic, son?"

I answered as politely as I could. "Can I ask why that matters?"

The priest leaned forward on his iron and smiled. "So you're a smart aleck, but you are not a Catholic, are you?"

"Not really, Father."

He chuckled, his wattle jiggling. "You'll have to do a good bit more than that, son. I understand your given name is actually Augustus. You remind me of another saint, Augustine. Are you familiar with him?"

"No."

"He was, I'm guessing now, a little older than you when he wrote a series of books—I suppose today they would be called memoirs—in which he renounced his sinful youth and embraced Christ."

"They'd probably be best sellers today."

"That they would. Ah, Lolly."

A woman in a gray sweatshirt stitched with the words LOUNGE STAFF appeared with a coffeepot. "Top you off, Father?" She poured without waiting for his reply.

"Anyone else like a cup?" the priest said.

All three of us demurred. Father Tim told the woman, "A three and a six today, Lolly. You'll mark them down?"

"Indeedy," she said. She lifted the Jameson and poured a splash into his cup before going back behind the bar.

The priest flipped the iron over and leaned the grip against the table. "I like to keep track of my scores," he said. He took a sip of his coffee, set the cup back down, and folded his hands on the table. "So, your mother," he said. "Beatrice Damico, yes?"

I was so startled that Joanie spoke before I could. "What's that got to do with anything?" she said.

"I met your mother, Augustus. Just briefly. A long time ago, before she was Carpenter. I was on a little vacation, a cabin at Burt Lake, and came down to visit St. Val's, met with a number of the classes. I recall that your mother had a devotion to the Blessed Mother."

"Did she?"

"When Mr. Regis told me your name was Carpenter and you had come from up north, I wondered if it could be Beatrice's son."

And I wondered how he would have known that Mom eventually became a Carpenter.

"So that's why you agreed to see me? To reminisce?"

"I wish," he said.

"You must have known Nilus then—Father Nilus, that is. And Sister Cordelia?"

"I'm sorry," Repelmaus said, "but Father Timothy, we really should go off the record."

I ignored him. "Are you representing the archdiocese, Father?" I said. "We asked to speak with somebody from the archdiocese. Excuse me if I think it's a little weird to be sitting at a golf course with a priest who's drinking before ten a.m., questions my religion, and then claims to know my mother."

I thought Joanie might flinch. She didn't. Neither did Father Timothy. Repelmaus said, "That's quite unnecessary, Gus."

I turned to him. "Who are you representing, Regis? Not the archdiocese, of course."

"My client is a Detroit law firm that represents the archdiocese."

"You mean Eagan, MacDonald and Browne?" I said.

"I have not been authorized to—"

"That will suffice, Regis," Father Timothy said. "Yes, Augustus, I speak for the archdiocese, and yes, Mr. Repelmaus is here on behalf of that firm."

"Then maybe you can tell me why the archdiocese is buying up land around Starvation Lake?"

I was taking a chance, jumping my question to a conclusion in the hope that they'd think I knew the answer anyway, so they might as well tell me. The priest shrugged. Repelmaus said, "The Detroit archdiocese hasn't had jurisdiction up north in decades."

"That doesn't mean they can't buy land," I said.

"Have you documented this?"

"I can document that your buddies at the law firm are buying land. But no way they'd be interested on their own. They must have a client who wants it, or wants control of it."

"Please tell me why you think that client would be the archdiocese," he said.

"Who's interviewing whom here?" Joanie said.

"Maybe the archdiocese is interested for the same reason Wayland Breck is."

I turned to the priest, who wore a purposeful smile.

"Ah, Mr. Breck," he said. "Our lost sheep. We had high hopes for him."

"He works for you," Joanie said.

"No," Repelmaus said, a little too quickly.

"Bullcrap," she said, pointing the notebook at him. "He digs up dirt on—"

"Please, please," Father Timothy said. "Can we all remain calm?"

Joanie sat back in her chair.

The priest said, "It is true that Mr. Breck assisted us with necessary research on litigation in which the archdiocese was involved. But that was some time ago. He is no longer in the employ of our counsel. Which is unfortunate, because Mr. Breck is afflicted with certain, shall we say, paranoid obsessions that we thought we were helping him with. Apparently we were mistaken."

"Obsessions with his grandfather?" I said. "And the murder of a nun?"

"Excuse me, Father," Repelmaus said. "Gus, you didn't hear this from me, but you might want to make a discreet inquiry about Mr. Breck with the state attorney discipline board."

"Noted," I said. "Father?"

The priest took up his club again, stood it on its handle. "I knew of Mr. Breck's grandfather. Joseph was a fine groundskeeper, a hardworking man who also played hard, as it was told to me. A man with good intentions. We know where those lead."

Repelmaus placed a hand flat on the table. "I'm sorry, Father," he said, "but we really must go off the record. If you say the wrong thing, Breck could sue for slander and—"

Father Timothy reached down and grasped the shaft of the golf club and raised the blade up and brought it down hard enough on the table that his cup spat up coffee and whiskey. Repelmaus pulled his hand away. Joanie sat back in her chair, wide-eyed. I kept my eyes on Father Timothy. His face had flushed red.

"I am quite capable, Mr. Regis, of determining what I can and cannot say," he said.

"Of course, Father, it's just—"

"Pipe down, man."

"I apologize, Father."

Father Timothy took the golf club from the table and dropped it on the floor with a thump. "I'm sorry for my lack of restraint," he said. He slipped a handkerchief from a pocket, wiped it across his mouth, dabbed at the spilled coffee and booze. "Forgive me, Lord."

He tucked the handkerchief away and turned to me. "You have done your homework, Augustus. But—some unsolicited advice?—you should worry less about Mr. Breck and more about your mother."

"Meaning what?"

The priest raised his shaggy eyebrows. "She hasn't told you about the poor Sister?"

"I know about Sister Cordelia, how she disappeared."

"But your mother, son."

"She told me she knew her, that she liked her," I said. "That's all."

He leaned forward, scrutinizing my face, searching for a hint of guilt in a tic, an exaggerated blink, an averted gaze. I imagined that I gave him nothing, but inside I felt as I did at the rare interview for which I hadn't had sufficient time to prepare, a reporter who not only didn't know the answers, but wasn't sure which questions to ask.

"That's all?" he said. "I see. All the better, I suppose."

"It would be better if you answered our questions," Joanie said.

He picked up his cup. It wobbled as he brought it to his lips, took a sip, set it back down. "I have answered what I can without violating confidences or the good Lord's trust in me. I will say, though, that for all of your enterprise, you may have stumbled onto a story that is not fit to print."

"Why? Because Nilus was a serial womanizer and you wouldn't want that exposed?"

The priest shook his head. "That's news that's almost older than me. I can't imagine anyone would care, but if it sells some more papers, have at it. The story I was talking about has more to do with you and your family, Augustus. I would assume your mother asked for God's forgiveness."

"For what?" I said.

Father Timothy picked up his wedge and stood, leaning on the club like a cane. "I'm afraid we have to wrap this up," Repelmaus said.

"Allow me to clear up one small item," the priest said. "Unlike most Irishmen, I am *done* drinking by eleven."

"Father," I said. "What did you say your last name was?"

"Reilly, son. Not like the life of, but Reilly: R-E-I-L-L-Y."

I wrote it down.

The priest nodded at Joanie, then offered his hand to me. "Thank you for your trouble," he said. "If you write your story, Augustus, please be kind enough to send us a copy."

TWENTY

Repelmaus walked Joanie and me to the parking lot.

"Well," he said, as the pro shop door swung shut behind us. "I thought that went well."

"For you or for us?" Joanie said.

"For all concerned, I hope," Repelmaus said. "I thought Father was candid. Maybe even a little too candid. Which reminds me, Gus." He reached into his pocket and pulled out a pink While You Were Out slip. "The archdiocese got a message this morning from Luke Whistler of the *Free Press*. Didn't want to return it until after we met. You know him?"

I tried not to look surprised. "Yep. He works for me."

"At?"

"The *Pine County Pilot*."

"Ah. Hadn't heard. I'm usually up to date on reporter comings and goings."

"He came up north after retiring, though you'd never know by how hard he works."

"As opposed to when he was at the *Freep*," Joanie said. "Come on, I've got to get downtown."

Joanie and I walked to Soupy's pickup as Repelmaus's Caddy pulled onto Six Mile.

"Well," Joanie said, "at least you got his name spelled, huh?"

"Don't be a smart-ass."

"It was like he interviewed you."

"I learned what I came to learn," I said.

"Like what?"

"Like, the archdiocese is buying up that land."

"He never confirmed that."

"Not so I could write it in the paper, but enough that I believe it. Also, he bullshitted us about Joe Wayland. That's why I asked about his name."

"What do you mean?"

"It dawned on me when he was drinking his coffee. His hand was shaking like a leaf, and I thought, man, he's old. And then I remembered there was a priest quoted in one of the old *Pilot* stories about the nun and Joe Wayland."

"That was him?"

"Pretty sure. I'll show you. In the truck."

"Hey." She stopped and faced me. "Can I ask you something?"

"Sure."

"Why didn't you come up last night?"

"Up?" I started walking toward the truck again. Joanie followed.

"To my bed," she said. "Am I too young for you?"

"Come on."

"Or are you intimidated because I work for a bigger paper? Your old paper?"

"No."

"For the record, I don't really care."

"Joanie, I didn't come—oh, what the fuck?"

The dome light was on in the truck. I ran over. As I got closer I saw that the driver's side door was ajar, and there was a jagged hole in the window. Someone had punched through the glass and unlocked the door. I pulled the door open, climbed across the front seat, and plowed through the garbage on the floor.

The lockbox was gone.

"Son of a bitch," I said. "My mother—" I stepped away from the truck and looked around the parking lot, up and down Six Mile. "Fuck."

"Someone broke in?"

"Yeah, and stole something. Something important. I'm an idiot. I shouldn't have left it."

"What was it?"

"A box. Something Mom gave me."

"How would anyone know it was there?"

"Nobody would. Except me. And Soupy." I looked back toward the clubhouse. "Maybe the good Father had the truck searched while we were in the clubhouse, and he got lucky."

"Too obvious," Joanie said. "But why would he care about your mother's whatever?"

"Your boyfriend didn't know, did he?"

"I told you I don't have boyfriends."

She blushed as she said it.

"Shit," I said. "Frenchy knew we were coming here, didn't he."

"He helped us, Gus. I'm sorry. Besides, I thought, you know, the small world of newspapers, he might know you from your time here."

"Oh, he knows me, all right."

"What do you mean?"

"Never mind. I'm such a jackass." I pointed at the clubhouse. "You don't think he's working for those guys, do you?"

"He works for a lot of people."

"Great."

"Should we call the cops?"

"No."

"I'm sorry."

"It's not your fault. I appreciate the help. Talking to the priest actually made things a little clearer. I've got to get back and make sure Mom's OK."

"Give her my best."

She stepped close and hugged me around the waist. The fragrance of her body wash was gone. She stepped back.

"I can't believe you're playing hockey," I said.

She smiled. "Maybe we'll get out there together sometime."

"Maybe."

"You know, Gus, you belong here."

I slid into the truck. "Sometimes I wish I did."

* * *

Brittle wind whistled through the hole in my window as I veered from Interstate 96 West onto U.S. 23 North. I didn't want to stop long enough to patch the hole, so I kept my hat and gloves on and turned the heat up as high as it would go.

I turned on my phone. A tiny red light was blinking, telling me the power was about to run out. I wondered if the blinking light itself was wasting power. I wanted to call Darlene but felt like I had to call my mother's attorney first.

Shipman was just heading into court. He told me he'd seen Mom in the morning and she was fine. The sheriff's department was keeping her in hot tea and magazines. He had advised her not to talk, and she had obeyed for the most part, except for a brief conversation she'd had in her cell with Darlene.

High beams flashed in my rearview mirror, somebody wanting to pass. I glanced at the speedometer. I'd been driving in the left lane at sixty miles per hour, about twenty-five too slow for the maniacs escaping Detroit on I-75.

I eased the truck into the right lane and asked what Mom had said. Mostly small talk, Shipman said, though she let on that she might have said something about, as he put it, "the new guy with Tatch and the other religious folks." You mean Breck, I said. Correct, he said, adding that he'd heard a rumor that Tatch also might have intimated something to the cops about Breck.

"Really?" I said. "Like what?"

Maybe, I thought, Tatch had had enough of his new "friend."

"Not sure, but Dingus seemed more jumpy than I've—"

That was the last I heard.

I looked at my phone. The red light had stopped blinking. A car horn beeped. I looked to my left. The man in the SUV next to me flipped me off before speeding ahead.

TWENTY-ONE

A blue Volvo station wagon was parked behind the *Pilot* when I pulled in. I didn't recognize it. You didn't see a lot of Volvos in Starvation Lake, or northern Michigan, for that matter. If you did, you'd be in Harbor Springs or Petoskey or Charlevoix.

A man was sitting at the desk mounded with old newspapers where the *Pilot*'s photographer had sat before Media North decided we didn't need a full-time shooter. He stood and offered his hand, and the first thing I noticed was that he was even shorter than me.

"Gus Carpenter?" he said. "Bennett Fuqua."

I shook his hand, thinking, The Media North bean counter, Fuckwad. Instinctively, I glanced over at the police scanner perched on a shelf behind Whistler's desk. Whistler had left the damn thing on again. I wondered if Fuqua had noticed.

"What brings you all the way over here?" I said. "Did the board authorize the mileage?"

He smiled uneasily. "Ah, ha, well, I was coming over anyway. United Way meeting in town, and I'm on the board. See, I specialize in nonprofits."

At first I didn't get that he meant the *Pilot*. "Funny," I said. As nonchalantly as I could, I walked over and turned the scanner off.

"Don't you need that?" Fuqua said.

"The cops'll call if there's anything important."

Fuqua considered that, then said, "How is your mother?"

"She's fine, thank you."

"Philo tells me you were quite close to the woman who died. My condolences."

"Thanks." I threw my coat on a stack of press releases atop a rusted Royal typewriter I hadn't gotten around to throwing away. "Excuse me a second." I plugged my cell phone into an outlet next to my desk. On my blotter I set a bottle of A&W and a brown bag holding a turkey-and-cheddar I'd picked up at the Twin Lakes Party Store. I sat and dumped the sandwich out, wishing I'd asked for an extra dill pickle.

Fuqua sat back down. A puddle of snowmelt glistened around his rubber-toed boots. In his creased black corduroy slacks and white turtleneck sweater, he could have posed for an L.L. Bean catalog. "I'm actually hoping to come back for the big game," he said.

"You're a hockey fan?" I said.

"Newly so." I was a little surprised at how young he seemed. I had pictured him as a bald man in his sixties with a bullfrog neck. But he couldn't have been much older than me, if at all. "My daughter started playing, and I got hooked."

"That's how it is."

"Growing up in Ohio, we didn't have much hockey around. But what a fast game. Pretty expensive, too. Of course my daughter had to play the most expensive position."

"She's a goalie?"

"That's right. I think I heard that you're a goalie, too, right? Someone said you played on the last great team around here. That must have been something."

I decided I wasn't going to let this guy soften me up. I'd imagined that Fuckwad was the kind of penny-pinching eyeshade who would piss on his grandmother's grave for a nickel, and I wasn't going to change my view because he helped the United Way and liked hockey. "It was something, all right," I said. "Mind if I eat?"

Fuqua knitted his fingers together in his corduroy lap. "You know how much we—actually, I—admire you and what you do."

"That and ten bucks will get me a fresh package of legal pads."

I took a big bite of my sandwich. Not bad. I wished Fuqua would wait outside until I finished. But he went on doing what he'd really come to do.

"As I think Philo told you, the Media North board of directors met yesterday. They deliberated for quite some time about the futures of a variety of our properties. They had to make some difficult decisions."

I went on chewing, looked up at the wall clock. D'Alessio's dog-and-pony show at Tatch's camp was supposedly going to start in a little more than an hour. "Hold that thought," I said.

"Gus, this is important."

I ignored him, took another bite, dialed my desk phone.

"Yo, Enright's," Soupy said. I heard the Guess Who in the background.

I swung my chair away from Fuqua. "Hey," I said.

"You got my truck?" Soupy said.

"Yeah. I'll pick you up in twenty."

"I'm working, man. Just leave it out front."

"Take a lunch."

"Trap, I'm up to my ass. Why?"

"It's a surprise. Bring some Blue Ribbons."

I didn't want a beer but figured it would hook Soupy.

"Oh, OK," he said. "I can't go long, but a six—that shouldn't take long, eh? But I'll have to kick Angie out. She drained half a bottle of Crow when I left her here yesterday."

"See you in a bit."

I hung up and turned back to Fuqua. "Sorry."

He was sitting straighter, his hands now flat on the chair arms. "The board had to make a particularly difficult decision regarding the *Pine County Pilot*."

OK, I thought. Whistler and I would have to wear gloves and hats in the office to stay warm. Copies would now be fifty cents a page, out of our pockets. At least that's what I hoped. Nothing worse.

"Let 'er rip," I said.

Fuqua told me as if he was telling me I had some mayo on my cheek.

"The last issue of the *Pilot* will be published this Friday," he said.

"Saturday."

"No. We're moving it up a day."

"Now? With all the stuff going on around here?"

"There's no good time to do this," Fuqua said.

An image of Darlene kneeling over her dead mother flashed in my brain. "There are some better than others," I said. "What about the hockey? What if the Rats win and go to the final? What if they win?"

When my Rats team had played in the state final against the Pipefitters in 1981, windows on every house and store and office in town were plastered with Rats team photos that had been printed across two full pages in the *Pilot*. I was front and center, sitting next to Tatch, our billowy leg pads touching. Even after we lost, people kept those pictures up for months until the tape dried out and peeled away. Then they folded them up and put them in the drawer where they'd saved front pages of the Tigers' 1968 World Series win and the day Kennedy got shot.

"There was some discussion of publishing into next week," Fuqua said. "Unfortunately, it's a business thing. Our printing contract expired at the end of February. They gave us a grace period, which is up Friday. If we go beyond that, we have to renew for six months."

"So the hell with Starvation, eh?"

Fuqua shifted in his chair. "After some discussion," he said, "the board calculated that the River Rats were unlikely to beat the Pied Pipers anyway."

"It's the Pipefitters. And what the hell do you and the board know about hockey?"

Fuqua pursed his lips. I swiveled away, afraid I'd say something even worse, and punched a key on my computer. I had an e-mail from Joanie. I called it up:

great seeing you.
call me about whistler

—j

I turned back to Fuqua. "Tell me," I said. "This difficult decision didn't have anything to do with a certain consultant charge, did it? Please tell me four hundred and fifty piss-ass little dollars didn't doom a paper that's been here since they named the place Starvation."

"Every factor was considered," Fuqua said. "Although I will say one or two board members expressed some concern that the charge you mentioned looked like it might be checkbook journalism."

"You have to be fucking kidding me."

"I realize you're upset," he said. "Which is why I let the language go the first time. Now I'd appreciate a more professional demeanor."

"My reporter used a consultant to help him get some information. It probably wasn't penny smart, but he wasn't whoring us out either. He even offered to pay himself."

"It wouldn't change our contractual situation."

"I see," I said. "Then I guess we'll just do our best online. If the Rats win it all, people can still print out the page and put it up. As for the other stuff, I guess maybe you're right."

"No, Gus."

"You just said—"

"No. No online. No anything. The *Pilot* is shutting down. It's over. We're closing the paper as of Friday."

My stomach turned over. Icy needles of sweat pricked the back of my shoulders. "Hold on," I said. "This can't— Philo told me nobody wants to close the paper. He said the board was considering how to rationalize print and online."

"That's what the board did," Fuqua said. He stood. "Philo said you yourself thought it would be a mistake to go online only. Something about antilock brakes."

"That's not what I meant."

"It doesn't matter. The money's not there."

I looked around the room and felt a sudden fondness for the clunky metal desks, the claptrap copier, the bubbling linoleum, the yellowing Pine County map peeling back from the wall, even the buzzing lamps. Fuck the board, I thought. Fuck every one of those fat-asses and the five thousand bucks they got for attending a two-hour meeting where they put a gun to the head of the only newspaper in Pine County. Fuck them and their fat-assed fucking wives and children. I hoped their fucking dogs died.

But I didn't say it. Instead I sat there feeling a little like I'd felt all those years ago when I let in the goal that gave the Pipefitters the state championship. Now the *Pilot* would die on my watch as executive editor. I would be left to wonder again, as I had for years after that goal, whether I could have done something differently to make things right.

Fuqua explained that the board had deemed that the *Pilot's* closing would be announced in its final edition, and nothing would be said about it before. I nodded without agreeing. He said a human resources person would call to go over our "separation options." By then I was too stunned to speak. I sat silent until Fuqua finished and asked me if I was all right. "I guess I'll have to be," I said, and he asked me if I would speak with Luke Whistler and I said I would. Then he told me he was sorry, he had to get to his United Way meeting, and I heard the back door close as he went out to his Volvo. I was facing my final deadline.

I dropped the rest of the sandwich in the trash. I threw my coat on and hurried out to Soupy's truck and pulled it onto South Street and took two lefts to Main and pulled up in front of Enright's, honking.

I forgot about calling Joanie.

"Jesus, Trap, it reeks in here," Soupy said. "What the hell did we come here for?"

"Sentimental," I said. "Want to get a last look before you sell it."

I hadn't been in Soupy's mother's house since an Easter dinner she had hosted when I was still living in Detroit. She made a leg of lamb with buttermilk mashed potatoes. That was the good part. The rest was Soupy's dad getting plastered and lighting into Mrs. Campbell for spending too much on the dinner. His marina wasn't doing well but, like his son, Angus Campbell was not a man inclined to find fault with himself. Soupy, his belly full of Blue Ribbons, had stepped in and soon the two of them were outside, threatening to kill each other while Mrs. Campbell and my mother yelled at them to grow up. Soupy threw one punch. Angus collapsed, unconscious, facedown in one of his own grimy boot prints in the snow. By the time we had carried him back inside,

Mrs. Campbell and Mom had taken my mother's car and gone. The first thing Angus Campbell said when he woke up was, "Goddamn broads."

Now Soupy and I stood in the little dining room where we had sat down to that meal. The table had vanished beneath mounds of moldy magazines and decaying *Pilots*, kitchen appliances, a rusting empty birdcage, an old Electrolux vacuum cleaner in a duct-taped cardboard box. The floors were covered. There were boxes and brown-paper bags and milk crates and plastic bags, all filled to the top with lamps and books and vases and coffee mugs. There were rolls and rolls of wrapping paper, mud-caked flowerpots filled with spoons and forks, a soiled cat-litter box, at least a dozen half-eaten apples, shriveled and brown. I nudged a box with the toe of a boot and heard glass clink against glass.

"What a mess," I said.

"Told you," Soupy said. He plucked a can of beer off the six-pack he was carrying and handed it to me. "No wonder it hasn't sold—yet." I didn't bother to suggest that Soupy clean the place up before showing it; the archdiocese probably wouldn't care. I put the beer to my mouth and drew in the smell to mask the pervasive odor of cat litter mixed with sodden paper.

Soupy's parents had separated in their final years. Mrs. Campbell stayed in the house in the woods, and Mr. Campbell usually slept on a cot at the marina when he wasn't ushering a woman into a room at the Hill-Top Motel. One night, Angus had come to the house, lit, looking for a mounted set of deer antlers to settle a bar bet. Mrs. Campbell took the antlers and locked herself in a bathroom. The police had to be called. Mrs. Campbell had the locks changed. She accelerated her hoarding of things. Every single thing, apparently. The antlers were now propped atop a stained lampshade.

Scattered amid the junk heaped on the dining room table were piles of photographs, dozens of them in color and black and white, framed and not. I picked up one of Angus standing at the end of a dock dangling a stringer of bluegills. I tossed it aside. I grabbed a handful of Polaroids leaning against the birdcage and fanned through them: Soupy and me in our Rats uniforms; a Thanksgiving dinner laid out on my mother's dining table; Soupy's old basset hound, Stanley, draped uncomfortably in a Red Wings jersey.

I showed the picture of Stanley to Soupy.

"That was one crazy-ass dog," Soupy said.

"Umbrellas, right?"

"Drove him mad. And motorcycles. He'd be quiet as a mouse, then he'd see somebody with an umbrella and go apeshit barking. Same with guys on motorcycles. Thank God he never saw a guy on a motorcycle with an umbrella."

I picked up more photos. There was my mother and Mrs. Campbell beaming in bathing suits and Ray-Bans on my grandfather's Chris-Craft. Mrs. Campbell cradling Soupy, a baby, in front of a Christmas tree. Another of Mrs. B and Mrs. Campbell curtsying together in bridesmaids' dresses, possibly at Mom's wedding. Seven little girls arm in arm wearing identical plaid jumpers over white blouses. It looked like the spelling-bee photo I had seen in the microfilm at the clerk's office, but without Sister Cordelia or the young Judge Gallagher.

I set those down and picked up a stack held together by paper clips. They looked more recent than the others. There were no people in them, just trees full of leaves and the forest floor covered with pine needles and cones sloping down and away, the same scene taken from different angles, probably at dusk, judging by how the shadows fell along the ground. I looked at Soupy. "Has anyone actually come to look at the place?"

"Nope."

"Doesn't that strike you as a little unusual?"

"Not if they're just going to rebuild anyway. They probably just want the land."

"Are there mineral rights?"

"Yeah, but no minerals worth anything. Why do you give a shit?"

"What if I want to buy it?"

Soupy watched me over the top of his beer can as he took a long pull. He belched and said, "Right. Or maybe the kids who broke in want to buy it."

"Somebody broke in here?"

"Didn't you notice the door almost fell off when we came in? Fucking kids about tore it off the hinges."

"When was this? Did you call the cops?"

"Couple of weeks ago. Came out here to make sure the pipes hadn't frozen and found the door all messed up and a bunch of boot prints."

"What'd they take?"

"Look around, Trap. How the hell would I know?"

Soupy was a month older than me, but sometimes he felt like a little brother.

"You didn't report it?"

"Report what? I didn't want to be one of those Bingo Burglaries or whatever you call them. No need to have my name in the paper."

I picked up the photo of the girls again. I counted seven. There had been five reported break-ins, six if you counted the one at Soupy's parents' place. Each had been at the grown-up home of one of the girls in the photo—except Phyllis née Snyder Bontrager. While it was unlikely that a burglar would have seen this particular photo, he might have seen the one I'd seen, with Sister Cordelia, too, in a newspaper clipping.

I grabbed another stack of photos leaning against the birdcage. There were probably twenty-five in all. My mother was in every one. Some included Mrs. Campbell or Mrs. B, a few Audrey from the diner. I put the stack down and picked up a framed collage of three photos hinged together. The photos were of Mom; Mom with Mrs. Campbell; and Mom, Mrs. Campbell, and Mrs. B in Mom's driveway, like the one I had seen at Mrs. B's counter at the *Pilot*. I turned the frame sideways, turned it back the other way, turned it sideways again. The Three Stooges, I thought. And then I thought something else.

I took the triple-frame of photos in both hands and twisted one of the three pieces against its hinges. When the hinges bent but didn't break, I braced the frame against the table's edge and broke it off with a crack. My right hand slipped and caught a sharp corner and I saw a trickle of blood along a fingernail.

"Ouch," I said.

"What are you doing?" Soupy said.

I put my finger in my mouth and sucked the blood away. I tossed the still connected frames on the table and held the one I'd broken off in front of Soupy's face. It was a picture of our mothers standing in front of Audrey's.

"It's a map," I said. "Your mom had a piece of it."

"Have another beer, Trap. It's a picture."

"I'm not talking about this."

I threw the photo aside and told Soupy about the lockbox, what was in it, the piece of paper I thought was a map, how it had gotten stolen, how it all had something to do with the murder of Sister Mary Cordelia.

"Fucking-ay," he said. "Are you sure?"

"Hell, no. But . . . that's got to be it. Mom tore the thing into three and gave the other pieces to her best friends."

"Which would be Mrs. B and my mom," Soupy said.

"Right."

"But for what? They rob a bank or something? You think that's what born-agains are digging for down the hill?"

"Something like that," I said. I rummaged through the junk on the table and found the photos of trees and leaves. I showed one to Soupy. "That look familiar?"

He squinted. "Looks like anything around here. Trees, dirt, pine needles."

"Could be right outside, huh? Looking down the ridge to where Tatch's people are?"

"Could be just about anywhere north of Grayling."

I recalled how the wiggly lines in Mom's drawing seemed to suggest a hill, the noted locations of trees. "Who took these pictures?"

"No idea, but, listen, that nun?"

"Yeah?"

Soupy walked slowly into the living room, his back to me. His empty can pinged on a heap of coat hangers. He yanked another beer off the ring, opened it, took a long pull.

"Ma got a call about some nun," he said. "Sometime after Angus died."

"Are you serious?"

He wrapped his arms around himself so that the beer can appeared beneath his left arm. "Man," he said. "I really haven't thought about Ma in a while."

I wanted to say, What about the nun, but I just said, "Yeah?"

"She was the one, you know, who got up at like five in the morning to haul my ass to practice. Angus was usually sleeping it off, if he was even home. I'd give her all sorts of hell about getting out of bed, and sometimes she'd have to just throw me out on the floor." He tried a chuckle, but it got stuck in his throat. "Then she'd have coffee made, and those cinnamon buns from the diner."

"I remember."

"She liked when your mom came along."

Mrs. Campbell and my mother had taken turns driving the two of us to our early morning practices. Sometimes both went.

"When she got sick—" he said. He stopped, then started again. "When she got sick, she started thinking over things, stuff she'd forgotten about, stuff that'd been bugging her forever, stuff she'd never had time to screw around with. You know."

"What about the nun?"

Soupy threw his head back and took another deep swallow. Then he said, "This woman called one night. I was over here helping Ma out with, I don't know, I think I was putting the storm windows in for winter. Anyway, she was frying up some perch I'd caught that day and the phone rang. And I was messing with a window and she got on the phone and next thing I know I smell this burning. All that sweet perch going to waste. I rush in and the pan's spitting grease and we're about to have a damn fire, but Ma's on the phone, talking real soft, like it's some big secret, and I go over and say, 'Ma, you're going to burn the house down,' and she takes me"—he grabbed himself by the collar of his shirt—"and shoves me away."

"Doesn't sound like Louise."

"Nope." He turned to face me. "Though she should have done it to Angus about a million times. Anyway, I go over and turn the stove off and dump the fish in the sink and go outside. But I slip down the wall out there"—he pointed outside—"and listen through the screen I haven't replaced yet, to see what the hell's got her so focused."

"And it was the nun."

"I think so. She kept saying something about a sister. But Ma didn't have any sisters."

"Did you hear the name 'Cordelia'?"

"That's the nun who got killed?"

"Yeah."

"I wish— I honestly don't remember. But I asked Ma after she'd calmed down. She said some woman was writing a history of St. Val's, and she might actually pay for some information, and I thought, great, because the marina was sucking wind, and I think that was about the time we had to get one of the lifts fixed, cost a shitload."

"You're sure it was a woman?"

"Pretty sure. After thirty-eight years with Angus, Ma didn't trust men much."

"Did she ever help the woman? Or get paid?"

"I don't think so. Then, it wasn't long before she passed away."

I sidled closer to Soupy, careful to avoid a cracked glass bowl filled with Mary Jane candy wrappers. "Why would you even remember this anyway?"

Soupy shook his head. "The smell, man. You ever smell perch burning? I still can't eat them. Love to catch them. Can't eat them."

I sat back against the table. "And that would've been about the time our moms stopped talking to each other, wouldn't it?"

"Goddamn broads, huh?" Soupy sat down on a pile of blankets on the sofa, the other beers dangling between his legs. "I can't tell you, man, how sick she was about all of that. It killed her that your mom never came to see her in the hospital."

"I'll bet it killed my mom, too."

"What was that all about anyway?"

By now it was clear to me that both Soupy's mother and Mrs. B knew things that were important to my mother. It appeared that Mrs.

Campbell had told or at least considered telling someone whatever it was she knew. Maybe what she knew about a map. Somebody had broken into this dump looking for something. I doubted it was kids.

"I don't know, Soup," I said. "I asked you once, you told me it was chick weirdness."

"You don't think it has something to do with this?"

"With what?"

"With what happened to Darlene's mom."

"Maybe," I said. "Maybe not."

I drained my beer, tossed the can on the table. "Let's go for a walk."

"Trap, I've got to get back."

"Come on." I reached with the hand with the bloody fingernail. "Don't be hoarding those beers."

TWENTY-TWO

We climbed the hill rising from the garage behind Soupy's mother's house. As a boy, Soupy had flooded a flat patch of ground behind the garage and used it to practice his stickhandling moves on moonlit nights. Sometimes his father would come out late, bottle in hand, and exhort his son to try this feint or that dangle, and Soupy would scoop up his pucks and say he was tired, he was going to bed.

Our boots crunched through the snow, Soupy bitching about the cold, nagging me about where we were going, me ignoring him, scanning the trees for a familiar pattern, something that resembled what I had seen in that peculiar set of photos on Mrs. Campbell's table, of trees and forest floor in fading light. The light now, as afternoon began to yield to evening, was the color of old snow. Thirty yards ahead of us, a thin streak of yellow glowed along the top of the ridge. As we climbed, I started hearing something from the other side of the hill, the sound of voices calling out in unison, as yet unintelligible.

"Jesus freaks," Soupy said.

"Hockey freaks," I said.

We kept climbing. The voices grew louder. As we crested the ridge, I heard behind me the snap and gurgle of a beer being opened, and then, as Soupy came up next to me, "What the hell, man?"

We stood between oaks, facing the long slope down to Tatch's camp. Lightbulbs in orange plastic cages dangled from nails driven into tree trunks. Extension cords snaked through the trees to the circle of trailers. Halfway down the hill, an idle backhoe crouched, its toothy scoop poised in midair like a dinosaur's jaw hovering over its prey. The ground surrounding it for fifty yards in every direction was torn into winding gullies and potholes blotting the snowy surface. The wooden handles of shovels and pickaxes jutted from mounds of snow and dirt amid the black hollows.

"I knew they were digging here," Soupy said, "but I didn't know it was this serious. What are they looking for?"

"Not gold," I said. "And not a septic field."

The voices below were rising. I saw the townspeople walking up the two-track from the beach road, their flashlights bouncing like fireflies in the gathering dusk. They carried signs and a banner, a shambling bunch of twenty or thirty people in parkas and hats and mufflers obscuring their faces in wool. D'Alessio led them, wielding a bullhorn in one hand and a hockey stick in the other.

"Septic field?" Soupy said.

"It's a dodge Breck's been using to get Tatch's born-again friends to chew up the ground looking for something else. Something he wants. Something your mother may have helped him with, intentionally or not."

"I hope not."

"Look."

I pointed up into the trees where the handmade crosses hung.

"Oh, man," Soupy said. "Creep me out."

We trudged toward the camp, stepping between potholes and ditches and the crisscross shadows on the snow. The chant of the mob from town became clearer: "We want Tex. We want Tex. We want Tex . . ."

The clearing between the trailers was a slop of mud. Women stood at the doors of each of the trailers, shovels held across their bodies like rifles. I knew two of them—Jody Frost and Lisa Royall—and wasn't surprised at all that they would go along with this drama, having seen them at play in their own personal theater on more than a few occasions at Enright's.

"Are we the fucking Hardy Boys?" Soupy said. "Jody Frost with a shovel? I'd sooner take on a flatbed full of Dobermans. Don't you think the Rats could get by without Tex? It's not like the Pipefitters are going to be scared of him."

"It's not about Tex," I whispered. "It's about Darlene's mom, and yours, and mine. And a bunch of other stuff I haven't figured out yet."

We stopped at the perimeter of the camp, peering into the clearing through an eight-foot gap between two trailers. I pulled Soupy behind one of the trailers so we could watch without being seen. At the center of the clearing stood Breck, hatless, blank-faced, his bare hands clasped behind his back.

The throng assembled on the far edge of the clearing. I saw the Fleder brothers, Floyd Kepsel, Shirley McBride, Clayton Perlmutter, others I'd seen around town but didn't know that well, people who had nothing better to do than shake their fists at the world. Handmade signs bobbed over their heads: Free Tex. He's a Boy, Not a Pawn. Where's Your Christianity Anyways? Two high school girls held opposite ends of a bedsheet banner painted with Free Tex Go Rats. Frank D'Alessio, clad in an unzipped deputy's parka, stepped out in front of them all.

Breck held up one hand. "Please stop there," he said. "This is private property. Please respect our privacy."

The crowd grumbled back, "Let the boy go." I noticed an unruly head of white hair moving behind them. Luke Whistler ambled along in his down vest, holding aloft what looked like a cassette recorder. His eyes weren't on the mob but on the hill behind me.

"We're calling your bluff, Breck," D'Alessio said. "Just let Tex go. We'll leave you alone. We might even put in a good word for you on your property taxes. We all know somebody on the appeals board."

"You can forbear, Mr. Candidate," Breck said. "Matthew is not here."

"Where's Dingus?" Soupy whispered.

"Good question," I said. "Maybe he's afraid to follow D'Alessio's lead."

D'Alessio stepped toward Breck. "If you've taken Tex somewhere against his will—"

"It's you who are trying to take from us against our will," Breck said. "We have sought recourse and been denied our rights to due process."

"What about due process for Phyllis Bontrager, sir?" someone yelled, then somebody else, "You ought to be the one in jail, Breck. Where were you Sunday night?"

Breck was unmoved "We are law-abiding citizens," he said. "We ask to be left alone. You violate our land in your vanity. You seek to empty our pockets in your greed. You imprison one of us in your vengefulness.

You are sinners. Your fathers were sinners, and their fathers before them." I thought of his grandfather, the sharpened spoon tearing into his neck, the blood washing into the water swirling pink in the shower drain.

D'Alessio took another step forward and pointed up the hill. "Looks like you're the ones violating the land," he said. "Still looking for that septic field?"

I saw Whistler sliding away from the crowd and ducking behind one of the trailers at the opposite end of the clearing.

"That's far enough, Frank."

Jody Frost stepped away from her trailer and raised her shovel like an ax. She and Frankie had had a tumultuous dalliance some years back, with rumors of sex in his sheriff's cruiser involving, of course, his handcuffs and baton. After Jody broke up with him, he kept pulling her over for minor traffic infractions and telling her she'd better take him back or she might wind up in jail. The last time he stopped her, she grabbed him by the collar and pulled him into the car and kissed him, thrusting her tongue hard into his mouth while rolling the window up on his neck, trapping him, and locking the door. Then she turned the radio up full blast, climbed out the passenger side, and walked home while D'Alessio screamed over the music. Nearly two hours passed before a state trooper happened upon poor Frankie, still screaming, his face smeared with lipstick. The trooper laughed so hard that it took him a few minutes to free Frankie, who never bothered Jody Frost again.

Now D'Alessio gave her an uneasy grin. "Hello there, darling," he said.

"Jody," Breck said. "This man is no threat to anyone but himself."

"Really?" D'Alessio said. "Who the hell are you anyway?"

Breck addressed the townspeople. "This is what matters to you?" I leaned into the gap between the trailers, looking for Whistler; I'd lost him. "A hockey game? You've lost one of your own, another two are in jail, and this is what matters? Perhaps even God cannot help you."

The crowd started yelling again and moving toward Breck. "Get back, goddammit," Jody yelled, stepping toward them, the blade of the shovel next to her head. "You're scaring our kids."

Breck turned to her. "Stay where you are, please, Ms. Frost."

"Thank you, Mr. Breck," D'Alessio said. "She's a spunky one."

Jody glared first at D'Alessio, then at Breck, threw her shovel to the ground, and stomped back inside her trailer, slamming the door.

"Look," D'Alessio said. "We're trying to meet you halfway here." The mob hear-heared. "Let Tex go and we'll put some pressure on Dingus to let Tatch go. Hell, nobody thinks he did anything anyway."

Breck took his wire-rims off, wiped them on his sweater, put them back on. "You are a fool, Mr. Candidate," he said. "Surrounded by fools. Matthew and the rest of us want nothing to do with you or your pathetic schemes."

Soupy poked me in the shoulder. "Trap."

"Shut up," I said.

"Look, idiot."

I turned and saw Whistler scrabbling up the hill behind us. He fell to one hand, then an elbow as his sneakers slipped in the snow and mud. He stopped at the backhoe and wrote something in his notebook. Then he disappeared behind it. I turned back to Breck.

"You are on private property," Breck told the throng. "I am asking you to remove yourselves now."

"Or you're gonna do what, mister?" someone shouted.

"How about we remove you, huh?" someone else cried.

The door on Jody's trailer swung open and she came bounding out, wearing a camouflage jacket, hair pulled away from her face in a rubber-band ponytail. Instead of a shovel, she was holding a double-barreled shotgun. She stopped halfway across the clearing and raised it to her shoulder, aimed in the direction of the throng. They gasped as one. "Call the police," someone shouted, and I saw cell phones come out, people punching keys.

"No," Breck said, turning to Jody. "We are not them, Jody. Please. Put the gun away."

"We've been pushed around enough," she said.

"Listen to him, Jody," D'Alessio said. "You're just going to get yourself in trouble."

She leveled the barrel at D'Alessio. "Back off, fuckface."

D'Alessio looked at Breck. "'Fuckface,' eh? That some new born-again—"

The boom of the shotgun cut him off and sent the crowd shrieking and diving into the snow, jumping behind trailers, racing down the two-track and off into the woods. D'Alessio keeled over backward into the mud. I clutched at the trailer next to me for balance and stepped into the clearing. Jody had lifted the barrel so that her shot flew into the sky. But D'Alessio remained on his back, apparently unconscious, perhaps fainted. I froze, watching to see if Jody, smirking at the fallen D'Alessio, would shoot again.

Only Breck saw Tex.

The boy burst from the trailer door behind another woman, almost knocking her down. "Dammit!" she screamed, while Breck swiveled and crouched for a tackle. Tex was barefoot in long johns and a T-shirt. "Tex," I yelled as Soupy pushed out from behind me and moved into the clearing.

Tex started first toward the scattering townspeople, but Breck scrambled over to cut him off, so Tex swerved and almost slipped down but held his feet and sprinted at Soupy and me, his eyes not seeing us, his feet churning snow, Breck gaining on him. I heard women and men bellowing from the other side of the clearing, some of the voices coming closer, Tex yelling as he ran, "Get away from me!"

Breck was close enough to try a flying tackle when Soupy jumped in front of him and threw a hip check that would have made a Red Wing proud. Breck flopped sideways with a grunt. He was back on his feet in an instant and, before Soupy could get his hands up, smacked Soupy hard in the shoulder with the heel of a hand. Soupy toppled over and I stepped up and took a run at Breck, but he jumped aside and I spilled face-first into the snow. Breck started up the hill as I got to my feet. "Don't do it, Matthew," he called out. "You are not their servant."

Jody Frost was shouting, "I'll shoot, dammit, I'll shoot again," as the Fleders and Clayton Perlmutter ran past her in pursuit of Breck. "Get that man," Perlmutter wheezed, a few steps behind the Fleders as they gained on Breck. The shotgun went off again. There was more screaming. Everyone but Tex and Breck flung themselves facedown in the snow. "Goddammit, Jody," Bart Fleder yelled. "You got some balls."

We all jumped up and started scrambling again up the slippery ridge, but Breck had nearly caught the barefoot, half-naked boy who wanted to play a game of hockey. Tex weaved left and then right and then left again, dodging the ditches, slipping Breck's grasp. "Stop now, Matthew," Breck kept calling, but Tex kept plowing up the hill through the twilight. About twenty yards beyond him I spied Luke Whistler, peering out from between a pair of birches on one side of the gullies, scribbling in his notebook.

"Luke," I yelled. "Help!"

Either he didn't hear or he didn't think he should intervene, because he kept looking around where he was standing and writing in his notebook, as a reporter probably should have. "Whistler!" I screamed again, and now he shuffled out from the trees, sliding sideways in his sneakers as he stuffed his notebook in his vest. His gaze was fixed on Breck.

"The boy," I yelled.

"Stop that prick," Soupy said.

"Grab him," Perlmutter called out.

"The boy."

Breck was almost in reach when Tex veered right to skirt a ditch and lost his footing. He slid legs first into the trench, grabbing in vain at the snow rimming the edge. There was a hard whump and then the cry of a boy in sudden, anguished pain. I saw his hair tossing back and forth above the lip of the ditch and then I came up to the edge of the hole alongside Breck and Soupy and saw Tex bellowing and holding his left leg with both hands, writhing in the blackened snow. The Fleders came up next and then Perlmutter, who took one look at Tex and lost his lunch. I noticed cop lights flashing on the tree trunks around us.

"I'll be goddamned," Whistler said.

An ambulance took Tex away.

Sheriff Dingus Aho cuffed Breck and read him his rights.

"Am I being charged?" Breck said.

"We'll get to that in due course," Dingus said.

Darlene stood to the side, staring at Breck. As Skip Catledge opened a cruiser back door, Breck screwed his head around to look back up the hill. Dingus clapped a hand on the back of his neck.

"You don't know what you're doing," Breck said.

"Shut the hell up," Dingus said, shoving Breck into the car.

I looked where Breck had looked and saw Whistler still poking around on the hill.

"I'm out of here," Soupy said. He went skittering along the edge of the clearing, around the back of the trailers, sidestepping the ditches as he climbed. He stopped briefly to pick up the last beer he'd dropped when he hip-checked Breck.

Two paddy wagons rolled up. Catledge and Darlene went to each of the trailers. The doors creaked open, the residents straggled out. There were about twenty in all, men and women, a few children. I'd seen them at the IGA, counting out pennies for their purchases; standing in line at the once-a-week food pantry maintained by the senior center; at Enright's, begging Soupy to extend them a little more credit for half a shell of beer to wash down the twenty-five-cent pickled egg they'd fished out of the jar on the bar. I had seen their faces but I hadn't seen them, knew their names but didn't know them. Soupy liked to say they were people with no lives. But here, I thought, on a lonely hill above the lake, they have a life, or at least they believe they do.

The police put the children in a trailer with Lisa Royall and told her to keep them inside while the other adults from the camp were taken for questioning. Catledge herded Jody Frost and the others into the paddy wagons while Jody tried to twist free, yelling, "Why aren't you arresting D'Alessio and those other assholes?" Lisa watched from her trailer door, trying not to cry, and I saw children's faces peeking through tattered drapes on a window next to her. "None of this would have happened," Lisa shouted, "if you all would just leave us alone."

D'Alessio, who'd been resuscitated by a paramedic, watched the arrests, then started down the hill on his own. Dingus ordered Darlene to bring him back and put him in a cruiser. "Are you sure, Sheriff?" she said. "Don't we have enough—"

"That's an order, Deputy," he said.

Darlene chased him down. As she cuffed him, he shouted at Dingus, "What the hell in the world can you charge me with, Sheriff?" Dingus glanced over his shoulder, said, "Trespassing," and then turned to me. "Get your boy," he said, pointing at Whistler, "and get out of here, before I arrest you, too."

Whistler drove us to town. The car reeked of garlic, its backseat piled with old Roselli's Pizza boxes. In a Toronado, that's a lot of boxes.

"You find anything on that hill?" I said.

"A lot of dirt under the snow," he said.

"You think this is it?" I said. "Is Breck the Bingo Night guy?"

"He's got motive, right? Avenge his grandfather?"

"Seems like," I said. "But you think he'd actually kill someone?"

"Maybe it was an accident."

"It's a dead body either way, remember?"

"Do the cops have any hard evidence? Anything that could really put anyone away?"

I recalled what Shipman had said about Tatch and Mom possibly saying something about Breck. "Tatch may have given him up," I said.

"You know what sucks?" Whistler said. "We don't have a paper until Saturday."

"It's worse than that," I said.

I told him about the *Pilot*'s fate. It wasn't clear what would happen to the two of us, I said, but I assumed we would either be laid off or farmed out to some other Media North property, maybe even Channel Eight.

"So it's Friday and that's it?" Whistler said.

"Look at the bright side," I said. "More time with Tawny Jane."

Whistler scowled. "I should have stayed at the damn *Free Press*."

We remained silent as he turned onto Main. He pulled to the curb in front of the *Pilot*, cutting across the angled parking spaces as if he didn't plan to stay. "You mind filing something about that circus to the Web? I'll drop by the cop shop."

"OK," I said. "You want to hear about my trip downstate? Pretty interesting stuff."

"Later, for sure," he said. He looked at his watch.

"Maybe meet for a beer." I pushed my door open. Snow had begun to fall. "Let's go out with a bang, eh?"

"Yep." He didn't sound like his heart was in it, though. Luke Whistler's survival, I thought, depended on having a newspaper to write for. "So they cleared that whole hill?"

"There's just the Royall woman and some kids left."

"OK. Call you later."

I wrote my story, locked up, and walked to my house through sheets of snow. A plow trundled past me on Main, blade clanking, yellow lights blinking in the whiteness. A bit late, I thought, but that's how it went in a county short of cash.

My pickup truck was covered in white. I opened the driver's door and stepped back so the snow on the roof didn't cascade onto my head. I reached in and started the engine to defrost the windshield and grabbed a long-handled brush and used it to scrape the outside of the truck clean. The snow brushed across my bare knuckles but I didn't feel it much because I'd been back in Starvation Lake long enough that I was accustomed to the cold.

My phone rang. I climbed inside the truck and turned up the fan and felt the heat blow around me. Coach Poppy was calling. He was at the hospital in Traverse.

"Tex has a high-ankle sprain," he said. "He's lucky he didn't break something."

"That's terrible."

"What the hell's the matter with this place?"

"I'm actually trying to find out."

"I know it's hardly the priority right now, and I hate to say it, but we don't stand a chance against the 'Fitters without Tex."

"Unless Dougie plays out of his mind."

"We'll show up," Poppy said. "The town needs something."

"Be thankful the Rats got this far. At least nobody's going to be blaming somebody for the rest of their lives. Tell Tex to hang in there."

I looked at empty Main Street, recalling the cars and trucks parading to the rink for the Mic-Mac game two nights before. Blaring horns and jam-packed bleachers would make no difference against the Pipefitters. Not without our star winger.

I turned the truck off. It had to be too hectic at the jail to see Mom yet. I thought I'd make myself some supper, take a quick nap, then go down. After that, I'd get with Whistler and make a plan for publishing the last issue of the *Pilot*.

"Gus."

The voice came from outside my window. Skip Catledge was playing a flashlight beam just below my face. I rolled the window down.

"Are you deaf?" he said. "Almost broke your window."

"Thinking."

"Follow me, please."

"Follow you where?"

The lights on the cruiser parked behind me began to flicker on my rear window. "Just do it," Catledge called out.

TWENTY-THREE

S
ilhouettes of reporters and cameramen and townspeople slid back
and forth against the fluorescent glow of the glass-walled lobby of
the Pine County Sheriff's Department. "Mob scene," I said to myself.

Catledge steered past the main entrance and headed toward the rear
lot where the cops parked. As I followed, I saw Tawny Jane standing
next to the Channel Eight van, smoothing her hair back in a side-view
mirror.

Catledge stopped his cruiser and stepped out and opened the chain-
link fence to the rear lot. After I pulled in, he got out again and closed
the fence. We parked near the back door to the jail. I stepped out of my
truck.

"Isn't that fence automatic?" I said.

"Froze up," Catledge said. "Dingus doesn't have the budget to fix it."

He ushered me through two buzzing doors. Everything was as
brightly lit as a school cafeteria. I saw Dingus emerge from his office
fingering a set of keys. "This way, son," he said.

Catledge peeled off. The sheriff led me into the women's wing of the
jail, through a locked door, then through another, and finally into a dim
gray corridor lined on both sides with cells. He stopped at the third one
on the right. Through the bars I saw Mom, curled up beneath a wool
blanket on a narrow bed, asleep. I felt the urge to reach in and stroke
her shoulder, comfort her somehow. Dingus held a finger to his lips and
shook his head. "Just wanted you to see," he said.

He didn't speak again until he'd closed his office door and indicated
the angle-iron chair facing his desk. "Sit," he said. The room smelled of
mustard and salt. A hot dog for dinner, I thought. Probably cooked in
the microwave in the shift room.

I sat. I'd been in the same chair many times while trying to wheedle information out of the sheriff, who usually leaned back and smiled through his handlebar mustache, his way of saying he wasn't about to help me.

Dingus wasn't smiling now. He sat and picked up his phone and hit a button and said into the handset, "Stand by," then hung up the phone. He brushed some crumbs off the blotter, set his bowling-pin forearms down, and leaned toward me. Besides the phone and the blotter, the only things on his desk were a stapler, a set of black handcuffs, a file folder half an inch thick with papers, and a framed picture of his girl-friend, Barbara. He opened a drawer, took out a box of staples, closed the drawer, and set the box on the desk.

"Did you give my mother a sleeping pill?" I said.

He ignored that. "Where've you been?" he said. His Scandinavian singsong made it hard sometimes to tell whether he was just fooling around. Tonight, I was pretty sure he was not.

"You brought me here, Dingus."

He plucked a row of fresh staples out of the box, then picked up the stapler and pulled the top half back to expose the carriage. "Figured you'd be out in the lobby with the other buzzards," he said.

"Has my mother been charged?"

He slipped two sheets of paper out of the file folder, fitted them into the stapler, and punched it down with a fist. "Should she be?" he said.

"I can't imagine with what."

Dingus set the stapled sheets aside, took two more from the file folder, and slammed the stapler so hard that it flipped on its side. "How about obstruction of justice?"

"That would only apply if she actually knew anything."

He righted the stapler. "What is it you hockey guys say? 'You can't hit what you can't catch'?" He slammed the stapler again, this time without any paper in it. "Well, you can't see what you can't see, can you? Excuse me." He picked up his phone and hit a button. "Now, please," he said into the phone. Then he addressed me again. "Be warned, sir, although she's your mother, you would be ill-advised to cover for her, legally speaking."

"You think I'm covering for her?"

"Have you retained legal representation?"

"Why should I?"

"Your prerogative," he said. "But let me tell you something: We do not believe that Bea slept as soundly Sunday night as she claims."

"She said she woke up to go to the bathroom."

"There's more to it than that. Or maybe she's told you."

"Told me what?"

His office door opened. Darlene walked in. She had doffed her deputy's hat and tied her hair back with a rubber band. She was carrying something behind her back that I couldn't see from where I sat.

"Stay right there, Deputy," Dingus said. Then, addressing me, "Can you think of a reason your mother would have left the house that night?"

My heart jumped into my throat. Because I could think of a reason.

"No," I said.

"Do not lie to me, son. I can and will hold it against you."

I wanted to ask Darlene what was going on. But of course I couldn't. I couldn't even look at her, which was why Dingus had brought her in, for maximum dramatic effect, to impress upon me the need to plumb Mom's fickle mind for whatever secrets she was keeping. Or had forgotten.

"I don't have to talk to you," I said.

"But you will unless you want to join your mother in a cell. I can charge you with obstruction of justice, too."

I grabbed my notebook and pen out of my back pocket. "That for the record?"

Dingus came out of his chair and leaned across his desk and pointed a finger so close to my face that I thought he might thrust it into my eye. "Do not trifle with me," he said.

"Don't trifle with me, Sheriff."

He held his finger there a moment longer, then sat back down. "Bea Carpenter," he said, "did not kill her best friend. And she might have slept through the assault on Phyllis Bontrager. But she woke up. And she got out of bed."

"Which she has willingly admitted."

"Here's what she has not admitted: She left that house." He turned to Darlene. "Put it here," he said, indicating his desk.

From behind her back, Darlene produced a clear plastic bag. She slid one end open and removed a green boot with a black rubber toe and fake white fur lining the opening. I recognized it as one of the pair I'd bought Mom for Christmas. Then I remembered the old galoshes she'd worn when we'd gone up to Dad's tree house.

"Tell me," Dingus said. "Did you buy Bea a pair of boots recently?"

"For Christmas."

"At Reid's."

"How'd you know?"

"Receipt. Credit card number."

"So what?"

He looked at Darlene. She said, "We found it stuck in the snow on the path up to your Dad's tree—garage. It was unlaced and pointing down the hill. The toe had gotten caught beneath a tree root under all that snow."

I wanted to help Darlene, because I loved her mother and I loved her. But I wasn't about to speak what I was now thinking: that Mom had left the house with the lockbox and gone up to Dad's garage and hidden the box in the trunk of the Bonneville, then hurried back inside.

Nilus, Mrs. B had said. Like Soupy's mom, she knew things that only they and my mother knew. I thought back to Sunday morning. Perhaps that's what Mom and Mrs. B had been talking about when I'd come in with Saturday's *Pilot*. Mom had asked why "they" hadn't taken anything. I now concluded that she must have meant the Bingo Night Burglar.

"Forgive me," I said, "but what does that prove? Maybe the burglar took the boot."

Dingus shook his head. "I'm not an idiot," he said. "Your mother lost this boot when she left the house that night. She was probably rushing, knowing we were coming."

"Why did you arrest Breck?" I said.

"You'll find out when he's arraigned in the morning."

"For murder?"

"Tell me why your mother left the house that night. Did she take something out of the house? Did she hide it somewhere? That garage?"

"I don't know. The burglar or burglars haven't taken anything. Have you figured out why? Or what they were really looking for? Feels like you're just fishing, Dingus. You've got a whole jail full of people and you don't know who did it, do you? What about your anonymous tip? Isn't that why you arrested Tatch in the first place? Now it's Breck? You don't really have any idea what happened, do you? The best you can do is cancel bingo."

Dingus ran a hand over his mustache. "Maybe the break-ins were for documents. You know, identity theft. These old folks have money stashed away."

Or a map, I thought. "I'm not an idiot, either."

"Perhaps you would like your own jail cell."

I risked a glance at Darlene. She rolled her eyes.

"You still have vacancies?" I said.

Darlene stepped closer "We think," she said, "the anonymous tip may have come from Breck himself. Tatch has been whining to other prisoners about what Breck did at his camp. Maybe Tatch had become an impediment to Breck."

"Tatch—Mr. Edwards, that is—is now telling us Breck wasn't at the camp that night," Dingus said.

That wasn't what Tatch had told me when he called me from the jail. He clearly was turning on Breck.

"How would he know whether Breck was there?" I said. "Tatch wasn't there either."

"We're checking that out with the others."

"Are you going to release my mother?"

"We did give her a sleeping pill," Dingus said. "I'm hoping maybe, with a good night's sleep and we let you take her home, her memory might improve a little."

Darlene moved around behind me. Dingus said, "The truth is, I wish we could slam a big door on all the pain-in-the-butt, nutcase downstaters who come here and mess up our quiet little town. Then maybe Bea could just go home and fret over whatever it is she doesn't want anybody to know. But it's too late to slam the door."

"You know, Dingus," I said, "back in the fifties there was a sheriff here who was in the middle of a tough election and he suddenly solved a big crime."

He pursed his lips. The tips of his handlebar jumped up an inch. "Get him out of my sight," he said. "I've got to go see the other vultures."

Darlene stuck a hand under my armpit and tugged me out of my chair. As we were going out the door, Dingus said, "By the way, way back in the fifties? Sheriff Spardell was re-elected in a landslide."

"What the hell was that all about?"

I whispered it to Darlene as soon as Dingus's door closed behind us. Darlene squeezed my arm hard, looked behind her, and yanked me down the hall, around a corner, and into a closet. She shut the closet door, plunging us into darkness. I backed up against a set of metal shelves, smelling soap and cardboard and then Darlene, as she stepped close to me.

She took one of my hands in both of hers and pressed something small into the palm.

"What's this?" I said.

"The button you left on the stairs at the tree house the other night."

"What are you talking about?"

She laid a hand on my chest. "When we came for Bea and you ran out the back."

"Dingus is off his rocker," I said.

"Shut up."

She grabbed my coat collar and pulled me into her and kissed me, her badge pressing into my ribs. The kiss was not long but it was wet and warm and I felt a shiver ripple across my belly like the one I had felt when she had kissed me in the dark courthouse closet almost twenty years before. She pulled away and pushed me back against the shelves.

"What was that?" I said.

"Breck insists on talking to you."

"What?"

"He has no lawyer and says he needs to speak with you. Dingus OK'd it."

"Dingus really is crazy."

She opened the door a crack, peeked out, closed it again, turned back to me. "Meet me later. My apartment."

My gut fluttered again. "Are you sure?"

"You're going to tell me all about the tree house and Bea." She opened the door. "Out."

Wayland Breck waited in orange coveralls at a long white Formica-topped table in the shift room. I was surprised to see a cigarette smoldering in a foil ashtray. He tapped a can of Vernors on the tabletop. Darlene sat me down across from him. His hands were unfettered, but I noticed shackles on his ankles.

"You have fifteen minutes," Darlene said. I assumed she had brought us to the shift room because the rest of Breck's group was being finger-printed and mug-shotted and Dingus didn't want them to see us talking. She closed the shift room door behind her. I saw the back of her head through the crosshatched observation window in the door.

"She's important to you, isn't she?" Breck said.

"Good evening, Breck. You wanted to talk to me?"

"Is she as important as your mother?" He smiled and took a drag on his cigarette before crushing it out. "You know, Mr. Carpenter, we are not so different. My mother kept secrets from me, too." He let that hang there. I chose not to respond. "For years," he continued, "I believed what my mother told me about my grandfather, that he died of emphysema in a hospital when I was a small boy. Only in her will did she leave a note telling me that was a lie."

"Why would she wait? Weren't you a grown man by then?"

"Yes. But as you, of all people, can appreciate, I can't be sure why she held back. Maybe she was embarrassed. In retrospect, I believe my grandfather's death tortured her for most of her life. She was"—he stopped and looked at the table—"an increasingly sad woman."

"But she kept the truth—or her version of it—from you."

"Perhaps she didn't want it to torture me."

"But now it does."

He chose not to reply.

"She didn't commit suicide, did she?" I said.

"Melanoma."

"And what is the truth?"

Breck looked at the shift room door. "Aren't you going to take notes?"

"On the record?" I said.

"Absolutely."

I took out my pen and notebook and opened the notebook and wrote BRECK, JAIL, WED at the top of the first blank page. I looked up at him. Only then did I notice.

"Did the cops confiscate your glasses?" I said.

"I don't wear glasses," he said.

"Go ahead."

"My grandfather," he said, "did not kill Sister Mary Cordelia Gallesero." He clasped his hands together on the table and leaned over them. "He may or may not have had romantic feelings for her. But he did not kill her. The truth is, he knew something about what happened to the nun, and so Father Nilus Moreau made sure he was eliminated. My grandfather wasn't even arraigned. He was tried, convicted, sentenced, and executed in this very building in a matter of two days on a weekend."

"That's all public record."

Breck continued as if I hadn't spoken. "He tried to call the only person in the world he trusted—his daughter, my mother—but she was away at a wedding, and there was no voice mail or mobile phones to track her down. She heard about his death a good twenty-four hours after it happened."

"He got in a fight with the wrong guy."

Again he ignored me. "As a fellow investigator, Mr. Carpenter, you'll be interested to know that I found the priest who supposedly heard my grandfather's confession."

"Impressive."

"Emile Waterstradt. Saint Robert Bellarmine. Otsego Lake. Glenfiddich."

"Glenfiddich?"

"Scotch. A bottle a day. Waterstradt finally left the priesthood in his shame. I found him living in an apartment above a bar in Hillman."

"How do you spell Waterstradt?" I said.

"He's dead. But if he were still alive, perhaps he would tell you, as he told me, that my grandfather didn't kill the nun, but that he did see what he believed to be the remains of the unfortunate nun."

"Where?"

"In a crawl space beneath the old church. They were about to start building the lovely new church, and Grandpa was cleaning things up. He found her remains beneath a pile of dismantled pews. At first he thought it was an animal. But there were shreds of cloth."

"Her habit."

"Correct."

"And he told the priest."

"The charming Father Nilus, yes. As for the 'wrong guy,' after Rupert Calloway was released on the pretense that he had acted in self-defense, he subsequently moved north and enjoyed splendid employment at a home for retired priests on Lake Superior. He mowed the lawn and plowed the walks and in return received room and board and the convenience of a whorehouse in Ishpeming."

"Rupert Calloway is—"

"The man who cut my grandfather's throat. He died in ninety-seven. Unfortunately I didn't find him in time to ask him a question or two."

"You're saying someone arranged for this Calloway guy to kill your grandfather?"

"I'm not saying it. Father Waterstradt said it, while crying like a child into his coffee cup of single malt. He and Nilus were close."

238 / *Bryan Gruley*

"Entertaining story. But you didn't go to the authorities."

"What did the authorities say happened to the nun, Mr. Carpenter?"

"Your grandfather dumped her in Torch Lake."

"But her body never washed up."

"Sometimes bodies don't wash up in that lake," I said. "Sometimes boats don't."

Breck smiled. "I've heard all about the underground tunnels that suck things out to Lake Michigan."

"Why should I believe a man who helped the church defend pedophiles?"

"Do not judge lest you be judged."

"Enough with the biblical claptrap."

"Believe what you like," he said. "I saved most of those men from much harsher treatment at the hands of my clients."

"Eagan, MacDonald and Browne, representing the archdiocese."

"Indeed. To say they were ruthless would be an understatement of the first rank. My research, which the lawyers put on the record quite selectively, didn't always help the archdiocese's case. So they were forced to settle on less-than-palatable terms, at least financially. The men were compensated handsomely, and they went on with their lives."

"You're a hero. Congratulations."

The door opened. Skip Catledge ducked in. "Five minutes," he said.

The door closed. Breck said, "You've no doubt noticed that my name didn't show up on any of these sex abuse cases until the early nineties, after my mother died."

"So that's why you got close to the church, to find out what happened to your grandfather."

"The law firm would be careful, of course, with an outside contractor like me. But I made a few friends, learned a few things."

"Like, they're buying up land on the lake."

"So you have done some homework. After I learned about the first purchases, last summer, I focused my research. And when I heard what they were offering for the Edwards parcels"—Tatch's property—"I decided it was time to act."

If only Tatch had taken the money and sold his land, maybe none of this would have happened. Maybe Mrs. B would be at Mom's house now, drinking rosé over a game of Yahtzee.

"Have you enjoyed your little messianic charade?" I said.

"It is nothing compared to your colleague's."

"My collegue?"

"I'm sure Whistler hasn't mentioned that he came to me a few years ago to ask about my grandfather. He said he was researching a story."

"Bullshit."

"He came with a woman. It was a hot summer day and I had a window open. I could hear them out in the parking lot, bickering. Then I heard tires screeching and he came in alone."

A woman? "How did he find you?" I said.

"My mother's name was in the papers when my grandfather died."

Of course. That's how I had made the connection. I felt a little sick. When Breck had told me outside the drain commission meeting that I was being "led astray," I hadn't thought he was referring to Whistler.

"But how would Whistler have known there was a story?" I said.

"He's fifty-six. Born in June 1943. And yet his father, supposedly one Edgar Whistler, was killed in April 1942 at Bataan. Which doesn't add up. But if little Lucas was born in one town—let's say Clare, an hour away, but another world back then—and his mother moved him back to Starvation as a baby, people there wouldn't doubt he was the son of the fallen soldier."

"But"—I hesitated, uncertain of the answer—"then he moved away?"

"To Allen Park. His mother was a night janitor at Superior Motors. But Whistler had to help support her. By the way, this is all publicly available information. I'm surprised you don't know it. Are you surprised you don't know it, Mr. Carpenter?"

Surprised wasn't the word. "I don't need to know the entire history of my colleagues."

"I see," Breck said. "It's funny. My contacts at the law firm called him Luke Chiseler. He knows more about any of this than anybody—or almost anybody. And he put a price on it."

"What are you talking about?" I said.

"Mr. Whistler called it a book deal."

"And?"

The shift room door opened again. Catledge stepped in.

"And . . . if you want to hear more, you should be at my arraignment tomorrow. It should be interesting. I dearly hope the entire town shows up."

"Why Tex? What's he have to do with this?"

"What better way to punish this town?" Breck said, then briefly lowered his eyes. "I am sorry about his injury. That was not intended."

"Why are you telling me all of this?" I said.

"In case I don't get a fair trial."

"Why? You think you're going to follow in your grandfather's footsteps?"

"Time's up," Catledge said.

Breck rose. "Ask Father Reilly."

TWENTY-FOUR

I didn't want to believe Breck.

Whistler didn't answer when I called him from my truck. I left a message, trying to sound nonchalant, hoping he was with Tawny Jane.

He was not.

Tawny Jane was finishing a stand-up in front of the sheriff's department when I rolled up. Other reporters milled around in the shadows outside the vestibule, deciding where to go for beers after calling in their stories. Dingus was gone. D'Alessio, who apparently had been released, stood off to one side, waiting for someone to interview him.

I didn't see Whistler or his Toronado. He had said he would be going to the cop shop, and I couldn't imagine he'd miss a briefing on this story. But maybe he'd thought I would babysit that. Maybe he was already at the *Pilot*, posting something online.

The wind kept blowing Tawny Jane's hair across her face, and she kept pulling it away with the hand that wasn't holding the microphone. I eased my window down to hear.

". . . will be arraigned tomorrow morning, a major turn of events in the spicy drama here in Starvation Lake, a quaint little town, which has seen its share of drama in the past. Channel Eight will be broadcasting live tomorrow from the Pine County Courthouse as Wylie Ezra Breck is arraigned before Judge Horace Gallagher . . ."

Not Wylie, I thought. And quaint? Not for a long time.

I threw my truck into park and got out and walked over to Tawny Jane. She gave me a look that said she wasn't interested and turned to her cameraman, Butch. "Good enough?" she said. "We can smooth it out back at the station."

"Yup," Butch said. "Couple of shots, your hair makes you look like Cousin Itt."

"Big news, eh, T.J.?" I said.

She tossed her hair back and pulled on a white wool hat. "A little late, aren't you?"

"Whistler was here, wasn't he?"

She pulled on mittens that matched her hat. "You'll have to watch me at eleven."

"Whistler was not here?"

"I didn't see him."

"You wouldn't happen to know why he didn't show?"

"I don't know a thing about that man."

She climbed into the van and it spun away in a whirl of snow.

The streetlights on Main glimmered through the frosted kitchen window in Darlene's second-floor apartment. We sat at her table with cups of tea. She had undone the top two buttons on her brown-and-mustard deputy's shirt and shaken the hatband imprint out of her hair.

I didn't wait for her to ask; she deserved to know. I told her everything Breck had told me, told her about the lockbox, my trip to Detroit, my meeting with Father Reilly, about Nilus's womanizing and my theory about the map and Mom's two best friends. Darlene listened without interrupting. If anything surprised her, I couldn't tell. Maybe she was so weary of the drama swirling around her mother's death that she could not register surprise anymore.

I reached across the table to take her hand. She let me.

"We haven't even made funeral arrangements yet," she said.

"Mom told me she was going to do it, then she said you were doing it."

Darlene shook her head. "She's mistaken."

No, I thought, Mom wasn't mistaken. "I can go with you tomorrow, after the arraignment."

"The arraignment," she said. There was scorn in her voice.

"What?" I said. She was staring at our entwined hands. "You don't really think Breck was there that night, do you?"

"I don't know what to think," she said. "I've never seen Dingus like this. You're right. He's off his rocker. Hauling in all those people. Even arresting D'Alessio. Come on."

"He's feeling the pressure. Do you have any hard evidence at all on Breck?"

"Just because we're here now doesn't mean I'm obliged to be unprofessional."

"I—"

"This is my mother."

She was fighting not to cry again.

"I understand. I can't believe you're still on the case. You're—"

"Don't. Don't say a word about courage or any of that bullshit. I'm just doing what I do, just like Sunday night with Mrs. Morcone and that damn raccoon."

"It's all right, Darlene."

"No, it's not, goddammit." She pulled her hand away. "Look—this is off off off the record. We have, essentially, nothing. No fingerprints. No witnesses. Nothing. Dingus is praying the DNA guys find something. We just keep filling up the jail with people who didn't do it."

"But you're going into court tomorrow."

"He couldn't let D'Alessio get away with rallying the people like that."

"Judge Gallagher's going to bite Dingus's head off."

"Well. We can certainly connect Breck to Nilus and make a case that he had motive to be in the house looking for something."

"Like a map. Or part of one."

"How would he know it's there?"

"No idea, unless . . ." I thought of the woman who had approached Soupy's mother. "I don't know."

"And why would my mother just blurt out 'Nilus'?"

"They were talking about it that morning," I said. "At least I think they were. I asked and they changed the subject."

"Do you think they suspected this burglar wasn't taking anything because he hadn't found what he was looking for?"

"Yeah. Reminds me. Someone broke into Soupy's parents' house."

"He didn't report it."

"What a shock."

"Probably just some drunk kids."

"Maybe." I told her about the microfilm photograph I had seen at the clerk's office, how all but one of the seven spelling-bee girls beaming with Sister Cordelia would, years later, have their homes broken into on bingo night.

"My mother's house didn't get broken into," Darlene said.

"Maybe she was next."

On the wall behind her head hung a framed aerial photograph of Starvation Lake. The water was indigo in the middle of the lake, shimmering to pale green along the shoreline. Pelly's Point jutted into the water, evergreens leaning out from the bluff. Darlene's father had ordered the photo for her from a shop in Suttons Bay. She had kept it because it came from him, although she said she didn't know why she needed a picture of the place she had lived in all of her life, since it never changed anyway. I looked for our houses. There they were, next to each other, the big yard where I'd once tried to kiss Darlene lying between.

"Tell me," I said. "Did your mother ever hear from someone supposedly doing a history of St. Val's?"

Darlene thought about it. "When would this have been?" she said.

"Couple of years ago maybe."

"If she did, she didn't say anything to me."

"Your mom wouldn't have." I told her about the woman who had called Soupy's mom. Money had been offered, I said.

"God," she said. "All these strangers."

"What's going to happen to you, Darl?"

"What do you mean?"

"If Dingus doesn't keep his job."

"I don't know. With Mom gone . . . I don't know."

"I hope you stay."

Darlene picked up our mugs and put them in the sink. Then she came and stood next to me. "My aunt Millie called," she said. "She said Bea was acting like she's getting ready to die or something."

"What?"

"They spent yesterday afternoon basically getting her affairs in order. Went to see a lawyer about her will and took a bunch of money out of the bank."

So it wasn't even shopping and cribbage. Same old Mom. I could see Millie going along with it, standing by Mom's side, then going home and rushing to the phone.

"She's safe for now," I said.

Darlene sat against the table facing me. "If I had just picked up my mom's call, maybe we'd all be OK now," she said.

"No, Darlene," I said. "This is not your fault, or mine."

Her eyes were filling with tears.

"What's wrong?"

"The rug. It's ruined."

"What rug?"

"Me Sweet Ho."

"Who cares?"

"I care."

"OK." I stood, put my hands on her shoulders. She looked up at me.

"I never told you," she said. "Your mom was going to give me the rug."

"When?"

"A long time ago. Before you went to Detroit."

"Why?"

"Because . . . I loved it. Because I loved teasing you about it. Because it reminded me of all the fun we had together as kids, in your house and my house, out on the lake, up in the tree house. They were sweet places."

"They were."

"Bea wanted me to have it so I could"—Darlene put a hand to her mouth, swallowed a sob—"so I could have it fixed. So it would say Home Sweet Home. So I could, we could . . ."

"So you and I could have it in our house."

She nodded.

"I'm sorry," I said.

"No. No. Everything—there's a reason."

"I don't know about that."

"I do."

She reached down and grabbed me by the belt and pulled me up against her. I wasn't sure I wanted this yet, wasn't sure I wanted to believe in this again. But I didn't stop her when she rose on her toes and kissed me, while she undid my belt and unbuttoned my plaid flannel, while she pulled my T-shirt out of my jeans and shoved it up on my chest. "Wait," I said, but she bent and flicked the tip of her tongue along the edge of my rib cage.

I woke up on my back, the living room carpet scratchy on my shoulder blades. Darlene was awake, looking at me from where her head lay on my chest.

"Gus," she said. "What do you believe?"

"I don't like the guy, but I don't think Breck—"

"Not that. I mean *believe*. Like faith. My mother, she believed in God, the church."

"Did you know your mom had a rosary at the office? Kind of like the one in my mom's lockbox. She'd set it next to her sometimes when she was writing obits."

Darlene closed her eyes. "What about you?"

"I don't have a rosary," I said.

"Please don't."

I looked around the room. My gaze fell again on the aerial shot of the lake.

"I don't know." I said. "I guess I believe in doing my best, trying to be a good guy, be nice to my mom, take care of the people I love. Is that good enough?"

"I don't know."

"Well," I said, "I hope it is. It has to be."

"Why? Why does it have to be?"

I knew the answer. I'd known it for a while, but I hadn't had the guts to say it.

"Because I'm here, Darlene," I said. "I'm here because you're here. You're why I came back after screwing up in Detroit. OK? Is that good enough?"

She picked her head up from my chest. I looked at her.

"Really?" she said.

"Yeah."

She leaned up and kissed my neck, then let her head fall back on my breast. My eyes drifted back to the picture of the lake. I thought of how we used to lie on our backs on the raft in summer, our eyes closed, our fingertips touching. I thought of Mrs. B, fingering her rosary beads, silently praying, then setting the rosary down and typing. I thought of my mother's rosary, hidden away in a metal box.

I nudged Darlene.

"Hey," I said.

"Hm?"

"Why didn't that body wash up on Torch Lake?"

She slid a hand down my belly and let it rest on the inside of one leg. "God, I'm tired. What are you talking about?"

"Sister Cordelia. You know. The sheriff who got re-elected way back when? Who solved the nun's murder? Breck's grandpa supposedly dumped her in Torch Lake. But the body never washed up."

"I don't know," she said. "Sometimes boats go down and don't wash up. The tunnels."

"Nobody's ever found one of those tunnels," I said. "It's like Bigfoot."

"You never really believe anything, do you."

"I guess not."

"Why does it matter whether the body washed up?" Darlene said.

I thought of my mother, lying in her cell, her hands crossed on her breast. I remembered her at my house, scrutinizing her fingers and nails, insisting they were filthy when they were not.

"Gus?"

"Mom knows," I said.

"Mom knows what?"

"Mom knows where that nun is." I sat up, dislodging Darlene. "We have to get her."

"She's in jail."

"No. We have to get her and get going. Now." Mom's words came back to me. "Before someone else gets there first."

TWENTY-FIVE

Darlene opened the back door of her sheriff's cruiser and helped Mom slide in next to me. She looked tiny in her gray parka.

"Gussy?" she said. "What is going on?"

"You'll see."

"I want to go home." She put a hand on the back of the seat, leaned forward, and addressed herself to Darlene. "Take me home, honey."

Darlene pulled the car onto Route 816 and punched the accelerator. She replied without turning around. "I'm sorry, Mom C. You're actually still in custody."

"I hope you don't get in any trouble," I told Darlene.

"Christenson was the duty guy," she said. "All those people from Tatch's camp were keeping him pretty busy."

"Where are you taking me?" Mom said.

Snow fluttered in the headlight funnels piercing the dark ahead of Darlene's cruiser. The rear of the car shimmied as she eased into a descending hairpin. Mom grabbed at the seat, squinted out the window.

"Why are we going here? I hate this road."

We were winding to the bottom of Dead Sledder Mile.

"Almost there, Bea," Darlene said.

"Oh, God, not this road. Especially in the dark."

Dead Sledder flattened. Darlene drove another mile, slowed, and came nearly to a stop. Mom was sitting up, watching. Darlene turned the cruiser onto a two-track, the tires groaning in the snow. The two-track wound upward through the dark trees.

"No," Mom said. "Please, I don't want to go."

"It'll be all right," I said.

"Stop," she told Darlene.

Darlene braked beneath a canopy of snow-laden evergreens.

"What's the matter, Bea?"

"I know why you're taking me here," Mom said.

"Good," I said. "Let's go."

Mom reached across the seat and grabbed my arm. "No."

"Why, Mom? What's up there?"

"Everybody has a past," she said.

"What does that mean?"

"Gus," Darlene said.

"The future is all that matters," Mom said.

"Sorry, this is gibberish. Darlene, go."

Mom moved as if to slap my face, but I caught her by the wrist.

"Darlene," I said.

"Let go of me," Mom said.

"Calm down."

"I will."

I let go. "You left the house the other night," I said. "You snuck out to Dad's tree house."

"I don't remember."

"Don't play the memory game." I pointed through the windshield at the two-track. "You know what's up there. Mrs. B knew what's up there. Soupy's mom knew."

She looked out her window. "Louise loved money more than me," she said. "Someone asked her. She told them. She wanted me to forgive her."

"She told them what?"

Mom's face fell into her hands. Her shoulders began to heave. I couldn't afford to care. Not then.

"Mother," I said, "I know you weren't playing cribbage yesterday."

"Go easy on her," Darlene said.

"Why were you taking money out of the bank? Why were you going over your will? What are you afraid of? You hid the lockbox, then you made sure I had it. Was that a slip? Or did you really want me to know?"

"Please," Mom said. She looked up, looked around, looked out her window again. "The sun. The sun was going down. I saw it on the leaves."

"Gus," Darlene said. "Leave her."

"She's playing us," I said. "There is no sun. There are no leaves. Enough of the secrets."

"You were not there," Mom said.

The car lurched into reverse. "She's had enough," Darlene said.

"All right. Stop. Now." It was Mom. "I'm not a 'her.' I'm not a 'she.' Don't talk about me as if I wasn't even here. I'm still here."

"I'm sorry, Bea," Darlene said. "We'll talk in the morning."

"No," Mom said. "No." She turned and looked into my eyes. "The truth will not set you free, son. The truth is a burden."

She told us.

Bea Damico had loved Rudy Carpenter since she was in the sixth grade. They had gone steady since the eighth. Watching sunsets from the beach at the public access, lake water lapping across their feet, young Bea and Rudy had talked of the day when they would marry and buy a house on the lake. It wouldn't have to be a big house, just one big enough for the two of them and maybe two children, a boy and a girl, and maybe a dog. The first time Rudy told Bea he loved her, she made him promise that they would paint the house yellow, her favorite color.

And then, one June, the summer before her last in high school, came Eddie McBride, Rudy's cousin from Ann Arbor. Like the other downstate boys who appeared at their family cottages in summer, Eddie had about him a confidence—Mama Damico called it swagger, as if the word was an obscenity—that made a girl think, for just a minute, maybe longer, that there might be something beyond Starvation Lake, beyond the Frostee Freeze and sock hops, beyond plunking for bluegill and water-skiing barefoot and making out on the dive raft at Walleye Lake.

Eddie was the cutest boy, too. All the other girls said he was the one they wanted to take them away, show them the big cities downstate. Bea didn't want to think about that, but it was hard not to, because Eddie was always with Rudy, and so always with Bea, and every now and then, when Rudy's head was elsewhere, Bea would catch Eddie looking at her, and she would try to pretend that she hadn't caught him, but his smile to himself let on that he knew she'd seen him, and he knew she liked him looking at her.

One night when Rudy had to work late at the marina, Eddie took Bea for a drive in his father's Ford. The car smelled of mothballs, Bea figured because his father owned a dry cleaners, but she didn't mind because she'd never been alone with a boy in a car, as Rudy's father wouldn't let Rudy drive his car until he was eighteen. One by one, Eddie pulled four bottles of beer out from under the bench seat and laid them between him and Bea. She felt a tiny thrill hearing them clink against one another, because she'd never drunk a beer alone with a boy in a car, never drunk more than one beer at a time anywhere.

Bea opened two bottles and they drove around the lake, twice. She opened the other bottles, feeling warm and a little giddy, as Eddie swung up the dirt road to Pelly's Point on the north shore. He parked near the edge of a high bluff and turned off his headlights and they gazed through elms at the reflection of stars twinkling on the lake surface. "It's so beautiful," Bea said, and Eddie winked at her and said, "Not as beautiful as you, little girl," and Bea felt her cheeks flush.

Eddie McBride talked about the stuck-up girls at his high school, how all they thought about was getting into the University of Michigan and didn't know how to have fun once in a while. Bea listened, watching Eddie's languid blue eyes, trying to imagine the Ann Arbor girls carrying books against the fronts of their boyfriends' baggy letter sweaters, wondering if they were all prettier and smarter than she was.

It happened fast. She didn't resist, as she might have halfheartedly with Rudy, when Eddie McBride leaned over and kissed her, nor when he slid his hand across her belly and up to her right breast, so much surer and more fluid in his movements than Rudy that she feared he might think she had never been touched like that before. The smell of the mothballs grew stronger after they climbed into the backseat. Bea focused on it while Eddie gasped into the crook of her neck. He licked her once behind the ear as his body went limp. He pushed himself up. "Whoa, little girl," Eddie McBride said. "I won't tell if you won't." Bea felt the urge to reach up and smack his face, but instead she closed her eyes and wrapped her arms around herself and shook her head no, she would not tell.

She held out for more than a month before she told Father Nilus in confession. Even though he could not see her through the confessional screen, she knew he would recognize her voice because he heard it almost every day when she worked with him in the sacristy and at the rectory, and she could feel him press his eyes closed in disappointment when she said, "I have committed a mortal sin." She wondered, as she admitted to having had intercourse, whether she would've given in to the boy if Nonny had still been around, if she could have gone to Nonny and told her she didn't understand why she would feel these urges for this boy when she knew she loved Rudy Carpenter and always would. These were not things she dared bring up with Mama Damico, who knew only that boys were bad and that her daughter, adopted or not, would not be bad.

When Bea finished her confession, Father Nilus did not speak for a long time. The confessional was stuffy and hot. Waiting, Bea imagined that she could smell the varnish evaporating off the wood, and she feared that she might faint, and that Father would have to come over to her side of the confessional and that then he would be absolutely certain that she was the girl who had had sex out of marriage, out of love, out of anything that mattered. It was a relief when he finally spoke and assured her that everything would be all right, that God was all-forgiving and would forgive her, but the extreme nature of her sin at such a young age would require a special sort of penance, and only after that could he give her absolution.

That night, Father Nilus drove her in his Studebaker up a two-track above the lake's northeastern shore. Bea had never been in these woods before. She liked how the dying sun flickered on the leaves and evergreen boughs as the car crawled upward. Father parked and told Bea to wait in the car for a minute. He opened the trunk and removed some things she couldn't see. "Come along, Beatrice," he called out. She got out of the car and saw Father Nilus with a wheelbarrow carrying a spade, a hoe, and other things beneath them.

It was August 21, 1950.

Nilus squinted up into the woods. "Go," he said, motioning Bea ahead of him.

"But, Father, I don't know—"

"I will guide you. The Lord will guide us."

They stopped where the foliage was so thick that Bea couldn't see down to the lake. Nilus pushed the wheelbarrow away from where they stood and returned with the spade. He used the blade to chop up the surface of the dirt. Then he instructed Bea to dig a hole, holding his arms out to show her how wide and how deep. She reached for the shovel, but he pulled it away and whispered that digging with her fingers would be part of her penance, that it would help to remind her that she had come from dust and to dust one day she would return.

"But, Father," she said, "why did you bring—"

"That is my concern," he replied. "Please now. Your penance. Dig, and I will pray for you, and your parents, and your boyfriend."

She dug with both hands, the dirt clotting black beneath her stubby nails.

"You are seventeen years old," Nilus told her. "You are not married. But you indulged in fornication. You gave your most precious gift not just to a boy who was not your husband, but to a boy who will never be your husband."

"Ouch," she said, catching the nail of a finger on a tree root gnarling through the pit of the hole. "Yes, Father," she said. "I'm sorry, Father."

Perhaps, she thought, he had brought her to do the burrowing because his arthritic knees were so hobbled that he might not have been able to climb back out of the hole. But why the digging anyway? What mysterious ritual was this? And what was in the wheelbarrow he seemed determined to keep from her?

She glanced up at Nilus. One of his arms was hidden beneath his black cassock. With his other he shifted the flashlight so that it shone into her eyes. She shaded them with a hand. His long face glowed pale in the reflected light.

"My heart remains strong with faith in you, Beatrice," he said. "But what of your boyfriend, what if he knew, how would his heart endure the knowledge?"

It would not, she thought. She ducked her head farther into the hole, digging harder as she swallowed a sob. Rudy would be off work by now, looking for her. "He doesn't know," she said, and whispered a prayer that he never would.

"And your parents, it would break their hearts, too."

"Please, Father."

"Your mother. Dear Lord, Beatrice. She wanted a daughter so badly that she went out of her way to find you, the jewel of her life."

"Yes, Father."

"To think that you could keep it from me. Haven't I been your friend? Haven't I done what I could for you since Sister Cordelia left us?"

"Yes, Father, you have."

He had prayed with her every day that Nonny was all right.

"More than anything, Beatrice, you have broken the Lord's heart. I could feel his sadness as I said a rosary for you today."

She drew a hand close and saw blood smeared in the grime on her broken nail.

"Keep digging, child."

"How much more?"

"A bit wider," he said, waggling the flashlight beam around the hole.

She clawed at the wall opposite her, scooping out the dirt and wriggling worms, careful not to smudge the priest's black leather shoes. She imagined she could actually smell the worms. She wished she had a yellow Life Saver to pop into her mouth.

"Here, child."

Nilus bent and set a gardening trowel at the edge of the hole.

"Thank you, Father."

She picked up the tool and began to hack at the hole's inner walls.

Sweat trickled down between her shoulder blades. She set the trowel aside and reached into the bottom of the hole for the loose dirt she had scraped away. Her shoulders ached. She kept working.

Finally she looked up at Nilus, brushed away the damp hair that had fallen into her eyes.

"Will that do, Father?"

He glanced back at the wheelbarrow, his eyes flitting about, scanning the woods. "That should suffice," he said. Bea started to rise from her knees but Nilus held his hand up to stop her. "Your absolution."

"Oh."

She folded her hands and bowed her head. Nilus placed his palm lightly atop her head.

"Please make a good act of contrition."

"O my God," she said, "I am heartily sorry for having offended thee, and I detest all my sins because of thy just punishments . . ."

When she finished, Nilus closed his eyes. "*Dominus noster,*" he said, "*Jesus Christus te absolvat . . .*"

She stood, her head still bowed.

"Thank you, Father."

"You understand that you cannot speak of any of what has happened within the bounds of this confession."

"I understand."

"You must promise."

She wasn't sure why she had to promise if it was already part of her absolution. But she felt itchy and hot and tired and she wanted to take a bath and go to meet Rudy. She decided to tell him she had to work late for Father Nilus, which was close enough to the truth. Father, after all, had sworn her to secrecy in God's name.

"I promise."

"Good. Go now in peace."

She gestured toward the wheelbarrow.

"Shouldn't I—"

"I'll be fine." He took the trowel from her, used it to point back down the slope they had climbed. The sunlight was gone.

"You can make your way along the lake, yes?"

"Yes, Father. I'll see you in the morning."

She started down the incline. A dead branch cracked beneath her shoes. She glanced over her shoulder and saw Father Nilus still standing over the hole, watching her descend.

Fifty yards down, the slope before her dropped off, so she veered right, stepping sideways across the grade, grasping at poplar trunks for balance. She chanced a look back up and across the incline. Nilus was invisible through the darkened woods. She crouched and scrabbled back up the hill, squatting behind a pair of entwined birches where she thought she was hidden. Staying low, she doubled back and up to a spot about twenty yards from Nilus and the hole, where she got down behind a section of oak that had been severed from its trunk by lightning. She lifted her head and peered across shreds of charred bark. Nilus was a shifting shape in the gloom. She thought he had his back to her.

The sound startled her. It was a thud, something hard striking something else hard. The priest bent his body down. "Oh, my dear Lord," he gasped. Then came a rattle, maybe rocks striking one another, then more thuds. "God, God," he said, and she ducked behind the tree, thinking he might have heard her.

"Lord Jesus," she heard him say. "What have I done?"

She raised her head again. Nilus had dropped to his knees and was gathering things from the ground and placing them in something she couldn't see on the other side of him. He bent again and lifted the thing in front of him.

A box, she thought. Some sort of box. Nilus leaned forward until his shoulders were nearly parallel to the ground, lowering the box into the hole. He remained still for a moment, regarding the hole. Then he reached into his cassock and came out with a thin leather pouch. She had to squint to see it in the dusk. She had seen it before in the sacristy. It was brown and Father Nilus's initials were engraved in gold lettering on one corner. He kept his money in it. Now he took it in one hand and, bracing himself on the rim of the hole with his other, leaned down into the hole. When he rose back up, he slapped his empty hands clean, then struggled to his feet.

He stood rubbing his knees, moaning softly, then straightened and moved to the wheelbarrow. He took up the spade. A scoop at a time, he refilled the hole with the dirt mounded around it, then patted it all down, first with the shovel, then with his feet. He shambled into the woods and returned with an armful of twigs and boughs that he scattered over the hole.

She surveyed the area where she lay and made a picture in her mind. She thought she could probably find the hole again, even in the dark, although she doubted she would ever want to come back. It would just remind her of the night with Eddie. It wasn't any of her business anyway. Father Nilus wouldn't have made her promise if he had intended for her to come back and dig up whatever he had buried.

The shovel clanged into the wheelbarrow. Nilus took the handles and began to push the wheelbarrow down the ridge. Bea watched. He had nearly vanished into the dark when a crack opened in the sky and a shaft of moonlight spread across the path before him. He lurched away from the light, ducking his head, and caught his foot on something, tumbling down as the wheelbarrow tipped tools across the ground.

He lay still for a while. Beatrice stood, wondering if she would have to go over and help. Nilus raised himself to his elbows, cradled his face in his hands. Later she would decide that he had been weeping.

We sat in the car in silence. My mother stared at the seat in front of her.

"My God, Bea," Darlene finally said.

"As you both know," Mom said, "Eddie and Rudy were best friends until Eddie died. Which is as it should have been."

"Did he force you, Bea?"

"We were children."

Eddie had died in Vietnam. My father dragged his death around with him until his own death a few years later. I remembered asking my mother once if she'd had a fling with Eddie. "I wasn't that kind of girl," she told me.

There was no point in bringing that up now. Mom was right. They were kids.

"I'm sorry about all of that, Mom," I said.

"I never wanted to think about it again."

"Did you ever find out what was in the box?" I said.

"Gus," Darlene said. "Leave it for a moment."

"I was curious. A few weeks later, maybe a few months, I asked him. He told me it was just some old vestments, some other altar ware that needed to be put away. He said it didn't matter, it was just a penance."

"Did you believe him?" I said.

"I wanted to."

"Did you ever go back?"

"Never," Mom said. "Five—I think it was five—years later, I married Rudy. We tried for a long time to have children. The doctor told me to stop. Then we had you, Gus."

"We're going up there now. Can you find it?"

Mom stared at her hands. "If I can find the birch trees."

Tree branches scratched the sides of the car, dropping tufts of snow as we climbed the two-track. Mom was glued to her window, watching.

We stopped at the edge of the clearing where the four trailers were circled. A strand of yellow do-not-cross tape lay on the ground between two trees. The trailers melted into dark when Darlene flicked her headlamps off. We got out of the car. She turned on a flashlight and aimed it at the clearing.

Lisa Royall stood blinking in the light. She had something cradled beneath her coat.

"Lisa," Darlene said. "Stay where you are."

"Now what do you people want?" Lisa said. She took a step forward, shaded her eyes with a hand. "You want the children, too? Who is that anyway?"

"Sheriff's Deputy Darlene Esper. Please remain still."

"Hello, Lisa," Mom said.

"Bea?"

"Yes, dear."

Darlene started walking in Lisa's direction. Mom and I followed. "You have nothing to worry about, Lisa," Darlene said. "We're just passing through."

"You're scaring the kids, you and everybody else tromping around up here. Why can't you just let us be?"

"Everybody else?" I said. "Who else?"

"I don't know. Somebody. A few hours ago." She waved at the dug-up hill above the trailers. "Guess he thought I didn't hear him. I yelled and he took off."

Whistler, I thought.

"Go back to bed," Darlene said.

"We're not bad people," Lisa said.

I looked at my mother. She was gazing up at the crosses in the trees. Darlene waved the flashlight beam at the nearest trailer.

"You better get that kid inside before he freezes to death."

"She."

"We're going to be moving through now."

Lisa watched from a trailer doorstep as we crossed the clearing to the ridge where the backhoe hunched amid the ruts and potholes. Mom stopped and surveyed the furrowed hill. She looked right, looked left.

"No," she said. "I can't—wait." She held a hand out to Darlene. "The flashlight, please."

Darlene gave it to her. Mom aimed the beam way up the hill and right, then swung it slowly to the left, beyond the area where Breck and Tatch and the campers had dug. She shifted the beam downward, then right again, then back, slower still, to the left, where she stopped. The beam had fallen on the crown of an old stump poking up through the snow. It was a good twenty feet from the nearest gully.

"There," Mom said.

"Are you sure?" I said.

"Follow me."

"Be careful, Bea, honey."

We skirted the holes as we climbed. Mom held the beam steady on the stump. I tried to take her elbow but she shook me off. Five feet from the stump, Mom stopped and played the beam slowly back and forth again on the trees and the rising ground beyond. She stopped it on a pair of dying birches wrapped around each other.

"Like yesterday," she said, to herself.

I thought I recognized the contours of the area from the piece of the map I had seen. Breck apparently hadn't seen any of Mom's map. He was guessing, based on the archdiocese's interest in the land. More of the systematic digging eventually might have reached the spot where Mom now shone the flashlight. She shifted the beam down and moved it along the ground a few inches at a time until it stopped on a dark spot on the surface of the snow.

"No," she said.

She rushed forward, the flashlight beam swinging wildly. "Mom," I said. She was whispering, "No, no, no." She dropped the flashlight and fell to her knees at the edge of the hole. Snow dusted the loose dirt at the bottom. The hole was fresh.

Mom reached down and dug her bare hands into the earth, tearing at it, throwing the cold dirt and snow up and out of the hole. Darlene and I got down on either side of her.

"No," she said. "No, no." She began to sob.

"Mom," I said, putting my arm around her, feeling her shrug me off. "What is it?"

"She's gone," Mom said. "Somebody took her." She stopped digging and covered her face with her hands, the sobs convulsing her body. "Nonny, Nonny, Nonny," she cried. "Oh, Nonny, I'm sorry, I'm so sorry . . ."

TWENTY-SIX

H ere, darling," Millie Bontrager said when we dropped my mother at her house. She wrapped Mom in a blanket. "I'll make you a cup of tea."

"I'll come for you in the morning, Mom," I said. "I love you."

"Yes, Gussy," she said. She looked sad. "I want to go to bed."

Darlene left me at the back door of the *Pilot*.

"I better go face the music at work," she said.

"I have to find Whistler," I said. I'd called him twice while we drove back to town. He didn't answer. I didn't leave messages.

Darlene reached across the front seat of her cruiser and squeezed my hand. "Call me if you find out anything."

In the newsroom, I hoped to see Whistler at his computer, pinkie ring snicking the keys. But all I saw was his desk, cleared of everything but his computer, a stapler, the blotter, and an empty Peerless *Pilot* Personals coffee cup full of paper clips.

I flipped on the black-and-white TV resting atop a pile of old *Pilots* on our fired photographer's old desk and tuned it to Channel Eight. The sports guy was yammering about the River Rats' chances against the Pipefitters. "Without Tex Dobrick," I heard him say, "this one seems piped for the 'Fitters . . ."

Go to hell, I thought.

I pulled out my cell phone and dialed Whistler's cell. It rang, and rang again. Then I heard another ring, clearer, from nearby. I went to my desk. Whistler's phone was lit up on my chair seat. I ended the call. He had left his phone sitting on a white business envelope. Typed on the front was simply GUS. I tore the envelope open. Something fell out onto the floor. Whistler's Media North credit card. I tossed it on my desk. The envelope also held a single typewritten page, folded in three.

I slid it out and read it:

> Gus,
>
> We had a good run together. You are a fine journalist (even if you're a Times guy—ha ha). I must regretfully resign from the Pilot, effective now. It's not like you need me around for one more paper. Besides, it's bad luck to hang around for the last issue of a newspaper. You know what they say about journalism careers ending badly. I had hoped we could get to the bottom of the Bingo Night Burglaries. Why bother now?
>
> Will send forwarding info.
>
> I'm sure the future holds good things for you.
>
> Always First!
> Luke
>
> P.S. Sorry again about that monitor I killed! It deserved it!

"Bullshit," I said. "Fucking bullshit." I balled the letter up and threw it at the wall.

A feeling came over me, a feeling I knew well from playing goalie. You're in the net and a guy is bearing down on you and you know you have the angle cut off but he's a sniper who can detect the tiniest gap you've unwittingly left between your legs or under one of your arms, so you tighten up from head to toe and slide out another six inches to cut off even more of his angle.

Then his stick unwinds and follows through and you feel the puck hit you at almost the same instant that you realize you saw it, or at least a black blur that must have been it, and you know you have it but you're not sure where, maybe your glove, maybe your gut, maybe your crotch, maybe beneath a leg pad, and you wrap yourself into a tuck while the shooter crashes in and your defensemen scramble around looking for the puck.

You're terrified that it will flop out from wherever you're holding it and lie there for the shooter or one of his teammates to slap into the net. You feel the fear in knowing that you have hold of something, but you don't really know where it is, and you might lose it before you ever get control. And if you let that happen, then it will be your fault, and your fault alone. Because your job is to keep the puck out of your net. You and only you.

I had to do something.

I went to my desk, picked up my phone, looked at my blotter. Scratched across one corner of the February page was a 313 number. Joanie. I'd forgotten to call her back. She had said she would ask around about Whistler.

I dialed.

"Yeah," she said.

Music blared in the background, and I thought I heard an announcer's voice narrating a hockey game, heard the names Maltby and Draper.

She's at the Anchor Bar, I thought. "It's Gus."

"What?" She was yelling. "I can't hear you."

"It's Gus," I shouted.

"Hang on."

I heard a clamor of voices talking over Hendrix and clinking bottles. I pictured Joanie stepping outside onto the sidewalk on Fort Street, coatless and shivering.

"What's up?" she said.

"I'm calling about Whistler."

"Why didn't you call before?"

"I was busy. What do you know?"

"Oh, jeez, this is weird."

"What?"

"So, long story short: Whistler had turned into this classic investigative reporter, always working on some big secret project that's going to win a Pulitzer and hardly ever getting anything in the paper. His career was in the crapper four or five years ago, the desk was trying to move him to one of the suburban bureaus, but he told them to stuff it. Then, a couple of years ago, he almost got fired."

"For what?"

"He was working on a story about a professional burglar."

"No."

"Yeah. A real pro. Rips off the rich folks in the Pointes and Oakland County. Apparently Whistler got a little deeper into this story than he should have. Followed the guy around, actually saw him pull some jobs."

I did not want to believe this.

"Are you sure?" I said.

I thought of my mother's house, and the sliding glass door I hadn't fixed.

"I'm sure," Joanie said.

Mom, I thought, had had Whistler and me to dinner one Sunday. She had complained about the door, how it wouldn't lock right. He was sitting there, hearing it as he finished his cherry cobbler.

"No way," I said.

I felt sick to my stomach.

"It's what I was told, Gus."

"By whom?"

"A couple of people, but mainly his ex."

Whistler's ex. The woman who always wanted to get to the crime scene before the cops. Creepy good, he'd said. I sat back on my desk, woozy.

"What's her name? Barbara something?"

"Beverly. Beverly Taggart. Byline had a middle 'C.'"

"Tags," I said.

"Whatever. She wasn't happy. Said Whistler owes her money."

"Hang on a second." Tawny Jane had popped up on the TV. She was standing in front of the sheriff's department. She had a news bulletin. The police had released Tatch and the other born-agains. Breck remained in custody.

"Sorry," I said. "How did Whistler not get fired?"

"How else? One of the top *Freep* guys is a drinking buddy. They just killed the B-and-E stories and told him he better come up with something else good. So he holed himself up in some fourth-floor cranny for months, locked the door, shooed people away. The bosses started looking for excuses to can him. He finally got in trouble spending money on long-distance phone calls and outside experts and other stuff regular reporters can't touch."

I picked up the credit card I'd tossed on my desk. Whistler had used it to pay a consulting firm $450. But what was the firm's name? I kicked myself for not asking Philo when he'd told me about it.

"Then," Joanie said, "on Christmas Eve, he just e-mailed them, 'I quit,' and disappeared."

"Christmas Eve?"

"Dramatic, huh? Why?"

"Because he started at the *Pilot* in November."

"Are you sure?"

"Might even have been late October. He wrote the annual turkey story."

"Oh. Well. Maybe my source got it wrong."

I dropped the credit card and grabbed the Media North cell phone Whistler had left behind. He had insisted, as if he were doing me a favor, on using his own Detroit phone until the end of the year, when his service contract was up. But now I thought, no, Gus, you dipshit— that's when the *Free Press* shut his *Free Press* phone off, when he tendered his resignation.

"No," I said. "I am a fucking idiot."

When Whistler joined the *Pilot*, he hadn't yet quit the *Free Press*. His bosses there must have assumed he was doing his investigative reporter thing, digging a dry hole, looking for news outside the newsroom, whatever vapid saying he used. He wasn't looking for a place to land in retirement. He didn't give a shit about fishing. He was in Starvation Lake looking for the very same thing Breck was.

"Fire his butt," Joanie said.

I almost laughed. "He fired himself," I said. "He's gone."

"Good."

"No, not good." Tawny Jane was on the tube again, recapping the day's Bingo Night Burglary news. The cops hadn't let the Channel Eight crew come up to Tatch's camp, so they shot from up on the ridge. I watched the camera pan the hill, passing Soupy's parents' house.

I had an idea.

"Could you get me that woman's number?"

"Who?"

"Beverly Taggart."

"Hold on. I might have it in my purse." She did. I wrote it on my blotter. "Is there anything—oh, wait, one last little thing. Not that it matters, but it's funny."

"What?"

"You know how Whistler's legendary for smashing computers?"

"Yeah."

"Seems it's not an anger thing. The guy would get freaked out on deadline and have like a panic attack. He wasn't mad. He just lost it under pressure."

"Really?"

"Typical investigative reporter, huh? Can't handle the real stuff."

"I guess. Listen, I owe you."

"That's right," Joanie said. "When are you going to come visit again? Maybe less business and more pleasure next time?"

"Soon," I lied.

I slid into my desk chair and let my head fall into my hands.

How had I missed so much? How had I let Whistler put so much over on me? I looked up to him. I trusted him. He was me. A reporter. *If you can't trust a fellow scribe, who can you trust?* he had said. *It's me and you and the rest of the world, right?*

I'd had the puck in my hands, and I had dropped it.

I sat up and looked at the phone. I heard one of the Channel Eight anchors babbling about a budget vote in Elk Rapids. I had calls to make. I was afraid of what else I might find. But I had to look anyway.

Philo was first. He was still up, watching the news. I told him I needed the name of that consulting firm Whistler had hired.

"Why?" he said. "It's late."

"I want to find out what the hell they billed us for. Maybe I can get it back."

"I'm afraid it's not going to save the *Pilot*," Philo said.

"Give me a fucking break," I said. "Just do it. In two days I'll be out of your hair and you can go back to playing newspaper exec."

There was a lengthy silence before he said, "Wait." I heard a keyboard clacking and Philo mumbling something about the idiots in accounting. I liked Philo, but I didn't have time to be nice to him now.

"All right," he said. "Something information services. Gawd-ralt? Gawd-ree-oh?"

"Spell it."

I wrote it down as he recited, "G-A-U-D-R-E-A-U-L-T."

"GAW-droh," I said.

"I guess. Gaudreault Information Services. Grosse Pointe."

I stared at the penciled word, recalling the voice I had heard, first around the pool table at Aggeliki's, later on the answering machine in Joanie's loft.

Frenchy. Albert Gaudreault. The computer geek.

Frenchy, whom Whistler had hired. Frenchy, who had lost one lover to me and thought Joanie would be next. Frenchy, who probably had known Joanie and I were going to meet with Reilly and Repelmaus at the golf course—and might have been working for them, too, for all I knew—and who had to have been the one who had stolen my mother's lockbox and given it, no doubt for a price, to Luke Whistler.

"I'll be goddammed," I said.

"Huh?" Philo said.

"Good luck shutting the paper down," I said, and hung up.

I dialed again, this time the number Joanie had given me. Eight or nine rings later, Beverly Taggart croaked, "What?"

I pictured her lying in bed. On the nightstand next to her would be a fake leather pouch for her cigarettes, probably pink, and an ashtray spilling over with butts.

"Tags," I said.

"Who's this?"

"I know where Luke is."

I heard sheets rustling. "That bastard," she said.

"I have to agree."

"Who is this?"

I told her. She asked me where Whistler was. Of course I had no idea, but I said headed for Canada, with the cops on his tail. That didn't seem to surprise her. I told her he had stolen something that had been buried on a hill overlooking Starvation Lake.

"He found it then?" she said.

"Found what?"

I heard the click of a cigarette lighter. "I wish I knew," she said. She exhaled. "He would never say, exactly. All I know's it had something to do with a nun his mother knew, and it was going to be our ticket out of the newspaper game."

"Big book deal, huh?"

"How do you know about that?"

"Everybody up here knows about it."

"That son of a bitch," she said. She stewed for a minute. I pictured her in a redbrick bungalow in Garden City or Inkster, a rusting gas lamp sticking out of the front yard slush. "I did a lot of work on that project."

"You talk to a guy named Breck?"

"The name sounds familiar. I don't think he helped much."

"It was you who found out about the map, though, wasn't it?"

"Lucas told you an awful lot. What did you say your name was?"

"Philo."

"That's a strange name."

"After my great-grandfather."

"Did he get the map? He wouldn't even have known about it if it wasn't for me."

"Somebody up here told you?"

She paused. I heard her lighter click again. "Some lady, I forget her name."

"Louise Campbell?"

"Could be. She was all hopped up to help us—for cash of course—and then she just clammed up, wouldn't talk again."

"She died a couple of years ago."

"Too bad. How?"

Cop reporters always wanted to know how.

"Broken heart," I said. "Your book was supposed to be about a nun?"

"Partly. A nun who died back when Lucas was just a baby. He never told me everything, but what I heard sounded like a humdinger. Priests, murder, buried treasure. Bitsy knew it was buried, she just didn't know where. Then again, Bitsy was just this side of crazy, and she was all drugged up on her deathbed when she told him, so maybe it's all BS."

"Who is Bitsy?"

"His ma. Elizabeth Josephine Pound Whistler. Bitsy."

I wrote it down.

"Is she alive?"

"No. Died, oh, mid-nineties."

Something was familiar about that name.

"Luke never said what the treasure was?"

"Nope. He just told me we'd be all set. So now the son of a bitch has it all to himself? I hope the cops—"

I hung up in the middle of her sentence. I'd gotten what I needed from Beverly Taggart. I got Darlene on the phone.

I told her I was now sure that Whistler had made off with Nilus's box. His mother had told him things. He had learned that there was a map. He'd acquired my mother's piece of it.

"He's getting away," I said. "You have to call the state police."

"Dingus doesn't like us sending the state cops on wild-goose chases," she said. "I'm lucky he hasn't asked for my badge already for kidnapping Bea."

"Come on, Darl."

"We don't even know that he took anything, let alone what he took. Even if it was what you say, what does this have to do with my mother?"

"It must have been him. He was looking for the map. That's why he never took anything. He left nothing behind. I'll bet he broke into Soupy's mom's house, too."

"All of those could just as well have been Breck. I mean, he was actually digging. And wasn't Whistler covering the story the night of the murder?"

I thought back, recalled seeing Whistler at the hospital.

"Shit," I said. "He was with T.J."

"Tawny Jane?"

"Yeah, they've been fooling around. He was with her that night. He heard about it on her scanner. Damn."

"Look," Darlene said. "I'll alert the borders at Sault Ste. Marie, Port Huron, Detroit. If he's got something strange in his trunk, they'll hold him."

I sighed. "OK."

"Get some sleep, Gussy. Tomorrow's going to be a long day."

I grabbed my coat. I was exhausted and hungry. I considered driving to the Hide-A-Way for a burger, decided I was too tired. I'd have to settle for peanut butter toast. I glanced at the police scanner perched over Whistler's desk. It was dark. "Now he turns it off," I said to myself.

I moved to the TV. Merv, the weather guy, was talking about a snowstorm expected that weekend. He was fat and bald and way too cheerful about the prospect of ten to twelve inches of snow. Tawny Jane Reese, I thought, would not make a good weather bitch.

Then I froze. I looked at the scanner, then back at the TV, then at the scanner again.

"I have a huge scoop for you," I told Tawny Jane when she answered.

"It's late."

"Two huge scoops."

"Why the hell would you give me a scoop?"

"Don't worry, you don't have to sleep with me. But I need to ask you something personal."

"You're an asshole."

"True. You want the scoops or not?"

I waited. "Give me the first one," she said.

I told her about the *Pilot's* imminent demise.

"Like the bosses at Media North are going to let me report that," she said.

"That's up to you," I said. As I talked, I stared at the name I had scribbled earlier: Elizabeth Josephine Pound Whistler. I drew circles around the four initials.

"What's the other one?"

"First I get to ask you."

"I might not want to answer."

"Understood. But at the hospital the other night, when they took Phyllis, you were late."

"Yeah. So?"

"You're never late. You're always on the ball."

She was. And if she'd heard the bulletin about the break-in at Mom's house at the same time Whistler had, there was no way she would have been late to the hospital. No way would Tawny Jane let a guy she was fucking beat her to the story—*especially* a guy she was fucking.

"Thanks," she said. "Except when my scanner goes bonkers."

"What scanner?"

"I have a police scanner next to my bed. It died on me Sunday morning."

The hairs stood up on the back of my neck.

"So," I said, "Whistler was not with you that night."

"Sunday night? No. Why?"

I told her everything I knew about Nilus, Sister Cordelia, Whistler, the box he had stolen away. She must have said, "Oh my God," ten times.

I called Darlene again and told her what I now knew.

"Calm down," she said.

"He's getting away."

"No."

"They got him?"

"No, I'm going to get him."

"You mean we're going to get him."

"Are you still at the *Pilot*?"

"Yeah."

"Wait there."

"Out back?" I said, but Darlene had already hung up.

I turned off the lights and the TV and locked the door and stood in the back parking lot watching for headlights. Ten minutes passed. Fifteen. I called Darlene's cell. She didn't answer. I walked out to South Street and looked up and down, as if that would make her arrive faster. At half an hour, I called again. It went straight to voice mail. I called the department.

"Pine County." It was Catledge.

"Deputy Esper, please?"

"Sorry, Gus. She's gone."

"Don't bust my balls, Skip."

"Not busting your balls. She hightailed it out of here forty-five minutes ago. Said she was going to make last call at Dingman's."

"She doesn't drink at Dingman's."

"Good night, Gus."

I stood listening to the wind hum through Starvation Lake, wondering where Darlene was and whether I'd see her again.

TWENTY-SEVEN

Half the town came to watch the arraignment of Wayland Ezra Breck. By the time Mom and I squeezed between Millie and Elvis Bontrager in the third row of the gallery, every fold-down wooden seat in the courtroom was taken. Reporters jammed the jury box. Dingus and county coroner Joe Schriver sat behind the prosecution table to the judge's left. There was no sign of Frank D'Alessio, whose campaign for sheriff appeared to be over.

Breck stood at the table opposite the prosecutor, alone. An orange jumpsuit bagged on his frame. Shackles bound his feet and hands.

I scanned the courtroom for Darlene. She was not there.

The night before, I'd gone home and moved an unpacked box from Mom off of the sofa and lay there with my cell phone within reach, waiting for Darlene's call. I dozed for snatches of ten or fifteen minutes, waking amid dreams of my cell phone ringing, only to see it resting silently on the end table. At six-thirty, I started calling her. Each time, her phone went to voice mail. Either she was choosing not to answer or she couldn't.

I considered calling Dingus, then recalled what Skip Catledge had said about Darlene—"One hell of a police officer, if you ask me"—and called him instead. I swore him to secrecy and told him Darlene had gone after Whistler.

Now I left Mom in her seat and walked up to where Dingus was whispering with Prosecutor Eileen Martin. When he saw me mouth the words "Where's Darlene?" he turned away in what looked to me like disgust. "What happened?" I said, too loud, and the prosecutor gave me a dirty look and pointed me back to my seat.

I sat again, patting my coat pocket for the tissues I'd brought in case Mom needed one. She and Millie were holding hands. I hadn't told her about Darlene.

From atop his bench, Judge Gallagher peered down through his horn-rim spectacles. He rapped his gavel once.

"We have before the court today a single arraignment," he said. "Counsel?"

Eileen Martin stood, wobbly as ever on her high heels. "Yes, Your Honor," she said.

"Thank you, Ms. Martin," Gallagher said. "Mr. Breck, am I correctly informed that you have declined counsel?"

"I will take my own counsel, sir."

"Sir?" Gallagher said. The judge smiled as he shuffled papers around. The residue of Brylcreem that usually made a circular shadow on his leather chair was gone. The judge had lost most of his silver hair while undergoing chemotherapy for an unspecified cancer. "I suppose 'sir' will do. But please tell me, Mr. Breck, that you are trained, at the very least, as an attorney."

"I am, sir."

"I assume you're familiar with the old joke about the lawyer who represents himself?"

"If you're saying I am a fool, so be it. I come to represent more than myself."

"Well, I'm interested solely in you. What do you plead, sir?"

"Excuse me, Your Honor?" Eileen Martin said.

Gallagher's head swiveled like a turtle's. "Ms. Martin?"

"Your Honor, we've just learned of new information that could—"

"Ms. Prosecutor, this is an arraignment. The purpose of an arraignment is to extract a plea from the defendant for the record of this court. Would it inconvenience you to let me accomplish that before you tell me whatever it is you wish to tell me?"

"Your Honor—"

"Or are you saying the prosecution wishes to withdraw felony charges of illegal entry, breaking and entering, conspiracy, and second-degree murder against the defendant?"

"Not at this moment, Your Honor," she said.

"That is a relief. Thank you."

Eileen sat, brushing a hair from her reddening forehead. She couldn't have been surprised. As a judge, Horace Gallagher was as unpredictable as cell phone service north of Gaylord. He ran his courtroom the way he saw fit, standard legal procedure and state judicial commission be damned. Lawyers whispered that he was unstable, but time and again, appellate courts agreed that Pine County's circuit judge, pushing seventy, had charted an improbable map to the correct destination. The judicial commission nannied him on occasion, most notably when he ordered a philandering husband in a divorce case to kneel before his soon-to-be-ex-wife and apologize. But the gripes from officialdom seemed only to encourage Gallagher's unique ways of pursuing justice.

He sat back in his chair, knitting his hands behind his head. "Your plea, sir?"

"Not guilty," he said. "But I would plead so first on behalf of my grandfather, Joseph Wayland."

A murmur coursed through the gallery. "Order," Gallagher said. "Mr. Breck, I will ask again, what—"

"For me, sir? Also not guilty. I've never been near the house that was broken into, and I dare the prosecution to produce a single piece of evidence that I have. But I will be heard by a community that has steadfastly refused, for five decades, to acknowledge the injustice it delivered upon my family."

The din rose again and the judge slapped his gavel twice. "Your plea is noted," he said. "As for your grandfather, no plea is possible, although I'm familiar with his case, being a bit of a history buff as well as a lifelong parishioner of St. Val's."

I recalled the photo of Mom and the other spelling-bee girls with the nerdy boy named Horace.

"May I speak, sir?"

"Proceed."

Breck cleared his throat. The sound echoed up past the seven oil paintings of dead judges on the walls to the pressed tin ceiling.

I glanced around again for Darlene, didn't find her.

"In 1950," Breck said, "the Archdiocese of Detroit endeavored to build a new church at St. Valentine's in Starvation Lake. The community was growing and the archdiocese desired a bigger building that would bring in more people and more money, most of which, incidentally, would wind up in Detroit."

"Your Honor, forgive me, but now I must object."

Every head turned to the man standing in the back of the gallery. I hadn't noticed him before. "You've got to be kidding me," I whispered.

"Who is that?" Mom said.

"Listen."

"Sir," Judge Gallagher said. "Have you properly noticed the court?"

"Your Honor, my apologies, I am Regis Repelmaus, representing the law firm of Eagan, MacDonald and Browne, counsel for the Archdiocese of Detroit. We cannot allow—"

Gallagher smacked his gavel down. "Sit now, sir, or you will be representing the archdiocese in the Pine County Jail."

Repelmaus frowned and sat.

"Mr. Breck."

Breck continued with the tale he had told me at the jail. He'd begun to describe his furtive research on sexual abuse victims for Eagan, MacDonald & Browne when Repelmaus again stood.

"Your Honor, I must insist," he said. "This is a slander against one of the most respected law firms in the state, against the Archdiocese of Detroit, against—"

"Are you deaf, sir?" Gallagher said.

The double doors at the back of the courtroom opened. Skip Catledge strode in and up the center aisle. He removed his earflap cap and stopped in front of the railing between the gallery and the bench. Dingus leaned over and whispered. Catledge nodded yes. Dingus's eyebrows went up. He said something else, but Catledge moved to the railing while Dingus watched, incredulous.

Gallagher raised a finger for the deputy to wait.

"I beg your pardon, Your Honor," Repelmaus said, "but Mr. Breck is seeking to use this court to engage in a smear campaign that has no basis in fact. The church, the archdiocese, and the law firm each have a right to counter these baseless charges before—"

"What would you have me do, Mr. Regis?"

"It's Repelmaus, Your Honor. I—we would ask that the court adjourn until we've had an opportunity to depose Mr. Breck so that we may prepare a point-by-point rebuttal."

"I understand your concern," Gallagher said. "But this is not a civil matter, it's—"

I jumped to my feet. "No, Judge. Don't even think about dealing with this slimeball."

I felt my mother's alarmed face staring up at me.

"Excuse me?" Gallagher said.

Now every head turned to me.

"Mr. Carpenter," the judge said, "I know you and your mother have had a difficult few days, but you are out of order. Please sit."

"With all due respect, Your Honor, no," I said. "If you want to put me in jail, fine, put me in with Repelmaus, who's just as out of order as I am. But if you allow him and his clients the slightest opening, they will keep this case from being solved forever. They've kept it from being solved for nearly sixty years, and they will persist, Phyllis Bontrager be damned."

"My God, Your Honor, this—" Repelmaus began, but Gallagher rapped his gavel three times and shouted, "Quiet! You will be quiet in my courtroom, Mr. Regis. And you, Mr. Carpenter, will sit down now."

I'd said what I had to say. I sat. Gallagher turned to a uniformed officer standing to his right. "Bailiff," he said, "please remove Mr. Regis to my chambers."

Repelmaus flushed red. "Your Honor, this is unnecessary," he said as the bailiff moved alongside him. "You will regret this."

When the chambers door behind Gallagher's bench closed, the judge addressed Catledge. "Deputy?"

"May I approach?" Catledge said.

Gallagher waved him up. Catledge whispered something. Gallagher replied, nodding. Catledge turned and left the courtroom.

"Mr. Breck," the judge said, "I assume you still have the note your mother left in her will."

"It's in a safe-deposit box along with other documents, such as canceled checks from Eagan, MacDonald and Browne payable to my firm, for services rendered, right up to October of last year."

"About the time you arrived here, is that right?"

"Approximately, yes."

Gallagher took off his glasses, set them down, rubbed his eyes with both hands, put the glasses back on. "You have subsumed much of your life to this cause, Mr. Breck," he said. "All for the sake of a dead man."

"For the sake of a dead woman, Your Honor."

The courtroom doors swung open again. The gallery turned as one to see. Standing on the threshold amid a small phalanx of officers, with an eye swollen shut and his hands cuffed behind him, was Luke Whistler.

Standing behind him was Darlene.

She was hatless. The top two buttons were missing from her uniform shirt, and the fabric was torn where her badge should have been. A wad of gauze was taped haphazardly beneath her left eye. I wanted her to look around the room for me, but she kept her gaze straight ahead. In her outstretched arms she held a plastic evidence bag containing what appeared to be a wooden box.

"Order," the judge said. "Mr. Breck, you may sit." Breck twisted around to see the back of the courtroom. His eyes went wide. Gallagher looked at Catledge. "Deputy?"

Dingus rose from his seat, looking as flabbergasted as I'd ever seen him. "Your Honor, I apologize," he said as he glanced from Gallagher to Whistler and back again. "Deputy Esper was suspended as of last night and should not be here now." I watched Darlene for a reaction, but her face remained a hard blank.

"Sheriff, can you please tell me what's going on here?" Eileen Martin said.

He ignored her, directing himself to Catledge. "Deputy, your orders were to take the prisoners directly to the jail."

"Yes sir, Sheriff." He glanced back at Darlene. "This seemed relevant to the matter in court."

"Deputy Esper is not even—"

"Never mind, Sheriff," Judge Gallagher said. "Deputies, please approach the bench and bring whatever you have."

Catledge prodded Whistler forward. Darlene followed. The box she carried looked to be about three feet long, two feet across, and twelve or thirteen inches deep. On the front was a hasp for a padlock, but no lock. The three of them stopped at the railing.

Darlene spoke. "Lucas Benjamin Whistler, Your Honor."

Whistler stared at the floor. "I want a lawyer," he muttered.

"He killed my mother."

A collective gasp rose from the gallery. I handed Mom a tissue.

"Your Honor," Eileen Martin said, "this is highly irregular."

"We passed irregular about twenty minutes ago," Gallagher said. "Mr. Whistler, you shall have a lawyer. But now, please approach."

Catledge, Darlene, and Whistler walked to the bench. Darlene set the evidence bag in front of the judge. "What is this?" he said.

"Your honor," Darlene replied, "I attempted to apprehend the defendant approximately twenty-five miles west of the border crossing at Port Huron. He disobeyed my instructions to pull his vehicle over, forcing me to—"

"She nearly killed me running me off the road," Whistler said.

"—take more forceful steps."

"Then she just broke into my car, clear illegal search and seizure. You'll be throwing this one out, Judge."

"Since when do we have jurisdiction in Port Huron?" Dingus called from his seat. "You didn't notify the state police?" He jumped to his feet. "Judge, I must ask that you allow me to remove these people immediately."

"I would concur," Eileen Martin said.

"Noted," Gallagher said. "Sit."

Dingus started to say something else, stopped himself, and sat.

"Deputy Esper," the judge said, "is it true that you arrested this man some—what?—two hundred miles from your jurisdiction?"

"Yes, Your Honor," she said.

"And where did you get this box?"

"It was in the trunk of the suspect's car. I believe it's stolen property."

Gallagher studied the box and the three people standing before him. In the gallery we waited, dumbstruck. I thought of Darlene chasing Whistler's Toronado, forcing him to the shoulder in the dark middle of nowhere. They must have struggled, I thought. How else could she have sustained a cut or Whistler a black eye? I wanted to ask her what had happened, why she had decided to go alone, why she had left me behind. I wanted to know how she had restrained herself from taking even more drastic action against the man she believed had killed her mother. I thought I knew what was in the box on Gallagher's bench, but I wanted to see it for myself, not hear about it days or even weeks on, when the state forensics guys finished with it.

I stood. "Your Honor," I said. "We can end this now."

Gallagher looked at me, his eyebrows high over his horn-rims. "Just whose courtroom do you imagine this is?"

"We can solve this case right now."

"We can, can we? I'll humor you—what do you propose before I have the bailiff roust you from this courtroom forevermore."

I glanced past him at the door to his chambers. He followed my eyes. "As you say, Your Honor, it's your courtroom," I said. "But we can solve this case as well as the one that's half a century old. But you will need me, and you will need my mother."

I looked at her. Her head was bowed over her handbag.

Gallagher looked at Whistler and Breck and Darlene. He picked up his gavel and stood. "In my chambers," he said. "Ms. Prosecutor, Sheriff Aho, Deputy Esper. All of you. Bring Mr. Breck and Whistler, please, and Medical Examiner Schriver." He pointed his gavel at me. "Augustus Carpenter," he said. "And Beatrice? You, too." He rapped once more. "This court is in recess."

TWENTY-EIGHT

The blotter on Judge Gallagher's L-shaped mahogany desk was framed in leather the color of blackberries. Gallagher pointed at it and said, "Remove the box from the plastic and place it here, please." Catledge did. The judge fluffed the back of his robe and descended into a leather-backed chair. "You may uncuff these men, Deputy."

I tried to get Whistler's attention as Catledge removed his cuffs, but he kept his eyes down, rubbing first his wrists and then his pinkie ring. I recalled picking the ring up off his desk, how heavy it seemed, and the initials engraved inside: *EJPW*. Elizabeth Josephine Pound Whistler. Bitsy. His mother.

He sat alongside Breck, facing the judge. Dingus stood behind them. Repelmaus stood with the bailiff. I sat with Mom on Gallagher's left, while Eileen, Darlene, and Doc Joe sat in a semicircle across from us. I finally caught Darlene's eye. She didn't smile, but she winked, and I thought maybe I'd done something right.

The judge opened a desk drawer and produced a package of latex gloves. He unwrapped it and pulled the gloves on. "Now," he said, looking around the room, "I plan to take a look at what is inside this box. Unless there's an objection."

"I must respectfully object, Your Honor," Eileen Martin said. "This risks contaminating what could be vital evidence."

"Really, Ms. Martin? How do you know what's in here? It could be nothing."

"But Your Honor, could we at least have some photographs—"

"Overruled."

Dingus spoke. "Your Honor, don't you think—that is, wouldn't you prefer, that the police handle the investigation and we'll come back to you—"

"With what? Yet another suspect?" Gallagher said. "You suspended the only deputy who's actually gotten anything done on this case, is that right?"

"Your Honor, the deputy did not follow—"

"You came into my courtroom this morning to charge this man"—he pointed at Breck—"with some very serious crimes, and an hour later we're sitting here with another man whom I would wager you plan to charge as well, am I right, Sheriff?"

Dingus shifted his bulk, folded his arms. "No objection, Your Honor."

"Thank you. Now, Mr. Regis?" Gallagher said. "I'll allow you to witness this, so long as you tell me you promise to behave, which is to say, keep your mouth shut."

"Yes, Your Honor." Repelmaus cleared his throat and showed the judge a cell phone he'd pulled out of his jacket pocket. "Although it's my duty to inform you that you may soon be getting a fax from Judge Wallace in Detroit."

"Federal judge Joseph Peter Wallace? A good man. Not much of a golfer, but a good man."

"Yes sir. My client has asked Judge Wallace for a temporary restraining—"

"No," Gallagher said, clapping his hands together. "Not another word."

"—order to halt this ad hoc proceeding and—"

"I'm sorry," the judge shouted over Repelmaus, "I haven't heard a word you said and if you speak another, Judge Wallace will have to post your bail."

Repelmaus pursed his lips.

Gallagher turned back to the box. Dirt was caked around its hinges, and it was tall enough that all we could see of the judge was his head and the few stray tufts of silver the chemo had spared. He motioned to Doc Joe. "Could you come over here?" Doc Joe came around behind the judge. Gallagher handed the coroner a pair of latex gloves, then turned to Whistler. "Mr. Whistler," he said, "can you tell us why you're here?"

"I demand a lawyer, Your Honor."

"Well, then, Mr. Breck?" Gallagher said. "Can you tell me why Mr. Whistler is here?"

A fax machine resting on a credenza behind Gallagher sputtered to life, chugging from hum to clatter as it began spitting out a page.

"Pardon me," Gallagher said, turning to Doc Joe. "It's impossible to conduct a conversation with that thing clunking along." Doc Joe reached behind the credenza and yanked a plug from its socket. The machine went silent.

"Judge, you can't be serious," Repelmaus said.

"Much better," Gallagher said. "Mr. Breck?"

Breck looked at Whistler. "He obviously made a mistake," Breck said. "He must have worried that my arrest would lead to his, and he panicked and went looking for that"—he nodded toward the box on the judge's desk—"and somebody figured it out."

Darlene and me, I thought. Finally.

"And why would Mr. Whistler care about what's in this box?"

Breck made a show of turning to look at Repelmaus. "Because he thought it might be worth a lot of money to the archdiocese. Like maybe five million dollars."

I looked at Whistler, who appeared ready to explode, his cheeks crimson, his pinkie ring tap-tap-tapping on his chair arm. I wanted to hear from him.

"Not only that," I interjected, "but he and his partner, one Beverly Taggart, sought to get women in town to help them with their little extortion plot under the guise of writing a history of St. Valentine's Church."

Whistler took the bait. "It wasn't a 'guise,'" he said.

"So, Mr. Whistler, you do want to speak," Gallagher said. "What would this history of yours say?"

Whistler looked around at his audience. He couldn't help himself. "Everything Breck says about the church framing his grandfather is true," he said.

"Preposterous," Repelmaus said.

"They had to frame somebody because Father Nilus Moreau had

killed Sister Cordelia with his bare hands and buried her beneath the old church. Later he moved the bones so they could build the new church."

"How do you know this, Mr. Whistler?" Gallagher said.

"My mother knew Nilus. Only too well."

"Why wouldn't the archdiocese just hand Nilus over to the authorities and wash their hands of him?"

"It was too late for that," I said. "They were already covering up years of Nilus screwing his parishioners."

"Your Honor," Repelmaus pleaded.

"If the murder of a nun came out, everything would come out," I said. "The archdiocese couldn't help but look complicit, and who knows what else." I looked at Repelmaus. "Your pal Reilly didn't tell you about the paternity suits, Regis?"

"Judge," he said, "this man has zero credibility as a journalist. Why is he even in here? What kind of crazy court is this?"

My mother jumped up. "Don't you dare say that about my son."

"Hush, all of you," Gallagher said. "Beatrice, please, sit."

"God damn you to hell, if he hasn't already," she told Repelmaus. She sat.

"Maybe Sheriff Aho should hire your son, Bea," Gallagher said.

"Hah," Whistler said. "He's clueless."

"Enough out of you," Gallagher said. Then, to Repelmaus, "This is not a courtroom, sir, this is my chambers. There is no jury. The rules of evidence do not apply. But since you're so keen on having the facts correct, please tell us: Did Mr. Whistler endeavor to extort money from the archdiocese?"

"I'm sorry, Your Honor, I would have to claim attorney-client privilege."

"Ah. Maybe Mr. Whistler isn't the only one with something to hide." He waited for a reply, but Repelmaus had none. "All right, let's see what could be worth the risks you people have taken."

Gallagher stood. He lifted the hasp on the box. He took hold of the lid with his gloved hands and eased it open. A musty odor floated up from the open box. I imagined the sort of line that would appear in a newspaper story: *The room filled with the smell of death.* I watched Gallagher's face as he examined the inside of the box. Doc Joe moved closer. His face blanched as the judge, whose face did not blanch, reached into the box and handed something to Doc Joe.

The coroner took the skull in one hand, rolled it over into the other. It wasn't much bigger than a softball and was about the same color and roundness, except for a small, irregular oval circumscribed by a hairline crack in the rear left part of the skull. The dent looked like one a ball-peen hammer might make in a sheet of drywall.

"Jesus God," Breck said. Whistler dropped his head to his sweatshirt.

I looked at Mom. Her eyes followed the coroner's hands as he turned the skull this way and that, peering in through the eye sockets and up through the neck.

"Your professional opinion, Doctor?" Gallagher said.

"Purely unofficial, of course," he said. "But on first glance, looks like a female skull, based on its size."

"Human," Gallagher said.

"Certainly."

"And this?" The judge indicated the dented area.

"Probably some sort of blunt force. Hard to tell whether it's passive or aggressive. It's possible she fell. It's possible somebody hit her with something. Not too terribly different from what happened to Phyllis, actually." He peered over his glasses at Mom. "I'm sorry, Bea."

She shook her head softly, pressing a wad of tissue against her lips.

Gallagher put a hand out and Doc Joe placed the skull in it. The judge set it back inside the box. He rested his hands on the edges of the box.

"Beatrice," he said.

Mom had begun to rock back and forth in her chair, her tongue bobbing inside her lips, making an "N": "Nonny Nonny Nonny."

"I haven't heard that name in a long, long time," Gallagher said. "Whatever was it supposed to mean, do you know?"

Mom shook her head again. "Nothing," she said, barely audible.

"Sister Cordelia made cakes for the kids' birthdays," I offered.

Gallagher's smile was gentle. "That's not quite correct," he said. "I was a couple of years ahead of Bea, but St. Val's was a tiny school. Sister Cordelia always made cookies for birthdays. She made cake for Bea's. Didn't she, Bea?"

Mom nodded.

"Bea was her pet."

"She used to keep me in from recess to work on my spelling."

"Did it work?" Gallagher said, still smiling.

"No."

Gallagher addressed the whole room now. "I used to listen to detective dramas on the radio," he said. "I always wondered why that body never washed up. Doc, is there a way to get positive identification?"

"Teeth are loaded with DNA, but I highly doubt we'll find family to match it with," Doc Joe said. "Maybe, with the help of the forensics guys in Lansing, we can reconstruct her smile and compare it to old photos, if we have any."

"Clerk's office," I said. "In the microfilm."

"Here, Horace," Mom said.

I watched as she loosed my hand, unzipped her handbag, and removed her wallet. She unsnapped a wallet pocket, dug inside it, and produced a small black-and-white photograph. She handed it to Gallagher, who looked at it, smiled, and then handed it to Doc Joe.

"This should do," the coroner said.

"There's something else here."

Gallagher reached into the box and plucked out a leather pouch that looked to be wound with white electrical tape. He turned the pouch around in his hands, inspecting it, then grabbed the scissors from the leather cup on his desk.

"Your Honor," Dingus said. "I wish you wouldn't do that."

"That is evidence, Your Honor," Eileen said.

Gallagher sliced through the tape and peeled it back from the top of the pouch. "The zipper's a little rusty," he said. He pulled on it hard and it tore open with a puff of reddish dust. Gallagher perched his horn-rims on his forehead and peered into the pouch. With two fingers he pulled out a yellowish envelope. He set the pouch aside and squinted at the envelope seal.

"Please be careful, Your Honor," Dingus said.

"Agreed, Your Honor," Repelmaus said. "I respectfully submit that these materials be left alone until their relevance and admissibility can be properly adjudicated."

Gallagher slid a fingernail beneath the seal. The envelope opened. The judge bent slightly and the envelope dipped below his desktop to where we couldn't see it. He paused, apparently reading. Then he straightened and set the envelope on his desk. In one hand he held some pages that had been folded in thirds.

"This is a letter, or appears to be," he said. "Written in what looks to be pen, in a rather florid hand, on the letterhead of St. Valentine's Roman Catholic Church, Starvation Lake, Michigan." He flipped to the last page. "It is signed by Father Nilus Moreau."

"Without objection," he said, "I'm going to read the first page." He waited, but by now even Repelmaus had given up objecting.

The judge read.

"Father, forgive me, for I have sinned. I have succumbed to the temptations of the flesh, to the venal allure of physical pleasure, to the enrapture of lust and all that goes before it, and with it, and alongside it. I have let sin reign in my mortal body and I have obeyed its desires. I have committed atrocity and tolerated it and sought the false and sinful asylum of denial. I have made company with men who would do the same, while demanding my silence and wicked acquiescence. I seek your divine mercy and everlasting forgiveness as I write these things down on the twenty-first day of August in the year 1950—"

Mom pitched forward over her knees, her hands clenched into fists at her breast. "Mom," I said, reaching across her shoulders, "are you all right?"

Gallagher looked up. "Beatrice?"

"Go ahead, Horace," she said. "Just go ahead."

*   *   *

Nilus met Sister Mary Cordelia at a convent in Midland, when he was an associate pastor at St. John Bosco Catholic Church. She was, he wrote, "as pure and delicate and lovely as a begonia open to the sun." And merely eighteen years old when she became pregnant with Nilus's child.

She refused an abortion. Her habit kept her from showing early but, before her belly became impossible to hide, Nilus arranged for her to stay for the rest of her pregnancy with his sister in Sandusky, about eighty miles east. In May 1933, Sister Cordelia gave birth to a girl who was immediately moved to an orphanage in Midland and then, the following year, to a different Catholic orphanage in the town that would soon become Starvation Lake, where Nilus had become assistant pastor of St. Valentine's. Sister Mary Cordelia followed. She became a teacher at St. Valentine's and helped at the orphanage.

Nilus and Cordelia vowed to remain chaste and be thankful that they had not been discovered, so they could take secret joy in watching their daughter blossom, if from a distance. Each night, they prayed that the family who adopted the child, unnamed in Nilus's letter, would never take her away.

"There followed several years of acute and unremitting pain as I struggled to sustain my faith while longings for Cordelia insisted themselves upon me," Nilus wrote. "It was then that Elizabeth Whistler entered into my life and lured me into the compounding of mortal sin that would damn my soul to eternity, Lord, if not for the saving grace and mercy which I pray you will bestow upon your unworthy servant."

It was the fall of 1942. Bitsy Whistler was a member of the Women's Guild at St. Valentine's. She saw Nilus on occasion at bake sales and pancake breakfasts the guild organized. "Elizabeth was a woman with a heavy soul," Nilus wrote, "having lost her heroic husband in the world war." She sought Nilus's advice—or so Nilus said—and, soon, counsel turned to consolation, which turned to love, or what passed for it between a despondent woman and a priest who labored under the weight of knowing he had made a mistake with the most important decision of his life.

Initially, Bitsy agreed to a quiet abortion of Nilus's child and moved south, to Clare, where she stayed with a cousin who convinced her that an abortion would be a sin for which she could never atone. When she returned to Starvation Lake in the spring of 1944, she brought with her a boy—also unnamed in Nilus's missive—who the townsfolk assumed was the son of her late husband, conceived on a leave shortly before his death at Bataan. Nilus gave Bitsy a job in the sacristy cleaning the chalices, cruets, and other furnishings used at Mass and paid her himself, in cash.

It wasn't long before Nilus and Bitsy were trysting again. After every few assignations, Bitsy would demand that Nilus increase the amount of money he paid her. Fearing exposure, and too weak to resist her enticements, he complied. "I was remiss, dear Lord, in countenancing the presence of Satan himself, or herself, in the person of Bitsy Whistler," Nilus wrote. "I was weak, weak unto my soul, weak in the flesh."

I looked at Whistler. He was shaking his head in disbelief, or denial.

"It was on such an evening, with my will at its most frail, that my sins came to bear the terrible fruits to which I confess. It was six years ago, almost to this day."

Sister Cordelia had gone to the sacristy looking for Nilus, to tell him their secret daughter had done well in a waterskiing contest. The sacristy was dark, but she heard voices inside. "She found us, O Lord, she found us," Nilus wrote, "and my life will never be the same, God forgive me, God forgive my soul." Cordelia, enraged, flung herself at Nilus. Bitsy stepped between them. The women struggled. Bitsy, the larger, took hold of Cordelia's cowl and thrust her away. The nun spun backward and smacked her head on the corner of a counter, crumpling to the floor. In seconds, blood had soaked her veil.

"You must forgive Elizabeth, Lord, for what happened next, for she knew not what she was doing," Nilus said.

Whistler came out of his chair. "No," he said. "He's lying." Darlene jumped up and grabbed him by the shoulders. He tried to wrestle free, but Dingus stepped between them and slammed Whistler back down into his chair.

"Bullshit," Whistler said.

Dingus snapped handcuffs off of his belt and said, "Judge?"

"My mother did not kill that nun."

"Are you finished?" Gallagher said. "Do you want to hear the rest?"

"He's lying, I'm telling you." He looked around the room as if someone might sympathize. "Goddammit. All right, I'll settle down. But Nilus is lying to save his own ass."

"We'll never know, will we?"

"I know," Whistler said.

Gallagher resumed reading.

Bitsy went to a closet and removed a black cassock. She folded it upon itself several times and, kneeling in the spreading puddle of Cordelia's blood, placed it tight over the nun's face.

"I told her no, Lord, but I was too weak, too selfish, too fearful for my own welfare, to stop her," Nilus wrote. "I thank you, dear Lord, that Cordelia did not appear to suffer."

"Liar," Whistler said.

Mom was doubled over now, quietly sobbing.

Nilus and Bitsy buried Cordelia in a crawl space beneath St. Valentine's. Two years later, in 1946, Bisty and her young son moved downstate.

"With temptation removed, I redoubled my efforts to dedicate myself to you, Lord, by raising the necessary means to build a church that would give you greater glory." Nilus wrote. "Circumstances arose, however, in which the Archdiocese of Detroit felt obliged to direct my actions. And so it is at the urging of Father Timothy Reilly that—"

"Your Honor," Repelmaus said, "I demand that this, this, this proceeding, whatever it is, be adjourned now, before more rank speculation and unconfirmed evidence is allowed to slander the good name of my client."

Gallagher looked at him. "You have a client named Father Timothy?"

"Actually, Your Honor—"

"Let me guess: attorney-client privilege?" Gallagher said.

"Father Timothy Reilly," I said, "was the spokesman for the archdiocese quoted in the stories about Wayland's murder in 1950."

"You may leave now, Regis," the judge said.

"Your Honor, you can't be—"

"Bailiff?"

When the door had closed, Gallagher read the rest of the letter.

Nilus told Father Timothy about the nun buried beneath the church. Father Timothy, Nilus wrote, came to see him one night that August of 1950. He told Nilus that someone tearing down the old church might find the remains. He suggested that Nilus disinter Sister Cordelia and rebury her somewhere she would never be found.

And so, on August 21, 1950, he had.

His letter didn't say that my mother had helped.

"Some confession," I said. "He blames everybody and everything but himself for the murder of a nun and the subsequent cover-up." I looked at Breck. "I'm sure you noticed there's no mention of your grandfather."

"I am not surprised," Breck said.

"Mr. Whistler," Gallagher said, "are you the son of Father Nilus Moreau?"

Whistler had turned pale. "Technically."

"Horace," Mom said. "I've had enough."

"I can imagine," he said. "Mr. Whistler, it would be prudent for you now to keep in mind that anything you say can and will be used against you." He turned to Eileen Martin. "Ms. Prosecutor, do you plan to file charges against this man?"

"I need to confer with the sheriff," she said.

"Then do so expeditiously. And what of Mr. Breck?"

"You have his plea, Your Honor."

"And a paucity of evidence. However, I suspect Mr. Breck may have information that could be useful to your investigation. Did you hear that, Sheriff Aho?"

Dingus was whispering with Doc Joe. "Sorry?" he said.

"Sheriff, you ought to listen up," Gallagher said. "You haven't exactly covered yourself in glory these past few weeks."

Dingus's mustache twitched. "Yes, Your Honor. May I interrupt?"

"Interrupt."

"That ring," he said. "I'll need it."

Whistler grabbed his pinkie ring with the other hand. "First I want a lawyer."

"They'll confiscate it at the jail," Gallagher said.

"Doc Joe, you've got the gloves on," Dingus said.

The coroner held a gloved hand out. Whistler slipped the ring off and handed it over.

"So," the judge said, "when we return to the courtroom, I will bind Mr. Breck over for trial in the hope that he might find ways to be helpful."

"Noted, Your Honor," Eileen said.

Gallagher placed the pouch back in the box and closed the lid.

"These items are now sealed until the court rules otherwise," he said. "Deputy Catledge, please cuff the prisoners. Sheriff, I turn Deputy Esper back over to you for whatever you must do. But now let's get back in court—everyone but you two."

He meant Mom and me.

"Why?" I said.

"You can leave through my clerk's office."

"What are we supposed to do, Horace?" Mom said.

"As your son said, solve the case."

"I don't know what you mean."

"I trust you'll figure it out."

Everyone stood. Mom and I watched the others file back to the courtroom.

"Wait," I said. "Darlene."

I started toward her. She turned around and came to me. Dingus didn't try to stop her. We embraced, Darlene burying her face in my chest.

"I had to go myself," she said. "I'm sorry."

"It's all right," I said. "It's almost over."

We held each other for a long minute. Dingus finally took Darlene by an elbow.

"Careful, Dingus," I said. "You don't want to lose your best deputy."

Gallagher was last to leave. "Take care of your mother," he said. "And Bea, you take care of your son."

TWENTY-NINE

When's the last time you were here?" I said.

Mom and I had left the courthouse and, at my insistence, walked down Main to Estelle, then turned north and gone six blocks. We stood now behind the empty rows of varnished wooden pews in St. Valentine's Roman Catholic Church. I wasn't sure why I wanted to go there. Maybe to jog Mom's memory, maybe to make her feel things she preferred not to feel. Maybe for me. It felt like the only way.

"Funerals and weddings," Mom said. "But Sunday Mass, not lately."

"It seems like a nice church."

"It's a building. They knocked the other down and they can knock this one down, too."

Stone columns embellished with gold-leaf carvings rose four stories to a vaulted ceiling painted sky blue with stars of gold. An enormous crucifix, Christ's head lolling to his right, hovered over the marble altar. A statue of St. Joseph was missing three fingers. The patterned rugs running the length of the church were worn to a pinkish gray.

"There was quite a row over the stained-glass windows way back when," Mom said. "The archdiocese said they were too expensive. Nilus ordered them anyway. There were special collections every Sunday for years to pay for them."

"So the parish paid for Nilus's guilt."

She walked to one of the windows, unlocked a transom, and pushed it open. Cold air blew into the church.

"Look," Mom said.

I walked over and leaned my head down so I could see out the transom. All I saw was a stand of snow-covered scrub pines at the bottom of a slope. "What about it?"

"That's where the old church was. See the foundation?"

In the middle of the trees, two jagged outcroppings of concrete jutted up from the snow.

"Right."

"That's where Nonny was. For six years, until . . ."

Her voice trailed off.

"So what else is there, Mom?"

"This is not about me, Gus. It's about Phyllis."

"No. You know it's about you. You've always known it."

"I wish I wasn't afraid."

"Afraid of what?"

"Of being somebody else."

"What are you talking about?"

"Some days I can't remember what I did ten minutes ago. I can't tell you how many times I've gone out to get the mail only to realize I'd already gotten it earlier. But I can remember everything from ages ago as if it was yesterday."

"Why don't you just tell me then? What else?"

"Son. I was seventeen years old and an accessory to murder."

"No. You didn't know you were burying a nun."

"Not then. But later."

"What do you mean?"

"That priest. That despicable man."

She met him in a conference room at a law firm on Shelby Street in downtown Detroit. It was the summer of 1971.

Father Timothy Reilly sat at one end of a long table. Beatrice sat to his left. The room was warm and smelled of cigar smoke. The priest wore a dark jacket and shirt with a Roman collar. He thanked her for coming. He told her that Father Nilus Moreau had recently died in a hospital on the Keweenau Peninsula.

"He was a friend when you were a girl?" the priest said.

"Yes," Bea said. "We lost touch."

"I see. He remembered you, even at the very end."

"That's nice. Is that why you asked to see me?"

She'd heard from a lawyer named Eagan that a priest who'd once met her when she was a child wanted to see her the next time she was in Detroit. She wondered why, but she wasn't eager to make the trip merely to satisfy her curiosity. When the lawyer called again to say the matter was "of a pressing nature" and mentioned Father Nilus Moreau, she decided she'd better get in the car.

Reilly didn't answer her question. Instead he said, "Your own husband died recently?"

"Last year."

The priest made a sign of the cross. "May his soul rest in peace."

"Thank you."

"Beatrice," Reilly said, "I need to take you into my confidence. What I'm about to say is of a rather delicate nature."

"A pressing matter."

"Indeed. I believe you also knew Sister Mary Cordelia Gallesero, did you not?"

The question startled her. She sat back in her chair. "Yes, Father. Why?"

Reilly folded his hands on the table and leaned over them toward Bea. "Forgive me for being direct," he said. Then he told her that, based on a confession Father Nilus had given as part of his last rites, she apparently had been party to the death of Sister Cordelia.

"No. That's ridiculous," Bea said. "Nonny—Sister Cordelia disappeared when I was a girl. I missed her terribly."

"Nonny. Yes, of course. I don't mean, child, to imply that you participated in the actual murder of Sister Cordelia."

"Murder?"

"We now believe she was murdered."

Bea felt nauseated. "By who?"

"It's not clear, unfortunately. What is clear, at least as Father Nilus confessed it to his God, is that you were involved in the disposal of the good nun's remains."

It all came rushing back: the humid evening forest, the smell of the earthworms, Nilus's shiny black shoes at the rim of the hole.

"No," was all she could think to say.

This was a crime, the priest explained, almost certainly a felony, and if she were to be convicted, she could land in prison. That would be especially tragic now that her husband had died, he said, because there would be no family left to care for her young son.

Bea felt the queasiness well in her stomach. "Father, what are you saying? I didn't know what Father Nilus was burying there. I didn't know what—"

"So you were there?"

She felt faint. She told herself to catch her breath. "Where?" she said.

"You don't know where? Beatrice, God is listening."

"Father, no, this . . . this can't be—he said they were vestments and other old things. It was just a penance for me to dig a hole, to remind me I came from dirt."

"Father Nilus took you into his confidence."

"He did not."

"Are you certain?"

She heard impatience in Reilly's voice.

"I am certain. I did not know that"—now her voice caught—"that Nonny was . . . was there."

"I see. His recollection differed."

"Then he lied."

Reilly offered his handkerchief. She waved it away.

"Beatrice, think. Why would a priest lie on his deathbed, standing at the gates of Heaven?"

Reilly rose and walked to a credenza that held a tray with glasses and a pitcher of water. He poured Bea a glass, set it down in front of her, and sat down again.

"Please, Beatrice, don't worry," he said. "You were only a child."

"I was."

"And you had sinned."

"What do you mean?"

"You were doing penance because you had confessed to a sin. A mortal sin."

Bea swallowed hard.

"But look," Reilly said, "the fact is, the church has no desire to unearth this regretful episode. There is nothing to be gained. You are a good, practicing Catholic who I assume has earned God's forgiveness. Let me ask you this: Could you by chance recollect where Father Nilus buried the poor Sister's remains?"

She thought about this, decided she could answer yes.

"Why do you ask?" she said.

"Well, we've thought that, perhaps if we could discreetly locate them, we could give Sister Cordelia the proper religious burial she deserves."

"But you don't plan to tell the police?"

"So many years on, Beatrice." He shook his head. "This is no longer a matter for men, but for God."

Bea picked up the glass of water and drank. She set it down empty. "I'm sorry, Father," she said. "I don't remember."

"Are you sure?"

"It was dark. We were way up on a hill somewhere in the woods where I'd never been before. It was a little scary, actually. I just wanted to get home."

"Nilus told us the northeastern corner of the lake."

"Maybe he remembers then. I don't."

The priest stood. Bea did, too. "Would you like my blessing, child?" he said.

"That won't be necessary."

He made a sign of the cross before her anyway. "I trust you'll keep all of this to yourself," he said.

"Why wouldn't I?"

"We may be in touch, from time to time."

She walked up Shelby and turned right on Lafayette, glancing over her shoulder to make sure she wasn't being followed. At Woodward she turned left and walked to Sanders, the ice-cream parlor. She took a stool at the counter and ordered a Coca-Cola with ice. She took a pen out of her purse. She flipped over the placemat and, on the blank back, drew a map.

* * *

"You remembered?" I said.

We'd sat down in the pew at the very back of St. Valentine's. A painting on the wall next to us showed a woman wiping Christ's face as he carried his cross.

"It was impossible to forget," Mom said. "The big stump. The double-trunk birch."

"And you gave pieces of the map to Mrs. B and Soupy's mom."

"Oh, God," she said. "Louise. She was so sorry."

"Because she'd talked to Bev—to that woman doing the history with Whistler?"

Mom looked as if she might cry again. "Louise came to me to apologize. She was a basket case. But I didn't care. She said she hadn't given the lady much. She so wanted my forgiveness. But I would not give it. All I could think about was my fear."

"It's all right, Mom."

"No, it's not. Never. I never should have done that to my friends. It's just—I was alone. I wanted someone else to know, just in case."

"In case that bastard Reilly did something."

"Yes."

"Why didn't you go to the police?"

"I don't—no. I do know. Because I didn't want that life."

"What life?"

"I didn't want to be the girl who helped bury a murdered nun, who helped a murderer and the terrible men who hid him. I didn't want to be the girl who cheated on her boyfriend. I just wanted to be Bea, Gus's mom, and live in the yellow house on the lake, like Rudy and I had always planned."

The shadow of a smile crossed her face.

"We used to go fishing," she said. "Do you remember throwing your pole in the lake?"

It was a casting pole with a button on the reel that let the line out when you flung the pole forward. I was four or five years old. I hit the button but didn't hang on to the pole. My dad was about to jump in after it until Mom grabbed him and they fell over laughing in the row-boat.

"Yes," I said. "Pretty stupid."

"I was happy, Gussy. That's all I wanted."

A happy family. I thought of my next-door neighbor, Oke Anderson, sitting down to dinner with his family. I took one of Mom's hands.

"And you hoped the rest would go away," I said.

"I could've just drawn Reilly the map. But when he said it was 'no longer a matter for men,' I just . . . I decided I wasn't going to tell him anything. I'm not sure why. But I didn't like what he said, or the way he said it."

We sat there for a while, Mom's hand in mine.

"So," I finally said, "what happened the other night? Can you remember?"

She sighed. "I remember this. I remember sitting at the dining room table that morning and Phyllis telling me I was imagining things."

"You were worried about the burglar not taking anything."

"Turns out I wasn't paranoid."

A noise awoke Mom in her bed that night. She wondered if maybe she'd been dreaming. She'd been dreaming a lot lately. In her dreams, she could remember what she'd had for breakfast and where she'd left her handbag.

She drifted back to sleep. She didn't know how much later, maybe an hour, maybe ten seconds, she heard a thump. She thought it came from the bathroom. Had Phyllis come over tonight? "Phyllis?" she called out. There was no answer. She thought she must have been mistaken about Phyllis being there. She went back to sleep.

She woke again later, needing to use the bathroom. She tried to push the bathroom door open but it stopped against something. She walked around to the door at the other end of the bathroom. Phyllis was sprawled across the Me Sweet Ho rug, unmoving, her eyes closed. Blood had splattered on the rug and pooled on the floor around her head. Her cell phone lay on the floor.

"Was she alive?"

"I don't think so."

"What do you mean you don't think so?"

"No. She wasn't alive."

"How long had she been lying there?"

"I have no way of knowing. I was asleep."

"So you called nine-one-one?"

"When I saw her lying there, I knew I was right to be afraid. I knew they'd come looking."

Whistler hadn't expected to find anyone there. After he slid into the bathroom and Mrs. B saw him, he must have panicked. When he'd panicked in the past, he'd put his fist through computer screens. The pinkie ring must have made the gash above Mrs. B's eye. That's why Dingus demanded it, I thought.

"And you called?" I said.

"Phyllis was dead, but I called. I had to hurry."

She went back to her room. She dug the lockbox containing the piece of map, her rosary, and the newspaper clipping out of the back of the closet. She threw her boots on and ran through the big yard, across the road, and up the hill to Dad's garage. She put the lockbox in the trunk of the Bonneville, neglecting to close the lid tightly, and stood there for a few seconds, willing herself to remember. Then she ran back to her house.

"You panicked," I said. "And you lost your boot."

"I couldn't stop. I could hear a siren. I had to get back. The next morning, I saw the one boot at the back door and couldn't remember what had happened to the other."

"But you remembered where the lockbox was."

"Yes."

"And you called nine-one-one before you went up to the garage?"

"Isn't that what I said?"

"Just making sure you remember correctly. That's a hike to get back before—"

"I know, Gussy. That's how I lost my boot."

She let go of my hand and stood and walked back to the transom. I followed, stopping a few feet behind her.

"I don't know what to say," she said.

"Why?"

"I might as well have killed Phyllis with my own hands."

"No. Let it go, Mom. There was nothing—"

"Stop." She spun to face me, her eyes filling with tears. "Stop telling me everything I did was all right. I made choices. Now my best friends are gone."

"It wasn't just your—"

"Stop, goddammit." Her voice echoed through the church. "You know the truth now. All right? I told you the truth. Everyone knows the truth. Are you all happy now? Are you free? Has the truth set you free, Gus?"

I stepped close and wrapped my arms around her. I whispered into her ear, "I'm glad you told me the truth." I held her longer and tighter than I had in years.

She sighed as she loosed my embrace. "I'm glad you're glad," she said. "Now can you take me home, please? I can't stay in this place any longer."

I dropped her at her house. Someone had plowed her driveway. I thought maybe I ought to stay awhile, but she told me she wanted to be alone. After all she'd gotten through for so long, I figured she'd get through this, too.

The last story for the final print edition of the *Pilot* went from my computer screen to the printing plant five minutes before deadline.

"Good-bye," I said.

I supposed somebody in Traverse City would plant a "Note to Readers" on the front page telling them Media North was ceasing publication of the *Pilot*. The note would thank subscribers for their loyalty and vow that coverage of their "region," never mind their county or their town, would continue unabated, because nobody was more devoted to the news than Media North.

There were no speeches or tributes or weeping staffers standing around with undone ties and dangling press passes. There was just me and the reek of toner and the buzzing of the lamps.

The single story I wrote concerned Judge Gallagher binding both Breck and Whistler over for trial. Of course, I couldn't report what happened in the judge's chambers. But I did plan to tell Darlene what Mom told me about her long-ago meeting with Reilly.

After sending the story, I dialed into the *Pilot* voice mail system, in case there was a message I wanted or, more likely, one I didn't want my bosses to hear. There were fifty-six messages in all. One by one I deleted them after listening to a few seconds of each, until I came to message twenty-two.

"Anyone checking on those whackaroonies at the Christian camp?" the muffled male voice said. "They're all agitated with the county. Maybe they're just messing with us, and now they made a big damn mistake."

Something about it bothered me. I played it again. The voice was muffled enough that it seemed to be intentional. In the background, I heard a clicking sound. I figured out how to turn up the volume and played it again. And then once more.

I knew that clicking: Whistler's ring on his steering wheel. And then I thought, Holy shit, I'll bet it was him, not D'Alessio, who tipped the cops that Tatch didn't show up for that hockey game. Whistler had heard me talk about it at the hospital that night. D'Alessio probably hadn't given it another thought.

I saved message twenty-two and made a mental note to tell Darlene about that, too.

Once I'd deleted the other messages, I packed up my Tigers beer stein, a few pens, a legal pad, a stapler, a box of paper clips, and a package of printer paper. I went up front and gathered up Mrs. B's photographs.

I snapped the lights off at twenty-six minutes past five. I was almost out the door when I remembered my keyboard. I'd written hundreds of stories on it and liked the feel of the keys. I went back and unplugged it and tucked it under my arm.

Seven hours later, I had to bring it back, because I had one more story to write. It was too late for the paper but I posted it online before I headed over to the celebration at Enright's.

UPSET! RATS SINK PIPEFITTERS, GO TO MICHIGAN STATE FINAL

By A. J. Carpenter
Pilot Staff Correspondent

In a triple-overtime thriller that ranks with the biggest upsets in Michigan hockey history, the Hungry River Rats of Starvation Lake beat the Pipefitters of Trenton, 2–1, to advance to Saturday's state championship final.

Goaltender Dougie Baker stopped a play-off record 71 shots in a performance River Rats Coach Dick Popovich called "absolutely stunning." Highlights included a diving glove save on a breakaway by Pipefitter star Bobby Hofmeister with 18 seconds remaining in the second overtime.

The victory marked the first time the River Rats (23–6–2) had ever beaten the Pipefitters (27–3–1). The teams came into the game ranked #7 and #2 in the state, respectively.

The Rats' other star was on the ice for less than ten seconds. Team scoring leader Matthew "Tex" Dobrick wasn't expected to play due to a severe ankle sprain.

But Dobrick showed up in uniform, skated in the team's pregame warm-up, and appeared at center ice for the opening face-off before retiring to the bench, in obvious pain, for the rest of the game.

"Tough kid," said Pipefitters Coach Ron Wallman. "We came into the building figuring he was a scratch, and seeing him out there messed with our heads."

A packed Starvation Lake Arena exploded nearly four minutes into the third overtime when Ethan Banonis banged in a rebound for the win.

"It's a great moment for a great town," Popovich said. "But we still have work to do."

The Rats will play for the state title in their home rink at 5 p.m. Saturday against the top-ranked Austin Painters (28–0–3), who beat Fife Electric, 6–3, in the earlier semifinal.

The Rats have played for the state title only once before. In 1981, they lost to the Pipefitters, 2–1, on a questionable overtime score allowed by goaltender Augustus Carpenter.

THIRTY

The sky was flawless blue outside the barred window behind Luke Whistler's head.

It was a morning in July. Whistler sat across from me with his manacled hands folded atop the metal table, his white hair trimmed to a crew cut, his pinkie naked of his ring. His black Toronado was parked outside in the impound lot of the Pine County Jail.

"Enjoying your stay, Luke?" I said.

He'd been refusing my requests to speak with him since his trial in May. On this morning, one hour before he was to appear in court for his sentencing, Darlene had rousted him from his jail cell and brought him to the interview room where I was waiting.

"Piss off, junior," he said. "You're a minor-leaguer and that's all you'll ever be."

"And your journalism career has ended badly, as predicted," I said. "What happened to your ring? The cops hock it?"

At trial it had come out that Bitsy Whistler, before departing Starvation Lake for the last time, had swiped a ciborium from the sacristy at St. Valentine's. After she died, Whistler had it melted down and made into the ring.

"These cops are fuckups," Whistler said. "You watch—I'm getting off on appeal. I didn't kill anyone. Yeah, I panicked, but I didn't hit anybody hard enough to kill them. She had a heart attack. I couldn't help that."

The jury had convicted Whistler of manslaughter. Dingus had wanted a charge of second-degree murder, but Eileen Martin didn't think she could make it stick. Except for a fingerprint Whistler could have left the night he had dinner at Mom's, there was no physical evidence that he'd actually been in the house. Whistler had learned well from the burglar he'd followed on that aborted *Free Press* story.

With a little help from me, Darlene dug up evidence suggesting Whistler had motive. There were canceled checks written to Whistler's mother by Nilus until just before his death, and then by various people at Eagan, MacDonald & Browne until Bitsy died.

"That's not what the jury said, is it, Luke?" I said. "If it was a heart attack, why'd you go to such lengths to point the finger elsewhere—the message on the voice mail, making me think I was discovering stuff about Nilus when you knew about it all along? Huh? Why didn't you just come clean?"

"I had a story to get."

"That reminds me. I know how you knew about your mother killing the nun—"

"Nilus killed the nun."

"Right. I know how you knew she was buried under the church, but how did you know about Nilus moving her?"

Whistler shrugged. "He made a few visits to see my mother downstate. You can read all about it in my book."

The *Detroit Times*, under the byline of M. Joan McCarthy, had reported that at least two New York publishers had expressed interest in a Lucas B. Whistler memoir. It infuriated me, but what could I do? People wanted to read that sort of stuff, so other people published it. It wasn't all that different from how I'd made my living.

Now, though, sitting within reach of the man who had killed a woman I loved who was the mother of another woman I loved, I recalled Poppy's advice to Tex. With one hard, unexpected right, I could shatter Whistler's nose, break his jaw, watch him suffer, if only until Darlene came in and dragged me away.

I stood and moved around the table to Whistler's right. He looked up at me.

"A book's a pretty good idea," I said. "Maybe I'll write one."

"Go fuck yourself."

"You too, Luke. I'll miss you in court today, though. Going fishing."

*   *   *

State troopers arrested Father Timothy Reilly one week after the arraignments of Breck and Whistler. The archdiocese and the state cops had arranged it so he'd be taken into custody in the middle of the night, when no reporters were around.

But Dingus got a heads-up. Catledge heard and called Darlene at home, where she was finishing up her suspension. She told me and I called Joanie McCarthy, who was waiting with a *Times* photographer when police brought Reilly out in cuffs.

Judge Gallagher bound Reilly over for trial on a charge of first-degree murder in the 1944 disappearance of Sister Mary Cordelia Gallesero. The priest refused to speak to the police and stood mute in the courtroom, where his lawyers from Eagan, MacDonald & Browne plied Gallagher's deaf ears with pleas to leave an old man be. Dingus and Eileen Martin knew the charge was over the top, but they hoped to elicit evidence that Reilly had conspired in the past year to conceal what Nilus and Bitsy Whistler had done.

In the meantime, Reilly, out on bond, went into hiding while the Detroit newspapers wrote story after story about the archdiocese's alleged cover-up of Nilus's chronic womanizing, the death of the nun, the reburial of her bones. I was able to slip Joanie a few tips on where to find paternity suits. One day I got an e-mail from her that made me smile: "Our buddy Regis is no longer in the employ of Eagan MacDonald." She said she owed me a Red Wings game, and I said that if I could bring Darlene along, that would be fine.

After his release, soon after Reilly's arrest, Wayland Breck rented a cabin on Crooked Lake so he could keep tabs on the trials of the priest and Whistler and assist the prosecution where needed. But when Tatch and his fellow Christian campers heard Breck was still around, they organized daily pickets at his cabin. If the *Pilot* had still been publishing, it would have run a three-column photo of people parading past his house, holding signs that said BRECK GO HOME and LIARS BELONG DOWNSTATE. Breck left Starvation in early June.

The Michigan State Bar's Judicial Ethics Committee came down hard on Judge Gallagher after learning of the shenanigans in his chambers. Rather than face censure, Gallagher retired. He posted his typewritten resignation letter on a bulletin board at Audrey's Diner amid ads for propane and landscaping services. The letter thanked everyone in Starvation, "especially those who both violate and enforce the law, for making my life so interesting for more than forty years." He said quitting wasn't difficult because his cancer had spread and he was moving to Arizona where he would "bask in the warmth of the Lord while preparing for the one verdict that truly matters."

The sun hovered just over the tree line at the lake's far end. I was sitting in the oak swing on the bluff at Mom's house. I felt a hand on my shoulder.

"What are you doing?" Darlene said.

"Just looking at the lake. The sun's still out and what is it? Nine o'clock?"

"About."

"I love July."

"So did your mother," Darlene said. She had a towel knotted over her bikini bottom. She sat, her bare knee grazing my thigh. "How was fishing?"

"Not much biting, but fun to hang with Soup."

"How is he?"

"You know. Polished off a six-pack by the time we got to the cove. Thinking of selling the bar. Or maybe not. He got a legit offer on his parents' place. That should tide him over for, I don't know, a month or two."

"Poor Soupy."

"And he got a dog."

"No."

"Yeah. My fault. I showed him a picture of old Stanley, he wanted another dog."

"Is this one afraid of umbrellas, too?"

I laughed.

"So," I said, "Whistler got the max?"

"Fifteen years."

"Did you get to usher him out?"

"No. Watched from the cheap seats. I'm not quite back in Dingus's good graces."

"You'll get there."

She stretched her arms over her head and wagged her neck back and forth. "I was so sweaty from all the unpacking, I had to go for a dip."

I had watched her from the swing. She swam freestyle straight out from the dock a hundred yards, then flipped on her back and paddled out to the middle of the lake, where all I could see was the wake of her kicking feet. I could have watched all night.

I reached into my pocket and pulled out a photograph and a folded piece of paper.

"Good thing I didn't toss that box," I said.

"Which box?"

"The one from Mom sitting on my sofa for weeks. It had a bunch of crayon drawings I did as a kid and report cards and other junk. But this is actually interesting."

I handed Darlene the Polaroid. She looked. I saw her eyes mist.

"Mom," she said. "And look how cute you are."

The photo was black and white. Mrs. B sat astride a hospital bed with an arm around me, her eyes wide and happy behind her big glasses. I was trying to smile but my throat probably hurt too much.

"Where is this?" Darlene said.

"A hospital downstate. I just got my tonsils out."

"Why was my mother there? I don't remember this."

"Supposedly she was there because Mom couldn't handle hospitals after Dad died. But this"—I brandished the folded paper—"suggests Mom was up to something else."

It appeared to have been torn from the kind of notepad Mom kept by her kitchen phone. I gave it to Darlene. "Oh, gosh," she said.

I'd found it stuck to the back of the Polaroid. Written on it in my mother's handwriting was the address and phone number for Eagan, MacDonald & Browne on Shelby Street in downtown Detroit.

"That's when she saw Reilly," Darlene said.

"Gotta be. He isn't going to get off, is he?"

"He has some good lawyers."

"Paid for by the collection basket," I said. "At the very least, he's dragging the archdiocese's name through the mud."

"Is that important to you?" Darlene said.

"I don't mind it."

She turned her body on the swing to face me. "I lost my mother, but I don't intend to lose my faith. She was too strong for that."

I wanted nothing but peace with Darlene. We were neighbors now, she in her mother's house, me in Mom's. We had agreed to live that close, maybe sell one of the houses later, move into the other together. For now, we were close enough that I could leave her bed in the middle of the night and walk home, and she could do the same.

I pulled an envelope out of my other pocket, feeling the raised letters within. "This finally came today," I said. "You know, Verna Clark could take a lesson from the clerk in Sanilac County. Her name is Bonnie Orwall and she's a peach."

Darlene took it. The return address said Sandusky, Michigan. "You haven't opened it?"

"I already know what's in it," I said.

To honor the River Rats' best season in nineteen years, the town council won the state's permission to post a commemorative sign at the Starvation Lake exit on I-75.

A sign-posting ceremony was held at noon on the Friday of Memorial Day weekend. Townspeople assembled in a cornfield along the highway. County commissioner Elvis Bontrager presented the sign to DOT workers who then anchored it on the shoulder near the beginning of the exit ramp. The sign, a rectangle of white lettering on a green background, announced the River Rats as the 2000 Michigan State Hockey Runners-Up.

The Rats had lost, 3–2, to the Austin Painters in the championship final. Dougie Baker played another acrobatic game, stopping forty-six shots. It wasn't enough. The Painters jumped out to a 2–0 lead, then made it 3–1 in the middle of the third period. They got to celebrating a bit early and Danny FitzGerald scored to pull the Rats within a goal with under two minutes remaining. The hometown crowd went wild, banging on the glass, waving the big blue-and-gold Rats banners. Coach Poppy pulled Dougie for a sixth skater. Maybe if that extra guy had been Tex, the Rats would have pulled it out, but Tex was standing on crutches behind the bench. We didn't manage another shot on goal.

But, unlike nineteen years before, when the town sank into an extended sulk following our state title loss to the Pipefitters, Starvation's leaders realized that great teams don't come along every year, and they decided to brag about the moment to everyone on Michigan's main north-south freeway.

I was as happy as anyone about that.

Which may be why my mother decided, without letting me know, that she was going to attend the posting ceremony. She'd said nothing about it when we met for breakfast that morning at Audrey's. She had tea and wheat toast. I had blueberry pancakes and ham. We didn't talk about anything important, except my reminding her that we were supposed to meet with her lawyer that afternoon to discuss her testimony in the trial of Father Reilly.

"Yes, yes," she said, annoyed. "Lawyers and more lawyers."

"I'll pick you up after the sign ceremony," I said.

"Fine. My tea is too weak."

I'll never know what she was thinking. She took a wrong turn off of Route 816, a road she had traveled maybe ten thousand times, and wound up atop Dead Sledder Mile, driving away from I-75 instead of toward it.

Later, Darlene and I would try to explain to ourselves how Mom had gotten off track. We agreed that she was tired, having just taken over Mrs. B's Meals on Wheels routes. But she'd also been withdrawn and quiet for weeks. Despite our efforts to get her out for euchre or a boat ride or anything, she'd sit for hours at the front window of her house, staring at the lake. We knew why. She was blaming herself for the death of one friend and the estrangement of the other. Trying to persuade her otherwise seemed only to sink her deeper into despair, as if the effort to soothe her proved that she was right, that she had failed two women she had loved, and who had loved her.

Dead Sledder's coiling descent wasn't as treacherous in the spring, but a morning shower had made the asphalt slippery. Mom probably felt the car slide left at the turn halfway down the hill and overcompensated to the right. She wound up in the ravine beyond the opposite road shoulder, her Buick crumpled against an oak. When I arrived at the scene, police officers were moving around in the twin halos of her headlamps glowing in the shadows of the trees. I smelled gasoline and oil. Darlene stopped me at the shoulder and told me I couldn't go down. I tried to fight past her but finally fell to my knees, wailing, No, this can't be happening.

A few days later, Dingus called me to his office. He sat behind his desk, I sat in my usual chair facing him. "You're not a thin-skinned guy, so I'm just going to tell you how it is," the sheriff said. "We hired two different mechanics to look your mom's vehicle over from stem to stern. It could have used tires but otherwise was in fine condition."

"She was going to testify," I said. "You don't think that they—somebody—could . . . I mean, she could have nailed Reilly to a cross."

"Maybe," Dingus said. "But these aren't stupid people."

"Have you ruled out suicide?"

"Well," the sheriff said, "you never can rule it out, really, not when there's one person dead and no witnesses. But I wouldn't—"

"So, no, you haven't ruled it out?"

"We cannot rule it out, Gus, no, but I wouldn't jump to conclusions."

Darlene had saved some of her mother's ashes from her funeral. We scattered those along with some of Mom's on the lake at sunset on June 20, the longest day of the year. We sprinkled the rest of Mom's ashes on the graves of my father and Louise Campbell.

The rosary Sister Cordelia had given her hung from my truck's rearview mirror.

Now Darlene tore the envelope open. She took out the paper inside and unfolded it.

She looked at me. "When did you know?"

"I had an inkling when I first heard my mom traveled to a spelling bee. I just didn't want to admit it. But I was damn near certain when Gallagher said what he said about the birthday cake, how Cordelia treated Mom special."

Darlene handed me the birth certificate. It had been filed in Sanilac County on May 31, 1933. It was for Beatrice Clare. The space for her last name was left blank. Her mother was listed as Mary Gallesero. The father's name had been typed over enough times that it was illegible.

"How does that make you feel, Gussy?" Darlene said.

"How do you think? It makes my skin crawl to think Nilus was, you know."

"Your grandfather. And Whistler, too."

"Yeah. My half uncle? Jesus. No wonder Mom—"

"Don't. Your mother loved you more than anything in the world."

I didn't say it. Instead I looked across the lake. The sunlight was almost gone. I felt Darlene's knuckles soft on my cheek.

"Your grandmother was beautiful and kind," she said. "And Bea loved her. Just think: Grandma Nonny."

An elderly couple passed in a canoe, their paddles dipping soundlessly into the silver water.

"I wonder if Mom knew," I said.

"That Nonny was her mother?"

"Yeah."

"At some point, she must have. It's almost like she was keeping a secret from herself. Then when her memory problems started, it wasn't as easy. She couldn't remember what she wasn't supposed to remember."

"Something like that." I leaned my elbows on my knees. "She was right, though."

"About what?"

"She told me, 'The truth will not set you free.'"

"Does that hurt you?"

"That the truth doesn't set you free?"

"No. That your mother kept things from you."

I smiled despite myself. "After all my years in the newspaper business, you'd think I'd have learned that the truth usually turns out to be bullshit."

"That's not what I meant."

"I know." I leaned back on the swing. "Do you think you would have left, Darl?"

"Left where?"

"Here. If D'Alessio had lasted and it turned out he beat Dingus in the election."

"I'm here now," she said. "We're here now. And I'm thinking, I don't know, maybe I'll even run for sheriff."

"Really?"

"Really."

"You should. Dingus has had his day."

We sat there, still and content, feeling the night breeze, watching the tree line etched against the sky disappear in the blackness.

Darlene snuggled into me. "Can I tell you a secret?" she said.

"You're kidding, right?"

"Nope. Do you know when I first fell in love with you?"

I grinned. "The night I played that amazing game against Grand Rapids in the regional final?"

"No, idiot."

"Sorry. When?"

"It was this one morning when we were kids. A school morning. I'd gotten up late and just got out of the shower. My hair was a mess, and I stood on my porch trying to fix it while the bus waited. You were standing out by the bus, and I kept waiting for you to yell at me, 'Get going, Darlene,' like you usually did. But you didn't."

"No, I didn't."

"You remember?"

"I do."

"Come on."

"You were wearing that white parka with the fake fur on the hood. Fats and Blinky were barking their asses off."

"That could have been any day."

"But it wasn't." I set a hand on her thigh and squeezed. "So, you keep secrets too, huh?"

"I just told you, so it's not a secret anymore."

"Uh-huh. Apparently, I'm attracted to people like you."

She pressed a toe to the ground and pushed so that the swing began to rock.

"Lucky me," she said.

ACKNOWLEDGMENTS

First, foremost, and forever, thanks to the readers who've given my books a chance.

This book was inspired by the true story of the 1907 disappearance of Sister Mary Janina in Isadore, Michigan. I became fascinated with her story after reading about it first in anthologies by the late northern Michigan writer Larry Wakefield, then later in *Isadore's Secret*, the splendid nonfiction book by Mardi Link. Full disclosure: In describing Nilus's search for Sister Cordelia, I borrowed a line from a newspaper story quoted by Link.

Thanks to my endlessly engaging agent, Erin Malone, and her boss, my old friend Suzanne Gluck, of William Morris Endeavor. I'm indebted to my patient, helpful editors at Touchstone, Lauren Spiegel and Stacy Creamer, and my publicist Jessica Roth, whose enthusiasm never flagged no matter how many times her Philly teams disappointed her. Thanks, too, to Marcia Burch, David Falk, Meredith Vilarello, and Marie Florio. In Chicago, I've been lucky to have gifted Web designers in Sunya Hintz, Justin Muggleton, and Quinn Stephens, and a new friend and way-too-young mentor in publicist Dana Kaye. Copy editor Amy Ryan has made all three of my journeys to Starvation Lake better. Thanks always to Trish Grader and Shana Kelly, who got this accidental trilogy started.

My wife, Pam, had a big influence on this book; as she has many times in life, she steered me back on track when I had veered off. My former *Wall Street Journal* colleague Scott Kilman advised me on how one can get sick in a chicken plant, among other things. Coach Michael Brown proposed the "one punch" theory. My sister, Kimi Crova, helped with cop stuff, as did my hockey pal and Chicago police detective John "Spin-O-Rama" Campbell. My future daughter-in-law, Kristy Stanley, offered geological advice. The eminent New York pathologist Michael

Baden talked to me about bones, and if I screwed anything up, it's my fault. I first heard Whistler's observation about journalism careers from Barry Meier of the *New York Times*, and Whistler's other favorite incantation from Phil Kuntz of Bloomberg News. I'm grateful for the counsel of early readers Joe Barrett, Julie Jargon, Andy Stoutenburgh, and especially Jonathan Eig, whose books on Lou Gehrig, Jackie Robinson, and Al Capone are models of honest journalism and evocative writing. His best advice to me: "Put this sentence on a diet."

Last but never least, thanks to the Shamrocks, the Flames, the YANKS, and all the boys of Thursday hockey.